The Unheard

Also by Nicci French

FRIEDA KLEIN NOVELS
Blue Monday
Tuesday's Gone
Waiting for Wednesday
Thursday's Child
Friday on My Mind
Dark Saturday
Sunday Silence
Day of the Dead

OTHER NOVELS BY NICCI FRENCH
The Memory Game
The Safe House
Killing Me Softly
Beneath the Skin
The Red Room
Land of the Living
Secret Smile
Catch Me When I Fall
Losing You
Until It's Over
The Other Side of the Door
What to Do When Someone Dies
The Lying Room
House of Correction

The Unheard

A Novel

NICCI FRENCH

WILLIAM MORROW
An Imprint of HarperCollinsPublishers

THE UNHEARD. Copyright © 2021 by Nicci French. All rights reserved. Printed in the United States of America. No part of this book may be used or reproduced in any manner whatsoever without written permission except in the case of brief quotations embodied in critical articles and reviews. For information, address HarperCollins Publishers, 195 Broadway, New York, NY 10007.

HarperCollins books may be purchased for educational, business, or sales promotional use. For information, please email the Special Markets Department at SPsales@harpercollins.com.

Published by Simon & Schuster in the United Kingdom in 2021.

FIRST U.S. EDITION

Library of Congress Cataloging-in-Publication Data has been applied for.

ISBN 978-0-06-313774-5 (paperback)
ISBN 978-0-06-313776-9 (hardcover library edition)

22 23 24 25 26 LBC 6 5 4 3 2

To Patricia

The
Unheard

The

Unheard

ONE

People say you can't die in your dreams but last night I felt I was going to die. I was falling, like she fell, and it was just before I hit the concrete—dark, rushing up at me—that I woke, gasping, sweating. I hadn't got away. It was happening again.

I tried to think of a smooth sea, of a blue sky, of a forest with the wind gently stirring the leaves. It didn't work.

I was awake but I was still in the dream. I was back where it all began.

I was sitting in the window seat of a café off Broadway Market. I was early and so I saw Jason and Poppy before they saw me. For a brief moment it was as if nothing had changed. Poppy was riding on Jason's shoulders, clutching his ears, her mouth open in precarious joy, her glorious red hair like a banner in the soft breeze. The father with his little daughter, walking down the street toward the waiting mother.

Even at that moment, even though I had come here

straight from being with Aidan, and had walked to the café in the glorious May warmth, feeling alive with hope and desire and excitement and a sense of life unfurling, I felt a ripple of sadness. Poppy was so small, so vulnerable and trusting. And Jason and me, we'd done this to her—split her life in half. But we would make it better, together.

I watched as they drew closer. Jason was holding Poppy's legs so that she was steady and he looked like he was singing. He had a nice voice; he always used to sing loudly in the shower. He probably still did.

As they passed the window, he saw me and gave that familiar, funny half-smile, as if there was a shared joke between us, like in the early days. He put Poppy's little overnight bag on the pavement so that he could lift her up and off and down to the ground. Poppy pointed excitedly at me, then put her face to the window, her nose squashing against the glass and her breath misting it. "Mummy," she was saying soundlessly.

I stood up and met her at the door and hugged her and she pressed her face into my shoulder. She smelled like sawdust and sap. I'd assumed Jason would leave immediately, but he ordered coffee for himself and a hot chocolate for Poppy and we all sat down at the table. Poppy wriggled onto my lap and I looked at Jason a little uneasily. I was always anxious to avoid any competition for her affection. But he just smiled.

He was still good-looking. There were gray flecks in his neatly trimmed beard; he was bulkier. He was a grown-up now, a headmaster, he had status, but I could see the young man I'd fallen for—the young man who'd fallen for me.

I had a sudden, vivid memory of that first evening all those years ago. It had happened so quickly, right at a time when I was thinking I never wanted to get involved with another man, ever again. I was emerging from a spectacularly distressing breakup. My boyfriend of seven years—my first real love—had gone off with a close friend, someone I'd known for most of my life. I lost them both. Even the past I shared with them was wrecked by lies. It had left me a frail, raw, sore, pulpy mess of a human being.

But on a spring day like today, full of blossom and fresh green leaves, my friend Gina had persuaded me to go to a party with her. She said it would do me good and wouldn't take no for an answer. She stood over me while I put on a dress that looked more like a sack, and brushed my long red hair, and refused to wear makeup. Jason was there, tall and rangy, with gray eyes, a cleft in his then-beardless chin, and a faded blue cotton shirt. I could still remember how he looked at me and didn't look away. We got talking. We danced together and I felt the heat of his body. I suddenly thought: so my life isn't ruined after all; so I am still desirable and I can still feel desire; so my boyfriend was a scumbag and my girlfriend crap, but I can still laugh and dance and have sex and feel life rippling through me. I can begin again.

We'd gone on to a bar in Camden High Street. I remember I had a tequila and my head swam and I was

3

thinking to myself that I had to be careful, I mustn't be a fool, not again. Jason laid his hand over mine, told me that he was with someone else and it was as if he had slapped me. I was suddenly sober. I said I wasn't going to get involved with anyone who was in a relationship. I knew what it felt like to be betrayed. Jason nodded, kissed me on the cheek, a bit too close to my mouth, and we said goodbye and I thought I would never see him again.

The next day, he texted me. I could still remember it word for word: *I've just broken up. No pressure. But I'd love to see you.*

Now we were here, all those years later, with our beautiful three-year-old daughter, and in July it would be the first anniversary of our separation. So much promised and so much lost. It hadn't been a divorce because we'd never married. But we'd shared a child and a house and a life.

The young, fresh-faced barista came over with the drinks. She put the large mug of hot chocolate in front of Poppy.

"This is for you, young lady, I guess."

Poppy glared at the woman, who looked disconcerted.

"She's a bit tired," said Jason.

"I'm not tired," said Poppy firmly, but she had that twitchiness about her. A storm was coming.

The woman raised her eyebrows and moved away.

"How was your weekend?" I asked.

Jason looked at Poppy. "How was it, Poppy?"

"It rained."

"Well, not all the time."

4

"It rained and it rained and it rained."

"I know, honey. You and me and Emily played games and you did pictures and you cooked with Emily."

Emily was Jason's wife. She really was his wife. This time Jason had got married. Poppy had gone to their wedding. I had made a yellow dress for her and washed her hair the night before, and later I saw the photograph of the three of them, a whole new family without me in it.

"That sounds good," I said, trying to sound like I meant it. I did mean it, I told myself. How could I not want Poppy to have a good time? I looked at my ex-partner. "Thanks, Jason."

Jason smiled again, his small, secret smile inviting my complicity: him and me against the world. He'd always been like that.

"We're doing OK, aren't we?"

"How do you mean?"

"Us two." He gestured toward Poppy, who was dangerously lifting her mug. "People make such a mess of it. They turn on each other. We haven't done that."

I slid my eyes to Poppy. She had chocolate round her mouth and she was carefully blowing into her drink. Poppy often seemed to be in her own world, not paying attention, but she was a human sponge, soaking up everything. It was impossible to know what she saw, what she heard, what she understood.

"We haven't."

"And we won't."

When we agreed to separate, we laid down ground rules: never to be angry with each other in front of

Poppy. Never to compete for her. Never to try and buy her affection with treats and toys, or not be firm with her about behavior or the structure of her days. Never to let any disagreements leak out into our relationship with her. Never to criticize the other to her. Always to collaborate on how we raised her. Always to assume that we had her best interests as a priority and to trust each other as parents. And so on. There were loads of them. It was like a self-help book. Jason wrote them all down and he emailed them to me, as if it were a contract. And by and large we had kept to it.

I looked at the man who was the father of my child. He used to hate buying clothes for himself, so I would buy them. The jacket was a birthday present I'd got him three years earlier. But I hadn't bought his patterned shirt. I hadn't been with him when he chose that pair of soft leather shoes. I unfolded a paper napkin and wiped Poppy's mouth.

"Shall we head off, poppet?"

As we stood up, Jason leaned close, almost as if he were going to kiss me, but instead he whispered something.

"Sorry?"

"Everything will be all right."

"What?" said Poppy.

"We're just saying goodbye," said Jason.

The shared entrance to my flat was always cluttered with junk mail. Bernie, who lived upstairs, kept his bike there and he was lifting it off its rack as I opened the door.

"Tess!" he said, as if I'd been away for months. "And Poppy!" He leaned forward with a look of concern. "Is everything all right?"

He was about my age, in his midthirties, thin, with muddy brown eyes, brown hair in a ponytail and a wispy brown beard. The tops of two of the fingers on his left hand were missing, which Poppy always found fascinating, and he had a habit of standing just a little bit too close to people. He stooped down to Poppy and she took a step back and stared at him with round eyes.

"She's tired," I said and slid a toe through the mess of letters. A couple of envelopes were addressed to me: more bills.

"If I can do anything," he said.

I mumbled something that I hoped was both polite and discouraging.

Our cat was waiting at the door of the flat. I'd taken Sunny when I left and I'd taken my old sewing machine and my garden tools and almost nothing else. I hadn't taken the pictures, the furniture and light shades and mismatched plates and glasses, the Christmas decorations, all the stuff that we had chosen together and accumulated over the years and which would remind me of those early days of happiness and then how they slipped away. I needed to shut the door on all of that but I couldn't have left Sunny behind with Jason and Emily in Brixton, even though he had lived in that house for years. He was my companion, old and fat and scruffy, his coat a fading orange, with disapproving green eyes, a limp and a ragged ear.

Poppy picked Sunny up, his legs dangling uncomfortably from between her arms, and hefted him into her bedroom. It was the first room I'd decorated when we moved in, putting up shelves, making the sky-blue curtains, painting the walls, assembling the bed, buying bed linen and bright throws and the little wicker chair. Poppy had helped me, choosing colors and standing beside me when I rolled on the paint, laying on small clean licks of paint with the brush I'd got for her.

I unpacked Poppy's bag, putting the dungarees into a drawer, tossing the tee shirt, knickers and socks into a corner to be washed. I took out the squashy teddy with button eyes and the slightly shabby rag doll, Milly, with her red felt skirt and hair of orange wool, and half-tucked them into her bed, according to Poppy's strict instructions. Poppy wouldn't go to sleep without them on either side of her. I returned Poppy's favorite picture books to her bookshelf and put the pouch of pens and crayons on the desk.

At the bottom of the bag was a pile of paper: Poppy's pictures from the weekend. I sat on the bed.

"Can you show me your drawings?"

Poppy sat beside me, the cat sliding off her lap. I looked down at the small figure. Pale-skinned, dark-eyed, with unequivocally red hair, redder than mine. A fierce, demanding, joyful little girl who still didn't understand what was happening in her life. The thought of it gave me an ache in my chest.

The first picture consisted of a bright orange splurge at the top and dotted streaks of blue below.

"Is that the sun?"

"It rained," said Poppy.

"It's beautiful."

This was followed by a creature I thought was a lion or a horse; a princess; a house; all of them in yellows and reds and blues.

"These are great. I'm going to choose one of them and put it above my bed, so I can look at it and think of you."

Poppy seemed unimpressed by this.

I lifted the house and came to the final picture. It was so different that for a moment I wondered whether there had been some mistake, whether it had been drawn by someone else. It was entirely in thick black crayon. It was simple and basic and violent. There was what looked like a lighthouse or tower and next to it, at the top of the tower, if it was a tower, was one of Poppy's triangular figures, with legs and arms like angry sticks coming out of it and a clotted scribble of black around the head. The figure was slanted, with its head pointed downward.

"Is that a tower?"

"It is a tower."

I wasn't sure that Poppy wasn't just repeating back to me what I'd said. I pointed to the figure.

"Who's that?"

Poppy put a finger on the head with the scrawl of dark lines around it.

"I done her hair."

"Did," I said faintly. "But who is it? Is it an angel? A fairy?"

"A fairy godmother."

I stared at the jagged lines with a sense of disquiet.
"Is she flying?"
"No."
"Is it a story? Is it a magic story?"
"She was in the tower."
"Like Rapunzel?"
"Her," said Poppy, jabbing at the figure in the picture.
"No, I mean, is that someone in a story?"
"He did kill her."
"What?"
"He did kill. Kill and kill and kill."
"Darling, what are you saying. Who?"
But now Poppy was confused and she said she was
hungry, and then she said she wanted to have been a
cat, and then she started to cry. I put the pictures on
the desk, except for the one in black crayon, which I
took with me.

Two

I dreamed someone was calling me and then blearily realized it wasn't a dream. I slid out of bed, still half asleep, and went into Poppy's room, turning on the bedside lamp. Poppy was sitting up, her hair wild and her face a tragic mask. I could smell and feel what had happened.

"Don't worry about that. Let's get you clean and dry and I'll put some new sheets on your bed."

"I did it."

"Did what?"

"I did wet it."

"It's just a little accident."

Though Poppy hadn't wet her bed for many months, I thought, as I pulled clean pajamas onto her and stripped the bed.

"Climb into my bed," I said, "while I get this done. Take Teddy and Milly with you."

"I did it. I did it." Her face puckered up and she started to sob.

"Never you mind."

"Don't hit me!"

"Hit you! What are you saying? Of course I won't hit you. I'll never hit you, my darling one. Come with me."

Poppy slept with me for the rest of the night. She pressed her strong hot body against mine and wriggled until she got comfortable. Her breath smelled like hay.

"Are you still dead?"

I gave a splutter of startled laughter.

"I've never been dead."

"You didn't die?"

"No. I didn't die, my darling. I'm here. Go to sleep now."

And Poppy did sleep until five in the morning, when a gray light was showing round the edges of the curtains, and then she woke with such a violent jerk that it woke me too. Her eyes were wide open and she stared at me as if I were a stranger.

"Jason, sorry to call like this, but I just wanted to know if anything happened over the weekend. Anything that might have disturbed or distressed Poppy."

I was downstairs in the conservatory—a room of glass and steel girders, and the reason I had bought this flat in the first place, in spite of its poky bedrooms and the miniature kitchen off to its side—speaking softly into the phone in case Poppy overheard. In the garden, there were two goldfinches on the feeder.

"It's not even half past six."

"I thought you'd be up. You always get up early."

"Nothing happened. Nothing disturbed her. She's fine. You shouldn't worry over every little thing."

"This isn't a little thing. She's acting strangely. And she wet her bed."

"She's just a kid, Tess."

I thought of the drawing, the words she had said. I thought of the way she had clung to me.

"It doesn't feel right."

"I've got to go."

"Right," I said tiredly. "I mean you're right. I'm sorry. I do worry."

I fed Sunny and emptied the dishwasher. I put clothes on Poppy (the stripy cotton trousers that I'd made for her a few weeks ago, a baggy tee shirt, her denim jacket and green pull-on sneakers), and clothes on myself (rusty-colored shirt dress, denim jacket, ankle boots). I brushed Poppy's red hair and plaited it and Poppy yelled. I brushed my own not-quite-so-red hair and tied it back. I made us both porridge. I put Poppy's lunch (sandwich, slices of raw carrot and cucumber, apple) into her lunch box and my own lunch (ditto) into mine. I cleaned Poppy's teeth and cleaned my own. Just before leaving, I put the drawing into my backpack.

At a quarter to eight, I dropped Poppy off at Gina's house. I'd known Gina since secondary school: we'd gone on holiday together, shared a house, shared secrets; we'd seen each other fall in love, go through breakups, get spectacularly drunk or stoned; we'd argued and made up. For a while, Carlie had been part of our small friendship group as well, until she went off with my boyfriend—and then Gina had refused to have anything more to do with her and still spoke of her with an icy contempt. Gina and I had been pregnant at the same time and given birth a couple of months apart.

I sometimes thought we were more like sisters than friends, bound together by a shared past. She was part of the reason I'd moved to London Fields. Her son Jake was in the same nursery class as Poppy. She had another child too, six-month-old Nellie, with chunky legs, cheeks like red apples and a roar like a motorbike accelerating.

Gina worked for a charity and she had returned to work three months after giving birth. It was her husband, Laurie, who worked from home and did most of the childcare. Sometimes I wondered if he actually worked at all. He genuinely seemed to love looking after the children: he was always baking with them, or painting, or going on outings to strange events he'd read about online. Poppy and I had accompanied him to a surreal rabbit gymkhana in Barking a few months ago and watched solemn teenaged girls tow their bewildered rabbits on leads over, and mostly through, miniature jumps. He was a slight figure, but I was used to seeing him with Nellie in a sling and Jake on his hip. Three times a week, he or Gina—but almost always he—took Poppy and Jake to school and collected them. Twice a week, on my days off, I did the same in return. While Jason had sailed upwards into his headship, I'd shifted sideways after Poppy was born, becoming a part-time primary school teacher on a salary that sometimes covered my outgoings and sometimes didn't quite cover them. How had that happened, I wondered, when we'd started out as equals? How had I let it happen?

That morning, Poppy didn't want to be left. She put her arms around my legs and hung on furiously. I had to pry her off me.

"Don't worry." Laurie gave me a little push out of the door. "She'll be fine as soon as you're out of sight."

"Something's wrong," I said to Nadine as we ate our sandwiches together. Nadine was head of inclusion in the school in East London where I taught Year Threes. She was tall and strong and had dark, very short hair. She wore hooped earrings and leather jackets and biker boots. She had three sons and whenever I went to her house I was struck by the amount of noise and mess they made, and by how calm she remained, like she was in a space of her own. The children at the school were quite scared of her. I loved her, and I wanted to be more like her—solid, confident, safe, married.

I took the drawing out of my backpack.

"She's never done anything like it before."

I told Nadine about what Poppy had said, about her wetting the bed, about her clinginess. Nadine listened attentively and then smiled.

"It's one drawing, one accident in the bed. Do you think that you might just be hyper-vigilant at the moment, because of everything you've been through with the divorce?"

"It wasn't actually a divorce."

"It was like a divorce. It was a crisis in your life and in hers. So one little thing triggers anxiety in you."

"What about 'he did kill'?"

She laughed.

"You should hear some of the stuff my boys come out with. They take everything in, things you didn't even notice they'd heard or seen. Something someone said on the street as they were passing by, something on TV, whatever."

I stood up.

"I'm sure you're right."

"If you go on feeling worried, you can always talk to Alex."

Alex was Nadine's partner and a psychotherapist.

"He wouldn't mind?"

"You can ask him."

"It's OK. I'll just keep an eye on her."

When I collected her from Gina and Laurie's, Poppy was bright-eyed and excited, with yellow paint smeared on one cheek and grass in her hair. She hurled herself into my arms and then pulled away to show me the stickers she'd put on her tummy.

"It looks like she's had a lovely time."

Laurie looked distracted.

"I think so. Yes."

"Was everything all right?"

"They had a little tiff. I'm sure it's all sorted now."

I put Poppy down and spoke to Laurie in a quieter tone. As a teacher, I'd always tried to deal with bullying wherever I saw it. I had always promised myself that I would never be one of those parents who refused to accept that their own children could do things like that.

"What happened?"

"Jake got a bit upset."

"Did Poppy hurt him?"

"I don't know. Jake was crying. I think Poppy said something."

"What did she say?"

"I don't know what it was exactly." Laurie gave a little shrug and smiled at her, a dimple in one cheek. "Jake just said it was something horrible. He was crying."

"Could I ask Jake about it?"

Laurie shook his head. "I've only just calmed him down. Don't worry. He's probably already forgotten about it. We both know what they're like at that age."

On the short walk back, I tried to let things be but I couldn't. When we got to the little patch of green near the flat, I stopped and knelt down so that I could look Poppy right in the eyes.

"Did you have fun with Jake?"

"He cried," Poppy said, matter-of-factly.

"Yes, I know. Why did he cry?"

"He was crying."

"Did you say something to make him cry?"

"I'm hungry," said Poppy. "Very hungry."

There was no point in pursuing it.

"That's good," I said, "because we're going to have a barbecue with Aidan. That'll be fun, won't it?"

I was being ridiculous, I thought. I was being just the kind of overprotective mother I promised myself I wouldn't be.

THREE

Aidan arrived with food and quick-lighting barbecue bags. He unloaded the food onto the kitchen table: corn on the cob, red peppers, two slices of tuna, a fishcake for Poppy, lettuce, tomatoes, a bottle of white wine.

"You know there's just the three of us," I said warily.

"It's the first barbecue of the year," Aidan said with an air of ceremony. "It needs to be done properly."

I turned to Poppy. "Do you want to help with the food?"

"No," Poppy said firmly.

Aidan looked a bit crestfallen.

"Sorry," I said.

"It's all right. Only men are allowed near a barbecue. It's the law."

The barbecue had collapsed during the winter and Aidan had to spend some time reassembling it before he could light it. I went inside with Poppy and gave her a drawing book and crayons and sat her down at her little red table and chair. Poppy immediately set to work with ferocious concentration, producing drawings at great speed: a page of violet streaks, one of green and yellow loops and circles, an orange blob that I knew to be Sunny—Sunny was her most constant subject. I looked over her shoulder: there didn't seem to be anything out of the ordinary.

In the garden, Aidan was still struggling with one of the legs of the rickety, rusty barbecue that the previous owner had left behind. It was probably time to buy a new one. He was wearing faded black jeans and a denim shirt, rolled up just below the elbows, and scuffed trainers. His dark brown hair was receding ever so slightly. His round-framed spectacles gave his a studious, slightly baffled air, owlish. He worked for an alternative energy consultancy and sometimes I heard him talking on the phone to colleagues about capacity factors, feed-in tariffs and more things I didn't understand. He was a neat, mild-mannered, courteous and slightly shy man who never pushed himself forward or interrupted or raised his voice: the opposite of Jason in every way. I liked everything about him, especially how he paid attention to people, listening to what they said with an air of studious concentration. He was like this with Poppy as well. I opened the bottle of wine, poured two glasses and walked outside. Aidan had got the barbecue steady and was lighting two bags of coal. He stood back and I handed him one of the glasses.

"What time will it be ready?"

He looked at his watch. "Seven. Sorry, is that too late for Poppy?"

"It's fine."

"Hello!"

We both had to look around to see where the voice was coming from. Bernie was leaning out of his window.

"This is Aidan and this is my neighbor, Bernie."

"I've seen you," said Bernie. "Going in, going out."

He said this in an appraising tone, as if he were keeping count.

Aidan lifted a hand. "Should we invite him?" he whispered.

"No."

"Barbecue," Bernie said.

"Yes, I hope the smoke from it won't—"

"If you're discussing whether to invite me down, don't worry, I've got a friend coming over."

The window went down. Aidan looked at me quizzically.

"He has a few of these friends," I said. "Some of them are very loud. You can hear it through the ceiling. Do you think I can ask him to be a bit quieter? It feels awkward."

"Does Poppy hear?"

"I don't know. I hope not." I noticed him smiling. "I know. It sounds funny but things feel a bit fragile."

He poked the coal with a stick and watched it brighten. "What's up?"

I took a sip of wine.

"I'm sorry. Sometimes Poppy comes back from her father's in a strange mood and then I worry and feel guilty about what we've put her through. Does that make sense?"

Aidan looked through the window at Poppy, still

21

deep in her drawing, that fearsome scowl, and the tip of her tongue on her lip.

"Is she all right?"

"I don't know," I said.

"I wish I could say something helpful. But probably it's just like the weather. It'll pass. I know that isn't much comfort when you're standing in the rain, but the rain will stop."

"I suppose so," I said doubtfully.

He put his hands up. "Or maybe it's not like the weather."

I leaned forward and kissed him on his stubbly cheek. He smelled nice.

"I know it's complicated, me and Poppy. I know I keep canceling on you at the last minute, or sending you away in the middle of the night. And that my mind can be on other things. I come with baggage."

With his free hand, Aidan touched the back of my head and then ran it down the nape of my neck and spine.

"I brought some work I need to get done after we've eaten. But after that, is it OK if I stay? For a bit at least. I mean, only if you want me to."

"I do want you to. Not for the night, though."

"OK."

"Not yet."

*

Poppy ate her fishcake and firmly refused to eat any salad or vegetables. Afterward she had a bowl of chocolate ice cream and then complained that her tummy hurt. I took her upstairs, undressed her and helped her into the bath, soaped her pliant body, blew a few bubbles for her, then lifted her out and wrapped her in a towel. I put her in her pajamas and read to her and she joined in with the lines she had by heart. When I put the book down, Poppy said she wasn't tired. She gazed at me fixedly and told me I had to stay. But almost immediately she was asleep.

While Aidan worked his way through a pile of papers, I brought the detritus of the meal in from the garden and cleared up. At one point, he looked up and asked if he could help.

"It feels bad," he said, "the man working and the woman doing the washing up."

"It should feel bad," I said. "Most of the time. But it feels good this evening. I want to be doing something. Get on with your work."

When I'd put everything away, I wiped the surfaces and rinsed out the sink. Then I lifted my sewing machine and the costume I was making for Poppy onto the table. She was going to a birthday party in a couple of weeks and insisted she wanted to wear a golden witch outfit. I wasn't entirely sure what a golden witch wore, but Poppy had very firm ideas. We had visited some stores in Spitalfields whose shelves were piled high with bolts of bright cloth, and Poppy had picked out a glittery length of blue and gold that almost hurt the eyes. Now I was making a hooded cloak. I slid the cloth onto the needle plate and checked the thread's tension.

I felt Aidan behind me. He put his hands on my shoulders and kissed the top of my head. I gave a small sigh and leaned back into him.

I could trace the course of my relationship with Jason through our sex life, from those early days when we couldn't keep our hands off each other, when it felt violent and almost dangerous, to the final months when it was almost like arranging a visit to the doctor, each of us removing our clothes on either side of the bed as if we were preparing for an inspection. I remembered once, years ago, when I had switched the light off and Jason had switched it back on: "I need to look at you," he had said. In the final years he had always switched the light off and I wondered now if it was because he wanted to pretend I was someone else.

With Aidan I'd discovered what it was like to be desired again, to desire again. My body had come alive. I abandoned Poppy's witch cloak and stood up and we wrapped ourselves around each other.

"Is she asleep?" he asked.

I pulled him upstairs and into my bedroom, pushing the door shut with my foot.

"Fast asleep. But we should be quiet."

"You don't want to disturb Bernie. If we can hear him, he can hear us."

Aidan wouldn't let me take my own clothes off. I felt he wanted to look at every bit of me, touch every bit of me. And then I lay under the covers and watched as he took his own clothes off, folding them up and laying them on the chair, his watch and his glasses on top of them. It was hard to keep silent and I pulled the covers over us so we were in our own dark cave. Even then, I worried we might have woken Poppy and waited, tense and listening out for any sound from the other bedroom.

I lay on my side and put my hand flat against Aidan's cheek. He looked different without his glasses, younger and less in control of himself.

"I'm sorry, you need to go. Do you mind? I want to do this right."

Aidan didn't speak but leaned over and kissed me and then I sat up, wrapped in the duvet, and watched him get dressed, liking the way he was neat and unhurried in everything he did, even in how he buckled his belt, laced up his trainers. I waited until I heard the front door close before I got up myself, pulled on pajama trousers and a tee shirt and walked through to Poppy's room. She was lying splayed out on her back, her arms spread out.

When Poppy was a newborn baby, I had sometimes looked at her asleep in her cot and, suddenly fearing that she was no longer breathing, I would wake her up. Even now I had to stop myself taking my daughter in my arms and hugging her. I thought of her violent, black drawing—a figure falling from a height—and a small shudder rippled through me.

"I'll protect you," I said, silently, and went back to bed.

FOUR

When I woke the next morning, Poppy was beside me. She had padded across from her room and got into the bed without waking me. I'd always been a good sleeper. Until she was born, I used to sleep ten hours or more at the weekends, lying in bed until midmorning while Jason went out to buy the paper and pastries. That felt a long time in the past. Now I felt dazed by the emotions of the previous day and by the crowded dreams I'd had in the night, although I couldn't remember any of them, just a sense of anxious chaos. I had to gather my thoughts, remember which day it was. Yes, it was Tuesday, my day off. Good. I snuggled down and closed my eyes for a few blissful seconds, then slid out of bed and went into the bathroom where I showered and got ready quickly. I woke Poppy and dressed her in jeans and a bright red tee shirt, which was a complicated business, since she stubbornly refused to cooperate.

I put on the kettle for coffee. I poured milk and oats into a saucepan and stirred them, hearing the familiar sound of Poppy talking to herself from her room above—Poppy always talked to herself—and then a banging sound. She was jumping on her bed. It stopped and there was a noise I didn't recognize and again, louder, and then really loud, as if something was breaking. I ran up the stairs and into the bedroom and saw Poppy in the act of violently hurling something at the wall. It was a small wooden cow and it hit the wall hard, leaving a mark.

"Poppy, stop!"

Poppy looked round, her eyes fiery bright.

"Kingcunt," she shouted. "Kingcunt."

I fell to my knees and grabbed her and held her close, partly to reassure her but also to restrain her and shut her up.

"What are you saying, Poppy? Where did you hear that?"

I held her away from me so that she could speak. Her face bore an expression I didn't recognize. Her mouth twisted. It frightened me.

"Poppy, what is it?"

"He did kill her."

"Poppy, Poppy stop!"

"Kingcunt, kingcunt, kingcunt!"

"Poppy, no."

I smelled burning.

"Wait one moment."

I let Poppy go and ran down to the kitchen to find the saucepan in an eruption of foaming, spewing porridge. I switched the gas off and took a deep breath and tried to calm myself. It felt like a bomb had gone off, two bombs: one in Poppy's bedroom and one in the kitchen.

As calmly as I could, I poured what remained of the porridge into two bowls and put them on the table, adding milk to cool the porridge and a teaspoon of honey to sweeten it. I fetched Poppy down and we both ate while I tried to think what to do. I couldn't get it straight. But first things first: I spoke in the most soothing tone I could manage.

"Darling Poppy, you know those things you said, just now? You mustn't say them to other people. You mustn't say them in nursery. Do you hear?"

"Why?"

"People will be sad. You can say anything to me. But you mustn't say them to anyone else."

"Are you sad?" She leaned toward me and squinted her eyes. "Did you cry?"

"No, Poppy. I'm not sad. But you mustn't say it at nursery."

"People will be sad."

"That's very good, yes." I waited a few seconds. "Who told you that word?"

"What word?"

I gave up and poured a glass of juice for her. While she was half-drinking it and half-playing with it, I found my phone and stepped out of the room, but only just outside. I dialed the number. There was a click and I heard a voice.

"Hi, Alex, this is Tess. Nadine said I could call. I've got an enormous favor to ask."

FIVE

"You probably think I'm being stupid, wasting your time."

"No," said Alex.

I'd wanted him to say yes. I'd wanted to be told this was nothing, it would all be all right, it would all go away.

After the phone call, I had rung Laurie saying that Poppy was missing the morning at school, so I wouldn't be taking Jake, if that was all right, but I'd pick him up as usual. Then, as he had requested, I sent Alex an email listing all Poppy's unusual behavior since the weekend: the drawing, the swearing, the bed-wetting, the way she had been more clingy. I had taken a photo of the black crayon picture and sent it to him. I had told Poppy that we were going to visit someone before nursery.

"A fairy godmother?"

"No, just a friend."

On the bus to Primrose Hill, Poppy had tumbled up the stairs and sat at the front, leaning forward, her little legs swinging, her face gleeful with interest. She pointed out the magpie sitting in the plane tree, the small dog that seemed to have lost its owner, the boy doing wheelies on his bike, the silver car, the puffs of white clouds in a sky that was blue, the gaggle of schoolchildren in their yellow reflective jackets, the bin that a fox must have raided in the night, spewing its contents onto the pavement. Her red hair shone and her eyes glowed in her pale, freckled face; she was like a small, bright flame.

The Warehouse was a recent conversion of an old industrial space, all steel and glass and wood. In the lobby we were met by a woman with a mass of curly dark hair who introduced herself as Paz. She was wearing a spotted yellow dress and had enormous earrings. Poppy gazed up at her with round eyes.

"Are you a witch?"

Paz grinned. "No. Or not a wicked one," she said. She had a faint accent: Spanish, I thought. "Are you scared of witches?"

Poppy considered. "When I was a witch, I did be," she said.

Paz looked confused by this.

"Alex is expecting you," she said to me. "This way."

I'd met Alex Penrose several times, but at parties or social gatherings. I knew him as a very thin and very tall man, a pourer of wine, a wearer of eccentric shirts, a teller of unexpectedly lewd jokes, an energetic but not graceful dancer. This was a different Alex Penrose, grave and courteous, who shook my hand briefly as if we were meeting for the first time, and then bent down from his unusual height to greet Poppy.

"Hello, I'm glad to meet you."

He talked to her respectfully, as if she were a small adult.

It didn't feel like a consulting room. There was a squashy sofa by the window, a striped rug on the floor, posters on the walls, children's books and toys spread out on a table.

"I hear you like drawing," said Alex. "Perhaps you can draw something for me."

He pointed to the box of chunky wax crayons. Poppy looked at him through narrowed eyes.

"Something for Mummy, not you."

Alex laughed. "Fine. Maybe Mummy can wait downstairs and it can be a surprise." My face must have shown my alarm, but Poppy seemed unconcerned. She was already seated at the table with an orange crayon in her fist, frowning in concentration.

"No looking," she said sternly.

"We won't be long," Alex said.

I sat in a chair that was too low, trapped in its capacious softness. It was only ten to nine, and the Warehouse was empty, its day not yet begun. I tried to read one of the newspapers spread out on the table, but the words made no sense to me and I soon laid it aside. Leaning back in my chair, I covered my eyes with one hand. I could feel hot tears start up and my body felt boneless with fear. How was it possible that I was sitting in this center for psychotherapy and mental health, while a doctor who specialized in child trauma was examining my daughter?

A few days ago I would have agreed with Jason that in spite of everything—the separation; the painful relocation to a different home in a different part of London; the careful restructuring of Poppy's life into time spent with Daddy, time spent with Mummy; the appalling sense that so early on in our child's life we had let her down—in spite of all of this, we had done all right. Poppy might be marked but she wouldn't be damaged. She had seemed miraculously unharmed, so sweet and sparky, that I'd let myself believe that we had done it, had survived. I had begun to believe I could be happy again, after years of happiness's gradual erosion. I had even let myself fall in love again, feel desired and beautiful and cared for.

Now, from the warm blue sky, this: this *ugliness*. What had happened over that one weekend with Jason to turn Poppy from a cheerful, settled little girl into one who had trouble sleeping, wet her bed, drew pictures of death, said "kingcunt" while her mouth twisted and her eyes glittered in her pale face?

I took my hand away from my face and let the light that shone through the large window dazzle me. There were flowers in the grass slope outside; birds were building their nests in the unfurling branches. I wanted Alex to walk toward me smiling, saying: *It's nothing at all, your daughter is completely fine.* But if he did that, I wouldn't believe him. I knew it was something. But what?

I heard a door open and a babbling voice and Poppy

appeared at the top of the stairs, Alex beside her. She was so tiny and he was so tall. He took one of her hands as they came down the steps, in the other she held a clutch of papers.

I heaved myself out of the low chair.

"There you are." My voice came out tinny.

"I did draw," said Poppy triumphantly. She pushed several drawings into my hand.

I smoothed them out on the table, scared that I would see a menacing black scrawl, but they were all bright with color. There was a fox, or at least something orange with an eye. A rainbow, wonky and bold, with the sun at one end and rain at the other. The beginning of a house: square box, two windows, door, tree to one side. The fourth drawing showed three triangles with circles on their tops from which messy spirals of hair sprouted. There was an enormous yellow circle to one side.

"That's you," said Poppy, tapping the smaller triangle. "That'—and she tapped the vastly larger one—"is me."

"And who's this then? Is that Daddy?"

"Daddy doesn't live with us. Daddy lives with Emily. That's the fairy."

"What about Sunny?"

Poppy looked at me reproachfully and laid a stubby finger on the giant yellow circle. "There."

"Of course."

"Do you want a sticker, Poppy?" Paz had joined us.

"Yes! On my arm and on my tummy."

"Let's go and choose you one."

Alex waited till they were out of earshot.

"You understand this isn't a formal assessment," he said.

"But what do you think? Is she all right?"

"Your daughter is a bright, friendly, inquisitive, outgoing child, Tess."

"I know. But is she all right?"

"I didn't find any sign"—he held up a long, bony finger—"with all the usual caveats, of abuse. I mean sexual abuse."

My breath came in shallow gasps. I needed to sit down.

"I didn't do a physical examination. But you said on the phone that there was no sign of soreness in the genital area."

I nodded. My head wobbled on my neck. Across the large room, Poppy was rummaging in a basket.

"No," I said. "Obviously I don't know what to look for."

"There's nothing that struck me as worrying. No sexualized behavior. She doesn't seem notably restrained." He allowed himself a smile. "To say the least. She is communicative. But"—the bony finger once more—"everything that you described to me, the sleep disturbance, the bed-wetting, the clinginess, the agitation, they can be symptoms of some kind of trauma. And they can also mean nothing at all."

"So you don't know."

"I can't know, without evidence. Young children are highly receptive. It's how they learn things. You know this as well as I do."

I thought for a moment. I felt dull and stupid and I wasn't sure whether this was good news or not.

"So you're saying this might all mean nothing."

Alex thought for a moment.

"Not exactly. I'm saying that I have no reason to believe that she has been assaulted but she may have witnessed something. Or she may just be feeling something."

"What do you mean by that?"

"You say that this began when she returned from visiting her father?"

"Yes."

"What's her relationship with him like?"

"Good. Fine. It's Jason—I mean, you've met him. He's fine. He—" I stopped and rubbed my face. My eyes felt gritty. "Oh, I don't know. I don't know anymore. She usually goes there every other weekend and every Wednesday and so I don't know that bit of her life anymore. She's only three, but what happens to her when she isn't with me is out of my reach. There's a bit of her I've already lost."

"It's hard."

"He's a good father. He adores Poppy."

In my mind's eye, I saw Poppy riding on Jason's broad shoulders, her hands clutching his ears, both of them laughing as he carried her down the sunlit street toward me.

"And is it just Jason?"

"You mean—oh, I see. No. He's married. He married pretty quickly after we separated. Emily's quite a bit younger than him." I grimaced. "Surprise, surprise. Anyway, I don't really know her but she seems sweet. Sweet—that's a word I don't usually like to use about a woman. But she does."

I was talking too much and too quickly. I took a calming breath.

"What should I do?" I asked again.

"Keep an eye on her. You might want to let her school know about your concerns."

"Yes, I will."

He paused again. He seemed to be thinking.

"This behavior of a small child," he said finally. "It can be about something else."

"What do you mean?"

"I was saying that children pick up on things. How are you?"

"Me?" I said, suddenly feeling self-conscious. "I'm fine. I'm doing my best. It's difficult sometimes."

He didn't respond. Instead he took a piece of paper from his pocket and unfolded it.

"Poppy did this picture as well," he said. He handed it to me.

I looked at it. It was a woman. I could tell it was a woman because of the hair and the triangular dress. There was a row of vertical black lines that almost covered the figure.

"What is it?" I said.

Alex looked across the space to where Poppy stood with Paz.

"She said it was you."

"What are the lines?"

"She said it was a cage, like at the zoo."

"A cage?" I said, dismayed. "Why has she put me in a cage?"

"A cage can be for keeping someone in," he said. "It can also be for keeping things out."

"So which is it?"

"I've no idea."

Six

At nursery, I let go of Poppy's hand and she raced into the melee of small bodies in the playground. I watched her for a few seconds: her red tee shirt, bright hair and small, strong body; that boisterous, throaty laugh. I realized that I was watchful and tense, as if waiting for something to happen. Would Poppy shout some obscenity, would she push someone, would her merriment slide into something dark and even violent?

I turned away and went into the classroom, where Poppy's teacher, Lotty, was eating her sandwich. She seemed alarmingly young to me, in her early twenties perhaps, with the smooth skin of a child, but she was always cheerful and calm and Poppy adored her.

It was suddenly hard to find the words: saying it out loud made it seem grimly real, as if I was bringing something dormant to life. I told her everything and Lotty listened without interruption, her head to one side, her sandwich uneaten.

"This must be upsetting for you," she said when I came to the end.

I couldn't trust myself to speak. I looked away and nodded.

"First of all, I have to say I haven't noticed anything out of the ordinary, but of course I'll be extra attentive now that you've told me this."

"She's been fine?"

"She's bright, she's energetic, she'll join in with anything. She can be excitable and boisterous and loud, but that's nothing to worry about. As far as I've noticed, she's been fine."

I swallowed. "I assume you'll report this to the safe-guarding lead?"

"It's policy," she said. "As you must know."

"So who will be informed about it?"

"Apart from her, then it's the head, the deputy head, and that's about it."

"And you'll keep an eye on her?"

"Of course."

"And tell me if there's anything I should know?"

"I will. But I'm sure she'll be OK."

I gritted my teeth: how could she be sure? "Thanks."

I stood for a moment in the schoolyard, in the silky warmth of the day. In the playground, Poppy raced past, unaware of me watching, her face radiant with purpose.

I turned away. Although both Alex and Poppy's teacher had been calm and reassuring in their different ways, I felt that I had set something in motion.

But what had I learned? Nothing, except there was probably nothing to worry about. Poppy was fine and I was a fretful single mother, the kind I often met in my job, the kind Jason complained about.

What had they said I should do? Nothing, except wait and watch and see and try not to worry too much.

I had three hours before I collected Poppy and Jake and I didn't know how to fill the time. Normally I would have gone home, done some yoga or had a run, and then continued with Poppy's witch outfit. Or I would have wandered round the second-hand shops in search of things that I still needed for the flat. Or met up with a friend. Once or twice I'd even gone to see a movie, sitting in the back row in the dark with the illicit pleasure of solitude. What I should really do was attend to the mounting pile of bills and reminders.

But I didn't want to do any of those things, because I was filled with a churning disquiet that made my limbs twitchy. If I'd still been a smoker, I would have smoked a cigarette and then another, lighting one from the tip of the previous one. Killing time.

I walked slowly down the street toward my flat, past the magnolia tree in sumptuous bloom, past the junkyard and boarded-up shops, then I stopped. I thought of the drawing, of Poppy's words and of the way that she had clung to me. What had she seen and what had she heard? What was she trying to tell me?

I turned round. I made my way on to the high street. I went up to the door of the police station and without giving myself time to think, I opened the door and stepped inside.

SEVEN

"I hope you won't think I'm wasting your time," I began.

Detective Inspector Kelly Jordan had come round from behind her desk as if she was trying not to be intimidating. I was relieved: for some reason, I had pictured a middle-aged, red-faced, beetle-browed and bulky man who would stare at me dismissively. But she was a woman. More than that, she was a woman who looked like she could be my friend. She was in her late thirties or early forties, I guessed, faint smile lines around her mouth and eyes, dressed in drawstring linen trousers and a long-sleeved black tee shirt. She didn't wear makeup and hadn't the time to do more than roughly bundle up her coarse dark hair. I felt I could tell my troubles to her.

"So you're reporting a crime," she said.

This was already starting to feel difficult.

"I think there's possibly been a crime committed."

Jordan frowned. "I don't understand."

I took a deep breath and began. I took Poppy's black crayon drawing out of my bag and showed it to the detective. I recounted Poppy's behavior and what she had said. I described our visit to the psychiatrist. I felt increasingly awkward. When I finished, there was a long silence.

"If you were me," she said finally, "what would you do?"

"I don't know." Though I did, of course. "You're a detective. You know how to deal with things like this."

"All right, then. Let me rephrase it: what are you asking me to do?"

"Investigate it."

"Investigate what?"

Jordan waited. She didn't seem scared of conversational silences the way I was. They always made me feel that they need to be filled.

"I'm not exactly reporting a crime because I don't know what the crime is. I said that you'd think I was crazy. But I think my daughter witnessed something bad. A three-year-old girl can't exactly report a crime but I think in her own way, in that drawing, in what she said to me, that's what she was doing."

"So where is the crime?"

"I don't know."

"Who's the victim?"

"You can go on asking these questions. I don't know."

"Do you have anyone you suspect?"

"I don't want to accuse anyone without any evidence."

"You must know that I'm going to ask this: do you suspect your ex-husband?"

"Actually, ex-partner. We weren't married. Not that it matters. And the answer is—" I stopped for a moment because I didn't know what I wanted to say. I just wanted someone to take me seriously and I could see that however sympathetic this detective was, she too was just going to tell me to go home and calm down. "No. I don't. I mean, of course I don't. He's a good man." I hesitated for a fraction—was Jason actually *good*? Charming, yes. Energetic, certainly. Interesting, for sure. But good? "He's one of the most trustworthy people I've ever met," I said, too emphatically. "If he says he's going to do something, then he does."

"So who?"

"What do you mean?"

"Who do you suspect?"

"Nobody. I'm not here to name people like that. I'm here because I think Poppy's witnessed something and you need to find out what."

"I've got two children myself," the detective said. "I share your impulse to protect your child. As a mother, I feel the same. I understand your fears. I also know that children are ..." She seemed to be searching for the right word. "Imaginative."

"You mean they make things up?"

"I mean imaginative. And therefore, to some extent, unreliable. If I believed everything that my daughter Layla said, I'd have gone mad long ago."

"So you're not going to investigate?"

"Tess—is it OK if I call you Tess?"

"Of course."

"Good. Tess, what is there to investigate? If there were a death you thought was suspicious, we would look at that. But there's not only no suspect, there's not even a crime. I can't just send my officers out to look for one."

"Why not?"

I sounded like a child. Jordan stood up.

"Since you're not a journalist or a politician, can I tell you a dirty little secret? We're so short-staffed here that there are whole categories of crime we don't even investigate. There are some forms of theft that we don't even send an officer to. It's difficult enough doing the ones we're actually doing. Being here with you, talking about a crime that doesn't seem to exist, has meant that I"—she looked at her watch—"am almost fifteen minutes late for a meeting about a current murder inquiry that has a real body and a number of very real suspects."

I stood up as well. "So you're saying I should just drop it?"

Jordan took a card from her pocket and handed it to me. "This is my direct line. You can always call me."

"You mean, if I find something?"

"For goodness sake, don't go playing the detective," she said. "In fact, don't do anything except look after yourself and your daughter."

"You probably think I'm being ridiculous. I probably am being ridiculous. I've already taken up too much of your time."

"That's all right. And if an actual crime occurs, you have my number." Jordan held out her hand and I shook it. "It's impossible with children. You never know if you're doing the right thing, but in the end things mostly don't go too badly."

"Except when they do."

"That's when we get called."

"I tried that," I said.

"It hasn't turned out badly yet."

"I hope not."

Maybe the detective was right, I thought as I walked home. I even spoke the words aloud: "Maybe she's right." I collected Poppy and Jake from nursery and tried to ask them in a relaxed tone how the day had been and they were uncommunicative in a way that seemed normal enough. At home, they ran around and shouted while I put a pizza in the oven and made a salad.

When Laurie came to collect Jake, Nellie fast asleep in the buggy, he ruffled the top of Poppy's head and bent toward his son. They looked alike: slender, with silky dark hair and blue eyes. Gina was tall and her hair was a dark blond, cropped bristle short.

"Hi, little guy. How's your day been?" he asked.

I waited, half-expecting Jake to start crying or to repeat something shocking that Poppy had said to him, but he just held up the little stuffed rabbit that he carried around with him all day and slept with at night.

Laurie stood up again. "How are things with you, Tess?"

He always asked me that. When Jason and I had separated, Gina had been one of the friends I'd turned to most for comfort and support. She had come to the house in Brixton and helped me pack up my things, hauling cases and boxes into her waiting car. She'd tried to make it into an adventure, determinedly up-beat. I remembered the first night Poppy and I had spent in the flat, and Gina and Nadine and a couple of other friends had come round with a takeaway. We'd sat on the floor, eating Thai food out of foil containers and drinking cheap red wine from mugs. Gina had lifted her mug and they'd toasted our new home and Gina had said: "Remember, Tess, you're not alone. You've got us."

She was someone I could say anything to, no mat-ter how intimate, and feel I wouldn't be judged. But I sometimes suspected that Gina had shared some of my secrets with Laurie, and he might know more than I wanted him to about my mistakes, my hurts and hu-miliations, rages and moments of disgrace. I looked at his smiling face and wondered what he'd say if I told him that I was seriously worried about Poppy, that to-day I had talked to a therapist and had also gone to a police station and talked to a detective.

"Fine," I said breezily. "How about you?"

"Knackered," he said. "Me and Nellie spent the day with my mother. She wore us out." He bent down to the buggy and spoke in a coo. "Didn't she, Nell?" I waited for his daughter to wake up and bellow. "She insisted we take her dog for a walk and I thought we'd be late."

"You didn't need to worry. We're not going any-where."

"Thanks."

He kissed me on the cheek; I felt the graze of his

stubble and a puff of warm breath. Eucalyptus, I thought.

After Laurie and Jake had gone, I kept a close eye on Poppy as she pottered around, had her bath, was read to in bed, tucked up, the light switched off. Was she being a bit louder than usual? Was she a bit too clingy? Was she more fearful than usual when the bedroom light was switched off?

I asked myself these questions as I lay waiting for sleep to drag me down. Probably every child seemed strange in one way or another, if you looked at them closely enough.

EIGHT

The next day was Wednesday, the day Jason usually had Poppy. I'd often felt it was an unsatisfactory arrangement, unsettling Poppy in the middle of the week. However, it was what we had agreed when we'd decided to part. It was what was fair. We were determined to be fair, to be civilized, to do it right.

Normally Jason collected Poppy from Gina and Laurie's but while I was still at school, setting things out for the next day, I got a text from him: *Work problem. Can you bring Poppy?*

I texted back: *You mean to your house?*

Yes.

Would you rather she didn't come today?

No.

You mean no she shouldn't come today?

I mean no she should come today.

I swore under my breath. I was meant to be seeing a film with Aidan, so I exchanged more texts with him, making the arrangement for later in the evening.

Everything was a rush. Even so, when I collected

Poppy, I paused to ask how things had been. Gina, who had left work early and who was now holding Nellie against her and jiggling slightly every time she was in danger of waking, just shrugged and said in a half-whisper that it had been fine.

"Did Poppy do any drawing?"

"No. They were both exhausted and Nellie's been a monster. I've only just got her to sleep, so I gave them some toast and honey and popped them in front of a cartoon."

Usually Jason and I arranged things, in an unspoken way, to avoid me having to come to his Brixton home, which until recently had been mine as well. When we separated, Jason took out a mortgage so that he could buy me out. It felt strange to be walking past the shops that had been my local shops, the greengrocer and the deli where they would greet me by my name. I noticed that there was a new bakery. It felt strange to approach my house, which wasn't my house. It felt strange to ring the doorbell. And it felt strange when my old front door opened and Emily was there, all welcoming smiles. She invited us in, she hugged Poppy, she put a hand on my arm when she was talking to me, she laughed at nothing.

She laughed too much, I thought, and smiled too much, and was too eager to please. Is that what Jason wanted, I wondered?

As Emily led us through to the kitchen—as if we didn't know the way—and put the kettle on and poured juice for Poppy, there was a scrabbling sound at the kitchen door.

"You can't make up your mind whether to come in or go out," said Emily fondly to the door.

"What?"

She pulled the door open and a creature not much larger than Sunny with coarse gray hair and a stubby tail hurtled in.

"Dog!" shouted Poppy.

"He arrived on Monday," said Emily to me. She turned to Poppy. "This is Roxie."

Poppy flopped down on the floor and put her arms around the animal, who stared at her with its baleful eyes.

"I thought Jason hated dogs."

I said it and then immediately regretted it. But I'd talked of getting a dog and Jason had always said no.

"She's not ours," said Emily. "She's just a guest. Aren't you?"

Poppy gave the top of Roxie's head a little scratch.

"Who does she belong to? Careful, Poppy, I don't think she likes you doing that very much."

"Oh, it's OK. Poppy and Roxie are making friends. Come and have some juice, honeybunch," said Emily. "It's in your special cup!"

Poppy's special cup was decorated with elephants and she held it with both hands as if she were even younger than three.

Honeybunch, I thought. I felt resentful and then angry with myself for feeling resentful. I hated seeing my old kitchen with the blue curtains I'd made but also with a gleaming new fridge. How could they afford a fridge like that when I could barely pay my heating bills? I hated the coats hanging in the hall that weren't mine, though it was me who had found the coat stand in a skip and repaired it. I hated the dog, because Poppy's face shone with delight as she patted it. I hated that Emily was so at home there. But, after all, it was her home. I hated that Emily was so young, still in her twenties I guessed, and lovely looking, a face round and soft as a peach. In fact her whole body was soft and curved and gentle. It made me feel thin and bony and harsh. And cross as well, which I had no right to feel because Jason had insisted that he'd met Emily after we parted. If Jason had married Emily when we'd told each other for years that marriage was unimportant, an outmoded patriarchal institution, and what was important was being in love, making a daily choice to stay together, and having a child together, then that wasn't Emily's fault.

Emily put a mug of tea in front of me and a small jug of milk beside it.

"Nice jug," I said.

"I was on a course," said Emily. "It's just a silly little thing I managed to make."

I heard some footsteps upstairs.

"Is Jason here?"

"No," said Emily. "It's my brother. Have you met Ben?"

"No." Because why would I have met her brother?

"He's staying here for a while. He had a few problems."

"What do you mean? What kind of problems?"

51

"It's nothing. He's just here while he sorts a few things out. Roxie belongs to him. She was with a friend of his for a few days, but Ben missed her so Jason gave in."

"How long's he been here?"

"How long?" Emily looked surprised by the question.

"Yes. When did he arrive?"

"Last Friday."

I heard the sound of the front door opening and a voice shouting a greeting. Roxie stood up and started growling. She had pointy yellow teeth.

It was Jason and I felt once again that coming here had been a bad idea. He entered the kitchen in his work suit, his tie loosened. He picked up Poppy and lifted her up almost to the ceiling. She shrieked with excited fear. He put her down and kissed Emily and murmured something to her. He glared at the dog, who glared back. He nodded at me and I felt horribly alone and lonely in this scene of domestic intimacy. It was as if everything in this house had continued in its old familiar ways, except with a different woman. My own life with Poppy in our small flat seemed suddenly threadbare and insufficient.

"Thanks so much," he said. "Panic at work."

"No worries." I swallowed painfully. "Emily was telling me about Ben."

"I'm Ben," said a voice behind her and I turned round sharply.

He wasn't in shoes and had entered the kitchen noiselessly. I saw his left toe was poking out of a thick orange sock. He was a large man, soft-bellied and round-shouldered. His face was slightly doughy. His straggly brown hair was tucked behind his ears, and he was wearing saggy drawstring trousers and a gray sweatshirt. He looked ill—not ill like someone who was sick, but ill like someone defeated by life.

At any other time, my heart would have gone out to him. Now I just felt a jolt of panic. He had arrived on Friday, just before Poppy's weekend here. Just before Poppy started her downward spiral.

"Hello, Ben," I said and held out my hand.

Slowly he took it. His own hand was big and cold and felt flabby.

"You've got a cute daughter," he said.

He leaned down and stroked his dog's bristly head. He did everything slowly, as if it was an immense effort.

Emily was pushing a mug of tea at him and Poppy was asking if she could stand on his feet while he walked. She put her arms around his legs in readiness and stepped onto his feet.

"Later," he said.

"Now, now, now!"

"Stop it, Poppy!" I said.

My voice was shrill. Everyone was looking at me. Neurotic, I thought, that's what they are thinking: a neurotic and bitter woman who can't let go. I glimpsed Emily's soft, sweet, dismayed face. Jason looked faintly embarrassed and also disapproving.

"How long are you staying?" I asked Ben.

"He's here for however long it takes to get things sorted," said Jason. "Don't feed Roxie, Poppy."

"And it's lovely having him," added Emily, smiling at her brother, showing her dimples and perfect white teeth.

Ben just stared at me with his mottled eyes and his hopeless smile and his face that would have been quite handsome except it had lost its elasticity and fallen into shapelessness.

"Ben is magic," said Poppy.

"Magic cards," explained Emily, beaming.

"Great," I said, looking down at my daughter who'd squatted down beside Roxie again. I felt sick.

"Tess," said Jason. He spoke to me quietly, the way he spoke to the children in his school when they had done something seriously bad. "Ben hasn't been very well and now he needs to live here a while."

"Of course," I said. "But you should have told me."

He considered this. I watched his face, the gray eyes and the smile marks round them, the trim graying beard that he'd not had when we were together. I had stopped seeing him as handsome, but now that he was distant from me, like a stranger with his pretty young wife, I could see it again. It was hard to believe that less than a year ago, we had slept in the same bed, held each other in the small hours, comforted Poppy when she had bad dreams.

"Excuse me." Ben's voice was hesitant, slightly slurred. He frowned, as if speaking was a mighty effort, words like boulders that he was heaving up one by one.

We turned to him. There was a long, uncomfortable silence.

"It's all a bit of a muddle," he eventually said.

"Muddle?"

"You know. I was in Lewisham with Fliss and it seemed good, but then things went wrong. It wasn't my fault."

"Nobody's saying it was," pleaded Emily. Her eyes were bright with kindness.

It seemed like there was a gap between something being said and Ben receiving it, like one of those phone calls where time delays make the conversation stilted and strange.

"Things just happened," he said.

"I should go," I bent toward Poppy. "I'll see you tomorrow, darling."

Poppy was cautiously poking Roxie and didn't answer.

"At school," I added. I raised an awkward hand. "Bye then, everyone."

"I'll see you out," said Jason.

"I know my way."

But he followed me from the kitchen and out of the front door.

"That was rude," he said.

"You should have told me."

"Really?" He raised his eyebrows high. "Like you tell me when Aidan comes round."

"That's different."

"Why?"

"Don't be stupid."

"No, really, Tess, why? Emily's brother is having a rough time. His marriage broke up and he lost his job. So he's staying with us. You think you have a veto?"

"Aidan doesn't stay over, anyway," I said uselessly. "Not unless Poppy's with you."

Jason looked at me and it was like he was looking at a professional acquaintance, not hostile but coolly assessing them. Once again, I felt the dizzying gulf between the life I'd had a year ago and the one I had now.

"I trust you to do what you think right for Poppy. I hope you trust me."

"Yes," I said, not quite meaning it. His eyes were still fixed on me and I remembered how some of his staff were scared of him. I wasn't going to be scared, though. I persisted. "We should tell each other things that are relevant to Poppy. Like the fact that there is a new person in your house."

"Very well."

He was using his patient voice. It made me want to shout. I smiled instead, through gritted teeth.

"Thanks," I said. "Because I want to tell you that Poppy had been a bit odd since her last weekend with you."

"Odd? How?"

"Clingy. And she wet her bed for the first time in ages. And had a bit of trouble sleeping."

Jason crinkled his brows. "You told me that already. I said I didn't notice anything."

"She talked about someone being killed and she swore. I think."

"What do you mean 'you think'?"

"She said 'kingcunt.' As in—"

"I get it." Jason laughed. "I wonder where she picked that up from! Not me, if that's what you're thinking."

"It all adds up."

"What does it add up to?"

"Something's not right."

"After she was with us."

"Yes."

"All I can say is she was fine. It really doesn't sound like anything to worry about."

"I am worried, though."

I thought of telling Jason about taking Poppy to see Alex and my conversation with the detective. I imagined the expression on his face changing to incredulity and then—what? Anger? Contempt?

"Mothers." He shrugged.

"What? *What?*"

"You're a worried mother. I see them every day."

"Don't you dare, Jason. I'm not a worried mother. I'm your daughter's mother, your ex-partner. Remember? This is Poppy we're discussing, not some random child."

"You've got to let go. She's at school now, out there in the world. You can't protect her forever."

"I'm not—"

"Remember how when she was a baby you would crouch by her cot, making sure she was still breathing."

What I remembered was both of us doing that, grimy with exhaustion, sheepish with a shared sense of our own foolishness. The anger went out of me and I wanted to weep at what felt like a betrayal of our past tenderness.

"Whatever you think about me and my anxiety, I thought you should know that Poppy seems a bit fragile right now. Keep an eye on her. Let me know how she is, yes?"

"Sure."

I saw a tiny flicker in his eyes.

"What?" I asked. "What is it? There's something you're not saying."

"I didn't want to mention it yet."

"What?"

But I knew. Of course I knew.

"Emily's pregnant."

"Oh. Congratulations."

"Thanks. It's early days."

I looked past Jason, at the house we used to share. Now it belonged to Jason and Emily and Poppy and soon Poppy's new sibling.

"When's she due?"

"Mid to late October."

I did the calculation: not so very early days.

"You must be happy."

He stared at me, his brows gathered together so that his face was almost ugly. He looked like he was about to say something, then changed his mind.

"Does Poppy know?"

"We haven't told her." He hesitated. "She may have overheard us talking about it."

"Does that mean that she did?"

"It means I think she heard us talking about it, but probably didn't understand."

"I see."

"She's fine, Tess. And Emily and I think it will be good for her not to be an only child, but be part of a proper family."

It felt like I had just been hit. "What did you just say?"

"I didn't mean—"

"Forget it."

"Tess—"

"I said, forget it."

"Let's not fall out. We've been doing so well."

I looked at his face. I'd seen it when it was contrite, exhausted, distressed, irritated, angry, joyful, full of love and of desire. Now it was just a handsome, blank surface, closed to me and unreadable.

"Another time," I said. "We'll talk about this another time."

NINE

Aidan and I had planned to see a film, but instead we went out for a meal. I wanted to talk; I needed to talk. We'd been to the local Italian several times before; in fact, it was where we'd had our first date almost three months ago, back when it was still winter. It was also where we'd gone on the day that Jason and Emily had married a few weeks later, and it had snowed so that when we stepped outside again it felt like a fresh new world had been summoned for them. We'd laughed and then kissed, our lips cold, and flakes caught on our lashes and melted in our hair. It had been like a bad movie.

We sat at our usual table by the window and studied the menu. It was a Wednesday evening and the place was half empty.

"Maybe I'll have the pasta," I said. Aidan grinned. "What?"

"Just that you can cook that at home," he said. "You *do* cook it at home."

I studied the menu. I felt hollow and wanted something comforting and filling.

"Sorry. It has to be the pasta. With wild mushrooms."

When the food arrived and the waiter had ceremo-
niously ground black pepper from a giant pepper mill
onto both dishes and we both had a glass of red wine
in front of us, I took a deep breath.

"Emily's going to have a baby," I said.

Aidan didn't say anything at once, just studied me.
I liked that about him. He never rushed: everything
he did was patient, considered, scrupulous. When
he cooked for me and Poppy, he did it just so, laying
all the ingredients out in advance, washing things as
he went along. I'd watched him when he brought his
work to the flat, sitting at the laptop with his long pianist's fingers on the keyboards and that steady look
of concentration on his face. He looked at me like that
sometimes, too: like he was taking me in. He was so
different from Jason, who was forceful and impatient,
insisting on things and sweeping everyone forward
with him. Jason liked to be the leader.

"Did you just find out?" he said at last.

"Yes. When I dropped Poppy off."

"How do you feel about it?"

"I don't know. A bit dejected."

I saw a barely visible wince tighten his face and put
my hand over his.

"This isn't about me and Jason. Or not in the way
you're probably thinking. We spent a long time drifting apart, hardly even realizing it was happening un-

til it was too late, and then we separated by mutual agreement. People say separations are never really mutual, but honestly I think this one was. It would have happened sooner, if it wasn't for Poppy."

Aidan nodded. I'd told him this before, of course.

"It's just a bit strange. We both said we didn't particularly believe in marriage, and then he marries Emily a few months after he meets her. It took a long time for him to agree we should try for a child, and by the time I was pregnant, we'd lost our way and however much we tried we couldn't find our way back. But with Emily, it took a matter of months. There's not one bit of me that regrets not being with Jason. He already feels a long time ago. I'm not jealous of Emily. I expected this really. I just felt, today, when he told me, kind of sad and not so young anymore and a bit drab and bashed about by everything. And, if I'm honest, anxious that Poppy would want to be with him and Emily and their new baby more than with me, which is stupid but I can't help it. I don't know, life doesn't go the way you think it will, does it?" I put my chin on my hand and looked at him across the table. "I guess I'm tired," I said. "I've had a few bad nights. Poppy hasn't been sleeping. I lie awake and you know what it's like in the small hours, when all the windows are wide open for horrible thoughts to fly in."

Aidan was still waiting. He had a thin, clever face and eyes that sometimes looked gray and sometimes blue.

"You're very nice to me," I said. "I've been so happy these last months. But it's been so quick."

"Please tell me this isn't a breakup speech."

"It's not a breakup speech."

"There's a 'but' coming."

"But I'm seriously worried about Poppy."

"Poppy? Why?"

"In the last year, her parents have split up, we've moved into a new flat, she's started nursery, there's a new mother figure in her life and then I met you. Now she's about to have a baby brother or sister. I wonder if it isn't all too much for her."

"Do you remember how we met?" asked Aidan.

Of course I remembered how we met. And since that day, we'd told each other the story over and over, correcting each other, adding new details, shaping memory into a shared narrative that pleased us both. It had been in the deli near my flat, on a raw winter afternoon, already getting dark and a cold rain falling. I had been buying fresh ravioli because a couple of friends were coming to supper and, as Aidan had just pointed out, pasta was what I cooked—especially when we hadn't long moved into the new home and everything was still in boxes and I hadn't made curtains yet, so the windows were hung with blankets.

Poppy, frantic with tiredness and impatience, had thrown a spectacular tantrum. She had lain on the floor, barking like a sea lion and thrashing wildly. One of the women in the shop had thought she was having a fit and asked if she should call the emergency services. Another said something, under her breath but meaning to be heard, about not taking your children into shops if you couldn't control them. I had bent over her, a writhing, heaving mass in her blue duffle coat, and tried to lift her from the floor, at which point Poppy kicked out, hit me in the face, and then sent a bottle of horribly expensive olive oil flying. It had shattered at the feet of Aidan, splattering his trousers. He hadn't seemed surprised or even annoyed, but had crouched to collect the shards of glass, making sure Poppy didn't get cut.

"Can you manage?" he'd asked, as I staggered out of the shop with Poppy a sobbing weight in my arms, and a bag of provisions gouging into my forearm and banging against my hip as I walked.

He'd chased after us with the pasta I'd left behind and walked with us to the flat, carrying the bags. The next day he'd posted a note through the door, asking if I'd like to have a coffee.

"You should have run a mile," I said. "In the opposite direction. As far as your feet could carry you."

"Yes," said Aidan, as if he was considering the idea. "There I was with my tidy life, buying supper for one, and this beautiful red-haired woman and her little red-haired daughter seemed to erupt into the shop. Into my world, actually. I met you both together. Poppy's not an add-on; she's part of you and part of why I fell for you. I know she comes first. We'll do it at your pace, whatever that is."

I took his hand and lifted it to my lips, kissing the knuckles.

"Even if I keep sending you away in the middle of the night or canceling on you or getting distracted?"

He made a face. "We aren't teenagers. We both have baggage."

I knew about his: his bi-polar father; the woman he'd lived with for nine years who'd had an affair for years under his nose; his subsequent immersion in the world of work.

"It's bound to be complicated, but you're still allowed to be—what is it? Tess?"

Because I was suddenly not looking at him, but out of the window, where a woman was standing quite still and staring in at us. She was small and slender, with a triangle of a face and short dark hair, and was wearing striped cotton dungarees and a white tee shirt and dangling what looked like a beret from her forefinger and thumb. She looked like a member of a circus troupe, I thought—or an elf: an elf who was smiling extravagantly at me and mouthing words. I looked around, thinking she might be looking beyond me at someone else, but no. It was definitely me.

"Who is she?" I asked.

"I've no idea." Aidan looked away from her, back at me. He pulled a face. "Do you think there might be something wrong with her?"

"I don't know."

"Pay no attention. What were we talking about?"

"Baggage," I said.

But now the woman was making gestures, then she hurried away from the window. A few seconds later, she was standing by our table.

"It is you!" She laughed and pointed at me.

I felt a sudden panic. Was she a mother from school? I sometimes bumped into one of them in the street and didn't recognize them out of context. Was she someone from college or school? Or someone I'd met at a party?

"I'm so sorry," I said and then was cross with myself. Tess Moreau, apologizing again. "Do we know each other?"

"Wouldn't you say so?"

"I don't think we've met. Have we?"

The woman was still smiling, one hand on her hip like she was waiting for the penny to drop.

"I think you know. Surely you do."

She looked young to be a mother of a seven- or eight-year-old. Perhaps she was a childminder. She was being so theatrically friendly I thought there was something faintly menacing about her manner.

"Are you going to tell me?" I said. "Maybe you're mistaking me for someone else."

"I don't think so. You've got a little girl."

"Yes. And?"

"Red hair like yours."

"Stop." I felt more and more alarmed. "Who are you?"

The woman, still staring and smiling at me, shook her head from side to side.

"Incredible," she said, then swung round to Aidan. "She's incredible, isn't she? Not to know me?"

Her smile was now so wide it seemed to take up her whole face.

She turned and left and we saw her pass in front

of the window. She looked toward me, put her hat on with a flourish and walked off.

"What was that about?" I sat back in her chair and took a large swallow of wine. I felt jangled by the encounter. I looked through the window to where she had been standing and then back at Aidan who had taken off his glasses and was rubbing his eyes.

"You weren't much help," I said.

"What do you mean?"

"You just sat there while that madwoman attacked me."

"She didn't attack you. She just mistook you for someone, I suppose."

"I felt you just stood by."

"It was really nothing. Maybe she was on something."

"It didn't feel like nothing to me. I felt under threat."

"What did you want? Did you want me to wrestle her to the ground?" he said with a smile that looked forced.

"Oh good," I said. "Our first argument."

"It's not an argument," said Aidan. "And if it was, it wouldn't be our first. Also, don't let something like this worry you. It's not important."

I shook my head.

"No. I think it is important."

I woke in the early hours with a lurch. For a moment I thought I was in my old house in Brixton and the man lying peacefully in the darkness beside me was Jason. Then memory flowed back into the strange gaps that sleep leaves. The world took shape. I put a hand onto Aidan's shoulder to feel his warmth. Sunny was heavy on my legs and I imagined his flanks rising and falling. I was in my home and I was safe. But still I was filled with a shapeless anxiety.

I got softly out of bed and went downstairs. Emily had been Emily Carey before she married and changed her name. I opened my laptop and typed "Ben Carey" into the search bar.

Dozens, hundreds, of entries filled my screen. Ben Carey the actor. Ben Carey the company director. Ben Carey the schoolboy who had won some math prize. Ben Carey the 103-year-old whose secret to a long life was half a pint of stout every lunchtime. Ben Carey who had died in 2013 in a fatal road accident. Too many Ben Careys. I clicked on the images and scrolled down through the faces, young and middle-aged and old, and none of them the one I was looking for.

I went on Facebook and typed in his name. Again, there were lots of Ben Careys and as far as I could see none of them was him.

I climbed back into bed at last and lay with my eyes open. I thought of that woman in the restaurant. Her beaming pixie face and the finger pointing.

Ten

There was something reassuring about reading the same stories to Poppy, night after night. The sleepy bear, the little worried owls, the Gruffalo. I'd almost never been to a church service, except for a couple of weddings and the funeral of a great-aunt, but I felt there must be a deep consolation in the familiar responses and rituals and hymns, day after day, year after year.

Poppy had been tired and subdued when I picked her up from school, so now I sat by her bed and spoke the words she knew by heart with the same intonations and pauses, showing her the pictures, licking my forefinger to turn the thick pages, hearing the rustle of paper. Sunny lay at the end of her bed, curled up on himself.

Gina was downstairs, baby-less and husband-less and waiting for a drink. Finally, the little bear was asleep for the second time under the big yellow moon, and although Poppy was not quite asleep, her eyes were starting to flutter and she was settling back on the pillow and wriggling under the duvet, finding a comfortable position.

I heard a sound through the ceiling, then another, a few sharp cries and a series of groans. Poppy didn't seem to notice. She was too tired. Was it time to do something? If I couldn't bear to say it face-to-face, what about a note pushed under Bernie's door? An anonymous note?

I picked up the teddy and tucked him in beside Poppy and then looked around for the rag doll.

"Where's Milly?"

Poppy just murmured something. She was drifting off to sleep. I knew that if she woke and found either her bear or Milly missing, she would get upset. I peered under the bed, pushed my hands behind the back of it, but came up with nothing except an old apple core. I looked under the covers, then stood up and tried to think. Could Poppy have left her rag doll at Jason's? No. I'd definitely seen it since then.

It wasn't anywhere around the bed. It wasn't in the crate where the less immediately desirable toys were kept. I was about to search elsewhere in the flat when, on an impulse, I looked in the wastepaper bin in the corner and there it was. Poppy must have dropped it in by mistake. I bent down to retrieve it and jerked back as if I'd suffered an electric shock. The torso was in pieces. The head and one of the arms and one of the legs had been torn off and the stuffing was coming out. The sight was horribly shocking, almost as if I had found a living creature dismembered in the bin. I knelt down by the bed and stroked Poppy's forehead. She looked very peaceful.

"Honey, what happened to Milly?"

"She died," said Poppy sleepily, without opening her eyes.

"But you—" I stopped. I didn't know how to describe what Poppy had done. "Why did you do that?"

Her eyes snapped open.

"She was naughty. She died."

I wanted to pick her up, grasp her by the shoulders, shake her and ask her what was happening. What had she done? What had she seen? What was happening in that restless brain?

Instead, I bent down and kissed Poppy on the cheek and rearranged the duvet around her.

"Go to sleep now. Sweet dreams," I said.

I picked up the pieces of Milly and took them with me.

"With you in a second," I called to Gina, trying to sound normal. I could hear her clattering around in the kitchen, the clink of glasses.

I walked out of the flat door and the front entrance and thrust the rag doll's severed limbs and head deep into the rubbish bin. I didn't want them in the house.

THE UNHEARD

ELEVEN

I peeled the cover off the plastic carton and tipped the olives into a little bowl. I pulled open a packet of crisps. Gina was making a Negroni, scowling in concentration as she tipped in the Campari, added slices of orange.

"I warn you, I've already had one," she said. "Just a small one. But you were ages up there."

"Sorry."

"Don't be. I know what it's like. It's my night off, though. No husband, no children, no chores. I'm going to get drunk and take an Uber home."

I tried to push away the image of the dismembered doll. I couldn't bring myself to tell Gina about it: this evening we were going to drink Negronis, get a takeaway and pretend we were twenty-one again, childless, partner-less, heedless, young.

We clinked our glasses together and took a sip; we both gave a small, almost identical groan of pleasure.

"Do you remember when we were drunk that time and you insisted I cut your hair?" said Gina.

"I do."

"I kept trying to get it even and it got shorter and shorter and you were sitting there so innocently. You had no idea what was going on. I was cutting away in a panic and all these thick locks of your beautiful hair were lying on the floor."

"Maybe you should cut my hair now."

"No way."

"Maybe I need a new look."

"I like your old look. So does Aidan."

"Starting over," I said.

"I am never going to cut your hair again. You can start over without looking like a scarecrow."

"OK."

I took another sip. It was bitter and sweet and warmth spread through me.

"We should do this more often," Gina said.

I laughed. "That reminds me of Jason. We'd do something like go to see a film and while we were there he would say: we should go to see films more. And I'd say: we're here, we're doing it, just live in the moment. I sometimes felt that whatever we were doing, his mind was on something else. Planning ahead. Making calculations. He has a devious mind."

"Devious? That sounds a bit sinister."

"It's more that I'm beginning to see him differently. The Jason I thought I knew and the Jason I see now don't seem to belong to each other. Which one is the real Jason?"

"Can't he be both? Lots of Jasons. And you can't be in relationship with all of them. There's something intelligent I want to say about multiple selves, but the Negroni is stopping me. Which is a good thing."

Gina took another swig.

"So you're saying that we can never be fully known," I said. I felt suddenly forlorn.

"Fully known? Christ, of course not. Do you want to be?"

"I don't know. No. Doesn't Laurie fully know you?"

Gina considered this.

"He doesn't know me the way you know me. And you don't know me the way he knows me. And neither of you know me the way I know myself." Gina squinted comically. "And sometimes I think I don't understand myself at all."

"Yes. I guess so. It's scary, though, isn't it?"

"It strikes me," said Gina, "that when you and Jason first separated, you seemed to feel freed from something, as if you could start over, as you put it. Find out a different self, away from him. I know it was painful, it was also a bit scary, yes, but exciting. I almost felt a tiny bit jealous. Which is stupid of course, but I did."

"Really? And I was jealous of you and Laurie and how you always manage to be so friendly and nice to each other. And equal. The way he's such a hands-on father. Still am a bit jealous, if I'm honest. Because now when I think about me and Jason, I find it hard to understand how I let our lives be so dictated by his wishes and his career."

Gina put her glass on the table with a click.

"Good," she said firmly.

"Good? What's good?"

"That you're seeing that now."

"You mean, you've thought that too?"

"Well, he's a bit of an alpha male, isn't he?"

Coming from Gina, that wasn't a term of praise. The Negroni was almost gone. I needed another.

"You think I was, you know, too submissive?"

"I think you do yourself down," she said. "Sometimes. You're too considerate of what other people are feeling. You go to such an effort to see things from their point of view that you can almost erase yourself."

"Erase myself! That doesn't sound healthy."

"But it was good as well. You gave it your best. You were amazingly tolerant."

"Tolerant? Is that what I was?" I leaned forward. "Submissive and now tolerant. What was I tolerant of?"

"You know. Jason being Jason."

"What does Jason being Jason mean?"

"I don't know."

Gina picked up her drink and took a swallow, so large that half the contents of the little glass disappeared. She looked at it in surprise, then pushed an olive into her mouth.

"The main thing is, when it didn't work out, I think the way you handled it was civilized and amazing really. You always put Poppy first, no matter what."

"I don't think Poppy's doing so well," I said. Suddenly I wanted to blurt everything out and be taken seriously. I wanted someone to see what was happening the way I saw it.

"Poppy's great! All kids have their ups and downs."

"You think?"

"Anyway, I always used to believe that there was no such thing as a good breakup. God, when I think of some of our friends. When I think of your *parents*: they were quite something when they were going through their divorce. You've been different, Tess."

"What about Jason? Has he been different too?"

"It was easier for him."

"Why?"

A little furrow appeared between Gina's eyes.

"Maybe it wasn't," she said. "But it seemed like it was. What with keeping the house. I never understood that. And his grand new job. And Emily."

"Emily came later."

"Right."

"Didn't she?"

"God, don't ask me. I only know what you told me."

But she shifted in her seat and looked away from me. A thought snaked its way into my mind, sharp and poisonous. It made me feel physically sick, and at the same time it was so obvious that I almost laughed at myself for being such a fool. Had I always known and chosen not to know? Was I that woman, who turns a blind eye?

"Can I ask you something about me and Jason? Was Jason unfaithful to me?"

Gina put her glass down on the table. She looked deeply shocked and distressed.

"What are you doing, Tess? Why are you asking things like that?"

I suddenly felt entirely cold and steely and stonily

76

sober. I looked at Gina full in the face, wanting to force her to continue.

"You're in a new part of your life now," she said a little desperately. "You're doing wonderfully with Poppy. You've met a new man. You don't want to damage any of that, do you?"

"You're my friend," I said. "I think maybe you're my best friend. Why didn't you tell me? Why didn't you *fucking* tell me?"

When Gina spoke, her voice was trembling. I thought she might even start crying. "Is this something you really want to do?"

"It's something I have to do."

Gina put her hand on my arm, but I pulled away.

"Tess, listen. I had this friend and she found out that the husband of *her* friend was having an affair. She told her friend and it broke up the marriage and I always thought my friend did it as an act of aggression or something. She'd never liked the man and I think she thought they were better apart." She gave a sniff and took a tissue from her pocket and blew her nose. "Mistakes happen in marriages—in all marriages probably. You know some of the things I've been through with Laurie. But you survive them. Sometimes you're better off not knowing. Christ, I agonized over it, but in the end I didn't think I had the right to tell you and wreck things."

I felt a heat of rage that was almost physical and I wanted to shout at Gina or hit out at her. The sense of humiliation swept through me like a sickness. Jason had had an affair and other people had known, had probably talked about me, pitied me, felt sorry for me. I couldn't bear it.

"So you knew this important thing about me and you decided I was better off not knowing, did you? So you didn't tell me. Who was she?"

"Tess," said Gina in a pleading tone. "What's the point? What are you going to do with this apart from tormenting yourself?"

"It's not what you think. Do I know her?"

Gina took a deep breath. "Ellen Dempsey."

"Ellen? *Ellen?* Lorraine's younger sister, Ellen? That one. The one who's years younger than us? Like a *child*."

Gina nodded miserably.

"How did you find out? *When* did you find out?"

"A year and a half, no, more like two years ago." Gina wasn't meeting my eye, but looking beyond me, out of the window. "Toward the end of the summer Ellen met me for a drink and it all spilled out. She felt terrible. I think she needed someone to confess to."

"She wanted to confess to my close friend?"

"I know. It sounds weird. Honestly, Tess, the whole thing was a torment."

"I'm so sorry for your pain," I said nastily and saw the hurt on Gina's face. Good. I wanted to hurt her.

I worked it out. Poppy would have been about one year old, newly walking, starting to say words, and Jason had been having an affair. And Gina had known. So many times when the two of us were having conversations about relationships, about our personal lives, Gina must have been thinking: I know some-thing about Tess that she doesn't know about herself.

"So when Poppy was just a baby, you knew. And when I went part-time while Jason sailed on upwards and became a head, you knew. And ..." I could hardly speak, I was so agitated. I pointed a wobbly finger at my friend. "When we were having *counseling*? I told you how it was going and you must have been aware that Jason hadn't said anything about an affair, and there I was thinking we were both being honest with each other and trying our best to repair things or say goodbye properly. And you knew. You knew all that. And you didn't tell me, when all these years we've had conversations about what it is to be a woman, a mother, stand on our own ground, keep our independence, have agency. Stupid bloody fuck-ing agency. Who was I kidding? And Jason was hav-ing an affair. And you knew. And probably you've told Laurie."

Gina didn't answer. Her face was slack.

"Right. So he knew as well. And who else?"

"I don't know. I didn't tell anyone else, of course I didn't. All I know is what I've said to you now." She finally looked directly at me. "I'm sorry. I'm really, really sorry. I know you're angry with me. I'd be angry with me, if I was you."

I rubbed the side of my face. I was suddenly tired, almost violently tired.

"I am angry. I'm so angry that I can hardly bring myself to look at you. But it's not really you I'm angry with. It's Jason. And me. I'm angry with myself for not seeing it. And humiliated. I feel such a stupid, stupid fool. Was it obvious? How could I not know? How could I be so blind?"

"You didn't know because you trusted him and that's how we have to live," said Gina. There were tears in her eyes and her lovely face was wretched. "I wish I'd told you. But honestly, I didn't know what to do, and then when you and Jason separated, I thought it was too late to tell you because it was over and you seemed sorted out about it."

"But it's not over."

"What do you mean?"

"It's not over. It's there, some horrible ugly stain that's spreading and spreading. Something's going on."

"What on earth are you talking about?"

I thought of Poppy, lying just above us in her bed; I thought of the mutilated rag doll; I thought of the violent drawing and the swearing and the night terrors. I was gripped by something I had no control over.

"Never mind. Does she work?" I asked.

"Ellen?" Gina screwed her face up in concentration. "Something in education."

"A teacher?"

"No. Some kind of educational organization."

"Which one?"

TWELVE

The man at the front desk started rummaging through the papers in front of him.

"She's not expecting me," I said.

"Who shall I say is calling?"

"My name is Tess Moreau. If she says she's busy, you can tell her it's about Jason Hallam. It's important and I'm not going away until I've seen her."

My own voice sounded unfamiliar to me—clear, sharp and commanding. He raised his bushy eyebrows and picked up the phone.

I barely had time to sit down before the lift door opened and a woman came out and walked quickly over to me. I stood up and we looked at each other for a few seconds, unsmiling. At least she wasn't going to pretend.

"Shall we go for a walk?" I said.

"We can go to Lincoln's Inn Fields. It's a bit quieter there."

We walked side by side, crossed the busy road and then passed through a narrow passage that opened up into a lush green space, trees rustling with new leaves and tulips blazing in the beds. I allowed myself to look at her properly. Ellen Dempsey had short hair and narrow dark almond-shaped eyes. She had a piercing in her eyebrow and one in her nose, and a rather beautiful tattoo, like a vine or a branch, running up her left arm. She was wearing a black leather skirt and wedged trainers. I took all this in, understanding what I had already known: she was young, so very young. Much younger than me; a whole different generation. It occurred to me that she was about the same age as my youngest half-sister, Polly. I'd been twelve when Polly was born and had always thought of her as a baby. Was this Jason's type? Ellen didn't look like Emily, who was also young, of course: she was slimmer, more angular, fiercer-looking.

After we had entered the gate into what was almost a little park, Ellen turned and faced me, wrapping her arms protectively round her body. Her lips were twitching slightly and she kept biting them.

"I'm not with him anymore," I said.

"I know."

"He's married to someone else."

"I know that too."

I waited. Ellen took a deep breath.

"He sent me a text saying that he was getting married." She swallowed and wiped her nose with the sleeve of her sweater like a small child. "I thought I was going to go mad. I tried to get in touch with him just so that he could explain what had happened and he said that if I went on pestering him, he would get a lawyer involved. Like I was stalking him or something. I just wanted him to explain."

"That's what you get for sleeping with married men."

"He wasn't married," she said, then screwed up her small face. "Sorry, that's a crap thing to say. I know that doesn't matter. He had you, he had a child."

"That's right. He had me. He had a child. Why did you do it?"

Ellen met my gaze; she had a punkish, slightly confrontational air.

"Have you asked Jason that question?"

I nodded. She was right: Ellen hadn't betrayed me. Jason had. I'd always disliked the way women blame the other woman, because it is less painful that way. It lets them avoid looking at what really mattered, what had really been done to them.

"Not yet. I will, though."

She grimaced and it was as if all the breath was going out of her.

"Oh fuck," she said. "I didn't mean to sound like that. It's just . . ." She shrugged her slender shoulders. "I didn't even want to have a relationship, certainly not one with an older man who was already with someone else and had a child. I'd come out of a bad breakup and I wasn't in a good place. We just talked at a party." She looked away and added, almost too softly for me to hear: "You were there, actually, a few feet away on the other side of the room, laughing with a group of people, so it was a bit weird. He rang me up the next day."

I tried to keep my face expressionless, but I felt a sharp pain, as if I'd been punched. She could have been describing the way Jason and I had first met, all those years ago when I was a young fool, vulnerable and ready for heartbreak.

"He was pretty persistent," Ellen continued. "I guess I was flattered. It wasn't even meant to be a date. You probably don't want to hear this."

"I'm trying to join up the dots, make sense of my past."

Ellen nodded. She got that.

"He was so in love with me, or at least he made me feel that he was. He made me feel like I was the most gorgeous woman in the world. He said he wanted to be with me, but it was difficult with everything. I thought—" Then she stopped.

"What?"

"I thought you maybe knew about it all. At the time, I mean. He kind of suggested you had separate lives and you'd be OK with it."

I squinted at Ellen through the glare of the sun and said nothing.

"So you really didn't know?"

"I really didn't. When did it start?"

"What a fuckup."

"When did it start?"

"About two years ago. Early summer. At first he made all the running and then, somehow, I fell in love with him. After a few months it seemed to get harder to see each other, but I didn't read the signals. I was such an idiot. In the end he sent me that text."

"That was a year ago?"

"Something like that."

"What happened then?"

"You really want to know?"

"I do."

Ellen wiped tears off her cheeks with the back of her hand.

"I thought I was going crazy. He'd made me believe he couldn't live without me, then he just behaved as if it had all been nothing, a fling. He left you and—"

"It was mutual," I said, interrupting. "We left each other."

But was that even true? I didn't know anymore and not knowing made me feel weak and untethered.

"Whatever," said Ellen cautiously. "You separated and he didn't want anything to do with me. I suppose he'd met this other woman."

I was about to interrupt again, to tell her that he had met Emily after we'd parted, but I didn't. Because who knew if that was the case?

"That word 'dumped,' that's how I felt." Ellen looked away from me, across the brightness of the park. "Thrown away. I tried to contact him and I wrote to him and I thought of going round there and slashing his tires or smashing his window, or going to the school and making a public nuisance of myself. He wouldn't have liked that. I went to a therapist instead, which was a much better idea, because now I don't want to kill myself and I don't even want to kill him, or shame him, I just want to get on with my life and never, ever be dependent like that again. I think he's an arsehole, a typical male shit who preys on the vulnerable, and I'm really, really, really sorry. But I think you're better off without him."

"You do? That's all right then."

"Sorry. That was a stupid thing to say."

"It was. Though I agree with you."

Ellen hesitated, then spoke in a rush. "Was he ever violent?"

"What! What are you saying? Did he hit you?"

"No." A flush moved up her neck and into her face. "But he . . . I always thought it was possible. You know."

"Right." I felt a bit sick.

"Every so often he was scary. So I wondered . . ."

"No."

"Good."

"Had he had other affairs?"

Ellen flinched. "I don't know. You'd have to ask him. I mean . . . I kind of assumed but I don't know."

"You said that you tried to contact him. When exactly was that?"

"When he left me and I was in a mess."

"Have you tried to contact him again or seen him?"

"Why on earth would I? I'm done with all of that. I never want to be that person again."

THIRTEEN

I rang Aidan and said I couldn't see him that night after all.

"You're doing this quite a lot."

"What?"

"Putting me off."

"I know. Sorry. It's just at the moment ..." I let the sentence trail away.

"Is there something you're not telling me? About us, I mean?"

"No. Honestly. I'll explain later."

I ended the call and sent a text to Jason saying we needed to talk, urgently and privately. A text came back almost instantly: *v busy can it wait?*

no, I replied.

Then added another: *Tomorrow before school? 8:15?*

I rang my school secretary. I'd told her early that morning I was ill, and now I said I wouldn't be coming in the next day either. Stomach bug, I added, very contagious. I didn't know when I'd be back. I called

Gina and told her I would collect Poppy today and tomorrow, but could she or Laurie take her to school in the morning. I could hardly bring myself to speak to Gina or picture her eager, pleading expression. I just wanted to take my troubled little daughter and go far away, somewhere empty and peaceful and healing. I pictured a hilltop, a lake, gentle heat: May was my favorite month, everything clean and new.

What would we do on a hilltop, though?

I was waiting outside Poppy's class when the bell rang. Poppy charged out and wrapped her arms tightly around my legs and burrowed against me. I stroked the top of her head, feeling the heat of her.

"Can I have a word?"

It was Lotty, Poppy's teacher. Her round, smooth face was serious.

I disentangled herself from Poppy's grip. "Get your coat and wait here a minute. We're going swimming."

"Swimming? Me and you?"

"Yes."

"Not Jake?"

"Just us."

I left Poppy with the nursery assistant and followed Lotty into the classroom.

"I know you've been worried about Poppy."

"Is she all right?"

"She hasn't had a good day. She bit Sadie."

"*Bit* her?"

"Sadie had to go to the nurse. She needed a bandage. Her mother is very upset."

"That's awful."

"It's not just that. It's what Poppy said." Lotty wrinkled her nose. "She called me a cunt."

I felt like I needed to sit down but I couldn't see anywhere. All the chairs were too small to sit on.

"I'm so sorry. But she doesn't understand."

"I know she doesn't. But we don't tolerate acts of violence and aggression in our class."

"I'll talk to her. I'll make that clear."

"I've reported your concerns to safeguarding already. I will have to add this incident."

"Right."

"Do you have any idea why Poppy's behavior has changed like this?"

"I don't. Her father and I separated, but that was a year ago and she's seemed fine up until now."

"Well. We'll keep an eye on her. Don't hesitate to come to me if there's anything I can do."

Tears pricked in my eyes. "Thanks," I said. "I'm sorry. So sorry."

We spent nearly an hour in the pool. Poppy was learning to swim: her strong pale legs paddled furiously beneath her; just the shallow disc of her face was above the water. Like a water lily, I thought, or a jellyfish. She had no fear. Every so often she would disappear beneath the surface and become a writhing shape, and then emerge spluttering and laughing, blowing spouts of water from her mouth.

Back home, we took biscuits and juice into the small garden and examined the flowers. When we'd moved in, one of the first things we had done—before we'd finished the unpacking and rearranging—was to plant spring bulbs and shrubs for the following year. The daffodils and tulips were gone, but I had also put in some aquilegias. Poppy squatted beside them and poked the tight buds that were beginning to open. She crawled over to where I was sitting cross-legged and put her head in my lap and we watched the goldfinch swinging on the feeder. Her face seemed almost luminous in the soft evening, and I thought how normal she seemed, how miraculous. It was hard to believe she'd sunk her sharp little teeth into her friend's flesh.

There was a sound of a window opening above us and I twisted round to see Bernie. There was a woman beside him with a shaved head and dark brows. He waved enthusiastically. I raised a cautious hand back.

"We've made some bread," he called. "Too much for us. Do you want some?"

"It's really kind of you but we have bread."

"Not homemade sourdough bread, you haven't."

He disappeared before I had time to reply.

We ate fish fingers and peas together, Poppy carefully peeling off the crisp shell of breadcrumbs to save till last, and then I ran her a bath and knelt beside her, trying to blow bubbles through the circle of my forefinger and thumb. I took her onto my lap to dry her, feeling the damp warmth of her clean, glowing body. Pulled on clean pajamas. Sat on her bed.

"Story," said Poppy imperiously. "Little Bear."

"In a minute. I want to ask you something. Your teacher said—"

"I didn't do it."

"You bit Sadie."

"I didn't do it. I hate her."

"And you used a bad word to your teacher."

"I hate her. I hate you. I *hate* you." She looked at me triumphantly. "Cunt," she said.

"You do not say that word."

"Kingcunty cunt."

"Poppy!"

But she turned away from me, wriggling her angry body further down beneath the duvet.

"I'm not going away. I want to talk to you. Even if you're upset or cross, you don't bite people. Or hit people. Or call people bad things. It's very wrong. It will make people upset."

"I want Milly. Where's Milly?"

"Listen, Poppy." I bit my lip, trying to find the right words. "I think you saw something that made you frightened."

"Yes. I did see. I did see!"

"Did Daddy hurt someone?"

"Yes, Daddy did hurt!" Poppy pulled herself upright, looking almost exultant.

"Who did he hurt?"

"He did hurt!"

"Who?"

"Milly?" Poppy sounded dubious.

I was doing this all wrong. It's the most basic rule with children: if you want to find out what has happened, never ask them a leading question.

"Or maybe it wasn't Daddy?" I said, hopelessly.

"Not Daddy?"

"Did Ben hurt someone?"

This was all wrong: I was just planting ideas into her fertile brain.

"Ben did do it." Poppy nodded vigorously. "Ben did hurt."

I rubbed the side of my face. I was like someone who had walked over crucial footprints, muddying them all. I plowed on.

"When you were with Daddy and Emily, did something happen to make you sad?"

Poppy gazed at me. Her eyes were bright, the pupils large. Her mouth was pulled into a straight line and her body was tense. I could see that a storm was building up inside her.

"Story." She pinched at my arm with fingers that felt like pincers. "Story now. Little bear."

When at last I leaned over her to kiss her good night, thinking her already asleep, Poppy's eyes flickered open. She stared at me as if I were a stranger.

"Are you dead now?" she whispered dreamily.

"No! I'm alive and I'm here."

"When you're dead, where will you be then?"

I looked at my daughter. Who are you? I thought. What are you thinking? What have you seen?

Bernie brought the bread round when I was writing reports. I had done three and I needed to do twenty-seven more in the next two weeks. He stood in the doorway, clutching the loaf to his chest and smiling.

"Thanks." I sounded rude. "It's very kind of you," I added.

"You're welcome."

He took that step forward, as I'd known he would, to bring him just a little bit too close.

"Being neighbors," he said. "We should do something. A drink or whatever."

"I just wanted to say," I blurted out, feeling it was now or never. "Your room is just above Poppy's. She can hear you."

He flushed slightly, but he didn't seem angry.

"I can hear you too," he said.

FOURTEEN

"I've got about fifteen minutes," said Jason, looking at his phone, laying down his briefcase, taking off his sunglasses, all business.

Even though I had had to drop Poppy off early and cross London, while he was a few minutes from his school, Jason was late. I had been in the café for more than ten minutes, watching my cappuccino go cold.

"What is it that's so urgent?"

"Poppy is urgent," I said. "So it might take more than fifteen minutes."

Jason sighed. "We've been through this."

"Is there anything you've forgotten to tell me? Apart from Emily being pregnant and Ben living in your house, that is. With a dog I don't trust."

"Tess, what's going on? Why are you being like this?"

"Nothing then?"

"I really don't have time for this. Look." He leaned forward and for a moment I thought he was about to take my clenched fist in his hand. "I don't understand your question. Is it about Poppy? She seems fine enough to me."

He sat back. I caught him taking a surreptitious glance at his watch.

"I just talked to Ellen Dempsey."

I looked at him as I said it and, despite myself, I was impressed. He gave the smallest start of surprise.

"Didn't you hear?" I said. I leaned forward and spoke more loudly. Another couple at the next table looked round. "You must remember her. Lorraine's sister, that one. The young one."

"Not now," he said, still calm. "Not here."

"When Poppy was tiny. When we were talking about our relationship and deciding to give it a go. When you were telling me that I was tired and emotional and that's why I felt dissatisfied. When we were having relationship counseling and being honest with each other, laying all our cards on the table. Remember?"

"Did you arrange this here so you could make a big scene in public?" said Jason. "Is that you?"

When Jason said that, he was being perceptive as well as unfeeling and manipulative. Because he was right. It wasn't me. I had spent my life avoiding confrontation, being the first to apologize, assuming everything must be my fault somehow. I was genuinely tempted to call his bluff and create a no-nonsense, horrendous public display. But I didn't. I knew I wouldn't be good at something like that and it would come out wrong and I would feel terrible about it afterward.

"That's not it at all," I said. "Once I knew, I thought it was important to tell you that I knew."

"All right," said Jason. "Now I know that you know. If you want me to apologize, all right, I apologize. It was a difficult time and it wasn't a big deal, but I apologize."

"She says you were in love with her and promised to marry her."

"She was angry and upset."

"Were there other affairs?"

"Let's not do this."

"Because your fifteen minutes is almost up? Or because there were?"

He sat up straighter, visibly gathering himself. It was as if he was willing himself into an attitude of contempt. Once there, he was more assured.

"We're over, Tess. We were together, we had a gorgeous child, and then we decided to go our separate ways. We don't have a relationship to talk about, except one that involves our responsibility toward Poppy. We've moved on. You have a new partner, I have a new partner. The past is gone."

"My past isn't what I thought it was. We weren't what I thought we were. Do you get how much I hate that?"

Jason stood up. "Is that Poppy's bag for tonight?"

He reached over and took it.

"You may not care about me, but I hope you care about Poppy. She bit a child at school yesterday. She called her teacher a cunt. Something bad is happening to her."

"I believe that," he said. "Have you looked at yourself? Don't you think that Poppy might be picking up on your resentment and paranoia? Maybe you're the one who's making her act up, not me, not some mistake of mine that happened years ago."

I stood as well. I leaned across the table so we were eyeball to eyeball.

"I keep thinking of all the lies," I said. "That's what gets me."

I watched him leave, picking up his briefcase, putting on his sunglasses, stepping out into the street and not looking back. Now what? I had taken the whole day off school, but for what? I felt scraped thin by the encounter and also full of a restless, itchy energy.

I walked the fifteen minutes to Brockwell Park and for a while wandered aimlessly through its large spaces. I used to come here when Poppy was a baby, pushing the buggy past the lido, the café, stopping by the beautiful ponds to feed the ducks. How long ago that world seemed. In just a few hours, my whole view of the past had been violently rearranged and everything seemed unfamiliar. I felt unfamiliar.

I sat on a bench, closed my eyes, tipped my head back to feel the kindness of the sun that came slanting through the tall trees. The light was dappled. There were birds in the branches above me. I didn't know what to do next. The detective, though sympathetic, had been no help; Alex had taken me seriously but could do no more than advise vigilance; Jason suddenly felt like an enemy. I could talk to Gina—but

I didn't want to talk to Gina. I didn't want to talk to Nadine, who would probably only say what she had already said. Or my friend Becky, who was in the middle of an acrimonious divorce. I briefly thought of turning to Aidan, but he was too new in my life, too affected by my emotional turbulence. I needed a woman and I also needed someone who knew the old Tess, the one who had lived for nearly ten years with Jason, who had loved and trusted him, who had been so blind.

On an impulse I rang my mother, but the call went to voicemail, and I realized that it was Friday morning, and she would be at the health-food shop where she worked three days a week. I had been four when my father left us and started a new family—not much older than Poppy was when Jason and I had separated. I remembered—or I thought I remembered—the vicious arguments that preceded it. The fallout had gone on for many years: a rumbling hostility between them that quite often flared up into something more dramatic. I'd witnessed my parents being transformed by rage and distress into people who no longer felt safe to me, their faces wrenched into ugliness, their words hard and bitter. They both used to tell me how wrongly the other was behaving, how they couldn't be trusted. It had been scary and nasty and it was what Jason and I had pledged to avoid ourselves.

My mother's face came into my mind, lined and anxious, always readying itself for bad news. I didn't leave a message.

I had no proof, no tangible facts, just a coiling dread

that Poppy had witnessed something terrible, and an instinct that she was, unconsciously, telling her mother what, if only I would listen carefully enough.

Then an idea came to me and I stood up. It was better than doing nothing.

FIFTEEN

I thought it would be really hard but it was easy. After just a few minutes searching online, I found a map of London murders organized by year. I had vaguely thought that there would be hundreds or thousands of murders to comb through, but so far this year, nearly six months in, there had only been sixty-two.

The statistics were searchable through different categories: age, type of weapon, gender of victim. I clicked on the box marked "female' and the number dropped to thirteen. Thirteen? Out of a city of nine million? It felt like an amazingly small number. The murders were represented by dots. It looked like south London was safer than north London: only three dots. West London was safer than east London, outer London safer than central London. I placed my cursor over one of the dots down near Brixton, clicked on it and the details appeared: knife, thirty-one years old.

That didn't look right. Poppy hadn't said anything about a knife. There was violence but her picture showed someone falling. I clicked on three more: knife,

knife, knife. The next one said "weapon: unknown'. That looked more promising. The woman was called Vicky Silva and she was 28 years old.

I opened a new window and searched for "Vicky Silva death" and immediately found a news report: her husband had pleaded guilty to strangling her. I went back to the map and clicked on another dot: blunt object. What was a blunt object? Yes, something that wasn't a knife.

I clicked on another dot: "weapon: unknown." Again I did a search on the victim's name and found a news story: "Suspected Murder Suicide." She had been found dead alongside the body of her husband. The circumstances of the deaths were unclear, but the police had concluded that the husband had killed the wife and then himself. Always that way round, I thought to myself.

Another woman had died in a fire started by an ex-partner. Another was weapon unknown and victim unidentified. What did that mean? It—whatever it was—had taken place in Dartford. This sounded too far out of the way to be significant but I wrote "Dartford?" on my notepad, though I didn't know what I would do with that.

The next one was also "weapon: unknown." A Russian woman living in Hampstead had been found murdered in her flat and two Russian men and a Russian woman had been arrested. Large amounts of money were involved and it all seemed a bit strange, more complicated, more exotic, and also entirely unconnected with what I was looking for.

Victim number eleven was eighty-nine years old.

For some reason, I had always imagined the victim in Poppy's drawing as young, but there was no reason to. I did a search on the name and found that it had happened during a burglary and the man had been caught and had confessed. Another blunt object.

Victim number twelve's cause of death was unknown. A search on the name showed that her body had been found in her flat in Stoke Newington. The autopsy had been inconclusive, but a man had already been charged with her murder: another ex-partner.

The thirteenth and final victim had been beaten to death by her boyfriend. He had confessed and been sentenced to life imprisonment. I read a local newspaper story about the crime and the condition of the body when it was found and the events that had preceded it and the previous offenses of the murderer, and I had to stop and look away from my screen and take a few deep breaths.

I thought of what had happened to each of those women. The youngest was seventeen and the oldest was eighty-nine. Even among this small number they were from different backgrounds, different cultures. Looking through my notes, I was struck by the fact that only two had been killed by strangers. The biggest danger to these women had been their husbands or their lovers, those they were intimate with, those they trusted. As far as I could make out, most of them had died in their own homes.

I looked around the living room and felt with a shiver that the place I had thought of as my refuge was where I was genuinely vulnerable. We're all safer with strangers because they don't care enough about us to kill us.

Still, I hadn't succeeded in what I had set out to do. I hadn't found a death that reminded me of Poppy's drawing. These tragic women had been stabbed or strangled or bludgeoned or trapped in a burning building. But none of them had been pushed off anything. None of them had fallen.

Fallen: not every murder was recognized as a murder. When a person was pushed from a high place, it might look like an accident or like a suicide. I did a search for UK suicides and quickly saw that this was going to be much harder. The UK was a country with few murders but many suicides. A government website told me that in the previous year there had been six and a half thousand suicides registered. Almost three quarters of those were men, but that still left almost two thousand possible cases to go through.

As I read on, I realized that the few murders in the UK are investigated rapidly with plenty of publicity, but suicides are different. They are just one part of the flood of deaths that happen everywhere all the time. They don't get much publicity, unless they are spectacular, and are investigated not by the police but by inquests that take months or years.

Unless they are spectacular. I read through an account of the different causes of suicide. A few deep breaths weren't enough. I made herself a mug of coffee and walked outside and stood in my little garden, in the sunshine, until I was ready to continue.

I returned to my laptop. The usual methods by which

people took their own lives were drab and domestic. A fall from a high window was the sort of thing that might get into the newspapers. I did a search for "falls deaths UK" and read a series of stories of little children and windows with defective window fastenings, scaffolding failures, mountain climbers' ropes coming loose, each of them a heart-stopping drama, none of them relevant. I narrowed it to "falls deaths London" and still there was nothing that felt right.

I closed my laptop and sat for several minutes thinking. I was still holding my pen, but there was nothing to write down. I drew little squares and attached triangles to the squares and filled them in with crosshatching. So where was I? I now felt almost certain that in Greater London, in the first four or five months of this year, no woman had died by falling or being deliberately pushed from a high place or high building. I tapped my pen on the paper. Was there something I was missing?

I reached for my mobile and called Laurie, who sounded surprised to hear from me.

"Are you all right?"

"I'm fine. I'm ringing about something that might sound a bit strange, but you've spent a lot of time with Poppy recently and I was wondering whether you ever read stories to her and Jake."

"Stories? Of course." Laurie sounded offended, as if I were criticizing his parenting skills. "I try to read to them every day, unless Nellie's having one of her screaming fits."

"I know, I know, you've been wonderful. I'm asking,

because Poppy has been doing some odd drawings and I just wondered where she got the idea from. For example, have you been reading any fairy stories to them?"

"I don't know. I just read a few of the books we've got around the house. I can show them to you if you want. I'm sure there's nothing that's unsuitable."

"That's not what I mean. For example, did you ever read them the story of Rapunzel?"

"Rapunzel?"

"That's the story of the girl in the tower and she's got long hair and—"

"Yes, I know what Rapunzel is."

He was definitely offended, I thought.

"Did you ever read it to them?"

"I have not read the story of Rapunzel to Poppy. Or to Jake for that matter. Or any other story involving princesses with long hair."

"It was more the tower bit of the story that I was thinking of. Of someone falling from a tower. Or jumping."

"I've not read any stories about princesses in towers. Or towers in general."

"Isn't there a Disney film about it?"

I heard Laurie laugh at the other end of the line.

"You're really pursuing this, aren't you?"

"I'm just trying to get to the bottom of what's been upsetting Poppy."

"I don't think it's likely to be a fairy story." Laurie sounded impatient. "Yes, I think there is a Disney cartoon about it, but I haven't got it or shown it to Jake or Poppy. I know I should encourage Jake to watch films about princesses, but he prefers adventures and fights and that probably makes me a bad father, but—"

"Of course it doesn't make you a bad father." I paused and he waited. "You're a wonderful father," I said. "Amazing. Anyway, that's all I wanted to know. Thank you. Poppy may have got the idea from somewhere, but she didn't get it from you and it probably doesn't matter anyway."

I rang off, hoping I hadn't sounded unhinged.

So Poppy hadn't got the idea from a story or film at Gina and Laurie's. I could check with Lotty. Could they have done a project about Rapunzel or something like Rapunzel in class? And what about Jason? Jason read stories to Poppy, and Emily too. I pondered this. Could a simple story have triggered Poppy's escalating distress?

There was, of course, another possibility. I had discovered nothing about the truth behind Poppy's picture or whether there was anything behind it at all. But I had discovered a new truth about my own relationship with Jason. Perhaps, in her unconscious, Poppy had picked up on the discord and the lies and the deceptions of her parents' breakup and that was what the picture was about.

Perhaps the figure in the picture was actually Poppy herself, in freefall.

SIXTEEN

It was barely midday. I opened the fridge and peered inside. There was milk, butter, four eggs, half a jar of green pesto, some Parmesan, a bag of salad leaves and a little bowl of mashed potatoes—left over from supper that Aidan had cooked, weeks ago. It must have gone off by now. I peeled away the plastic wrap and dipped a finger into the mash. It had definitely gone off. I threw it in the bin then stared around. I wanted to do a binge tidy of the kitchen, but everything was clean and in its proper place. I might not be an amazing cook, but I was a good tidier and cleaner. Like my mother, like my grandmother. Women down the generations washing, sorting, folding, putting away, bringing order to mess and to chaos.

I looked around the large downstairs room. There was a damp patch spreading above the baseboards that needed attention. The fridge was old—bought second-hand and failing already—and through the winter the heating had been inadequate. I worried about the leftover money from the Brixton house leaking away.

I worried that this place wouldn't feel like home to Poppy, that she would prefer to be with her father, in a house with many rooms and a larger garden, full of the comforting clutter that had been built up over the years.

I went into Poppy's room, adjusted the covers on her bed unnecessarily, opened her drawers and peered inside at the bright-colored tee shirts, the paired socks. I thought of Poppy at school. It would be lunchtime now, and I pictured her tearing round the playground with her red hair flying, her pale face and shining eyes, that look of ferocious joy on her face.

I pictured her shouting at her teacher, biting her friend, making Jake distressed, and had an impulse to run to the school now and pick her up and carry her home where she was safe. But today Poppy was supposed to be going to Jason's again: he was only having her for a few days over the half-term week, so they had arranged long ago that this weekend she would stay with him from Friday to Saturday afternoon.

The thought of not seeing her until tomorrow afternoon was unbearable. The thought of her being with Jason, in that house full of new people and old memories, impossible. Something might happen; she might come back freshly traumatized.

I paced through the flat, unable to keep still. On an impulse, I snatched up my mobile from the kitchen table and wrote a text to Jason, pressing "send" before I had a chance to read it over or change my mind:

Really sorry for late notice, but Mum has arranged

some kind of treat for Poppy tonight—she didn't tell me until now! Hope that's OK.

I looked at the sent message, frowning, then added: *I am sure you'll understand.*

I pressed "send" and then regretted it because after our last meeting it sounded so patently false. I added a postscript.

Will pick Poppy up from school.

It occurred to me that when he next saw her, Jason might ask Poppy about the treat. I found my mother's number on my phone and rang it, but it was engaged. I cursed and went online to search for kids' event in Abingdon over the weekend—after all, it had been weeks since Poppy and I had visited my mother, so this was an opportunity to turn the lie into the truth. There was a puppet show on Saturday morning. I opened the link, while trying the number again.

My mobile rang as I did so, startling me. Jason.

"Hi," I said breezily. "Sorry about the mix-up."

"So your mother's taking Poppy somewhere this evening?"

"Yes." There was a silence and I filled it, like I always did. "Apparently she arranged it ages ago, but she only just let me know." I gave a brittle laugh. "Typical."

"Is that so?"

Something about his tone sent a spike of unease through me.

'I told you as soon as I heard. I know it's a bit irritating, but you saw Poppy on Wednesday and you can have her for a day next weekend. Is there a problem?"

"I think I'd call it a problem."

"Oh?"

"I've just come off the phone to your mother."

Sweat was breaking out all over my body.

"Why were you talking to my mother? I mean, you never talk to my mother. You don't even like her."

There was another silence. I thought of throwing the mobile away and unplugging the phone and closing the curtains and curling up in a small ball of shame.

"I rang her," said Jason eventually, "because I wanted to know if she was expecting Poppy this evening."

"You shouldn't have done that." I had closed my eyes, as if being in the darkness would make my humiliation easier. "You had no right," I added uselessly.

"She was very surprised to hear from me, and very surprised to hear that she was taking her granddaughter out this evening."

"OK. I lied." I opened my eyes and took a deep breath. "I want to have Poppy this evening."

"She's coming to us. As planned. Emily will pick her up from school."

"Please, Jason. I just need to have her with me tonight. She's not her usual self. I won't keep doing this. I shouldn't have lied. But I knew you'd say no if I just asked."

"You were right. I am indeed saying no."

"I'm worried about her."

"And I'm worried about you." He was enjoying this, I thought; he liked hearing me squirm. "Have you thought of talking to someone?"

I wanted to shout, to hurl the phone into the garden, to scratch his handsome face.

"You don't get to say that to me. Not anymore."

"I'm just looking out for my daughter. I'm sorry for whatever it is you're going through, Tess, but I don't want Poppy to suffer."

I went for a run, sprinting as fast as I could down the little side streets, into London Fields, relishing the pain in my calves. I had a long shower. I wrote two more reports, then sat at my sewing machine, feeding Poppy's golden witch cloak through the steadily ticking needle. I picked up my mobile to call Aidan because I needed to hear a kind voice, I needed someone who was definitely on my side, then put it down again.

I picked up my jacket, my keys, and walked swiftly toward Poppy's school, ignoring the voice inside me that was telling me it was a bad idea. I stood under the plane tree and watched as Emily arrived, looking so pretty in a flowery dress, her dark blond hair falling round her face. I watched as Emily greeted Poppy, leaning down toward her, and there was my sprightly little daughter in her yellow cotton skirt and her red hair flying, holding onto Emily's hand, dipping and weaving and skipping along beside her as they left. I felt ready to cry with tenderness, with jealousy.

I was being stupid. Stupid stupid stupid stupid.

Jason had lied to me and he had had an affair—or probably affairs. Poppy had been going through a bad patch. And I was behaving like a madwoman.

SEVENTEEN

That evening, Aidan and I went to a party together. I put on my green silk dress and piled my hair on top of my head. I applied red lipstick that made my face look unhealthily pale and squirted perfume behind my ears. When I stood in front of the mirror, I seemed like a stranger, which made me feel both triumphant and uneasy.

We both drank a large gin and tonic before we left and I filled my glass to the brim with red wine when we arrived at Lex and Corry's house near Victoria Park. It was a fortieth birthday celebration. There were lots of people there and most of them were pretending that they were still young and childless. I hugged old friends and introduced everyone to Aidan—he still didn't know many of my circle and I knew few of his. I smoked a dizzying cigarette in the narrow garden with Lex and a man called Geoffrey and felt a bit nauseous. The moon was up, a buttery yellow and almost full. I could smell roses. As the evening wore on, I danced, my body loose and free. I put my face close to my old friend Simon's and said:

"Did you like Jason?"

"Jason? I liked him because you were with him."

"But did you *like* him?"

"Is this a real question?"

"Yes."

"I would say he was a bit arrogant. Some of the time. Not always."

"Did Jason ever make a pass at you?" I asked my friend Megan as we sat together on the stairs, propped against each other.

"You're drunk," said Megan affably. "So am I."

"But did he?"

"No. But he always felt"—she made a flapping gesture with her free hand—"available."

"Available," I repeated.

I felt dangerous, as if the self I had carefully kept under control was coming loose and unraveling. I sought Aidan out and wound my arms around his neck and he kissed me on my jawline.

"Beautiful woman," he said softly.

"Nice man," I said.

"What I said was nicer."

"No. That's the sexiest thing you can be. Nice, nice man." I kissed him hard on the lips. "If you ever cheat on me, we're over. No second chances."

At half past four in the morning, I woke with a dry mouth. Aidan was lying on his back beside me, straight as a log and with his hands gathered on his chest, which rose and fell peacefully. He looked younger in his sleep, more vulnerable.

I quietly climbed out of bed and went into the main room, which was washed with moonlight, though day was already coming. I made myself a mug of tea and sat by the French windows looking out into the garden. Miles away across the city, Poppy was sleeping. I could picture her, her hands pressed together under her cheek as if in prayer and her mouth very slightly open, all the heat and fret of the day gone from her.

But was she safe? The question made my heart hammer faster. I cradled my tea in my hand and tried to turn my mind onto other things. But the fear that, far from me, Poppy might be in danger, had rushed back and was filling me with a churning dread.

At last, I tiptoed into my bedroom and in the dim light put on a pair of jeans, a shirt and sneakers. I left a note on the kitchen table for Aidan—*Couldn't sleep so gone for a walk; back before long xxxx*—took my light jacket from the hook in the hall and left the flat, shutting the front door with a quiet click as I went.

The curtains were all closed in the house in Brixton, but there was a light on downstairs. At twenty to eight, the front door opened and Emily appeared in her dressing gown. She put out a bag of recycling, then went back inside.

At ten to eight, the curtains were opened in Poppy's room, which looked out onto the street. Standing on the other side of the road against a lamp post, I waited to see Poppy herself, but only made out a larger figure move briefly across the space. Jason? My tummy rumbled. I needed breakfast. I could be sitting in my flat right now with a pot of coffee in front of me, while Aidan made scrambled eggs for us and the goldfinch came to the bird feeder.

Half an hour later, the front door opened once more and Emily's brother Ben came out, Roxie at his heels. He was moving slowly, as if carrying a heavy weight, and dragging his feet on the ground. His hands were deep in his pockets and his head was lowered.

Ten minutes later he was back, carrying a bundle of newspapers. Jason had always liked to get the Saturday papers.

Another half an hour went by and then the door was flung wide and out came Jason, Emily and Poppy. I knew where they were going: they were going where Jason and Poppy and I used to go on a Saturday morning—the little café on the edge of the park. Jason would have granola with blueberries and two mugs of coffee, milk on the side. Poppy would probably have the pancakes with maple syrup. It was the same tradition, just a different cast of characters inhabiting it.

I followed them at a safe distance. Poppy held Jason's and Emily's hands. Sometimes she would drag down on their arms and I knew she was asking to be swung. Twice they gave in and I saw Poppy lifted high in the air and heard her whoop in delight.

Now Poppy was refusing to walk. She tried to sit down on the road and Jason held her up by one arm so she dangled like a rag doll. He was dragging her along. I groaned out loud. I watched as they went into the café. I dithered uselessly on the pavement, then edged a bit further toward the entrance.

"Tess? It is Tess, isn't it?"

I spun round. Ben was standing there, holding Roxie on a lead and looking confused.

I couldn't think of anything to say.

"I thought you weren't collecting Poppy until later."

"I was in the area. And I remembered there was something I forgot to give Jason."

"He's in there." Ben jerked his head toward the café.

"It's not important."

"Give it to me then." He held out his large soft hand, palm upwards. "Whatever it is."

"I've changed my mind." I stepped back.

"Give it to me," he repeated.

"It doesn't matter. Got to go."

"You don't like me, do you?"

"What do you mean? I'm just sorry I bothered you."

I half-turned, but as I did so the door of the café swung open and there was Jason and he was striding toward me.

"Tess," he said. Ominous voice.

"I'm just going. Passing. You know. There was something I was going to— But it's OK. Poppy can wait till this evening. Silly. No worries." I lifted a hand in histrionic farewell and began walking away so fast I was practically running. My breath was ragged. Where was the hole I could hide in? Where was the ground that would open up and swallow me?

116

Jason easily caught up with me.

"What?"

"You're spying on me."

"I'm not."

"Yesterday Emily said she saw you at the school when she went to collect Poppy."

"I needed to speak to the teacher."

"Stop it."

"I'm going now," I said.

He put a hand on my shoulder and I jerked and pushed it off.

"Careful," said Jason. "Poppy might see you behaving like this. Is that what you want?"

"What do you have to say then?"

He leaned in closer. Stubble. The smell of coffee on his breath. "You're this close . . ." He held up a thumb and forefinger, almost touching. "This close to me getting lawyers involved."

I made a scoffing sound that sounded more like a squawk.

"I'm serious. This is serious. You tried to stop me seeing Poppy. You lied about arrangements. You spied on my wife." The phrase "my wife," spoken so pompously, made me smile nastily. "You're here now, spying on our family. Stalking us. You need to get a grip on yourself, Tess, and quickly."

"Is that it?"

"That's it."

"Right. I'll leave you to your wife, your family."

"Make sure you do that."

EIGHTEEN

"Do you want a glass of wine?" asked Aidan.

He was preparing pizza for when Poppy got back, his shirtsleeves rolled up and a striped apron tied round his waist. I was sitting at the kitchen table, ragged with exhausted emotions, but I liked seeing him at work. It soothed me. He had already made the dough and it was rising soft and spongy in the bowl; now he was making the sauce, chopping onions and lifting them into the pan where they sizzled, squeezing garlic, adding a tin of tomatoes.

"No," I said. "Or actually, yes, but I think I'll wait till after Jason's brought Poppy back."

He glanced across at me. "Are you OK?"

"Not really."

"Do you want to tell me about it?"

"I'll have herbal tea, I think."

"The excitements of Saturday night," he said, but agreeably.

It took some rummaging around in the cupboard before I found a carton at the back with two remaining bags of peppermint tea. Making it was the sane thing to do and I needed to do something sane.

When it was ready—it smelled disagreeably like toothpaste—I sat back at the kitchen table and tried to calm myself before Jason arrived. When you feel stressed, you should breathe slowly and look around your environment and take a note of every object and ... then what? I couldn't quite remember. It was something about looking as it is, in itself. Not judging it. Not making plans about it. I looked at the carpet that was badly worn (really it needed either replacing or removing altogether and just having the floorboards, which would probably need sanding and polishing, but that was the kind of job I liked doing). I looked at the green vase on the mantelpiece, with tulips in it that were starting to splay and collapse.

Aidan was tearing a ball of mozzarella into pieces, then grating Parmesan. He was very serious about it all, almost comically so. There was a rich smell of tomatoes and garlic in the kitchen.

"Shall I put some music on?" I asked.

"Good idea."

Soon a deep female voice, a glorious smoker's voice that made you think of whiskey and sex and heartbreak, was singing about being half crazy. I had become half crazy myself. Or at least, I had done the sorts of things that madwomen did. Jason would be here soon and I knew that I must be careful not to give him any more ammunition. He had a way of twisting things so that even when he was in the wrong, he appeared to be in the right.

In one of our counseling sessions, Toni, a middle-aged woman with a strange taste in cardigans, had told us that we both needed to take responsibility. I could have wept as I remembered how I had opened up to Toni and to Jason about my own failings, my own bad thoughts, about how I had been changed by motherhood and maybe I hadn't paid enough attention to the relationship and that I could understand how hard this must be for Jason—and Jason had nodded with a sad smile and all the time, all the fucking time, he had known that he was still sleeping with someone else, that all this was a grim charade. You could unhinge someone like that. You could make them think everything was their fault, their weakness, their failure.

I took another sip of the hateful tea. Aidan was stretching the dough in his hands like a piece of elastic that sprang back on itself as soon as he loosened his grip. He laid it out on the baking tray, ladled on the rich sauce and scattered the cheese over. He sensed me looking at him and crossed to the table. His glasses were steamed up so I couldn't see his eyes, but he took them off and bent down and kissed me.

"Whatever it is, it'll be OK," he said.

"Will it?"

"Yes."

He tucked my hair behind my ears, put his glasses back on and returned to the stove.

"Aidan?"

"Yes."

"Thanks."

I felt a new fragile calm which hadn't dispersed

when, shortly before seven o'clock, the doorbell rang and I went upstairs and opened the front door to find Jason and Poppy standing on the step. Poppy was wearing her little backpack and her hair was in unraveling plaits. Jason's expression was entirely impassive, as if he were looking at a stranger.

I resisted the impulse to lift Poppy up and hug her close.

"Did you have a lovely time, darling?"

Poppy only yawned, so widely I could see the clean pink of her throat.

"She's tired," said Jason. "She needs her sleep."

"Do you want to come in?"

"I'd better get back."

"It's kind of you to come all the way," I said formally. "I know it's a big journey. I could have met you halfway like we usually do."

"I thought it best." Jason's tone was clipped, as if he were rebuking me.

There was a pause. I was aware that it was a silence I was supposed to fill, probably with an apology. I had to make a physical effort not to do that, biting down on the words jammed up in me—sorry, so sorry, I didn't mean, I'm a bit stressed . . .

"Was everything all right?" I asked instead.

"In what way?"

"You know." I gestured toward Poppy, who was clutching Jason's hand and yawning.

"Maybe this isn't the time," he said.

I lifted Poppy into my arms.

"Say goodbye to Daddy, sweetie."

She only buried her face in my neck.

Jason was still holding Poppy's overnight bag and also a bulging black trash bag. He leaned forward and deposited them just inside the door.

"Emily put out some old clothes she thought Poppy's school could use for their dressing-up box," he said.

"Great."

"I'll call you."

He turned and walked away, his hands in his pockets.

I closed the door and carried Poppy downstairs and into the kitchen, where Aidan stroked her head and told her that the pizza would be ready in a jiffy. But Poppy's face was still deep in my neck.

I mouthed a few words at Aidan about how she was always in a strange mood when she got back from Jason's. I unhooked her miniature backpack, slung it on the ground beside us and carried her into the garden to find Sunny. She still didn't want to let go of me. She wrapped her arms fiercely around my neck and her legs around my waist like a scared koala. Her body felt squashy and soft and it smelled slightly sour. Her hair needed washing but I would do that tomorrow.

We ate outside, sitting at the rickety little table that I had found in a junk shop shortly after we'd moved in. Poppy insisted on staying on my lap. She barely touched the pizza that Aidan had spent so long making and she didn't want any of the strawberries he'd bought.

"No bath tonight," I said. "Bed."

"Story," said Poppy.

I picked up the backpack and the bag that Jason had left by the door and carried Poppy to her bedroom. I dressed her in her clown pajamas and selected the happiest stories I could find. I noticed that her eyes were starting to close.

"Shall I turn the light off?"

"I want another story," Poppy's eyes clicked open and she stared at me. "Then another and then another."

"Tell you what. I'll unpack your things and put them away and I'll find Teddy and when I've done all that, I'll read you a story."

I unzipped the bag. The sight of the little dungarees, the tee shirts, the miniature knickers and socks made me feel sad. I suddenly had a vision of my daughter as a vagabond moving from place to place, still too young to realize what had happened to her. She could only express it in behavior, in pictures. She didn't yet have the words.

I put things in their various drawers. I found Teddy and tucked it into the bed next to Poppy, now almost asleep. The small backpack had a few items in it that must be for the school's dressing-up box—a couple of chunky necklaces, a few bangles, a corduroy cap, Emily's cast-offs. I tossed them into the corner of the room, to sort out later. The backpack felt empty now, but I put my hand in to make sure. It touched a soft object and I pulled it out, then felt a jolt that was so severe that I fell backward and sat on the floor of the bedroom, holding it in front of my face, staring in disbelief.

I was holding Milly. Milly the doll. Milly the rag doll that Poppy had ripped into pieces and that I had taken outside and thrown into the trash because I couldn't bear it being in the house.

123

I could hardly bring myself to look. The doll had been crudely repaired with thick black thread, and the whole point was to clearly show that it had been stitched together. Its head was sewn on back to front. Its arm had been attached too low down, so it dangled like a mutant limb. The foot on the mended leg was pointing outward. Bits of its stuffing pushed through the large, clumsy stitching, like the fluff inside a ripped jiffy bag.

I stared at it with horror. In my distress, had I suffered a form of amnesia? Was it possible that I hadn't actually thrown the doll in the trash? I tried to imagine a scenario where I had repaired the doll and forgotten about it. It was inconceivable. In all the murk and mess, one thing was clear. Someone had retrieved the doll from the bin and they had repaired it horribly and given it back to Poppy.

I was still sitting on the ground and now I edged over to the bed.

"Poppy?" I said.

But Poppy was asleep, her right arm thrown back above her head.

"Look," I said to Aidan, sitting in the garden in the dusk. "Look!"

Aidan took the mutilated doll. He stared at it, an expression of distaste of his face. 'I don't get it," he said. "What happened to it?"

I realized how much I hadn't told him.

"Poppy tore it up."

"Why on earth—?"

124

"No. Wait. That's not the point. I found it in her room a couple of days ago, all dismembered, and threw it away. In the outside trash." I could hear my voice rising and stopped for a few seconds to calm down. "And now it's reappeared. Like that. In her overnight bag. What's going on?"

"Hang on," said Aidan slowly. He was still holding the doll. "You're telling me that someone got it from the outside bin, mended it—if you can call this mending—then gave it back to Poppy?"

"Yes. I don't know. Who would do that? Why?"

"That's hideous," said Aidan. I felt a new terror rising in me. "Are you sure about this?"

"What shall I do?" I wasn't really talking to him.

"It was in her overnight bag?"

"Her backpack."

"And you're sure it wasn't in there before she went to Jason's?"

"How could it have been? I threw it away."

"When was this?"

"When? Wednesday? No. Thursday. Thursday evening. It was when Gina came round."

"Who did you tell about it?" He lifted his eyes from the doll. "Not me, anyway."

"Who? Nobody. I didn't want to think about it."

"What about Gina?"

"No. I'm sure I didn't. We had other things to talk about," I added grimly.

"You didn't tell Jason?"

"No. I probably should have done but I can't really talk about things with him just now."

125

"Poppy couldn't have got it back herself?"

"Poppy? No. Surely not. And even if she did, what then? She definitely didn't sew it back together."

"And you're quite sure you threw it away?"

"Yes. In the outside trash."

"It's easy to get memories wrong."

"So people keep telling me!" I sounded waspish. "Sorry. I'm rattled. I remember doing it. I'm sure I remember. I didn't want it in the house. It gave me the creeps. Now look at it! I feel like I'm going out of my mind."

Aidan nodded. He was staring at the rag doll.

"What do you want to do?" he asked at last.

"Do? What can I do?"

"You can go to the police," he said.

"What good would that do? What am I asking them to investigate? My little daughter's having a bad time and she ruined her precious doll and then someone sewed it back together again."

"If you put it like that," said Aidan.

"It feels like a message. Like a warning or a curse."

NINETEEN

For once I let Aidan stay, but when it was almost light I nudged him awake.

"Sorry," I said.

I felt a pang as I watched him dress. I would have liked the three of us to spend the day together. We could have gone to the park and fed the squirrels. But we were still leading our separate lives. Aidan was meeting his colleague, Frederick Gordon or Gordon Frederick, I couldn't remember which way round it was, in Birmingham at a weekend conference on bio-energy, and Poppy and I were taking the train to visit my mother on the outskirts of Abingdon. It was the right thing to do. As a mother, she had been anxious and fretful, but as a grandmother she was a figure of kindness and comfort. She had arranged for Poppy to have a ride on a neighbor's ancient donkey. "Sam the gonkey," Poppy called him, as she sat on his coarse back, wearing an expression of ardent solemnity.

We had lunch in the garden, which was as immaculate as her living room, scarcely a leaf out of place, then went to the playground. I watched Poppy as I pushed her on the swings, perched opposite her on the seesaw, helped her clamber up the climbing frame. She was still quiet, but seemed less feverishly clingy; it was as if a storm had passed.

Walking back to the house, Poppy wheeling and skipping ahead of us, my mother said in a low voice: "Tess, I have to ask you, that time Jason phoned . . ."

She let the sentence trail away. I saw that she was embarrassed.

"You mean when he asked about Poppy and me having an arrangement to see you?"

"Yes. Which was the first I'd heard of it."

"That was just a mix-up," I said airily. "Nothing to worry about."

"He didn't seem very happy with you."

I looked at her anxious face that was softening and loosening with age, the frown marks and folds of worry deeper than I remembered.

"He isn't very happy with me, Mum, that's the truth, but it's all right. We're separated. I don't have to worry about his moods anymore. The only relationship I have with him now is as the father of Poppy."

Poppy, a few feet ahead of us, lifted her foot and brought it down firmly on a large snail.

"She seems fine," said my mother.

I opened my mouth to say that actually Poppy wasn't fine at all, that she was in some kind of trouble. I thought of telling my mother everything that I feared and suspected. I imagined how her shoulders would sag and her mouth would draw down in that expression of helpless sadness.

"Yes," I said. "Poppy's great."

"Then that's all that matters," said my mother placidly.

But that evening, as I sat by her bed, Poppy suddenly said: "Naughty girl."

"Who's naughty?"

Poppy gazed at me.

"You're my lovely, good girl," I said. "Did someone say you were naughty?"

"Bad," said Poppy. "Watching you."

The following day started peacefully enough. We were both up early. Before breakfast, at Poppy's insistence, we went through the dressing-up clothes for her school. I lifted each item out of the bag and held it up for Poppy to agree or disagree: she had strong opinions about such things. She enthusiastically accepted two flowery dresses that must have belonged to Emily, an old leather bag that snapped shut, white gloves that came up to the elbow. She loved the beads and the bangles that had been in the backpack. She wasn't so keen on Jason's natty waistcoat (which I had given him shortly after we met) and she wavered for several minutes over the flat cap, corduroy with a maroon-colored peak, before trying it on in front of the mirror, giggling at how it came over her eyes and finally taking it. Her favorite was a large scarf in a green and pink zigzag pattern.

Then we ate buttery crumpets with honey for breakfast and walked to Gina's house hand in hand. Poppy jumped over cracks and counted how many dogs we passed. I left her there and caught the bus to my school. I had a meeting with a parent after school, but managed to get back to collect Poppy by five.

Gina answered the door.

"I was expecting Laurie," I said.

"He's with his mother. I took the day off. I just suddenly felt I had to. Honestly, Tess, I'll look back at these times and see how I missed my children's growing-up years. But I'm completely exhausted. How does Laurie do this day after day? Come in and excuse the mess. We've made cupcakes. Nellie's asleep for once, so I had time. They're decorating them now."

"This is so nice." I looked around at the chaos in the kitchen. Jake was covered in flour and Poppy had green and yellow dabs round her mouth and in her hair, and thickly sticky fingers. She barely looked up from her misshapen little cakes violently slathered in icing.

"It's been fun," said Gina.

"Thank you."

Gina turned and spoke in a low voice. "Are we OK?"

"We are. Of course we are. It wasn't your fault; I know that. You were just the messenger and I do know you were in an impossible position. It just caught me off balance. And I've been worrying about Poppy."

"She's been fine today."

"Good. Did Lotty say anything?"

"No." Gina took my hand. "What's up?"

"There've been things—it's a long story. Not for now."

"We need another Negroni."

"We do."

"God, I'm relieved we're OK. I've been so worried. I'm really sorry, Tess."

"It's me who's sorry."

We both gave strangled little laughs and I hugged Gina and Gina sniffed loudly and kissed me on the cheek.

"We need to look after each other," she said.

"Yeah."

She looked at me more closely. "No, I mean really. I know the state of mind where you're already feeling anxious and then some random thing triggers you and it plugs right into your anxieties."

I nodded automatically at this and realized that I had no idea what she was talking about.

"What do you mean 'triggers'?"

"I've been exactly like that with Jake. Some horror that's got nothing to do with you makes you worry about your child. Laurie told me about it."

I felt completely confused. Was I being stupid?

"I'm sorry, Gina. I've no idea what you're talking about."

"You see a story about a woman falling from a tower block and then you get worried that Laurie will tell the children about it. He wouldn't do that."

Now I felt even more confused.

"You've got this wrong," I said.

"Really? I know that my mind tends to drift when Laurie is talking but I'm sure he said something about a woman falling from a tower."

"I was just asking about fairy stories."

"Oh, I see. Sorry. My mistake."

131

"Hang on." I beckoned Gina out of the kitchen into the hall. "A woman falling from a tower block? What happened? Did she die?"

Gina shrugged.

"I just read it online on some local news website. I can't remember where. A woman found at the foot of a tower block. I don't know whether she fell or jumped."

"Was it in London? When did it happen?"

"I've told you everything I know." Gina looked at me with concern. "What is it? I mean, it's awful, but it's got nothing to do with anything, has it?"

"No," I said slowly. "No, of course not. How could it?"

I only allowed myself to go online once Poppy was safely asleep, her mouth slightly open, her chest rising and falling, her face untroubled.

I opened up my laptop and searched for "Woman dies falling from building." And my screen filled up.

A young woman had fallen to her death during the early hours of the morning from her eighth-story flat near Elephant and Castle. No one else was involved. There wasn't much. No name, no photos, no explanation.

It was just an everyday kind of tragedy—a young woman losing her life, or taking her life, falling from a block of flats.

A young woman falling from a tower.

I reread the story. It was exactly what I had been looking for, what I had searched through the murder statistics for and had failed to find. But there was a problem. It had happened today, Monday. The woman had died after Poppy had drawn her picture, not before.

I felt as if I had captured something and then it had run through my hands.

TWENTY

Poppy wet the bed again in the night. I carried her to the bath and washed her down. I dried her and pulled on a clean pair of pajamas, murmuring to her all the while as reassuringly and lovingly as I could. I carried her to the soft chair near the window and stripped her bed, giving silent thanks for the plastic sheet.

When the bed was ready again, I picked Poppy up, but when I tried to put her back in her bed, she wouldn't let go and started crying desperately. I could feel her sharp little fingers clutching me so tightly that it almost hurt. To release her, I would have had to pry the fingers off one by one.

"It's OK, honey."

I carried Poppy through to my own bedroom and laid her down and fetched a large bath towel and spread it under her. I switched the light off and got into bed beside her. Poppy was already asleep, but still whimpering. I could feel the vibration of the sobs rippling through the bed.

For what felt like hours, I thought about our situation. It couldn't go on like this. I needed help, but what kind?

Finally I slept but it was as if I was continually waking and sleeping for the entire night, until what was real and what was a dream became confused.

When I properly woke, I felt as if I was being dragged into the light out of a deep, dark cave, my eyes glued together, my head stuffed with spiky straw. Poppy was clambering over me and began bouncing on the bed. After a few heavy jumps, she lost her balance and fell heavily across me. I felt an impulse of anger and then remembered the events of the night and the anger changed to relief. Wild boisterousness was way better than last night. Anything was better than last night.

I looked at the clock. I had forgotten to set the alarm and it was ten past eight. There wasn't much time. I felt sticky and battered. I had the quickest of showers and then carried Poppy into the shower too, and washed her all over while she yelled furiously and squirmed beneath my hands.

I pulled on my clothes and found underwear and a pinafore dress for Poppy. Breakfast was a cup of coffee for me and a bowl of cornflakes for Poppy. Finding Poppy's school folder and her jacket, remembering the bag of dressing-up clothes, remembering my laptop and school lanyard, and getting out of the door was so frantic that it was only once we had collected Jake, and were halfway to school, that I realized that Poppy seemed a little more like her old self, looking around and commenting on almost everything she saw: a woman on a bicycle, another woman leading one very small dog and one very large dog.

"That's the baby dog," Poppy told Jake.

I tried to explain that there were different kinds of dogs and that different breeds of dogs were different sizes. Poppy was still looking around and I wasn't sure if she was paying attention.

"I did see a lion," she said suddenly.

"What? Where?"

"I did see a lion and . . ." Poppy was frowning with effort. "And a parrot. And a dog. And a . . ." There was another pause as she searched for the word. "A fant." She paused. "An elfant," she said.

"That's a lot of animals." I was quite impressed with Poppy's vocabulary. "Where did you see them?"

Poppy gazed at me as if she were baffled by my ignorance.

"They live in the zoo."

I found it difficult to reply to this. One of the things parents did with their children was to take them to the zoo, and I had vivid memories from my own childhood of the sour reek of the lion house and the shrieks of monkeys. I remembered feeding time when a white tiger had clambered up a tree trunk to retrieve a joint of meat. But even as a child I hadn't really enjoyed seeing animals behind bars. So I had never taken Poppy to a zoo and I was almost certain that Jason hadn't either. And Laurie wouldn't have taken her, not without saying.

"Did you go to the zoo with your school?" I asked.

"Yes," said Poppy. "When I used to be a lion."

"No," said Jake equally firmly.

It was hard to believe Poppy. Normally even the most routine school excursion needed parental permission and form filling. Was it possible that the school had taken the children to the zoo and I hadn't known, and Poppy was only mentioning it now? Probably she was making it up, imagining it from a book or something, but after I dropped Poppy and Jake off and left Jason and Emily's cast-offs with the nursery assistant, I approached Lotty. She had a mildly harassed air and looked worried when she saw me. I knew the feeling. Parents were usually bringers of bad news.

"It's really nothing. I just wanted to ask about something Poppy said on the way to school today. She said she'd been to the zoo. We've never taken her to one. I wondered if somehow she might have gone with the school without me realizing?"

"Don't worry. We'll send you a form."

"What do you mean? What form?"

"It won't be for ages. We told them about going to the zoo next term. We talked about what they are, what animals are there, we'll get them to draw pictures and then we'll go and see them. But you'll get a handout with all the details."

I was so confused by this that I couldn't think of anything to say, but it didn't matter because Lotty had run across the classroom to rescue a little boy who had clambered onto a table. I left the school feeling like I was in a fog.

Suddenly I stopped. There was nothing wrong with Poppy. And I knew what I had to do.

I rang my school.

"I'm so sorry to do this yet again. But I've got a dreadful migraine." I heard the faint sigh at the other end. "I won't be in till later."

TWENTY-ONE

The detective sat down opposite me. She had an expression of wary patience.

"I'm having a busy day. So?" Kelly Jordan made a gesture inviting me to speak.

"You remember I showed you the drawing by my daughter? The drawing of a woman falling from a tower?"

"Yes, I remember."

She said this like she was talking of a faintly unpleasant memory, a headache or a twisted ankle.

I took out my phone and looked at it.

"Sorry. I've lost it. Hang on, it won't take a minute." After a little more than a minute of frantic clicking and scrolling, I found the local news story and handed the phone to the detective, who read it and handed the phone back.

"So what do you think?" I said.

"What do *you* think?"

"Isn't it significant? A woman falling from a tower. It's like Poppy's drawing."

139

Kelly Jordan took a breath.

"As I'm sure you've noticed, this happened yesterday. So the woman fell from the tower *after* your daughter did her drawing, not before. I don't really see the point of this."

"Yes, that's what I thought. It's not just the picture. When I talked to Poppy, she said that a woman *did fall* from the tower. So obviously I thought it was about something that had happened."

"Or that she thought had happened. Or imagined had happened."

"Yes, well, whatever. But this morning I was taking Poppy to school and she said that she'd been to the zoo. That seemed weird to me because I didn't think she'd ever been to one; I would have known if Jason had taken her. So I asked her teacher and it turned out that they're planning a visit to the zoo next term. In the future."

There was a glazed expression on the woman's face, but I persevered.

"It was like this glimpse into the brain of a three-year-old. Poppy's not that clear about the difference between what has happened and what will happen. Or at least she's not clear about it in her language."

Now there was a long pause. Kelly Jordan's eyes were almost closed, like she was doing a complicated mental calculation. Finally she shook her head.

"I don't get it," she said. "What problem does that solve? Are you saying that your daughter is some kind of clairvoyant?"

"No, no, not at all. Poppy's picture scared me and

she was obviously scared in some way. And still is. But I couldn't work out what exactly it was a picture of. But now I think I've got an idea. Poppy heard someone saying, I'll push you over the balcony. Future tense. Poppy drew the picture. And then a few days later they did push the woman off the balcony."

"They?"

"He. Her. It must be a he, mustn't it? He threatened to do it and then he did it."

"That's an awful lot to extract from a little news story that says nothing about a third party. It just says she was found at the bottom of the block of flats. She may have fallen. She may have jumped. It doesn't even give her name."

"I came in before and you said that there was no crime to investigate. Now there's this. If a woman is found at the bottom of a block of flats then surely there's some kind of police investigation, isn't there?"

Kelly Jordan drummed lightly on the desktop with her fingers.

"How's your daughter doing?" she said.

"Not well. She's sleeping badly. She's behaving strangely. She's rough with her friends and clingy with me."

"I know it's not my place to say, Tess, but maybe you'd be better thinking about your daughter than looking around for a crime that doesn't exist."

"You're right. It's not your place to say. It's your place to investigate crimes when people like me report them."

"Careful," said Kelly in a sharper tone. "Most of my

colleagues would have thrown you out the first time and not seen you at all today. Remember that when you come in here and tell me how to do my job."

"Sorry," I muttered.

"When I have time—if I have time—I'll make a call and if there seems any point to it at all, I'll send someone over. If anything comes up, I'll let you know."

"I'll call you and find out what you've discovered."

"No!" She looked alarmed. "Don't call me. Just go home and play with your daughter."

I bit back a sharp reply. After all, she was being nice to me. She had listened to me when others might have turned me away. That was something.

I didn't go straight to work because suddenly, as I was walking out of the police station, a fragment of a conversation floated into my mind. I stopped at a café where, sitting by the window with a cup of coffee, I took my laptop out of my backpack and opened it.

In Lewisham with Fliss. That's what Ben had said when I had first met him in Brixton. So I didn't just have his name, but that he had lived in Lewisham, with someone called Fliss. Was she his wife? Jason had said his marriage had broken up.

Fliss Carey wasn't a common name. I typed it into the search bar. Nothing. I added "Lewisham." Nothing.

I took a sip of my coffee, typed in Carey, Lewisham. And I found her, or at least, I found someone called Felicity Carey Connors who lived in Lewisham and was a cello teacher. Could that be her? I hadn't imagined Ben being married to a cello teacher. I clicked on her image: she had a pleasing face, softly oval, with pale brown hair tied back and round glasses.

There was a phone number and an email address. After some hesitation, I wrote her a message:

Hi, I was hoping I could meet you and ask your advice. I am free a couple of evenings midweek, and every other weekend. Thanks, Tess.

Vague enough for her to think I wanted a cello teacher, but not a lie—not quite.

THE UNHEARD

TWENTY-TWO

Poppy was feverishly excited when I collected her from school. Her cheeks were blotchy and her voice like a drill.

"I'm Red Riding Hood," she had shouted. "Big eyes! Big teeth! All the better and gobble you up!"

"Has she been all right today?" I asked Lotty.

"A bit hyper. As you can see." She turned to Poppy. "We had to tell you to be quiet and to sit on the carpet, didn't we, Poppy?"

Poppy didn't reply. She was staring ahead of her so intently that both Lotty and I followed her gaze to see what she was looking at. But there was nothing. I turned back to Lotty.

"But not worrying?"

"The meltdown didn't quite happen," said Lotty. "Look. I took a few Polaroids of the class. Here she is today."

I glanced down. There was Poppy on the slide, arms raised and a ferocious smile on her face. There was a close-up of her face, eyes half hidden by the cap Jason had donated, mouth open in a yell. She looked like a miniature football hooligan. Another in which she was holding hands with Sadie, the girl she had bitten: Poppy was staring straight at the camera, but Sadie was looking at her timidly; maybe even with fear. The last was a fuzzy one of her pointing and shouting.

"Thanks."

"Take them."

I didn't really want them; there was something a bit wild about Poppy in them, on the brink of hysteria. She was holding Sadie's hand as if she had taken her captive.

We went to the park and she gradually calmed down. We fed the ducks and played Grandmother's Footsteps. We had our supper together in the little garden, where birds were singing. I made cauliflower cheese and then cut a mango into slices that Poppy ate with a greedy delight, her mouth smeared orange.

But now I felt drained, unsteady on my feet. When I glimpsed myself in the mirror, I looked thinner and older, new lines round my eyes. My hair needed washing. I would have a long bath, I thought, then sit outside in the fading light. It was quite nice that Aidan was away and I had nobody to think of but Poppy and myself.

When I looked at Poppy curled up in bed, clean and peaceful, her lips puffing slightly with each breath, her lashes long on her cheeks, I wanted to weep with love.

I put the kettle on for tea and attached a couple of the photos from school on the fridge with a magnet, but threw away the one of Poppy and Sadie. Then the

145

doorbell rang and I cursed under my breath and went to answer it. I thought it was probably Bernie with more sourdough, but it wasn't.

"Is everything all right? Have you found out anything?"

"Can I come in?" Kelly Jordan looked past me into the hall. "I'm on my way home from work. It's been a long day."

I led the detective into the downstairs room, looking around to make sure that the supper things were cleared away, the toys tidied. There was one of Poppy's picture books on the table. Outside, long shadows lay across the garden. Everything looked orderly, well cared for.

"Nice place," Jordan said. She sat down at the table, picked up the book then put it down again. "Is your daughter here?"

"She's asleep. Tea? Coffee? Wine?"

"No, thank you. I won't be long."

"It's kind of you to come. So you haven't discovered anything? I mean, about that woman."

"I have her name and some information on the facts surrounding her death."

"Yes?"

The detective opened up her little briefcase and withdrew a piece of paper. She studied it, taking her time.

"Her name," she said at last, "is Skye Nolan."

"Skye Nolan." I felt no tingle of recognition. "I don't know a Skye. Or anyone called Nolan as far as I know."

"There you are then. I have a few details about her. She was twenty-seven years old. She was single." Kelly Jordan studied the paper again. "She moved to London about a year and a half ago, to a flat just off Elephant and Castle."

"Did she work?"

"Bits and pieces. For the last year or so, she earned most of her money, cash-in-hand, as a dog walker. Apparently that counts as a job."

"I've heard that," I said. "There are a lot of dogs that need walking."

"The main thing you should know, however, is that there are no suspicious circumstances involving any other person. The police believe she took her own life by jumping from her eighth-floor balcony. Apparently she was subject to violent mood swings and prolonged depressive periods."

"They're sure?"

"I'm just telling you what they told me. So maybe you can stop looking for some mystery that doesn't exist. I have her photograph." She dipped her hand into the briefcase and bought out a small plastic wallet. "Here."

I took the photo. For a brief moment, I looked with simple curiosity at that happy, smiling face, not knowing what was coming for it, what fate had in store, and then suddenly I felt something prickling in my mind, like a noise that I couldn't make out. It must have shown on my face because I heard Kelly Jordan's voice, as if it were coming from far away, asking me if I knew her.

"I don't know," I said. "She sort of looks . . ." And then, oh yes, I remembered. "I think I saw her."

"What do you mean, you saw her?"

I gazed at the photograph. A narrow triangle of a face. Short dark hair. Big dark eyes. Like a pixie, an elf, full of life and mischief.

"In a restaurant," I said, very slowly. I was remembering it now, bringing back the strangeness of that encounter. "I was there with my boyfriend, sitting at the window, and she was outside, waving at me and making gestures. She was wearing striped dungarees."

"But you didn't recognize her?"

"No. Not at all. I'm sure I'd never seen her before. But she knew me, or she thought she did."

"Or she knew your boyfriend, perhaps? Or someone else in the restaurant, sitting at another table?"

"It was me. She came in and she started talking to me."

"What did she say?"

"She said . . ." I frowned. "She pointed, and said 'You.'"

"You? Is that all?"

"I asked her if we knew each other. Because I couldn't place her at all. I thought maybe she was one of the mothers from school—or from the school I worked at before, or a childminder maybe, and I'd forgotten her."

Kelly Jordan frowned, alert but unconvinced. I bit my lip, trying to get it clear.

"She kept grinning, in an odd way. I didn't like it. She said we did know each other and then—" I stopped abruptly, lifted both hands to my mouth. "She asked me about my little girl."

"You're sure?"

"Yes. Yes, I'm absolutely sure about that bit. She knew Poppy had red hair."

"Go on."

"I said something, I can't remember what, and then she said something like, 'astonishing.' No. 'Incredible,' that was it. She smiled at me and said 'Incredible' and then she left."

"Nothing else you can remember?"

"No."

"Did you see her again?"

"No. But I don't understand. What does it mean? I mean, what does it *mean*?"

"I don't know." Jordan waited a beat, not taking her eyes off me. "I don't know if it means anything."

"Of course it does. How can it not mean something?"

"Try to see this from my point of view. No, try to see it from a complete stranger's point of view. One of my colleagues, for instance. You're already in an agitated state, and a woman you've never met comes up to you in a restaurant and because you are nervy and suspicious, it spooks you. And then, several days later, you see a picture of a woman who died and she looks a bit similar, is the right kind of age, and you convince yourself it's her. That everything bad is connected to you and your daughter. Do you see?"

"No, you're wrong."

"Maybe I am and maybe I'm not. I'm trying to see it from all sides and I'm just giving you another way of seeing it. The world feels like a hostile place to you, Tess. Everything is falling into an ugly pattern. Perhaps this isn't about you and your daughter at all."

"You don't believe me," I said dully.

When Kelly Jordan answered, it was in a gentler tone.

"It's not about believing or not believing."

"I met this woman and she said she knew me. I swear."

I stood up and walked round the room, standing at the French window and pressing my forehead against the cool glass, before returning to where the detective sat, looking puzzled and dissatisfied.

"I need to get this straight," she said. "First of all, your daughter makes a drawing showing someone falling and she says someone did it. Whatever *it* is."

"Yes. I mean, she's not yet four. You've seen the drawing. She said 'he did kill,' to be precise. 'Kill and kill.' "

"She starts showing signs of distress."

"Yes."

"So you come and see me and I tell you there's nothing I can do."

I nodded.

"Then you hear about a woman falling from an eighth-story balcony and you wonder if it's got anything to do with Poppy's drawing."

"Yes. It's obvious."

"I don't think it's at all obvious. The woman died several days after Poppy drew the picture, so it looks unconnected, until you realize that she often gets tenses the wrong way round. So you think that perhaps she is not talking about something that has happened, but is reporting a threat she overheard: something that *will* happen."

"Right."

"And now you believe you actually met this woman."

"I know I did."

"I won't give you a lecture about the unreliability of eyewitness testimony."

"There's something else."

"What?"

"I've recently discovered that my ex-partner, Jason, was being unfaithful to me. I had no idea. Nothing was as I thought. Everything was wrong and I didn't see. How could I have been so blind?"

"Listen, that's obviously very upsetting and—"

"And then Poppy ripped up Milly."

"Sorry?"

"Her rag doll Milly. Who she couldn't sleep without. She ripped her up."

Jordan started to speak but I held up my hand to stop her and continued.

"Wait. I put the doll in the outside trash. I just wanted to get rid of it. Then, two days later, when Poppy came back from being with her father, it was there in her little backpack. All sewn up. But crudely and horribly sewn up, with legs the wrong way round and her head askew."

Kelly Jordan was staring at me, her face blank.

"Can I see this doll?"

"Hang on."

I ran upstairs, tiptoed into Poppy's bedroom and retrieved Milly from the high shelf above her wardrobe. My instinct that night had been to throw the doll away again, but in the end I had hidden it out of reach. I handed it over. Jordan examined it and then gave it back to me.

"It felt like a threat. Malevolent." I heard my voice half-break and paused to steady myself. "You do believe me, don't you? You have to. Someone has to. I didn't know what to do. I don't know what to do. What shall I do?"

Kelly Jordan shook her head slowly. "I don't know what to make of this: children's drawings, dolls. I'm not sure this is a police matter. I'm not sure whether it's connected at all. Look, you're anxious and in your anxiety, you might very well be putting together lots of things that bear no relation to each other and insisting they all belong together."

I saw her face close down and felt a desperate anger rise in me.

"Everything's connected, don't you get it: Poppy's drawing, her words, her strange behavior, this poor young woman's death, Milly. Everything. I knew something was going on. I knew it. I wasn't just going mad. But it's Poppy. I mean, Poppy—she has to be all right. I need to make it all right for her. Do you see?"

"Tess." Jordan held up a hand. "Listen to me."

"Help me," I said. I gripped the detective's arm. "Please. You have to help me stop this."

TWENTY-THREE

They came at ten the next morning, Kelly Jordan and a child-protection trained officer, Madeleine Finch, a tall, angular woman with an unruly mop of dark hair and a fierce handshake.

"How does this work?" I asked. "I mean, can I sit in with you? I don't want her to feel anxious."

In truth, Poppy didn't seem anxious. She was squatting in the garden, talking earnestly to Sunny, wagging her finger, occasionally prodding the cat whose long tail twitched ominously. I had told her we were spending the first half of the day together and some friends might come by to talk to her, and she'd nodded and said airily, "About the zoo."

"That would be all right," said Madeleine Finch. "As long as you don't say anything. This is just to capture key information as swiftly as we can. I will be asking open questions. As you know, children are very vulnerable to suggestibility and it's crucial to avoid contamination."

I had an uneasy sense that I had already severely contaminated anything Poppy might say.

I signed the consent form that Madeleine Finch passed to me and opened the door to the garden.

Poppy came obediently enough, though when she opened up her fist, she was holding the glistening remains of a snail. I washed her grubby hands, then sat her at the table with her juice. Madeleine Finch and Kelly Jordan sat opposite her and Poppy regarded them benignly.

"I did see a lion," she said. "I did see a fant."

I opened my mouth to explain she meant elephant, but closed it again.

"That's nice." Madeleine Finch spoke in a gentle coo that I found annoying. Poppy took a biscuit from the plate I'd brought and stuffed it into her mouth. "So, Poppy. You did a drawing." And she held up a photocopy of that menacing picture in heavy black crayon: the triangular-shaped figure standing on what looked like a tower or a lighthouse, its head pointing downward.

Poppy glanced at it without interest. Her cheeks were bulging.

"Can you tell me what it's about?"

An indistinct sound came from Poppy. Both women waited.

"I did draw a lion," she said eventually.

"But this drawing." Madeleine Finch pressed a finger on it. "What does it show?"

"Zoo?"

"What is this?" Pointing at the triangle.

"Lion?" Poppy waited. "Fant?" she added helpfully.
Kelly Jordan drew the photo out of her case and passed it across to the other woman.

"Now, Poppy," Madeleine Finch said. "I am going to show you a picture."

The photo was slid across the table.

"Who is that?"

Poppy lifted up her glass and very noisily drank her juice. She pushed another biscuit into her mouth. Her legs were drumming against the chair she was sitting in.

"I want Sunny," she said through a spray of crumbs. "I want Teddy. I want Milly."

"Who is this woman, Poppy?"

Poppy slid off her chair.

"Do you know her?"

"Know her." It was impossible to tell if this was an agreement, a repetition or a question.

"Do you know her name?"

"Milly. I did do it."

A faint twitch of a frown crossed Madeleine Finch's face.

"Is Milly your doll?" asked Kelly Jordan.

Not an open question, I thought. I watched Poppy as temper boiled up in her.

"No." Very loudly. "No no no."

"Poppy. When you see this picture—?"

"I want Sunny. I want my green mug. I want Teddy. I want Milly. I want Gruffalo. I want Little Bear. I want Owl Baby. I want cornflakes." Her voice was rising to a roar. "I want *anything*."

Madeleine Finch looked across at Kelly Jordan. "This is what you're putting yourself out on a limb for? You know you're going to have to sign off on this?"

Kelly Jordan nodded. She didn't look happy.

I stood up and went round the table. I crouched beside Poppy.

"It's OK."

"Mummy?"

"I'm here."

"I was naughty."

"No, darling."

"Milly did die?"

"No. She's a doll. She isn't alive and so she can't die."

"Did you die?"

"I'm here."

"But did you?"

I looked up at the two detectives.

"I think we've done all we can," Finch said.

At the door I put an arm out and held Kelly Jordan back.

"What did she mean, putting yourself out on a limb?"

"You don't need to concern yourself with that."

"But I'd like to know."

She gave a small sigh. "It's going to be quite hard to justify the time and resources I have spent on your anxieties."

"Will you get into trouble?"

"Maybe a bit of a dressing down—and loads of forms to fill out, which is worse."

"So why?"

"Why am I doing it, you mean?"

"Is it because you believe me?"

"I don't know, Tess. Maybe it's because I'm a mother too."

"Thank you," I said softly.

TWENTY-FOUR

"We're not staying."

Aidan was standing at the front door, holding a pink peony in a large terracotta pot. A portly man with silver hair stood behind him, carrying another one.

"What's this?"

"A client gave them to me but as I don't have a garden, I thought of you."

"Are you sure?"

"Of course."

"You should have warned me you were coming," I said. I smiled as I said it but I meant it. I didn't like surprises. "I might not have been in."

"We would have just left them outside. But now we're here, can we come in before we drop them?"

Aidan introduced his colleague, Fred Gordon, who gasped a greeting. His face was red and sweat was running off it.

I stood back and they staggered into the hall just as Bernie flung open his door. All four of us stood crammed into the little space while I maneuvered open the door to the flat.

"Let me take that, mate," said Bernie to Fred. "You look like you're about to have a heart attack."

"Where's Pops?" asked Bernie as they carried the plants downstairs into the conservatory.

I pointed into the corner of the garden, where Poppy and Jake were squatting.

"They're finding worms," I said. "It's their latest obsession. There's a jug of elderflower in the fridge. Can I get you some?"

"Yes, please."

Bernie had sat himself down as if he was settling in. Fred stood by the glass door, wiping his brow with a tissue.

Aidan collected glasses, yanked open the fridge, poured out elderflower juice into glasses for everyone, including Bernie.

"Cheers," he said, passing his glass to me and putting a hand on the small of my back.

Now Bernie was walking around with his drink, looking at my pictures and my books.

"How was the conference?" I asked Aidan.

He touched my hand and spoke in a low voice so that only I could hear. "I missed you."

"Are you staying for the evening?"

"I can't. We've got a work event."

The doorbell rang once more.

"I'll go," said Aidan, leaving the room before I could stop him.

"The little guy doesn't look too happy," said Bernie.

I looked out into the garden. Jake was curled on the ground, his hands over his face, while Poppy tried to push a handful of mud through his spread fingers. I pulled open the door.

"Poppy! Stop it!"

I pulled Poppy off Jake, who immediately started crying.

"When I was a little boy," Bernie said from behind me, "I ate worms."

Poppy gazed at him and Jake stopped his crying mid-gulp.

"Yum yum," said Bernie and rubbed his stomach. Jake giggled.

"What's going on?"

Both Laurie and Jason had come into the garden, Aidan behind them looking flustered. He made a gesture to me, palms up in apology and helplessness. I realized that while he and Laurie knew each other slightly, this was the first time he and Jason had met.

Jason was looking at Aidan appraisingly, his head slightly to one side and a slight smile on his face, and my heart lurched because Aidan looked small beside him; his hair was thinning and his glasses were slightly lopsided. But Laurie was looking down at his son, whose face was smeared with mud and tears. Nellie was in a canvas baby carrier on his back; her round face peered over his shoulder accusingly.

"What's happened to Jake?" asked Laurie. "Jake, are you OK?"

"I'm Aidan." Aidan held out a hand to Jason, who took it firmly. I could see the two of them doing battle over the handshake. Aidan's mouth was a thin line and Jason's smile didn't meet his eyes. It was almost funny. Almost.

Laurie hauled Jake to his feet. Aidan and Jason let their arms drop to their sides. Then Poppy squeezed her eyes tight shut and opened her mouth so wide it seemed to take up her entire face and a roar came out.

"Kingcunt," she yelled. "Kingcunt kingcunt kingcunt."

"Someone's tired," said Bernie.

"Now then, Poppy, that's enough." Jason spoke in his head teacher's voice and tried to lift her into his arms, but Poppy squirmed and kicked him hard on his shins.

"Mummy," she said and she wrapped her arms around my legs and burrowed into me. "I want to go home."

"We are home, darling."

"I want to be good."

TWENTY-FIVE

The next morning, as I was taking Poppy to school, I was called by Kelly Jordan.

"Are you at home?"

"I will be. I mean, after I've dropped Poppy off. I'm not at work today."

"Can we come at ten?"

"Sure. But what do you mean, *we*?"

"See you then."

At two minutes past ten, I opened the door to Kelly Jordan. A man was standing beside her.

"This is Chief Inspector Durrant," she said.

"Ross," said the man, but without smiling.

He looked like he had dressed in a hurry and chosen a gray suit that was slightly too small for him, a dark tie that was loose. He was flushed and jowly. Even the exposed scalp on the top of his head had a red tinge, surrounded by unkempt curly gray hair. He was breathing heavily as if the walk from the car had been too much. When he sat down on the sofa, I saw there were beads of sweat on his forehead.

"I'm sure you're pressed for time," I said.

"Why?" asked Ross Durrant.

The question was so brusque, almost aggressive, that I was taken aback and struggled for a moment to answer.

"I didn't actually mean anything by it. I was just being polite."

"That's all right," said Kelly Jordan. "Chief Inspector Durrant is the detective responsible for the Skye Nolan death."

"You're not saying 'murder.'"

"That's why we're here," said Ross Durrant.

"Do you want me to make a statement?"

"That won't be necessary at the moment." He took a little notepad from his outer pocket and a ballpoint pen from his inner pocket and laid them on the table. It seemed like something more for writing a shopping list than for serious police business.

Ross Durrant looked at me directly and I saw that he had deep dark brown eyes. He didn't smile reassuringly and he didn't frown. He looked entirely impassive as if he were explaining the detail of an insurance policy. I immediately felt like I was in the wrong.

"Let me put the situation from one point of view," he said. "We have the body of Skye Nolan."

"Do you think she jumped?"

"I think it's plausible. Or perhaps she fell. Against that, we have a drawing by a three-year-old girl, evidence that, in my view, would be inadmissible in court. The police interview with her was, in any case, unproductive. We also have your own statement that

163

you met the dead woman. I won't insult you by telling you about the problems with eyewitness evidence."

"I've already heard that. But I did meet her. I'm a hundred percent sure. You can ask my boyfriend if you like: he was there as well. And there's the doll."

"Yes, of course. There's that."

Ross Durrant picked up his ballpoint pen and tapped it against his notebook but didn't open it. He looked across at Kelly Jordan and she looked back at him, making a slight tip of her head. It reminded me of the looks that married people exchange and I thought I could interpret it: we've already had this conversation.

"All right," Ross Durrant said. "This is an unusual situation. Because you have approached us with your concerns, I'm obliged to investigate if there is anything substantive in them." He was telling me he didn't believe me. "You've been through a difficult breakup, I understand. With the father of your daughter."

"Yes, that's right," I said. "I don't know if it's relevant, but I just wanted to be straightforward. I went through what I thought was a good breakup. But after all of this happened, I ..." I paused. "I asked some questions and it turned out I'd been misled about various things."

"Your partner, Jason Hallam, was unfaithful," said Durrant.

"Yes."

"You know of one person, but you suspect there were others."

It felt terrible and shaming having this conversation with a stranger.

"It's possible."

He thought for a moment. "According to your theory—"

"It's not exactly a theory."

"All right, according to the concern you've raised, you think your daughter witnessed a threat."

"She may just have overheard it."

"Overhearing is witnessing. So we need to consider the people your daughter has spent time with in the last few weeks. It seems like the obvious place to start is with Mr. Hallam."

"It's just because she came back from his house with the drawing."

"And that's the place where she's spent the most time," he said. "Apart from here."

"Yes."

"Who would she come into contact with there? Apart from Mr. Hallam."

"His new wife, Emily Hallam. She's pregnant, by the way. And she seems very nice. And nice to Poppy, so far as I can tell."

"Good," said Ross Durrant.

He still hadn't opened his notebook and he wasn't referring to any notes. I was moderately impressed. Clearly he had done his homework.

"Her brother is also there," I added. "Ben."

"Ben who?"

"Carey."

"What do you make of him?"

"He's clearly a bit troubled."

"Troubled? In what way?"

"I think he has some issues, some kind of depression. He's out of work. Now his wife has left him. That's why he's living with them. He's only been there a week or so. The same amount of time that Poppy's been acting strangely. Maybe it's a coincidence. Anyway, I've only met him once." Twice, I thought, if you counted our meeting in the park. I was trying to forget about that. "He seemed quite passive."

There was a pause. Once again Durrant barely reacted.

"Do you trust him with your daughter?"

"Trust Ben?"

"Yes."

"I wouldn't want him to look after Poppy. He can barely look after himself." I checked myself. "That's my impression anyway. It may be unfair. But as far as I know, he's never been left alone with her."

Now Ross Durrant picked up the little notebook and opened it and clicked his pen and wrote something that I couldn't make out.

"I saw in the file that you've got a new partner."

I swallowed, suddenly feeling self-conscious. The stepfather. Of course, he wasn't a stepfather. It didn't even seem right to describe him as my new partner. But the words already felt suspicious, including anything I might say about it, or him. It hadn't even occurred to me that Aidan would be dragged into this. That he would become a figure of suspicion. I suddenly realized that this was going to have an effect on everyone around me, the guilty and the innocent and the in-between: Jason and Ben and people at Poppy's school and my friends. And Aidan.

"Yes," I said. "Aidan."

"Last name?"

"Otley."

"I was hoping you'd say a little more about him."

"I don't know what you want me to say. We've been seeing each other for a bit."

"A bit? A week? A month?"

"About two and a half months."

Ross Durrant made a note.

"He must have seen a lot of Poppy."

"I don't think a lot, actually. I felt very cautious about that when we started seeing each other. I worried that Poppy would get attached and then it might not work out. So he hasn't been around that much and I've always had clear boundaries. Even now, he doesn't stay the night when Poppy is here. It's complicated."

"Does he mind that?"

I hadn't even talked about this with Gina. I hadn't thought about it in any coherent way.

"I don't know. It's probably frustrating. But he knew what he was getting into when he met me. *Us*, I should say."

Ross Durrant closed his notebook and laid it down.

"You know, of course, we'll be interviewing every-one."

"Yes, now that you that say so, I can see that."

"And it won't be a problem?"

167

"What do you mean?"

"I mean with your ex-husband or his brother-in-law or your new partner? Will that feel awkward for you?"

"Of course it's awkward for me and it's awkward for them as well. But that's not the point. I'm thinking about Poppy and I'm thinking about a dead woman." I paused. "But you'll be careful?"

"Careful?"

"I mean, you won't be heavy-handed?"

He looked unconcerned. "People who are innocent don't have anything to worry about, do they?"

"I don't think that's true at all."

Once again he didn't smile. He closed his notebook, put it in his pocket and stood up. It felt like an effort for him and he gave a small groan.

"You're the one who thinks there may be a murderer out there," he said. "You're the one who contacted us. Don't you want us to find him?"

TWENTY-SIX

I walked to my school. It was three and a half miles away, though only a mile and a bit from Poppy's school. I went slowly, barely noticing the cars and buses rumbling past, the cyclists weaving along the pavement to avoid the traffic, the tangle of deflated balloons hanging from the magnolia tree, limp among the triumphant candles of flowers, or the sun breaking through the clouds, or the sound of London all around me: never silent, never still, a city in perpetual motion and perpetual change.

I was thinking about what I had started. Soon, today perhaps, the police would question Jason; they would question Ben. Jason was going to be furious. They would question Aidan. It was all in the open now.

I trudged along the road and considered the three men. I didn't know Ben. He was obviously in a bad way: his wife had left him for reasons I could only imagine; he didn't work; he looked like someone who was wretched and unraveling, and he had ended up in his sister's house, with my little daughter. I had no way of knowing what went on there.

But I did know Jason. I would have said, just a few days earlier, that although we were no longer together, I knew him intimately, better than Emily or anyone else knew him. I knew him as a lover, as a partner, as a father, a friend. I knew him as a young man and now as a man who was no longer so young. I had seen him grow and change and solidify. I had seen him at work, seen him succeed and rise on the wave of his ambitions. I had seen him ill, drunk, hungover, stoned, tender, angry, insecure, kind, derisive, petty.

Now I knew there was a side of him that he'd kept hidden from me. I hadn't seen it because you have to trust each other in a relationship: that's what we had said to each other at the heady start, when it was inconceivable that we would ever want anyone else. Trust is like faith. It's an act of will and of optimism. Once you start distrusting your partner, it's over.

I no longer trusted Jason. He had cheated on me and lied to me over the course of his affair with Ellen Dempsey—and if with her, why not with others?

But could he *kill* someone? Jason? Poppy's father? In my mind I saw his face when we had last argued, disfigured by anger and contempt. Perhaps he could. But then, if he could, what did that say about everyone else?

No. I didn't mean everyone else, of course. I meant Aidan: lovely, modest, slightly shy Aidan whose face brightened when he looked at me, who listened to me with the kind of attention that made me feel recognized, who treated Poppy with unpatronizing respect.

Aidan, who arrived at my flat with his bags of complicated ingredients and spent hours cooking meals that
Poppy prodded at dubiously with her fork, who felt
that in meeting a single mother and her small daughter, he was the lucky one. Did I trust Aidan? Did I
think—I crossed a road and a motorist jammed on his
brakes and blared his horn—did I think Aidan could
kill someone?

No.

I didn't. Of course I didn't.

And then I made myself think of Aidan again. He
had met me at my weakest. Had he met me because I
was at my weakest? Always, ever since I was a teenager, I'd felt like the one on the outside, on the edge of
the group, ignored. I think I'd always been grateful,
too grateful, for any attention. Once or twice I'd slept
with people as a way of saying thank you for wanting
me and only then discovering they were the sort of
people who would want anyone.

Was that Aidan? Was Aidan's attentiveness, his ac-
ceptance of Poppy and me together, just a form of control? Even as I considered this, probing it like an open
wound, I felt, that's me again, that's Tess. Because I'd
always felt so unsure of myself that I also felt unsure
of anyone who fell in love with me because why would
they fall in love with me?

Until I met Jason. I'd been sure that I was loved by
Jason and I'd given myself up in a way I never had before. But I'd been wrong. Now I was discovering that
he had lied to me as well and it had destroyed my trust
in everyone. Nobody was quite what they seemed.

Everyone—that man in shorts crossing the road with his terrier straining at the lead, that one in his pin-stripe suit and his briefcase, that one in the car with his elbow on the open window, that young one, that middle-aged one, that old one—carried secret selves. And the world in all its May brightness suddenly felt like a dark and scary place.

I came to a halt. People flowed round me as I came to a decision that I hadn't known I was going to make but must have been growing inside me.

It was over with Aidan. It had to be. If I had the tiniest shred of doubt about him, I couldn't be with him.

Even if I trusted him entirely, it had to end. He was the right person at the wrong time.

It was about Poppy. There was no room for anyone else. Sadness spread through me like a stain.

That afternoon we finished making the witch's cloak. Poppy stood on a chair wearing the garment while I took up the hem, my mouth full of pins. When it was done, she refused to take it off. She raced round the garden, her face fervent under its glittering hood.

I stood and watched her. A ping came from my mobile: Aidan. My heart was erratic and I felt a squeeze of panic in my stomach.

Can I come round this evening? Tell me when Poppy's asleep x

I will.

Aidan took my hands in his and held them.

"We need to talk." His face was grave. Did he know

what I was going to say, or was this about the police? I couldn't tell.

"Come in."

One of the lenses on his glasses had a slight smear on it, which was unlike him. He normally looked so neat and prepared.

We went into the conservatory and sat facing each other. He was wearing the dark green shirt I liked.

"Aidan, listen," I began because if I was going to do this I needed to do it at once, like ripping off a bandage. But he held up a hand.

"This is hard, but I need to say something first."

"All right." I watched his face. He didn't look angry.

"The police came and talked to me." He gave a slight grimace. "That makes it sound civilized."

"Oh God. What happened?"

"They came to my workplace. One of them was in uniform, just to make sure that everyone noticed. I was in a meeting, but they said it couldn't wait."

"I asked them to be careful," I said.

Aidan let his gaze settle on me. "What have you done?" His mildness was awful.

"I should have told you before all this happened. I went to the police last week about my worries about Poppy. Obviously they thought I was being ridiculous. Which is why I never mentioned it, because of course it did sound stupid—Poppy starts wetting her bed and using swearwords and I go to the police! I went again when I heard that this woman had died falling off her balcony because it was like Poppy's drawing. You must know all this; they must have told you."

He shook his head mutely.

"So then it got weird because the woman who died wasn't someone I knew as such, but she was that woman who we saw in the restaurant." His face remained blank. "You must remember that woman."

"What are you talking about?"

"The one in the Italian the other night. Who thought she knew me."

Finally I felt I had got through to him. He took a step back.

"She was the one who died?"

"Yes."

"And you knew her?"

"No, you were there. She said she knew me."

I could see him frantically thinking.

"That makes no sense," he said. "If she knew you, you must know her."

"But I didn't. I told you at the time I didn't. I've been going over and over it, but I can't remember her at all. Maybe I'm being stupid and there's something obvious. And that name: Skye Nolan. If I'd ever met anyone called Skye, I'd remember it. I could have met her somewhere and not known her name. But I'm sorry about all this. Was it awful?"

He gave the very faintest of smiles.

"You know how it is. Being interviewed by the police is . . ." He searched for the word. "Unsettling. They were fine. I wish they'd been more discreet about it."

"But I had to tell the police, don't you see? Once I realized that I'd met this woman and it all linked up with Poppy's drawing and her behavior, I had to tell them."

"Tess," he said gently. "Try to see this from my point of view for a moment. I fall in love with this woman, who has a little daughter, and we start going out. I'm happy. Happy like I haven't been ... well, ever, almost."

"Oh, but so was I—"

He held up a hand. "Why didn't you *tell* me?"

"I should have. I see that now. I just thought ... I was so bewildered."

"I can't believe I'm saying this, but did you not trust me?"

I was about to babble out an apology, but I stopped myself.

"It's not about that. I don't know what trust means anymore. The police just have to investigate. I feel terrible about it."

He stared at me and I could hardly bear to meet his gaze.

"I'm in love with you," he said. "And I love you and I like you. And I love and like Poppy as well. I just—" He stopped, rubbed his eyes with back of his hand. "It's not just about what happened with the police. I tried to do what you wanted. You canceled on me, I said fine. You didn't want me to stay the night, so I got up and left. You didn't want me to pretend to be Poppy's father, and of course I accepted that. At the same time, you wanted me to see that you and Poppy were a unit.

I accepted that too. I'm not blaming you, but there's something we're not managing. I want you to tell me how to do this better."

I shouldn't have let him talk for so long, but I wasn't used to ending things, knowingly giving pain, saying goodbye. That wasn't what I did. I dragged in a deep, hurtful breath, made myself speak.

"Please, Aidan. There's something I need to say."

He gazed at me. He knew; I could see in his eyes that he knew, and in the way he put a hand to his face, adjusted his glasses, readying himself. He suddenly looked smaller, bonier, and I felt monstrous.

"Recently I've felt so taken up with my worry about Poppy and what's going on with her that it's all I've been able to think about. Nothing else really matters right now and I will always put her first. Always. You've known that from the start."

"Of course I've known it."

"Just now that means not having someone else in my life."

There was a thick silence in the room.

"You mean, not having me."

I nodded. I wanted more than anything to put my arms around him and draw him close and comfort him, stop him being lonely and alone.

"It's been so nice. That's not the right word. It's been lovely. You've been lovely—" I halted. I could feel a tear making its way down my cheek. "It's just at the moment, I can't do it. I don't know what to do, but I can't be . . . I just can't . . . I'm so sorry."

I did everything I could not to cry—I was the one

who was hurting him. My throat ached with the weeping that would come when he was gone, and my eyes stung.

"You're saying it's over."

"Yes."

"I thought we were happy. I thought I made you happy."

"We were. You did. I just can't. I can't."

"But what did I do wrong?"

"No! Nothing, nothing at all. It's me. Poppy. Everything. It's the wrong time. Sorry."

"Is there nothing—?"

"I'm so sorry, Aidan."

There was a silence. I looked at him and his face was pale and his mouth set. Our eyes met and for a moment I thought I would reach out and take his hand and pull him toward me and call him my darling, but I didn't.

He picked up his jacket and left, not slamming the door behind him.

Twenty-seven

I stood in my school's playground and watched the children as they surged around me, forming groups and breaking up again, whispering to each other, barging into each other. It was the afternoon before the half-term and they were more excited than usual. I kept an eye on Fatima, who sat alone in the far corner, trying to be invisible, trying to look as if she didn't care. And on little Georgio, newly arrived in the school, with barely a word of English and half the size of the other boys in the class. He had sharp wrists and knobbly knees and his eyes were dark and huge as saucers; I wondered what he'd seen in his short life. I thought about Poppy, in a different playground. I pictured her shouldering her strong, determined little body through jostling groups of children to get whatever she wanted.

Poppy was going to spend a long weekend in Brixton and I would have her the rest of the Whitsun holiday. I knew I should make plans for what to do with her, but the thought of arrangements defeated me. What I really wanted was to be in an isolated house in a raging storm, where I could read books to her and we could eat hot buttered toast in front of the TV and close the doors on the world.

I felt tired and numb. Last night with Aidan now felt like a slow-motion dream of a breakup. It was like I'd been in a car crash and I was playing it over and over in my mind. Several times I'd thought of calling him, and even picked up my phone to do so, but then drew back. What was there to say?

I looked at my mobile, knowing there was no message there from Jason. Had the police visited him yet? We had agreed to see each other in Vauxhall Park for the handover of Poppy. But of course that was before I had given the police his name.

"Miss, Miss," shouted a boy, running toward me, and I came out of my reverie. I glanced down at my mobile one last time. Still nothing from Jason.

A couple of hours later, one look at Jason told me he was furious. Just the forceful way he walked toward us, crunching his feet down on the gravel path, was a warning. He looked like a large, consolidated mass of masculine rage.

"Daddy!" cried Poppy. "I did see a quirrel."

Jason stooped and picked her up and whirled her round and she laughed ecstatically and kicked her legs out. Over her shoulder, Jason's eyes bored into mine.

"I've got some bread," he said, setting Poppy down. "Shall we go and feed the ducks?"

"Ducks and baby ducks!"

"That's right. Let's go and find them."

"I'll say goodbye," I said.

"We'll feed the ducks together," Jason said.

"Yes," cried Poppy. "All of us: Mummy and Daddy and Poppy. Hold my hands. Swing me! Swing me high!"

"One, two, three, and up you go," said Jason, and as Poppy rose into the air shrieking, he said to me, "The police came to my school."

I didn't reply.

"Again," said Poppy. "Again. Higher."

Up she went.

"What are you up to?"

"Didn't they say?"

"It was in my school, in front of my teachers and my parents. Do you know what that means for me?"

I thought about the way Jason talked about "my" teachers and "my" parents, in the same way that he talked about "my" wife and "my" family.

"I'm sure you found a way to explain it," I said.

"They also came to the house and talked to Ben. He's not doing well as it is. What do you think this does to him?"

"Again," said Poppy, dragging down on both our hands so her bottom was practically on the ground.

"No," said Jason, too forcefully so that she shrank back. "Here's some bread. Tear pieces off—little pieces so it will last—and you can throw them to the ducks."

"A woman died."

In front of us Poppy hurled scraps of bread into the water and chortled as the ducks found them.

"Your three-year-old daughter did a drawing and wet her bed. Are you insane?"

"Look," I said, crouching beside Poppy and pointing. "A duckling. There! On the other side."

I stood up again. To my surprise, I was feeling quite unmoved in the face of Jason's whispered onslaught.

"Only a madwoman would think that has anything to do with a woman dying," Jason continued in his carrying hiss.

"I met her. She tracked me down."

"I don't care. I don't care about this strange paranoid world you're living in."

"Jason," I said. I could see myself in his pupils, and I could see the tiny pricks of stubble on his chin. "All this is beside the point. Did you know Skye Nolan?"

"Of course I didn't."

"But you would say that."

"Then don't ask me."

"Daddy," said Poppy, running into him and holding out a hand. "More bread."

He pushed another stale slice into her imperious fist.

"They knew about the marches we used to go on. And"—he lowered his voice again—"they asked about my personal life."

"You mean your affairs?"

"My affair."

"Just one?"

"I had an affair and that was wrong, but you can't go calling in the police and suggesting I killed a woman because you want some kind of revenge."

"Is Daddy angry?" Poppy was back.

"No, Daddy isn't angry. Last bit of bread and then I must go."

I waited till Poppy moved away again. "Is that what you think? That I'm doing all of this to get back at you?"

"Either that or something's very wrong with you."

"Has it occurred to you that there's a third possibility? That I'm genuinely anxious about Poppy and genuinely scared that she is in some way connected to what happened to that woman? To Skye Nolan," I corrected myself. "That I am just trying to stop something happening, or find out about something that did happen, something that feels horribly close to home, to our home, to Poppy. It feels like a nightmare that I kept trying to tell you about and you kept not paying attention, or maybe—" I stopped abruptly. Poppy looked round at me and I smiled reassuringly.

Jason muttered something under his breath.

"You know what? I don't really care what you think," I said, and found as I said it that it was true. "Poppy is in a vulnerable and anxious state: that matters. A woman is dead: that matters. Other stuff, not so much."

We stared at each other and, for a fleeting moment,

something unexpected passed between us, a glimmer of recognition, a softening. I saw that if one of us held out a hand in friendship, the other would take it. I almost thought we could laugh together, at our anger and absurdity. I could sense him seeing it too. One word, one gesture, from either of us. The moment passed, like the sun going behind a cloud.

Poppy turned and ran toward us, clasped each of our hands.

"Push me on the swing now," she said. "Or we can seesaw!"

"I've got to go."

I bent down and kissed the top of Poppy's head, nodded at Jason and walked away.

It was Friday evening, and the beginning of half-term. I was alone: no Poppy, no date night with Aidan as we'd arranged. No more date nights with him ever. The flat was tidy, the fridge was empty, the phone didn't ring.

I went for a short run, had a shower, looked at my emails. I wondered why I'd never heard back from Felicity Carey Connors, and then a thought struck me and I went to the junk mailbox, and there it was.

Dear Tess,
So sorry not to have replied before; it's been one of those weeks! I'd be pleased to meet with you. You said you had every other weekend free—this Sunday afternoon, about 4, would work

for me if you're free, though it might be too short
notice? I'm at 12a Faversham Drive. Maybe bring
your cello and we can see where you're at.
Felicity

I replied saying Sunday was good, making no mention
of the cello, but not daring to tell her I just wanted to
ask about Ben.

Then I made myself a gin and tonic, which was light
on the tonic, and tipped a small bag of spiced nuts into
a bowl. I had a strong desire for one of my rare ciga-
rettes, so I went into my bedroom and rummaged in
the underwear and the tee-shirt drawers until I found
a squashy packet. There were five left. I pulled one out
and went into the garden. The light was softly silver
and wind rustled in the leaves.

I lit my cigarette, which was stale with age, took a
sip of my drink, put a nut into my mouth, watched the
goldfinch. I felt lightheaded from the unaccustomed
cigarette and from my sense of being in the aftermath
of a derailment. I was estranged from Jason, had left
Aidan, was without my little daughter for three days,
and had made no plans. All the events of the past two
weeks lay behind me in a wreckage and the future was
a glare of blankness.

I closed my eyes and a memory swam toward me:
Jason and I, shortly after we'd met, walking up a
mountain in the Tyrol. The fog had come down, until we could barely make out the path in front of us
and the summit was hidden from view. I had a vivid
recollection of turning round to look back and seeing

the vague shape of Jason beneath me, almost wiped out by the fog. I felt like that now. Everything that had been vivid about our life together, everything that I'd taken for granted, seemed to be dissolving; everything that lay in front had become invisible.

I dropped the cigarette and crushed the ember with my heel. I finished the gin, the spiced nuts. The goldfinch was gone and the light had thickened.

What was going to happen next?

TWENTY-EIGHT

On Saturday morning, Kelly Jordan rang and asked if she could come round.

"Can't you just tell me over the phone?"

"It's better face-to-face."

"Is it good news or bad news?"

"I'll tell you when I see you."

I felt so agitated and confused that I tried to do some mindless tidying up as I waited for her to arrive. I was scrubbing the toilet bowl when the bell rang.

Five minutes later, the detective was sitting at the kitchen table while I poured coffee for us both. I was burning with anxiety and curiosity, but I also had something to say and couldn't stop myself from saying it.

"Why did you have to go to Aidan's work? Why did you have to do it in public? And you went to Jason's school. He was furious. With me."

"I'm here to talk about that."

"Have you found out something?"

Kelly Jordan gave a half-nod. I couldn't tell whether

that meant yes or no. I brought the two mugs across to the table and placed one in front of her.

"I can't remember whether you take milk. Or sugar."

"It's fine like this."

I sat down so we were facing each other across the table. She looked tired. There were very fine lines extending from the corners of her eyes. She had other things to deal with, other cases, other people to see. It was Saturday morning. Maybe her children were waiting for her to come home. I was just another name on her crammed schedule, and one of the more tiresome ones.

"You've been very patient with me. And kind." I paused. "Can I get you a biscuit?"

Kelly Jordan was sipping coffee and gave no sign of having heard. She replaced the mug on the table.

"Skye Nolan's inquest is on Monday," she said.

"That's quick, isn't it?"

She gave a faint shake of her head. "It'll just be a formality. It'll be opened and then adjourned almost immediately because of the murder inquiry."

It took me a moment to realize the significance of this.

"You mean there really is a murder inquiry now? It was murder?"

"We got the autopsy report back yesterday. I wasn't expecting much from it. I didn't think you could learn a lot from a body that's fallen a hundred feet onto concrete."

"So what did you learn?"

"There was a lot of damage, as you'd expect, multiple fractures. The funny thing is that among all those broken bones, there was a bone that shouldn't have been broken."

She raised her chin and touched her throat gently with her fingers.

"There's a funny little bone here. It basically never gets broken. It doesn't break if you fall, even from eight stories up. What does tend to break it is the direct force when two hands are applied to the neck."

I had to think about that for a moment.

"You mean like when someone is strangled?"

"Yes."

"You mean that Skye Nolan was dead when she fell?"

"Yes. And more than that. The pathologist also identified dark patches on the skin. This happens after death when the blood stops flowing and starts to be pulled down by gravity. It's called pooling. It's like when you hang up a wet towel to dry. The bottom bit of the towel gets wetter. It's like that."

"Except with blood."

"Yes."

"So you're saying that she was strangled before she was ..." I hesitated because the reality of what I was saying suddenly horrified me. "Before her body was pushed over the balcony. But you're saying more than that. That stuff with the blood settling in the body, it would take time. It must have lain there for some time."

"The report estimates that it would have taken a minimum of half an hour."

"Why? Why would you kill someone and then wait all that time?"

"We don't know," said Jordan.

I felt a moment of exhilaration. I had been right. I had gone to the police and they hadn't believed me. I had said the death of Skye Nolan had been murder and they had been dubious about that as well. And now I had been proved right, scientifically, in black and white. But the moment quickly passed.

"There's something else, isn't there?"

"This is an ongoing inquiry," the detective said, "and I can't talk about all the specifics. But it's clear that Skye Nolan was a troubled young woman. She had a turbulent private life."

"Turbulent? What does that mean?"

"Problematic relationships."

"With men?"

"Yes, with men. And she has also had psychological problems. We found a significant amount of prescription medicine in her flat."

"What has that to do with anything? She was still murdered."

"What I'm trying to say is this: we've talked to her mother and to her one relatively long-term partner. We have checked her phone records and her social media. The simple fact is that we have found no connection to any of the people you mentioned to us."

"So?" I said. "Couldn't that just mean you haven't been looking hard enough?"

Jordan's face tightened. "Tess, we've been very patient with you and your worries. We've taken them seriously, which, believe me, some police forces wouldn't have done. We've looked at the people whose names you gave us as thoroughly as is practical and, for that matter, legal. We've interviewed them and we've searched for any connection with Skye Nolan's life and we haven't found it, not even the most tenuous one. It's not there."

"What about Poppy's drawing? What about the doll?"

She made an impatient gesture. "Police investigations simply don't work that way round. I admit that you brought this tragic case to my attention and because of that I thought it was vital that we investigate your concerns. But we have finite resources. In fact, we have worse than finite resources. You have a feeling about this murder, based on a child's drawing. We investigated it. We drew a blank. Fine. These things happen, though I am not looking forward to explaining to my boss why I investigated it. As it stands, we have a victim who led a chaotic life and had a series of hook-ups with strangers. I think it is likely that one of them got out of hand and she was killed, possibly in the course of a robbery. She may have picked the wrong person to take back to her flat."

"So you're not following up on what I told you?"

"Have you not been listening to anything I've been saying? We did follow it up. Scrupulously. We didn't find anything."

"It was that other detective, wasn't it? I could tell he didn't believe me."

"No, it wasn't him. We couldn't find anything. There was nothing to go on."

"What about the drawing?" I asked weakly.

"One drawing by a child is not enough," said Kelly Jordan. "It's just a drawing. And maybe the woman is flying, not falling, have you thought of that?"

"Poppy said she was falling."

"Poppy is three."

I was breathing heavily. I could feel my pulse racing. I wanted to shout. Punch the wall. Punch Kelly Jordan. I made an effort to calm myself down.

"You realize," I began, forcing myself to speak in a level tone, "that if I'm right and you're wrong, that somewhere out there is a murderer who may be starting to suspect that the only witness to the murder he's committed is a three-year-old girl. Have you thought of that?"

Kelly Jordan leaned forward across the table.

"This is getting out of hand. You need to stop. Now."

"How do I do that?"

"You have my number. If anything happens, you can always pick up the phone and tell me. I'll talk to you anytime. Just give us something to investigate and we'll investigate it."

"This is my daughter. She's all I've got."

Kelly Jordan stood up.

"I'll keep you informed," she said. "You keep your daughter safe and we'll find the murderer."

TWENTY-NINE

But I couldn't keep my daughter safe. My daughter was with Jason, with Ben.

I ate half a croissant in the garden and scattered the rest for the finches.

I opened my laptop to write more reports, *Kadijah has been a pleasure to have in the class . . .* closed it again.

I picked up my mobile to call Jason and then put it down, remembering his face. He hated me. How long had he hated me?

I thought of calling Aidan. Then I remembered his words. *You need to sort things out and yourself out.* And he was right. I did. But I didn't know how.

I wandered into Poppy's room and sat on the bed. I looked at the pajamas tucked under the pillow, the absurd Easter bonnet we had made together for school still perched on top of the wardrobe, the little crate of toys with the chunky green caterpillar on top, the pile of clean clothes on the top of the chest—miniature tee shirts, trousers and knickers.

I picked up the little cardigan that was draped over

the chair and held it to my face, breathing in the smell of my daughter.

Tears came into my eyes as I remembered bringing Poppy home from the hospital and lying in bed with her, staring at the scrunched face and blue eyelids, the tiny stork mark on her forehead. Heavy with milk and dreamy with love, I had whispered a promise that I would always protect her. Always. Until she died, I would make sure my daughter was safe—as if I could do that, as if mothers were all-powerful beings who needed no one else.

I sat down at my sewing machine and stood up again. Opened the fridge and closed it, seeing the image of Poppy's smiling face pinned to the door by magnets. Watered the garden. Paced about, itchy with the sense that I needed to do something and had to do something and would go mad if I didn't do something, but I didn't know what it was.

A message pinged on my phone and I glanced down.

Sorry for late notice. Girls' get-together this evening, at the usual place? Do try and come—it's been ages! L xxxxxxx

"Tess! Over here!"

It was hard to miss them—five women round a table already strewn with bottles, talking loudly. There was Liz with her mane of hair, waving her arms as she made some point; there was Cora giggling as if she was seven. There they all were.

"We thought you weren't coming," said Kim, standing up to give me a hug.

I was late because I'd felt nervous about seeing them all, even though we had been friends since university and had continued to get together over the years, shedding partners and children to gather in restaurants or pubs or one or another's house, sometimes even for weekends away. It had been nearly twenty years since we had first met, I thought, as I looked around the group. They had lines on their faces, a few of them had gray hairs, some had gone through serious illnesses and one of them—energetic and loud-mouthed Tilda—wasn't there; she had died of breast cancer three years back. Some were married and some single, two had got divorced, most had a child or children—though Liz was on her third round of IVF.

Seeing them was a marker of time, I thought, and I hugged each of them and then squeezed my way into the chair waiting for me. Perhaps that was why I had stupidly worried over what to wear and how to get there and nearly hadn't come.

"We've ordered already."

"Small plates."

"Bloody small plates. Since when did everything have to be shared?"

"Look at you—how do you stay so skinny?"

"Have some wine."

"How long has it been?"

How long had it been? I wrinkled my brow, sipped my drink.

"God, I don't know. Before Poppy—can that be true?" I paused. "And before Tilda died. Where have I been?"

"Well, you're back." Cora held up a glass. "Welcome back."

"Here comes the food. Move some of these bottles. Who wants—well, whatever these are. What are they?"

For about half an hour, I was swept up in a torrent of talk, which lurched between the gossipy and the confessional. Then Becky turned to me, "So you finally got free."

"What do you mean?"

"You're divorced."

"I was never married, but yes."

"Is it OK?"

"Being alone. I don't know." I opened my mouth to say something about Aidan, closed it again, and had some more wine instead.

"It's hard," said Kim. "But everything's hard, isn't it? Fucking life." She knocked over a glass of wine and ignored the red stream trickling toward her.

My phone rang. I looked at it: the Brixton landline.

"Sorry. One moment. Hello? Jason? Is something up?"

I could hear a voice—Emily's voice—saying something and then Poppy was on the other end.

"Mummy?"

"Poppy, darling. Hello! Aren't you in bed?"

"Yes."

"Are you all right?"

"I want Milly."

"But—"

"I want Milly!"

"Listen, Poppy." I got up from the table and moved

away, gesturing apologetically to my friends. "You have Teddy there, don't you?"

"Yes."

"Cuddle up with Teddy. We can talk about Milly when you come home. But now it's time to go to sleep. Is Daddy there?"

"Emily here."

"Where's Daddy?"

"Emily here, not Daddy," said Poppy again. "Mummy?"

"Yes. Here I am."

"I want Sunny."

"Sunny's waiting for you. I'm waiting. I will see you very soon. Give the phone back to Emily and cuddle Teddy and close your eyes and soon it will be morning."

"Morning," said Poppy.

"Night night, my lovely love."

There was silence. My heart was a bruise. I ended the call and made my way back to the table, trying to smile at them.

"Everything OK?" asked Liz.

"Poppy's having a bit of a hard time. Transitions." I turned to Becky. "Wasn't I free?"

"What?"

"You said I'd finally got free. Wasn't I free before?"

"Well, were you?"

"I guess a relationship, any relationship, is a kind of—?"

"No! I mean, of course that's true. But you, specifically. You know."

"No."

"You and Jason," said Liz and the table was suddenly quiet. They were all looking at me and suddenly I wanted to jump up and run away from their shrewd and tender eyes.

"Me and Jason?"

"He was always a bit of a control freak, wasn't he?"

"Was he?" I felt a bit giddy.

"Hang on." Miriam, who had barely spoken, raised her voice. "I don't think Tess needs us bad-mouthing the man she lived with for years, who's the father of her child. I want to see pictures of her, by the way," she added.

"No, I want to hear this," I said. "I want to know what you thought of him. Honestly."

Liz didn't need much encouragement. "He didn't like it when you disagreed with him, did he? I always wanted you to tell him to fuck off, but you just took it. He never knew how lucky he was to have you, that was his problem. He thought he was the catch. As if."

"He liked being the one to make the decisions," said Miriam.

"Someone told me you left, and he kept the house."

I nodded. "Yes," I said. "It seemed to make sense. It's near his work and anyway I kind of thought I needed a fresh start." As I spoke, I wondered if that was the true explanation.

"Bloody hell. Really? You put so much into that house, Tess. I remember you making all those bookshelves and the curtains, and painting all the rooms, and digging up the garden as well. It was your house way more than his. You loved it."

I looked round the table. "You thought he bullied me? You thought I was being *bullied*?"

"I wouldn't put it like that," said Miriam hastily.

"He didn't like us much, did he?" Becky picked up a stick of celery, dipped it into a creamy concoction and chomped it.

"Didn't he?"

"Not as a group, anyway," said Cora.

I leaned forward. "Now what does *that* mean?"

"Nothing."

"We're all a bit drunk. Honestly, Tess, all we're saying is we're glad you're here and you're OK."

"No, really. What does it mean? Listen, don't all look so worried. I'm not upset at what you're saying. Actually, I recently discovered that Jason had started on what was to be a long affair just after I had Poppy, and what felt worst about it was that I'd been in the dark all that time. Other people knew this big thing about me that I didn't. Friends knew." I looked from face to face. "It feels important to me to recognize what he was like. So: did he try it on with any of you lot?"

"No." Kim was flushed. "But I always thought that he wasn't the faithful type."

"He wouldn't have dared," said Liz. She had a smear of beetroot on her cheek. "You don't think any of us would have? Tess?"

"Course not," I said. "You're my dear friends."

But in truth I felt nothing would surprise me anymore.

"I heard a rumor," said Cora. "Don't ask me anything else. It was years ago and it was just a rumor. I wanted to ask you—but you were very defensive at that time. The drawbridge would go up."

"Was I? Would it?" I rubbed my face. "I didn't know."

"I thought so anyway."

"I just thought he took you for granted," said Miriam softly. "When he should have been thanking his lucky stars for being with someone beautiful and clever and kind like you."

"It turns out nothing's like I thought it was," I said. "What shall I do next?"

"Eat pudding."

It was nearly two when I got home. I made myself a mug of tea and was about to climb into bed when I heard a scrabbling sound from Poppy's room. I went onto the landing and put my ear to the door, my skin prickling. Silence, and then a piteous meow.

"How could I have shut you in!" I said as, full of relief, I pulled open the door.

Sunny shot out and down the stairs, an outraged orange streak. I wandered into the room and sat on Poppy's bed, cradling my mug of tea. I had a sore throat and my eyes stung. The barrier between me and the world had grown as fragile as parchment and any new thing could pierce it; I would flood out and the world would flood in.

I finished my tea, put it on the floor, lay down on Poppy's bed, put my muzzy head on Poppy's pillow beside her favorite pajamas, which were purple and decorated with pink seahorses. I thought about everything my friends had said and how with love and kindness they had rubbed out the picture I had of myself.

Maybe Jason and I hadn't separated. Maybe he had left me, while making me believe we were deciding together what was for the best. Hot tears filled my eyes.

I wanted my daughter. I wanted Aidan. I wanted to go back and do everything again and do it better. I didn't know what I wanted: I just wanted.

A fat tear rolled down my face and into my hair, then another. I wiped my face with the sleeve of Poppy's pajama top.

And as I did so, I felt a strange and nasty tingling on my skin, as if I had a high fever or was going to be violently sick. My stomach knotted. I sat up.

Why were Poppy's pajamas on top of her pillow? I felt sure that earlier they'd been tucked under it. Hadn't they? I shut my eyes for a moment and tried to remember. Memory is fickle—that's what everyone had told me, over and over again during these last days of nightmare. A child can't be trusted to distinguish between memory and imagination, and nor could I be trusted when I said that the woman who accosted me in an Italian restaurant was the same woman who had died falling from a tower. My memory of my life with Jason had turned out to be a tattered thing made from anxious hope and blindness. Memory is a lie, a creative act, a flimsy shield against the truth.

But Poppy's pajamas? I could see them as they had been that afternoon, *under* the pillow. I stood up, looked around, my eyes scanning the room. My gaze froze on the Easter bonnet. Surely, *surely*, when I had looked at it earlier, the dried flowers I had stitched on had been facing me full on. Now they were at the back.

The chunky green caterpillar—that had been on the top of the toy basket and now it was half under the patchwork quilt. The drawers on the chest had all been closed and now the top one was a few inches open.

Someone had been in here. They had shut Sunny into the room, because now when I thought about it, I knew I had fed him just before I left and watched him tumble his old body through the cat flap. Someone had come in here and they had lifted up Poppy's toys, her pillow, her Easter bonnet. I stood absolutely still, not breathing, and strained to hear a sound. Nothing, just the intermittent rumble of a car passing, the faint sigh of the breeze in the trees, the complaining creak of the water pipes.

Very quietly, I went out of Poppy's room and shut the door. I went into my bedroom and tried to remember exactly what it had been like when I left. I opened my wardrobe and a dress had slid off its hanger. I picked it up and put in back on the hanger: had it been like that?

Had there been a robbery? I opened my jewelry box, though I didn't have anything of value—no gold or diamonds. I gazed around.

In the conservatory, everything looked as I had left it. Except a cupboard door hung ajar: one of its hinges had come loose and it had to be lifted up to shut it properly. I didn't remember it being open. I didn't think I would have left it like that, because I was pretty obsessive about returning to a tidy house. I hated beds not being made, cupboards and drawers left open, chairs not pushed into the table.

I moved slowly round the flat, running my hands over surfaces. I checked the windows, the doors to the garden.

I was sure, but what was my evidence? Just a memory of how a cat was not shut into a room, pajamas were folded under a pillow, a cupboard door was open. And who would believe me? After all, I was the woman who had already cried wolf.

THIRTY

It took me over an hour and a half to get to Lewisham and find Faversham Drive, but I was still twenty minutes early. I paced the side streets, hot and itchy with nervousness and the sense of doing something underhanded.

At five minutes before four o'clock, I rang the bell at 12a and heard its chime, then footsteps. The door opened and Felicity Carey Connors stood before me, an expectant smile on her face. She was my height, my kind of age. Before she even spoke, I liked her.

"Tess?"

"Yes. Good to meet you."

"You too. Come in."

She led me up stairs and into the living room of her flat. It was light and tidy, with bare sanded floorboards, pale wooden furniture, a few paintings on the walls, and a smell of baking. There was a cello on its stand in the middle of the room and some sheets of music beside it. I felt bewildered. Perhaps this Felicity had nothing at all to do with Ben's Fliss.

"You didn't bring your cello."

"No."

"Never mind. Have a seat. Do you want a cup of tea? And I've made some biscuits."

"I don't have one."

"Oh? Then—"

"The truth is, I don't want lessons."

She turned her calm face to me. "I don't understand."

"I know. Sorry. I want to talk about Ben."

"Ben?"

"You are married to Ben? Or were, that is."

"Who are you?"

"Tess. I'm Tess Moreau."

"Yes, but who are you? Why are you here?"

"It's hard to explain."

"Either explain or leave."

We were both still standing, the cello between us. I realized that she was angry—but also that she was the Fliss I was looking for.

"I was married to Jason before he married Emily." I coughed unnecessarily; I couldn't think how to tell the story so it made any sense. "I met Ben at their house a few weeks ago."

"And?"

"And he didn't seem in a good way."

"What business is that of yours? What right have you got to come out here to tell me that? As if I didn't know already."

I tried to explain, stumbling through the story, telling her about Poppy's drawing, Poppy's nightmares, the mutilated doll, the death, the fact that it was a murder, my gathering dread. She stood with her hand on the neck of the cello and listened to the end.

"And you think poor Ben might somehow be involved in all of this?"

She spoke with a kind of contempt and I felt my whole body flush hot. "I just need to make sure it's safe for Poppy to be with him," I mumbled.

"I don't know why I'm not showing you the door."

I tried to smile, but my mouth was the wrong shape, stiff and square.

"Oh God, let's have some tea in the kitchen," she said.

The kitchen was small, with a little table against one wall and two chairs. Felicity gestured to one and I sat and watched her while she made a pot of tea and took some biscuits from the wire cooling rack.

"Oat and ginger."

"Thanks."

"When we met he wasn't like he is now."

"Right."

"Look." She pointed at a photo on the wall and there they both were, in a different world. I barely recognized him: he had a placid face and short hair and a smile. Only the eyes were the same.

"He gets depressed," she said. "I mean, *really* depressed. You're probably thinking it cruel of me to chuck him out."

"No," I said. "I'm not thinking that."

"He wouldn't take his pills. Then he started drinking too much. He lost his job. Everything went downhill. I thought I could stick it out, but the truth is, I couldn't. I kept giving him ultimatums, but it was like sliding into a nightmare. In the end, I just couldn't take it anymore."

"Of course you couldn't," I said. I'd seen Ben and could imagine how awful it must have been.

"At least he has Emily."

"So you think he couldn't do ..." I couldn't finish the sentence.

"I've never seen him violent. Only sad and kind of ..." She searched for the world. "Vacant. Like he's taken leave of himself. He's just a poor sap who can't cope with life. And I let him down, which was probably the last straw. I don't feel good about it."

"It wasn't your fault," I said.

"Oh, I don't know." She picked up a biscuit and dipped it into her tea. "I feel very bad about him; I can hardly bear to think of it. But I wouldn't have him back, not the way he is. I wasn't any help to him. He was like a drowning man who was pulling me under with him. And I quite like living on my own. It's simpler, anyway."

As I left, a few rich notes from the cello floated into the street. Poor Ben.

THIRTY-ONE

When I rang her on Monday morning, Kelly Jordan was as unimpressed as I had expected her to be.

"Were there signs of forced entry?"

"Not that I could see."

"And you say that nothing was stolen."

"You know that feeling where you can't put your finger on it, but you know someone has been in your room?"

"No, I don't."

"Things had been moved around, like someone was looking for something." There was a pause. "I know this all sounds vague, but I thought I should tell you. I know that your heart must sink every time you hear my voice."

She didn't contradict me. "Normally I'd tell you to report it so that you'd get a case number, but to be frank I'm not sure what there is to report. Or, to put it more baldly, there is nothing."

"I just thought I should tell you anything that's relevant."

"Relevant?"

"Yes. To the case."

"I'll make a note of it."

I doubted whether she was making an actual note.

"There's something else I should mention," I said.

"What?"

"I'm on the bus. I'm going to the inquest. Maybe I'll see you there?"

When Jordan responded there was a new note of incredulity in her voice. "You mean the Skye Nolan inquest?"

"Yes."

"No, you won't see me there. Why on earth are you going?"

"I was hoping to learn something about the case."

"There won't be anything to learn. It'll just be a formality. More to the point, you shouldn't be going."

"Why?"

"Because you're obsessed."

"That's what you call it. I call it—"

"I don't care what you call it. I am seriously advising you to stop your wild goose chase. For our sake; for your sake. Also, these are people who've lost someone in the most terrible way."

"I'll be sensitive," I said.

I ended the call. I wasn't sure the exchange had improved my situation.

THIRTY-TWO

The coroner's court was on the side of an abandoned-looking building on the edge of St. Pancras churchyard. The only sign of the proceedings was a little typed schedule pasted up on the window next to the door. The inquest was due to start in less than five minutes. I pushed at the door, but it was locked. I pressed a button and heard an unintelligible voice.

"I'm here for the inquest," I said and the door clicked open.

As I stepped in, I was met by a large man in a gray suit.

"Are you friend or family?" he asked.

"Friend."

The man gestured toward an open door behind him. I walked inside. I had expected some kind of municipal office, but this was more like a chapel with a gabled roof, six chandeliers and old oak pews arranged at the back and two more rows on one side. There was a somber dignity to it, as if I were attending a wedding or a funeral. At the front was a raised dais, like in a courtroom, with a large video display and a computer screen and whiteboard, all facing forward.

The room was almost empty and I sat in the back row, a few feet away from a young man in a dark suit who was looking at his phone. Perhaps he was a journalist. Two people were seated in the front row on the right-hand side. I could only see them from the back. A woman with purple hair, a bright scarf round her thin shoulders, sitting very straight. Her companion turned his head to see who had come in. He was younger, midthirties, with tortoiseshell glasses, a neat beard and one earring. He was wearing a tie, but didn't look comfortable in it. He looked like someone going to church or to an interview.

Two uniformed police officers, a man and a woman, were seated in the same row on the other end. The man was whispering something in the woman's ear.

The burly man who had admitted me came into the room from a door at the side and faced the front.

"All rise," he said.

There was a shuffling of feet and all of us stood. A door in the far wall opened and a woman emerged. She was dressed in a severe gray suit and carried a bundle of files under her arm. She stood in front of the long desk and bowed slightly. I reflexively bowed back along with the rest of the—what? Audience? Congregation? Even though I knew the public had the right to be there, I felt like an intruder.

The woman sat down and laid the files on the desktop and there was a little rustle as everyone else sat down too. There were so few people. It seemed inadequate. But this wasn't a memorial service after all.

The woman gave a preparatory cough.

"Good morning. My name is Charlotte Singer. I'm the deputy coroner for this district." She narrowed her eyes and looked around the few seated people. She settled on the man and woman at the front.

"Are you the family?"

"This is Skye's mother," said the man. "I'm an old friend."

Singer inclined her head slightly.

"I'd like to offer my sincere condolences. It must have been terrible for you. I'll try to make this as painless as I can. You may know that the purpose of a coroner's inquest is simply to answer four questions: the identity of the deceased, where they died, when they died and how they died." She was addressing the mother directly. I couldn't see her face, but her head was bent forward and she seemed to be trembling. The man put his hand on her back.

"I hope it's been explained to you that today's proceedings are a formality. I've been informed that, following the autopsy, this is now a murder investigation. As a result I shall be opening and immediately adjourning the proceedings."

"Is that it?"

Singer looked up. The man sitting next to Skye Nolan's mother had spoken.

"I'm sorry," said Singer. "Mr. . . . ?"

"Beccles. Charlie Beccles," said the man. "I'm Skye's friend. I wondered if we were allowed to make a statement."

211

Singer began to fidget with the files in front of her, arranging them into a neat pile.

"There will certainly be opportunities for that, in due course."

"When is due course?" said Beccles.

"I'm afraid that's out of my hands."

"Days? Weeks? Months?"

"Months," said Singer. "But it all depends on what happens with the investigation and criminal proceedings. The one thing I need to say today is that I can't order the body to be released." She looked at the police officers. "Have you anything you need to ask?"

But the officers were there for the following case so the coroner gathered her files, nodded a farewell in the direction of Skye Nolan's mother. They were ordered to rise once more and Singer stood up, bowed to them and left.

I sat for a few moments, uncertain of what to do. Was that it? But the mother was here and a friend. That was an opportunity that might never come again. I waited for them to make their way toward the exit and then I stood up. For the first time, I was able to see the mother's face and suddenly I had a sense, like a physical blow, of what it must be like to lose a child. The cheekbones were prominent, the skin almost gray, the large, dark eyes seemed to be staring at nothing. She looked like her daughter, small-boned and pale-skinned, except her hair was dyed a pale purple. She was not nearly as old as I'd expected; in her midforties, I guessed. She must have been a young mother, and of course Skye had been young when she was murdered. She was wearing a long, paisley-patterned skirt, Doc Marten boots, a faded indigo-blue shirt, a bright scarf, large rings on her hands and a clatter of bangles round her sharp wrists—as if she were about to go on a protest march or on a picnic with friends.

"I'm very sorry," I said to her. "This was a terrible thing. I don't know what to say except I'm so, so sorry."

The woman barely reacted. Her face turned slowly toward me.

"Thank you," she said. She sounded numb; I wondered if she were on medication.

The man looked at me suspiciously. He was quite short, but broad-shouldered. There were tiny streaks of gray in his neat beard.

"Did you know Skye?" he asked.

I realized that I hadn't thought of what I was going to say in response to this obvious question. I mustn't lie to them. I mustn't do anything to damage this woman who had suffered more than anyone should ever suffer.

"Only a bit," I said. "It's difficult to explain. But I wanted to come here because I hoped I could talk to you about her. I completely understand if you don't want that at the moment."

"I like to talk about her," said the mother. She had a light, silvery voice. "It's the only thing I want to talk about. You know, they wouldn't let me see her body. That's terrible, don't you think?"

I could imagine why the police hadn't let her see

her daughter's body and the thought of it was indeed terrible.

"I'm sorry," I said. "I don't even know your name."

"Peggy. And this is Charlie."

"Hello."

I held out my hand and shook both of theirs in turn: Charlie's strong and warm; Peggy's chilly and thin as a bunch of twigs.

"Charlie's been a very good friend. I'd always hoped that he and Skye would get married. But it didn't happen. Skye didn't have many proper friends. But Charlie, you were a proper friend."

I'd worried that Skye's mother wouldn't want to talk about her daughter, but she was desperate. It seemed she would talk to anyone, even a stranger.

"Can we go somewhere? Perhaps I could buy you a cup of tea," I suggested.

"We're going to the station," Charlie said. "I'm not sure if this is the right time."

I could feel the opportunity slipping through my fingers. If this ended now, I might never see them again.

"Of course," I said. "Perhaps I can walk some of the way with you. I think we can go along the canal. It's not far."

We came out into the sunshine. Charlie stood on one side of Peggy, taking her arm, and Peggy took my arm too, as little and as trusting as a child. We crossed the canal on the new bridge and descended to the towpath.

"Tell us how you knew Skye," Charlie said.

I tried to think of an answer that was not entirely untrue, but that would also encourage them to keep talking to me, even to stay in touch.

"This will probably sound a bit strange. We only met once, very recently. Just a couple of weeks ago. But it stayed in my head. I've thought about her a lot. And then I saw she had died. I hope you don't mind that I'm here, a virtual stranger."

We were walking past rows of houseboats. I was conscious that every second of this conversation was precious.

"One of the reasons I remember Skye so clearly"—I felt fraudulent calling her Skye, fabricating an intimacy—"is that she seemed very agitated about something."

"Yes, that's my daughter," said Peggy. "She'd been like that for a long time."

"Was it worse in the weeks before she died?"

Peggy swung her head from side to side. She was tiny between the two of us. "I didn't see her in the weeks before she died."

We walked up the broad steps from the canal and reached the path that led to King's Cross Station. I halted.

"Could I come and see you?" I asked Peggy. "I'd love to talk to you about your daughter, if you would like that."

Charlie knitted his brows, but Peggy seemed grateful.

"I would," she said. "I feel I need to talk at the moment. Otherwise it is like she's . . ." She lifted a fist and then opened her fingers. "Disappeared, into thin air. As if she was never here at all. So few people to miss her or really remember her."

"Then I'll come."

"I live out in the wilds." She smiled. "Chelmsford, I mean."

"That's no problem."

"I'll probably just cry all the time."

"That's no problem either. You're allowed to cry."

We exchanged addresses and then the pair turned to go, but after a few paces Charlie turned back. He spoke to me in a low voice.

"What the hell are you doing?"

"What?"

"Do you have any idea how vulnerable she is?"

"Of course I do."

"She might want to talk to you, but I don't get why you want to talk to her. What are you up to?"

What was I up to? I looked up the path at Peggy, her face pinched and prematurely aged with grief, staring blankly at the brown water.

"It's complicated. I honestly don't want to make things more painful than they are."

"That would be hard."

"I know."

"Give her a bit of time, anyway, wait for it to be not quite so raw."

"OK." But time was my enemy. "Can I talk to you then?"

"Me?"

"Yes."

"About Skye?"

"Yes."

He scowled at me, then gave a heavy shrug.

"Can you make tomorrow early evening, at the Parliament Hill Lido? I'll be in the café just after six."

"I'll be there."

THIRTY-THREE

I was supposed to be collecting Poppy from Jason's at three. Even though the bus I was on took a circuitous route and I had to walk the last mile, I was half an hour early. As I made my way up the familiar road toward the house where I used to live, a message pinged on my phone from Jason:

Delayed. Back at 3:30/4-ish.

I cursed him under my breath but rang the bell anyway, just in case. I heard shuffling footsteps and the front door opened. Ben stood there, barefoot and wearing checked trousers that might have been pajamas. I couldn't tell.

"Sorry," I said, remembering our last meeting in the park. "I know I'm early. I only just got Jason's message."

"Jason and Emily aren't here."

I could hear the dog barking from inside the house and electronic music playing somewhere.

"I know. I'll just go and grab a coffee and come back in an hour."

"I worry about Emily," he said, as if I hadn't spoken, or as if I were somebody else entirely. "I'm her big brother. Maybe not much of a big brother recently, but you know."

"Why do you worry?"

"You more than anyone should know."

"What are you saying?"

"I just worry."

"But is something wrong? I mean, wrong with her and Jason."

"She's not like you," he said.

"Like me?"

"Able to stand up for herself."

Was I able to stand up for myself? Had I ever done so with Jason?

"What does he do?" I asked.

The dog barked again.

I took a small step forward.

"I hope you don't think I'm interfering. I know we got off on the wrong foot. But I wanted to ask you something."

"I need to clean my teeth now."

"But before that, can you just—"

"Mummy!"

I half-turned toward the street, but stopped, dislocated. The voice came from inside the house.

"Poppy?"

And there was my daughter, bounding toward the door. She was only wearing knickers and her witch's cloak, and there was a thick smear of jam on her cheek. Her hair was unbrushed.

"Poppy?" I repeated. "But I thought—"

"I did do a wheel."

"What is this? Come here."

I picked up Poppy and held her close.

"How long have Jason and Emily been gone?" I asked Ben.

"They're coming home soon. You're early."

"I said, how long have they been gone?"

Poppy's breath was hot in my ear. "When I was a fant."

"Tess!" I heard Jason's voice behind me.

I spun round, still holding Poppy. Jason and Emily were at the little iron gate. Emily looked tired and her eyes were puffy.

"You're early," Jason said.

I ignored him and spoke to Poppy.

"Come on, darling, let's get you dressed and home."

"Roxie did growl."

I climbed the stairs, Jason behind me. I shouldered open the bedroom door and put Poppy on the bed, then started throwing her clothes into her bag.

"Sunny will purr."

"He will. Here," I said, tossing over a tee shirt and pinafore dress. "Why don't you wear these?"

"No."

"You can wear the witch cloak on top." I looked up at Jason, who was still standing in the doorway. "How long were you gone? Was it overnight?"

"We didn't leave her with a stranger."

"Let me help you with that." I found the armholes for Poppy and tugged the dress over her head and down her wriggling body.

"Does Sunny love me?"

"Here. Your cloak."

"It was a one-off."

I stared briefly at Jason, loathing everything about him: his solid bulk, his square jaw, his masculine good looks, the way he stood with his arms folded and his legs slightly apart. Like a bull: how did I ever let him come near me?

"We're done here. Let's be on our way."

We had less than twenty-four hours before Poppy went to stay with my mother.

We went to the park together and I pushed Poppy on the swings and watched her as she clambered up the climbing frame. We fed the ducks and Poppy rolled down a hill and she tried to stroke all the dogs that came past. There was a black Labrador that stood peacefully and let her pull its silky ears, and a terrier with crooked legs that jumped up at her and licked her face. I thought about Skye walking dogs. Ben had a dog.

Back home, we started making a house from a large cardboard box, cutting out windows, a door, a hole for the loo-roll chimney. I was taping the wall to the ceiling with such deep concentration that when I finished and looked up, I hadn't noticed that Poppy wasn't there. She wasn't even in the room. I called for her and then heard a scraping sound from another room. I guessed it was something on the hard floor of the kitchen. I ran toward the kitchen and saw Poppy coming out of it. She was holding something and it took me a moment to see that she was holding a knife—a really big sharp knife, the one I used for cutting bread and carving joints of meat.

I wanted to scream. I wanted to shout at Poppy to put it down. But I knew that if I scared her she might drop it and cut herself. In an absent moment while using it to slice an onion I had once cut my finger to the bone and I hadn't even noticed it until the blood welled up and then I couldn't stop it.

"Poppy," I said in the warmest and most casual tone I could manage. "Why don't you give that to me?"

"It's for Mummy," she said.

"Just stand still."

It would take just one false step, the kind of falling over or stumbling that she did ten times a day and the blade would go right through her. Slowly, still smiling, I got to my knees in front of her and leaned forward, closer and closer, until I was able to grasp her little fist with one hand and her arm with the other and then gradually ease the knife out of her fingers, keeping the blade away from both of us.

When I had it away from her, I put it up on a high shelf and turned to her.

"Poppy, you must never, never, ever touch that knife again."

"It's for Mummy," she said.

"Yes," I said. "It's Mummy's. Not Poppy's."

I looked in the kitchen and what I saw made me want to vomit. Poppy had pulled one of the chairs over to the counter, climbed up on it, leaned over the counter and pulled the knife off the magnetic strip on the wall. Then, somehow, she had climbed back down off the chair, still holding the largest and sharpest knife in the house. All of it while I was in the next room sticking a paper house together.

"Why for Mummy?" I asked her.

"What?"

It felt like she had already forgotten the whole thing. I reached for the knife and held it in front of me.

"This. Why is it for Mummy?"

"It's a sword," she said with a frown. "For Mummy."

We made rice pudding together and ate it in front of a cartoon. I ran a deep bath and lifted Poppy in, then sat beside her, soaping her pink body, cutting her nails, and at the end washing her hair and combing out the matted knots. Poppy wailed and punched me in the face and said she hated me.

I read stories to her until she fell asleep, and then sat for several minutes watching her as she twisted and turned on the pillow, put two fingers into her mouth, then burrowed into the covers.

She wet her bed in the night and cried, I cleaned her and changed her pajamas and lifted her in beside me and lay for what felt like hours listening to her breathing, feeling the heat of her little body.

In the morning we ate cinnamon buns in the garden and Poppy persecuted Sunny and dug up worms and picked a peony blossom for me to wear in my hair. There were two golden butterflies dancing in the warm air.

Then we packed a little bag for her and took two buses and arrived with time to spare at Marylebone

Station. But my mother was already there. She was wearing a thick jacket in spite of the heat; her graying hair was coming loose, and the bag she was carrying had a broken strap. There was a faint air of dishevelment about her that gave me a pang. She needed me to be protecting her, not adding to her worries.

I put my arms around her and kissed her on the cheek. She smelled the same as she always had done: the floral perfume she wore every day, and a whiff of face powder.

"I got an early train, just to be sure," she said.

Poppy put her hand trustingly in her grandmother's. "Will I go on Sam the gonkey?"

I watched them leave, Poppy wearing her little backpack and clutching her teddy, and I thought about all the arrivals and departures, all the meeting and goodbyes, in her short life. Did she mind? Was she homesick? Where was home for her?

And I thought about the events of the previous evening, about the knife and what Poppy had said about the knife. It was "for Mummy." It was a sword. What kind of sword? Was it a sword to attack me with? Or was it a sword for me to defend myself? Was Poppy, my mysterious little child, my visitor from another planet, threatening me or trying to protect me?

I could have wept, but I wasn't going to do that. Not yet. I had things to do and places to go.

THIRTY-FOUR

I arrived at the Parliament Hill Lido shortly before six, bought a cup of tea and found myself a seat outside the café, overlooking the water. It was a warm, soft evening and the pool was full of swimmers, some of them slow and splashy, others surging strong-shouldered through the chemical blue. It was impossible to know if Charlie was among them. I could barely remember what he looked like, except that he had a trim beard and round tortoiseshell glasses.

Then a young man, broad-shouldered and with a slight pot belly, hauled himself out of the water, took off his swimming cap and goggles and squinted toward the café. When he saw me, he lifted a hand and gestured, then disappeared into the changing rooms. A few minutes later, Charlie was sitting opposite me. He was wearing shorts and a long-sleeved tee shirt and his hair was damp, his face pink from the swim. He rummaged in his rucksack for his glasses and put them on. I felt like I was looking at him for the first time. This was the man who had cared for

Skye. But also: this was the man who hadn't been able to save her.

"I don't have much time."

"It's good of you to see me."

He held up a finger. "Before you say anything else, I want to know why you're so interested in Skye. You met her just the once, you say, but then you turn up at her inquest and you want to go and speak to her mother. Are you a journalist?"

"No. I'm a teacher, if you want to know. What about you?"

"Does it matter?"

"I don't know. Sorry for asking."

"I work for a tech company and if I tried to explain what my job is, you probably wouldn't understand anyway."

"All right, fine," I said.

"So what are you up to? Almost no one cared about Skye, so why do you care? After one meeting."

I took a deep breath.

"This will sound strange, but I believe I'm tied to her murder in some way."

Charlie sat back in his chair. "So why are you talking to me? You should go to the police."

"I have."

"What did they say?"

"They're investigating," I said, hoping that this vague answer was enough. "It's all complicated, but I think Skye might have had a connection with someone I know and maybe they killed her."

"Who?"

"I don't know."

"What kind of connection?"

"I don't know."

"You're not making sense."

I paused because I wasn't even making sense to myself. "I don't know what to tell you. You just need to accept that I'm acting in good faith. I need to find out about Skye because I need to know why she tracked me down just before she died."

"She tracked you down?"

"Yes."

"What did she say?"

"She came up to me in a restaurant and behaved like she knew me."

"What restaurant?"

"It's called Angelo's. Just a little Italian place near London Fields."

"And you didn't know her?"

"Not that I could remember."

He considered this. At least he wasn't running away.

"Why not just let the police get on with it?"

I thought of Poppy with her little backpack, hand in hand with her grandmother and clutching her teddy.

"It's important to me," I said softly.

"I don't know," said Charlie grudgingly. "It feels like there's something about this I don't understand."

"It's strange to me as well."

"All right," he said, looking at his phone. "I've got to go in a few minutes. What do you want to ask?"

227

"I'd just like to know what Skye was like, the places she hung out. And I guess most of all I need to know about her and men. If that's not too painful."

He looked away for me for a time, staring at the water. Even when he turned back toward me, he didn't look me in the eye directly.

"I'm not sure what to say. She would have been twenty-eight next month. She wasn't born in London. She used to talk about herself as an Essex girl. She went to school in Chelmsford. She was an only child, never knew her father. She was—" He stopped and grimaced. "Was was was. I find it strange saying that. She said that she was a bit of a wild teenager. Drugs and all that. She was really smart, but she didn't go to uni or anything like that. She worked as a childminder for a bit, before she came to London, and then she did bits and pieces. She worked in a bar in Enfield first of all. The Crown and Anchor," he said before I could ask. "Then an Italian place that closed down. She said they took her on because she looked a bit Italian. She was a waitress and she worked in the kitchen sometimes. She used to cook a mean pizza."

Charlie looked out at the pool, the people thrashing past.

"I thought she was a dog walker."

"That was in the last year or so. She really liked that. She loved dogs. She loved all animals. Her dream was to have a refuge place for stray dogs and cats. I don't think she ever had a realistic business plan for it." He trailed off.

"Where did she walk them?"

228

"Where? Mostly in that park near Kennington and in Burgess Park too, I think. It depended on which dogs she was looking after. She'd go to other parts of London as well."

"How did you meet?"

"Is that relevant?"

"I don't know. It probably isn't."

He pushed a hand into his damp hair so it stood up in peaks.

"We got talking on a coach journey to London. At the end of it, she wrote her phone number on my wrist in felt tip. We were together for years, on and off, though we never moved in together." He paused. "She was fun. Really sweet. That's the thing you have to know about Skye: she could be the sweetest, kindest, sparkiest person in the world. It was like she was giving off energy, do you know what I mean?"

I nodded.

"You're probably wondering why someone like her was with someone like me?"

"I wasn't," I said, not entirely truthfully.

"She was a bit what I wanted to be more like and maybe things would have been better for her if she'd been a bit more like me." He gave a little smile. "I mean stolid, organized."

"But you got on."

"For a time. I was her . . . I was going to say, her rock. That's the cliché, isn't it? But it's not quite right. I was more like her scratching post. You know, the way cats find some chair they like to run their claws down."

"She could be difficult."

229

"Yes. Difficult and destructive. Christ, she was destructive. Destructive and self-destructive."

"Like how?"

"Drinking too much, smoking too much, too much of whatever. Letting friends down. Getting into fights. Anyone who got in her way, which was me mostly. And yeah, like fucking other men sometimes, or rather, letting them fuck her, because she felt like a worthless piece of shit and so why not behave like one? And then she'd feel awful, terrible. She hated herself. It was like a spiral she went into."

"So it ended between you?"

"It kept ending. And then it ended for good. She was very lovable, despite everything, but I couldn't deal with it anymore."

"When was that?"

He thought for a moment.

"About eighteen or twenty months ago. I didn't see her for a few months, but we stayed friends. I don't think she had any other friends by the end. She was too much for them. It took a lot to stay friends with her."

"So there's no one else you can think of who I should talk to?"

Charlie shrugged. "Not really. Which is terrible when you think of it. Or if there is I don't know who they are."

"Did she tell you about the men after you?"

"She'd come and cry on my shoulder sometimes, weeping over the mistake she'd made about this one; the way that one had let her down, how she was a fool for never learning from experience."

230

"How did she meet them?"

"She used dating apps sometimes—but the police must have checked those. And then, I guess she just met guys here and there. She was very good at that. You'd be out with her and she'd strike up conversation with the homeless guy, or the woman at the checkout, or whatever. She was always interested in them." Charlie's eyes looked slightly red; perhaps it was the chlorine.

"Was there anyone like that just before she died?"

"She told me about a guy," he said. "He'd picked her up when she was out of it. That's not what she called it, mind. She said he'd come to her rescue. She said he was handsome and kind and she was sure he wasn't going to let her down."

"So did she see this guy again?" I kept my voice light.

"A few times, I think. She said there were complications, but it was going to be all right. She wasn't going to let this chance of happiness get away."

"Nothing else?"

He shrugged. "I don't think so. It was the same old story."

"Did she go to his house?"

"I don't know. I think she said he had a nice place. But maybe that was another guy, another time."

"Right."

"I shouted at her, told her not to be so childish and idiotic, but she just laughed at me and told me not to be so cynical. She said she was following her dreams." He ran his fingers through his damp hair. "The thing is about Skye, she was born with fewer

layers of skin than other people. She was so unprotected. Like a little kid really. A lonely little kid. She
thought someone would save her, make her all right.
But they didn't."

"It wasn't your fault," I said uselessly, just as I had
said to Felicity.

Charlie turned back to me. "Who are you to say
that?" His voice was harsh and grating. "You met her
once. She left me a couple of crazy messages just before she died and I never got back to her. I was busy,
but the real reason was that I couldn't quite face it."

"What were they about?"

"Nothing really. She was gabbling."

"Do you still have the messages on your phone?"

He blinked slowly. "I never thought. Maybe."

He took out his phone, scrolled down, then laid it
flat on the table between us and pressed play. And then
Skye was speaking.

"Charlie, Charlie!" Her voice was high and clear,
like a girl's. "Darling Charlie, where have you got
to? Pick up!" There was a brief silence. "Something's
happening. I've got this plan. It's like that film we once
saw. What was its name? I can't remember. I want to
talk to you. I'm desperate—no, not desperate." A rippling, silvery laugh. "Excited." There was a clatter of
noise in the background. "Got to go. Call me."

The voice ended. Charlie put the phone back in his
pocket and stared out at the blue receptacle of water.

"What film?" I asked eventually.

"I have no idea."

"Can you think of—?"

He jerked his head up and glared at me with blood-shot eyes.

"I told you. I don't know! She was probably imagining it anyway."

"Right."

"All that chaos."

"I'm sorry."

"I'll have to live with it, I guess. Letting Skye down."

"I'm going to give you my details in case you remember something," I said. "Anything. Can I have your email?"

I took out my phone, keyed it in, wrote down my address and mobile number.

"Also," I said. "I wonder if you'd email a couple of photos of her to me."

"Why?"

"So if I'm asking people about her, you know."

"I guess so," he said. "I should go now. I'm running late."

"Thank you for giving me this time."

"I've got a girlfriend," he said. "It's only been a few months, but I like her."

"Talk to her," I said. "Tell her how you're feeling."

He stood up and slung his rucksack over his shoulder.

"The weird thing is that everything I've just told you, I've never said that to anyone. I've never spoken it aloud."

I could see he was close to tears. "I'm sorry if I've made things more painful."

He shrugged. "Go carefully with Peggy. I can't imagine how she'll live with this."

233

I watched him as he walked away, then bought another cup of tea and a cinnamon bun. I sat for a long time, eyes on the swimmers moving up and down the pool, flickering abstract shapes in the blue water.

On the bus, I took out my mobile. Charlie had sent me three photos of Skye. One was a close-up, slightly out of focus. Her hair was cut short, almost to a bristle, and she had a piercing in her nose. She was smiling widely and there was a dimple in her left cheek. The second was of her sitting on a chair with a yellow shawl round her shoulders and a large black cat on her lap. In the third she was outside, wearing walking boots and a padded jacket. She was holding onto several leads and leaning back slightly as if she was being pulled, although the dogs were out of the picture. I studied her: small, slender, pretty. And young, I thought. So young.

THIRTY-FIVE

The first dog I saw was a chocolate-box spaniel with a glossy coat, long silky ears and sad, adoring eyes. Its owner wore a dress in sprigged cotton and dark glasses pushed back on top of her head.

"I'm so sorry to trouble you," I said, my mobile already held out with the picture of Skye on its screen. "I'm wondering if you knew Skye Nolan. She used to walk dogs in this park."

"I don't think I've seen her. Sorry. Has she gone missing?"

As if Skye were a dog herself.

Next, a scruffy and cheerful-looking terrier that scampered around me as I spoke to the man with a big beard.

"Never, I'm afraid. But I'm not usually the one to take Noodle out for his walk."

Two golden retrievers, one young and the other old and stout. They were accompanied by a woman in running clothes who stopped when I accosted her and unplugged herself from her earphones before replying.

"Maybe. Maybe I've seen her. But I don't know. And I've never talked to her. Sorry."

And off she ran, the dogs loping behind her, their pink tongues hanging out.

A dachshund in a coat, so overweight I could barely make out its legs. The teenage boy cajoling it along the path looked embarrassed to be seen with it.

"I'm on half-term. My gran asked me to walk it. It just waddles a few yards then sits down. Look at it!"

"So you haven't seen this woman?"

"No."

A moderate-sized cross-breed with inquiring eyes and a coarse coat. A poodle. A Vizsla (I only knew that because its owner told me). Two Staffies. A chocolate-brown puppy that ran round in circles.

A mangy dog that looked like a fox. An enormous dog that was the size of a pony and had ropes of saliva hanging from its jaws. A tiny dog the size of a mole that lifted a leg against a tree and stared reproachfully at me as I spoke to its owner. Three dogs on leads held by one teenage girl who was battling bravely to keep them disentangled. No one had met Skye.

Then came a dog with a golden-brown coat and a white bib and a look of eager puzzlement.

"She's a Duck Toller," said the woman.

"I've never heard of that."

"Not many people have. She's very clever. Aren't you, Primrose?"

"I'm sure she is."

"I think she understands half of what I say and most of what I mean."

"That's nice. I was wondering if you'd ever come across this person."

I held out my phone. The woman peered at the screen then straightened up.

"Skye! Of course. She loved Primrose."

"So you knew her?"

"Well, I didn't *know* know her, if you see what I mean. But she was often in the park and I'm here twice a day."

"With her dogs?"

"The dogs she walked, yes." The woman sniffed disapprovingly. "Sometimes she had four or five of them. I mean, how can you properly look after five dogs all at once?"

"I don't know."

"You can't. Mind you, she did always clear up after them, which is more than you can say for some dog walkers. I don't know why people have dogs if they need to hire a walker."

"Did you talk to her?"

"I certainly did. We had nice chats over the last few months."

"What did you talk about?"

"Dogs," said the woman. "What else?"

"Do you know whose dogs she walked?"

"What is this? Is something the matter?"

"Actually, Skye died," I said.

The woman looked down at her dog, as if for consolation, and Primrose looked back up at her. I'd never noticed before that dogs have eyebrows.

"Now I think of it, I haven't seen her. Was she ill?

She didn't look ill, though she did smoke an awful lot. I used to tell her."

"She fell from a building."

"That's horrible! Dear oh dear. What were you asking? Yes ... I don't know whose dogs she walked. It wasn't the same dogs all the time and there were weeks when I didn't see her. Why? Are you her friend?"

"Yes."

"I'm sorry. Who'd have thought it? She didn't have much luck, did she?"

"What do you mean by that?"

"With her men friends. When she wasn't talking about dogs she was talking about men. She said she was a fool when it came to men."

"Did she mention any by name?"

"It was just in passing. I think she was the same with loads of other people in the park. She would just come up and start chatting, like you'd known each other forever."

"Was she always alone?"

"She was with a man once."

"Did you see him?"

"Only from behind."

"What did he look like?"

"I really don't remember."

"Tall or short or fat or thin?"

"Just a man, seen from behind," said the woman.

"When?"

"When? Maybe a few weeks ago. I don't know."

"Did they seem close?"

"I really couldn't say. I was walking Primrose and

238

she was there with all these other dogs and a man. Excuse me, but why are you asking all these questions?"

"She was a friend," I said.

I looked down at my mobile. Skye looked back, smiling. Smiling at me, her eyebrows slightly raised.

Dogs, I thought. All these dogs.

And then I thought of something else and the air went out of me.

THIRTY-SIX

I sat at Gina's kitchen table and she poured two coffees from the French press. The house was strangely quiet.

"Where is everyone?"

"Laurie's taken the kids to see his mother. They left just before you came. It's weird, being here on my own. I can't remember when that last happened."

"I don't want to make you late for work."

Gina looked at the clock on the wall: it was twenty past eight. "I have half an hour before I need to leave. It's OK to be late once in a while." She picked up her coffee, took a sip, sighed luxuriously. "Isn't it good that it's just the two of us, sitting at the table. Sometimes I have a moment on my way to work, or when Jake and Nellie have gone to sleep, when I look back at us before all this happened. Maybe we forget what it's like just being friends, hanging out."

"That's true." I felt like a spy in my own life. Now I was being dishonest with my best friend. "I was thinking. Sometimes I wonder if I should get a dog. It might be nice for Poppy. What do you think?"

Gina's expression turned to alarm. "I'd think about it very carefully. People say it's like getting a new child. You can never just go away and leave it. Approach the idea with caution. And what about Sunny—I don't think he'd take very kindly to a dog in the house."

"So you wouldn't get one?"

"Christ, no. It's as much as I can do to cope with two children—even though it's mostly Laurie who does the day-to-day coping. The thought of coming home in the evening and having to take a dog out for a walk is too much. And then picking up their poo. And the way they smell when they're wet. And that thing when they put their dribbly snouts on your lap."

I laughed.

"No, seriously. And leave hairs everywhere. And yap."

"I get the picture. You're not a dog person."

"I might let Jake have a hamster or something."

"Laurie likes dogs though, doesn't he?"

"Laurie? Does he?"

"He told me he sometimes takes his mother's dog for a walk."

"If you can call that little rat a dog. I guess he likes dogs more than me, anyway. Actually, if he had his way, we'd be living in the countryside surrounded by mud and with hens and goats and stuff. Fatherhood's gone to his head." She grinned. "He says that whenever he goes out with Winston—that's his mother's dog—he gets into more conversations with people than in all his years of going to London parks put together."

"So where does he walk him?" I hated myself as I asked these questions.

"Where? I don't know. She lives in Kensal Rise so maybe he goes to the cemetery. He does love a good cemetery. But then, Winston is a small dog and I think he only needs small walks. Twice a day, mind."

"Does his mother ever hire a dog walker?"

Gina laughed. "What is this? Are you working for the RSPCA?"

"I just wonder what people do about their dogs when they go away."

"The answer is, I don't know. Now then, enough of the dog interrogation, all right? Tell me how it is without Poppy."

"Strange. Very quiet. I miss her. I've talked to her several times a day and she seems cheerful. Though last night she had night terrors, and my mother says she isn't really eating much."

"I'm sure she'll be fine," said Gina airily. "And at least you and Aidan can spend time together, just the two of you. That must be nice."

"That was the original plan."

Gina turned an inquiring glance on me.

"We broke up." I tried to smile, but my mouth quivered and I turned away.

"No! Tess, darling, what happened? You seemed so happy together. When did it happen?"

"A few days ago."

"Was it you?"

"It was the wrong time. But now I wonder why I did it."

"It's not too late," said Gina.

"Oh, I don't know. Everything's a mess."

"If you think you made a mistake, tell him."

"I can't. The reasons I ended it haven't changed. It's just that I miss him and I feel a bit crap about everything. This is the dangerous period, when it's all fresh. When it came to it, I just wasn't ready. We met at the wrong time. I thought I was doing so well, but I'm not really, Gina. And more to the point, neither is Poppy."

I looked at Gina's solicitous expression and felt a stab of guilt. Here I was, harboring sinister suspicions about her husband and at the same time opening my heart, confiding in her, wanting her comfort.

"Oh dear, oh dear," said Gina. "I'm so sorry, Tess."

"Me too. Oh God, look at the time."

"Sod the time. Let's have another coffee and you can tell me properly."

"I can't." I stood up. "I've got to catch a train. I'm off to Chelmsford."

"Chelmsford? What's in Chelmsford?"

"A friend of a friend."

THIRTY-SEVEN

Peggy Nolan opened the door before I even had time to knock. I wondered if she'd been standing at the window, watching for me. She was wearing a green jumpsuit that was missing a couple of buttons and had a checked scarf tied round her head. She held out her hands and I took them in mine: thin fingers, chipped nails, tiny grains of mascara embedded in the skin round her eyes, a cold sore on the side of her mouth. She looked a bit grubby, a bit starved.

She took me straight through her house to the garden at the back. I could see why. The house—a short taxi ride from the station—was a tiny two up, two down in a suburban street that could have been anywhere in England and it was crammed with objects: shoes piled up in the hall, posters on the walls, mobiles and wind chimes and dream catchers hanging from the kitchen ceiling, dozens of jugs on the windowsill, three clocks, only one of which was working, a guitar leaning against the wall with a string broken. But the garden was different. It fell slightly away from the house down to a second level and then beyond that looked across woodland. Peggy had made the garden her own and it was lushly green, brimming with flowers and, at the end, there was a neatly tended vegetable patch.

"If it wasn't for this, I would have gone mad years ago," she said. "Maybe I did go mad for a while. I'd be at the checkout at the supermarket and the person would ask how I was and I would tell them what was happening to my daughter, how she was running wild or breaking down or whatever she was doing at that particular point, and after a few moments I would see in their eyes that they were embarrassed and they just wanted me to stop and go away. The one thing that comforted me was this." She gestured around her. "I used to want to live in a commune and we'd all dig the land and feed ourselves off it and weave things and bake bread. Then Skye came along and ... oh well. That was just a stupid dream. Probably it would never have happened anyway." She looked more closely at me. "Are you a mother?"

"I've got a three-year-old daughter."

"Look after her," said Peggy. "Hold her close."

"I try to."

"I want to talk about Skye. It's all I want. The only time I feel a bit better is when I'm talking about her; then she doesn't seem so far away. It doesn't seem like I'll never see her again." There was a rising sob in her voice. "That's why I was happy you wanted to come out here to see me. But if I talk too much, just shut me up."

"I want you to talk as much as you need."

"Shall we have tea out here? I think it's warm enough."

"I'd like that very much."

I sat on a slightly wobbly metal garden chair on the paving just next to the house. After a few minutes, Peggy emerged, carrying a tray.

"I made a carrot cake," she said. "It's vegan. Can I cut you a slice? It might be a bit heavy."

"Just a thin piece."

Before pouring the tea she took a small square flat piece of pottery, glowing amber and green, and placed it in front of me.

"It's a coaster," she said. "It's to put the hot mug on."

I picked it up and examined it. "It's beautiful."

"I made it. I do pottery. I used to have a fantasy of doing it as a job. But it gives me pleasure."

"It's gorgeous."

"Please, take it."

"What?"

"Have it. It would make me so happy to know that it was owned by someone who liked it."

"Really?"

"Yes. Go on, put it in your pocket."

I laughed. "That's incredibly kind. I'll put my mug of tea on it first."

As I drank the tea, Peggy talked about what Skye had been like as a child, how happy and impulsive, with intense and volatile friendships, and subject to violent enthusiasms, usually to do with the natural world: pressing wildflowers, volunteering at an animal sanctuary, learning to identify birds. But something

246

had gone wrong when she was a teenager and Peggy had often wondered whether it was to do with not having a father around.

"It was me and Skye," she said. "Our safe little world. I thought I could protect her."

I repressed a shudder at that. "You don't know how children will react."

"I kept thinking it would just be a phase," said Peggy. She was looking past me at something beyond. She could have been talking to anyone—or talking to herself. "She got involved with a group of people when she was about fourteen and it was horrible. I didn't know what to do. There were drugs, of course, and she had a couple of boyfriends who treated her badly. It was like having a stranger in the house, a stranger who hated me. Sometimes she stole from me, and from my mother too. That was awful.

"When she moved to London, it was like she was escaping. She only told me little bits about her life there but it worried me. When she met Charlie, it was like a miracle. But in the end he couldn't save her. Nobody could."

There was a pause.

"Can I say something?" I asked.

"What?"

"You're talking as if your daughter killed herself. Or died of an overdose. She didn't. Maybe she didn't need saving. Maybe she would have saved herself or was in the process of saving herself. She just had the terrible luck to run into the wrong person."

Peggy shook her head slowly. "You don't understand.

You don't get it. When she and Charlie broke up—when he left her, I should say—she was heartbroken. You've never seen such despair. Skye never did things by halves. When she was happy, she was so happy it was almost frightening. And when she was sad—oh my, she was sad, like the whole world had ended. The truth is, when she cut herself off from me, I was—"

She stopped, putting up a hand to shield her face from the sun. Her eyes were bloodshot. I waited.

"I was *relieved*. That's the truth. It had all gone on too long. I didn't want to think about her. I didn't want to know, day by day, how she was going off the rails. I didn't want to know about the drugs. Or the men. I didn't want to be responsible. I'd spent so many years in dread, panic in the pit of my stomach every single day. So I was relieved she didn't want to see me."

"I can understand that," I said. "It doesn't mean you didn't love her. Did she say why?"

"It wasn't like that." Peggy was speaking quickly now, trying to keep ahead of her sobs. "I don't think it was a decision. She just stopped coming home to visit, or calling, and didn't answer my texts or anything. Maybe it was because I reminded her of the life she wanted to get away from, or maybe she was ashamed. I don't know. But I do know that I didn't really try very hard to keep in touch with her or find out how she was. I told myself that if she wasn't contacting me that was good. No news is good news, that's what they say. But sometimes no news is terrible news. My little girl. Murdered." Her voice shook. "I should have known. I should have insisted. That's what a good mother would have done. So I blame myself. I'll always blame myself. And I don't know how to bear it. I literally don't know how."

I put my hand over hers. It felt like a claw.

"I'm so, so sorry. I can't begin to imagine what it feels like."

We sat together in silence. A blackbird whistled from the garden wall.

"Have the police told you what's happening with their investigation?" I asked at last.

"They haven't told me anything. A young police officer came round and sat where you're sitting and asked me if I was feeling all right. I don't need the police to give me therapy. I'm already seeing a therapist. And I do yoga and meditate. I just want them to find who did it."

"Didn't they interview you?"

"I couldn't tell them much. They wanted to ask me about the people she'd been seeing, but I didn't know who she spent her time with."

"Didn't she stay in touch with any old friends?"

Peggy took a long time to reply.

"I think mainly she left all that behind when she moved to London. I think she may have seen one or two who also moved down there."

"Do you know their names?"

"Why do you want to know?"

"I wanted to talk to someone who knew her in London."

"There's one I always liked, a girl called Hannah."

"Do you know her second name?"

"Yes, of course. Hannah ..." She hesitated. "Flood. Hannah Flood. She was good with her hands. She used to have a market stall selling candles and things like that, beautiful things, and I think she opened a shop in London."

"Do you know where?"

"Marylebone, I think. Just off the high street. But I don't know whether she was in touch with Skye. I haven't seen her for ages and I hadn't seen Skye for a long time either. When I went to her flat last week, it was the first time I'd been there for almost a year."

I felt a prickle of interest. "Why did you go?"

"To clear it out. I'm her next of kin." She sniffed. "It was just a couple of years ago that I cleared my mother's house out when she died. I'm only forty-five." She gave a laugh that sounded like a sob. "I always thought I was too young to be the mother of a grown-up. Now I feel about a hundred years old and probably look it." She rubbed her thin hands over her face as if to wipe away the lines of grief. "But it made me think of my own house and what it would be like for Skye to deal with all my old clothes and things in drawers I should have thrown away years ago. I never thought I'd be the one to do it for Skye."

She took a tissue out and blew her nose.

"That must have been so painful."

Peggy shook her head. "It was helpful in a way. We can't have the funeral yet, and anyway that will probably be awful, but going through everything in the flat felt right somehow. It was a way of saying goodbye to her. This sounds stupid, but it felt like I was taking care of her. Taking care of her like I didn't when she was alive. Folding up her clothes and putting things in order. She lived in such disorder." Tears were rolling down her thin cheeks and she made no attempt to check them. "I'm not exactly tidy myself; I'm a magpie, I like collecting stuff. But Skye made a mess wherever she went; her whole life was a mess. Charlie went down with me and we went through it all together. I don't know how I would have managed this without him. It was mostly rubbish, of course. It felt strange putting her knives and forks and dustpan and brush and tea towels into cardboard boxes. We should probably have taken them straight to the dump, but I couldn't bear to. She had some nice clothes. She looked so pretty in them. I don't know what to do with those. I don't think I can bear to get rid of them. What do you think?"

"I think you shouldn't make decisions about anything like that at the moment."

"That's what Charlie says too." She paused. "But there was something. Would you like to see it?"

"Yes, of course."

Peggy got up and walked into the house and while she was away I thought about Charlie, the devoted ex-boyfriend, the keeper of the flame.

I remembered looking at the list of murdered women in London. It was a very small sample but even so, the perpetrators were mainly the husbands and ex-husbands, the partners and ex-partners and people who wanted to be partners. Charlie, the ex-boyfriend, must surely be the first on the police's list of suspects. And he had gone round with Peggy, helping her clear out the flat. It was something to think about. But how did Charlie and Skye connect to me and Poppy?

Then I had another thought. What if I died? Would Jason, as Poppy's father, be allowed to help "clear out" my flat? Was he still some kind of next of kin? I would have to check up on that. The thought of it made me almost physically sick.

Peggy came back out into the garden holding a shoebox. She placed it on the table and took the top off.

"This was the most emotional part for me," she said. "This was Skye's jewelry. Sometimes I just pick up one of her sweaters and I can still smell her perfume on them. But more often I go through these, looking at her earrings and the necklaces." She picked out a silver flower on a thin chain. "I got her this for her twenty-first birthday. It's nothing valuable, but I found it in a second-hand shop and thought it would suit her."

I felt such sadness, looking through these intimate possessions of a woman I had only met once. I picked up a copper bracelet, a clutch of thin bangles, an anklet with tiny charms hanging from it, a pretty moonstone necklace, some large hooped earrings and some other smaller ones, several studs, a brooch in the shape of a fish, a handful of tortoiseshell hair slides, a delicate floral headband. I pictured Skye standing in front of a mirror in her disordered room, trying things on, studying herself, preparing herself for the world, and then

I let the jewelry pour through my latticed fingers, back into the box.

As I did so, I felt a sudden puzzlement and turned to Peggy, but Peggy's pinched and tear-stained face made me pause so I didn't ask.

THIRTY-EIGHT

On the train back to London, Peggy's coaster in my pocket, the events of the day swarmed through me till my head ached. I thought of Skye's sad, short life, but I also thought of my own life. The story I had told myself had been scribbled over and ripped up. Firm ground was now quicksand. My own sense of who I was and what I meant had been dislocated.

A man walked through the carriage and, although there were several empty seats, he sat opposite me, spreading his legs, occupying space. He was fleshy, with brawny arms and jowly cheeks, and he let his gaze linger on me. I looked away, feeling queasy. Men, all men, had become figures of dread and menace. I had been so focused on Jason, but what about Ben, there in Jason's house with his mean dog and his sad eyes and his pallid, slack face? What about Laurie, who I hadn't even considered until now, although he had been in plain sight all along? Or Bernie, who always seemed to be around, meeting us in the hall, staring down at us from his window as we sat in the garden, bringing round bread, being a good neighbor? And of course, there was Aidan, who had been in my actual flat as much as anyone. Not anymore, of course. Men with dogs and men without dogs. And now there was Charlie, who had no connection to me, so far as I knew, but was deeply connected to Skye.

Who was I meant to be suspicious of? Who was I meant *not* to be suspicious of?

I couldn't wait; it felt as if every second counted. I phoned Kelly Jordan.

"I'm very busy," she said instead of hello.

I stood up and walked to the place between compartments so that the man wouldn't be able to hear me.

"You said I should get in touch if I had any concerns."

"What are your concerns?"

"As far as I understand, the basic police theory is that Skye Nolan was killed as part of a robbery that went wrong."

"It's one possibility."

"If it was a robbery, then why wasn't her jewelry taken?"

There was a pause. I looked at my phone, wondering if I'd lost signal.

"How do you know that?"

"Skye's mother showed me her jewelry box."

"Why did she do that?"

"She invited me to her house."

"How do you even know her?"

"I met her at the inquest. Remember? I told you I was going." There was a silence on the line. "It's open to the public."

"I know it's open to the public, Tess. Lots of places are open to the public. But talking to witnesses—you could even call it interfering with witnesses—is not ..." There was another pause. "Not something you should be doing."

"I just wanted to offer my condolences and she wanted to talk to me. I think that's all right. But what about the jewelry?"

"I don't have to explain the police investigation to you."

"I know. I just wanted to inform you in case it changed your mind."

"All right, Tess, in this case the jewelry was found scattered on the floor. Presumably by the murderer."

"But why wasn't it taken?"

"Because we're only seeing what was left. It looked as if the jewelry had been hastily tossed around as if someone had rummaged through it. Presumably more valuable items were taken."

"Peggy Nolan didn't say anything was missing."

"Perhaps you don't know that Peggy Nolan had lost touch with her daughter over the past year. There is no reason she would have been able to identify missing pieces of jewelry."

"But you don't *know* that any jewelry was stolen."

"That's true. But it may have been or it may have been that nothing was stolen because nothing was worth stealing. Is that all?"

"Sorry," I said. "I don't mean to tell you how to do your job. I just want to be helpful."

I heard Jordan take a deep breath.

"I need to warn you that this is a murder investigation."

"I'm just talking to people."

"You're talking to Skye's mother, who is extremely vulnerable."

"I know that. Also—" I took a deep, steadying breath, knowing that I might be about to make a neighbor into an enemy and also wreck my friendship with Gina. "There are other men I think you should take a look at."

"What other men?"

"Other men who Poppy sees a lot of. Like our neighbor, Bernie, who lives in the flat upstairs, and then there's the husband of a friend of mine who looks after Poppy after school several times a week. And I don't know if you've thought of investigating Skye's ex-boyfriend, Charlie. He seems distraught, but I've heard that—"

"Tess."

"What?"

"Can you hear yourself?"

"That's not the point. Do *you* hear me? Are you listening?"

"I understand you are worried."

"Justifiably."

"Let me say this. You are now accusing people left, right and center—"

"Not accusing them. Mentioning them."

"Have you thought of seeking help?"

"I'm seeking your help. Right now."

"I don't mean that kind of help."

"You think I'm mentally disturbed?"

"I think you have allowed yourself to be swamped by anxiety." Kelly Jordan spoke carefully. "So that you are not seeing things clearly or being rational. It might be worth talking to someone. Instead of ringing me up every time a random new fear pops into your mind."

Looking up, I met the man's gaze; he didn't drop his eyes. I turned my back and walked into the next carriage.

"The trouble is," I said, "the only way you'll take me seriously is if something terrible happens."

"I can assure you the police are working very hard to find out who murdered Skye Nolan. You can leave that to us. You are not helping us; you are not helping yourself or your daughter; you are simply getting in the way of our investigation, and if this means anything to you, I'm already in enough trouble as it is because of the time and energy I have spent on you and your fears."

She broke off the call without saying goodbye and I found myself holding my phone and staring out of the window, through the back windows of houses in east London.

I returned to a different seat. I couldn't stop myself thinking of Jason walking through my house after I was dead, going through my things.

I waited on the station forecourt, my heart racing. Soon I would see Poppy.

I had ten minutes before their train arrived. The detective's words echoed in my mind. *You need to seek help.*

Maybe she was right, maybe I did. Maybe I was like Poppy and a story had taken hold of me and I could no longer tell what was true and what was a fiction born out of tenderness and fear. My hands were trembling as I called the number.

"I want to make an appointment with Dr. Leavitt. For tomorrow."

"He has no appointments tomorrow."

"It won't wait. I need to see him at once."

"You can come to the walk-in tomorrow. We open at eight."

Thirty-nine

Poppy flew round the flat. She picked up Sunny and clasped him to her chest, till the old cat reached out and batted her; then her mouth opened in a square of wounded distress and she dropped him and howled.

She hit out when I insisted on washing her hair that was clotted with something like marmalade. Her naked, soapy, angry body was slippery as an eel's.

She lay on her tummy in the downstairs room, dreamily arranging her collection of toys in a circle and talking to them, while I cooked a meal.

Lying in bed, clean and sleepy, she said, "When did you die?"

"I won't die for a very long time."

"But who will look after me then?"

"You will be all grown up," I said. "Maybe with children of your own, maybe with grandchildren."

"With Milly?"

"Milly's gone, darling."

"She did die."

"She was just a doll; she didn't die."

I stroked Poppy's hair. Her forehead was slightly damp. On the edge of her hairline, a faint stork mark was still visible. She was still so little; the residue of babyhood clung to her.

"Story," demanded Poppy.

I picked up a book.

"No. My story."

"Once upon a time," I began. "There was a little girl called Poppy. She had a mother called Tess and a father called Jason."

"And a cat."

"Yes. A cat called Sunny."

"And Sam the gonkey."

"And Sam."

"And a fant."

"All right. An elephant too. And her family and her friends loved her and she was kept safe."

"But she was a bad girl."

"No! She was a good, lovely, kind and clever girl."

Poppy gazed up at me. She put a finger on my top lip and traced its shape; she traced the faint smile lines at the corners of my eyes.

"Are you very old?" she said.

"I'm not young like you, but I'm not old."

"When I was old, I did die."

FORTY

Poppy had to come with me to the GP surgery. I gave her a piggyback there and she sat on my lap in the waiting room while I read to her. She seemed miraculous to me: the warm weight of her, the shine of her hair and the blue veins under her pale skin, the smell of soap and shampoo and that indefinable fragrance that was hers alone. My daughter, I thought—but she wasn't mine, she was firmly her own precious self. I was hers, though. I belonged to her.

I didn't know Dr. Leavitt very well. I'd only been to see him twice since moving here, once because Poppy had an ear infection and once because I had a suspicious mole on my stomach. But I instinctively liked him. He was in his sixties, with pouches under his tired eyes and a kind and respectful manner that made you feel listened to.

Tears filled my eyes even before I entered his room, Poppy holding my hand. He gestured me to a chair, and I hauled Poppy onto my lap, where she wriggled round and pushed her face into my neck.

"Hello, Poppy," he said.

She didn't respond at all. She stared straight ahead at nothing.

"Poppy," I said. "Say hello to Dr. Leavitt."

She gave no sign of having heard me at all.

"That's all right, Ms. Moreau. What can I do for you?"

I didn't know where to begin and felt horribly self-conscious.

"It's probably stupid," I said. "I don't want to be wasting your time."

He waited. I saw that the collar of his jacket was turned in on itself and had an absurd impulse to lean forward and rearrange it.

"I'm not doing so well," I said, speaking softly so Poppy wouldn't feel disturbed. "It's hard to talk about."

I made a gesture toward Poppy and he nodded.

"I have some animals that need looking after," he said.

He leaned down toward a tub beside the desk and pulled out a soft rabbit and a panda bear.

"Here. Sit in that corner there and see if they are ill."

Poppy climbed off my lap and took the soft toys very carefully.

"Milly did die," she said. "I did kill."

"Her doll," I explained.

"You tell me if they need bandages," said Dr. Leavitt to Poppy. "To make them all better." He turned to me. "In what way are you not doing so well?"

I swallowed. My throat felt constricted and my eyes pricked with tears.

"Poppy started behaving in a strange way." I spoke

in a whisper so she wouldn't hear. "She drew a disturbing picture and she began swearing and she tore her precious rag doll to pieces."

"Milly."

"But that's not why I'm here. I mean, it is, it is in a way, but I took her to see someone and ... sorry. I'm not explaining myself and I know you don't have much time."

In the corner, Poppy was bent over the rabbit, saying something I couldn't hear.

"Go on."

"I'm feeling anxious. I mean, so anxious I don't know what to do with myself. I thought she must have witnessed a crime. That she was in danger. I thought it was her father."

"I'm not sure I understand."

There was a deep furrow between his eyes.

"I don't understand either. I began to believe he had done something terrible that she had seen. And then I thought it was his wife's brother. Then in the middle of this, someone died, a young woman. I didn't know her exactly, but I think she was the person Poppy was talking about. I think it is all connected to Poppy."

I stopped abruptly because I saw the expression on his face, a mixture of incomprehension and sympathy.

"Rabbit is nearly dead now," announced Poppy. She sounded quite cheerful about it.

"I know I'm not making sense," I continued quietly, desperately. "But I feel she's in danger. No." I pressed a hand against my chest, hearing the thump of my heart. "I know she is. I *know*."

I heard my voice, the words tumbling out all mixed-up and disconnected: danger, affairs, Milly, detectives, inquest. I saw the doctor's eyes flick toward the clock over his door. I saw Poppy put her hands round the rabbit's neck.

"No one believes me. The police think I'm a crazy woman. But everywhere I look, I see danger. Danger so I can hardly breathe. From Jason or Ben, that's the brother, or Aidan—he's my boyfriend. Was my boyfriend. Or from my friend's husband, or my neighbor, or ... oh, I can hear myself," I said. "When I say it out loud like this it sounds mad, when I look at your face as I say it, I understand what I must seem like."

There was a long silence. Poppy shook the rabbit.

"He did die," she said triumphantly and turned to the panda.

"Ms. Moreau."

"Tess."

"Tess." Dr. Leavitt spoke very gently, as if he was trying to calm me down. "I'm not sure I understand everything you've said, but I do understand that you are distressed and anxious, and I want to ask you a few simple questions."

"Like what?"

"Do you often have a racing heartbeat?"

"Yes. Yes, of course. Wouldn't you if you thought your child was in danger?"

"Do you sometimes feel faint?"

"A bit. But that's maybe because I'm not eating as much as usual."

"Nausea?"

"Yes. Because I'm scared."

"Do you have chest pain?"

I put a hand against my chest. "I don't know. There are times I feel my heart is hammering so hard it's going to burst through and it feels really horrible."

Poppy wandered over.

"Home," she said.

"Soon," I told her and she climbed back onto my lap and started winding my hair through her fingers.

"Pins and needles?" asked Dr. Leavitt.

"Yes. What does that mean?"

Dry mouth? Yes.

Churning stomach: God, yes!

Shaky limbs? Yes.

Choking feeling? Every so often.

A need to go to the toilet? Maybe.

Insomnia? Of course.

Exhausted? How not.

A dread of dying? Haven't you been listening . . . ?

"How often do you feel these things?"

"How often? Almost all the time."

"And how long have they been going on."

"A couple of weeks."

"Mummy, I want to go home."

"These are classic symptoms of severe anxiety and of panic attacks. Am I right that you recently separated from Poppy's father?"

"Almost a year ago now."

"And so most of the time you look after Poppy on your own."

"Yes."

"And work?"

266

"Yes."

"And can I ask, are you worried about money?"

"Of course I am." I said it cheerily so that Poppy wouldn't pick up on it.

"Tess," he said carefully, neutrally. "Do you have any thoughts of self-harm or suicidal feelings?"

I held Poppy close and rested my chin on her head. It was impossible to know if it was her heart I could feel beating, or my own.

"No, I don't."

He moved back in his chair.

"You obviously have many stresses in your life and it's quite natural you should feel anxious. Panic is a severe form of anxiety and while panic attacks are not dangerous in themselves, they are very unpleasant and frightening and can become a vicious cycle. I could prescribe you a type of antidepressant, but I don't want to do it just now. I'd like to suggest a course of cognitive behavioral therapy. It would just be a few sessions. It can be very helpful. I can give you a list of therapists you can contact directly or, if you want, I can refer you."

"I can do it."

"I'm also going to print out a set of breathing techniques that can help you through your panic attacks. And there's a mindfulness app you can download. Some people find it helps them through anxiety. Here."

He wrote down the app's name on his pad, tore off the piece of paper and handed it across. I took it.

"And when you leave, I want you to make an appointment to come back to see me in two weeks' time, so we can see how you're doing."

"All right."

"Are you able to continue working?"

I suddenly saw this was an opportunity. I could take Poppy to school every morning and collect her every afternoon and not let her out of my sight.

"Maybe I'm not," I said. "I work with primary school children. I can't do it halfheartedly."

He nodded. "I'm going to write you a sick note signing you off for the next week. We can see how it goes."

"Thank you. Thank you for being nice."

"I hope this will help," he said. "Find a CBT therapist. Meditate and practice the breathing techniques. Go for walks. Rest. Look after yourself. Come back and see me."

"Yes."

"Do you have any questions?"

Yes, I did. I had this question screaming inside my head: *Everyone thinks this is inside my head, but what if it isn't? What if I'm right to feel such fear and dread?*

But I didn't ask it. I was too used to the expression of pity that would appear on his face. I lifted Poppy to the floor and held out my hand to shake his.

"Look after yourself," he said.

Pills, I thought as we walked out. Mindfulness. Therapy. Maybe, in the future. But now, I had a sick note. I had a free week.

FORTY-ONE

I helped Poppy get ready for her party: brushing her hair till it crackled and for once she didn't roar, wrapping the tulle skirt I'd stitched together round her waist and adjusting it so it wouldn't drag on the ground, pulling on her unicorn tee shirt and finally putting on the glimmering witch's cloak. She stood in front of the mirror and gazed at herself with awe. Iridescent with color, quivering with excitement, she looked like a hovering dragonfly.

She wanted a flower crown so I went into the garden and cut a lush peony from the pot Aidan had brought and then rummaged in the kitchen drawer of odd bits and pieces for some ribbon. My fingers touched a jangle of keys and I drew them out. Among them were the keys to the house in Brixton. I'd forgotten I still had them, and seeing them now I had a thought that was like an itch.

I ignored it, took out a length of silver ribbon and tied it round Poppy's head, then tucked in the flower.

"There," I said.

"I can fly," said Poppy.

I thought of Poppy trying to fly.

"No, you can't fly."

I took her by the hand. As I passed the drawer, I took up the Brixton keys and slid them into my pocket.

After I left Poppy, I called Jason's landline. Jason and Emily had said they were going away, but Ben might be there. It rang and rang. Good.

I walked up the familiar street, the sun warm and the trees in their new green, but I stopped a few doors down from the house. I took out my mobile and rang the landline number once more. Again, no reply.

I edged forward and squinted up at the windows, seeing no sign of life. I stood at the front door, hesitating, listening for any sounds of life. Nothing.

I rapped: nothing.

I inserted the key in the lock, turned it and pushed open the door. There was a small pile of unopened letters on the doormat. I stepped inside and the door closed behind me with a click.

I walked through the empty house and I was like a ghost in my old life. I knew everything intimately—the marks on the wall made from Poppy's old buggy back when we were a family, the step that creaked, the bald patch on the stair carpet, the tap that still dripped, the poster from a Van Gogh exhibition we'd been to together, one corner coming unstuck, that old chair I'd rescued from a second-hand shop and mended, the mirror hung slightly askew and my face as I passed in front of it, tense and white with an unruly tangle of red hair—and everything had changed. I was an intruder, the crazy woman who was haunting her old, abandoned home.

I passed Poppy's room and gave the door a nudge and it swung open and for a moment I thought she would be in there with me, among her toys.

And then I was in Jason's study, overlooking the garden that I had made, all those hours of levering up paving stones and hacking at overgrown shrubs, digging rubbly soil and planting flowers and herbs, blisters on my palms and dirt under my nails. Jason and Emily weren't looking after it properly. The roses hadn't been pruned or the beds weeded. I pushed the door until it was nearly closed. I was relieved to see that Jason hadn't taken his laptop with him. I sat at the desk, pulled it toward me and lifted the lid. It came to life with a muted ping and I cursed under my breath when it asked for the password.

I thought for a moment. He couldn't have kept it, could he?

I typed: "14aWaverleyStreetMarmie'. It worked. It was the address of the flat we'd lived in when we first met and the name of the funny little cat that belonged to the woman downstairs. Had he kept it as a sentimental gesture? More likely he'd used it so long, he never even thought about it.

His desktop appeared. I quickly looked over the contents of the screen. There were folders and documents with names I didn't recognize. There were icons representing different games. I could ignore those. But what about the rest? There was so much. This particular laptop was probably not more than a year or two old, but I knew that Jason had been using versions of it since he was at university. Each time he bought a new one he would transfer the contents from the old one. It contained his life. I had a sudden vision of his computer being like a city and I had wandered into the edge of it, a little path into an outer suburb and I was looking for something and I didn't even know what that something was.

If I were a computer genius, I'd do something clever. But I wasn't a genius. I barely knew how to find anything on my own computer. I was wasting time even thinking about this. I was also trying not to think of how unimaginably awful it would be if someone came back and found me in the house. At the same time as trying not to do that and failing, I was also listening to every creak in the house, every movement. Even the sound of a car passing outside made me shiver, waiting for it to maybe stop and park outside.

And then I heard something. I really did. At first I hoped it might be outside, branches being blown against a window, but it was inside the house. I could feel it. It was a rattling sound, something was moving, but I couldn't tell what it was because I couldn't decide whether it was close or distant.

The sound felt like it was coming into focus, a rustling became a pattering and then stopped altogether. I looked round and I was looking down into the face of the little dog, Roxie. She looked back up at me. I felt a wave of fear that almost made me vomit. What if she went for me?

"Hey, Roxie," I said.

She responded with a low growl that wasn't much more than a purr. I leaned down and put my hand toward her. I heard somewhere that dogs were attuned to human emotion. I tried to seem as gentle and calm and reassuring as I could.

"Come on, Roxie." I stroked her wiry fur. The growl became a low whine and she lay down and turned over on her back and I stroked her tummy. "Now you'll let me get on with this, won't you?"

She seemed content to lie on the carpet and I turned back to the screen. I'd already been doing this too long. I looked at my watch. Three minutes, I told myself. Then I'd go.

I clicked on his email icon. That seemed the most promising spot. There were 25,865 messages. I swore silently. His email was another whole city in itself. I scrolled down. It was utterly hopeless. Mainly they were ads of various kinds, announcing various deliveries, hardly any of them were personal. I clicked on a few random examples: mainly they were to do with school, there was a confirmation of a date for a drink—copied to two women and three men. There were no messages from Emily or Ben or, for that matter, me, not that there was anything strange about that. We'd barely used emails for years. We communicated by text or WhatsApp and even then it was generally little more than a "running late be there in five" kind of thing.

I looked at my watch. The three minutes had passed. It was really time to go. I gave myself one more minute.

I clicked on the list of folders. The categories looked straightforward: "Work," "Accounts," "House," "Party 2016." I smiled at that last one and clicked on it and saw a familiar list of names. It was the party we'd had here, in this house, just after we'd moved in. There were still unopened packing cases and the fridge hadn't been delivered, but it was a beautiful autumn evening and we'd put candles in jam jars in the garden. I closed it. And looked at the remaining folders: "Holiday," "Sport," "Wedding." I swore again. Fucking wedding. And then something occurred to me, something odd, like when you feel a stone in your shoe. What was it? Sport. What sport did Jason play?

I clicked on it and right away I knew. The bastard. At the top, most recently, there were a few, a dozen maybe, messages from a Lara Steed. Further down there were a couple from a Nicole and still further down a few more from an Inga. I clicked on an Inga message and just fixed on certain phrases: "last night," "I want you." I felt sick all over again. These were Jason's secret emails. He could have deleted them with a keystroke, but he had kept them like trophies.

And then I heard another sound. There was no doubt about it. They were footsteps. Human footsteps. They were inside the house. I turned my head trying to locate their direction. It was from upstairs, a creaking, and then I heard them on the stairs. At first I just felt frozen. What could I do? What could I say? I looked round. Roxie had pushed the door behind me open. It was too late to close it and what good would it do anyway if Jason came into his office. The door opened inward. Almost without thinking I stood up and tiptoed across and stood behind it.

Now I was starting to think desperately. Didn't this just make things worse? If I were found just sitting normally in a chair, then maybe—just maybe—I could come up with some kind of pathetic excuse about using my old key to find something that Poppy needed for school. But if I was found hiding behind a door, there was no feasible explanation at all. It was too late.

The steps were close now.

"Hey, Roxie, come on, girl."

It was Ben. He had been up in his room. He had been there all the time. How could I have been so stupid?

Roxie barked twice, but didn't get up.

I slowly turned my head toward the wall. If I looked at Roxie and she looked back at me, she might take that as invitation to walk across to me. Also, I just couldn't bear to see. Ben was just a couple of feet away from me on the other side of the door. I could smell him, a mixture of sweat and smoke. Wasn't it possible that he could smell me, even if he couldn't see me?

"Roxie, what is it, you fucking dog?"

Roxie just growled and curled up. She didn't want to be disturbed. I stared at the wall and my skin crawled; I was horribly tempted to step out and reveal myself just to stop the terrifying stress of it all.

"Fuck off, then."

I heard the steps recede, but instead of going back up the stairs, I heard them going down. What was he going to do? If he was going out, then I could wait a few minutes and leave. But what if he was going to make himself something to eat? Perhaps he would get some food and go back to his room. I imagined that was how he spent his days, up in his bedroom, online or playing computer games.

I listened intently. It was difficult because everything seemed drowned out by the beating of my heart and by my breathing. I could make out the fridge door opening and closing. So he probably wasn't going out. Something rattled, glasses or cutlery or glasses. It sounded like he was preparing food.

I waited one minute, two minutes, three minutes. I looked at my watch. Why hadn't I left sooner? Then there was another sound, voices, a snatch of music, what sounded like applause. I realized with another ripple of nausea running through me that Ben had settled down in front of the television.

I cursed myself once again. How could I have got myself into this situation? I could be arrested. I could lose Poppy. I pushed the thought away from me. That was no use to me. Instead, I pictured the layout of the house downstairs. The stairs from the first floor led down to a hallway with the front door straight ahead: that I was sure of. On the left of the hallway were two rooms that had been knocked through into one large room. The kitchen was at the back of the house, with a door that led into the garden with high, unclimbable walls.

Ben was presumably sitting in front of the television. But where was the television nowadays? Which way was he facing? Was the door to the hallway open and, if it was, would he see someone passing? I tried to remember where the television was, but I couldn't. I had no idea.

I took a deep breath. I had two choices and the answer was horribly simple. I could just wait for him to finish watching television and then perhaps he would go out or go back up to his room. In the meantime someone else could arrive and I would have no chance at all.

Or I could try to leave now.

It felt unbearable, but I had to do it.

I tiptoed back across to Jason's laptop. Those names, what should I do about them? I forwarded one of each of them to my email address.

I shut the computer down, turned and almost trod on Roxie.

"Please, please," I whispered to myself.

I took a step out onto the landing, then another one. Each step creaked and I could feel each of them, as if I had an abscess in a tooth and I was prodding at it.

I looked down the stairs. I could only see the doorways sideways on but one of them was definitely open. For all I knew, Ben could be looking straight out of it. There was only one way of finding out.

I needed to be quieter. I raised my right foot and slipped off the shoe. As I pulled my left shoe off, I lost my balance and tipped against the wall, only just stopping myself from falling headlong. How could he not be hearing this?

But in my socks, my footsteps were almost silent as I moved down the stairs, step by painful step. As I reached the bottom I saw that the first door was completely open.

I froze. From where I stood, I could obliquely see the TV screen and I could see Ben, sideways to me, leaning back in the armchair. I almost moaned and put my knuckles into my mouth to stop any sound. He was wearing tatty boxers and nothing else. I could see his hairy shoulders and his soft white belly, which, as I stared, he scratched at luxuriously. He had a plate beside him, a huge sandwich with bits of pink ham protruding, a large blob of tomato ketchup on the side, a can of Coke that he pulled the tab off and gulped at, wiping the back of his hand against his mouth.

He was watching a game of darts. If he turned, he would see me. If I made a noise, he would hear me. But I had no choice. I had to walk past and there was nothing I could do about it: either he would see me or he wouldn't.

He belched, scratched again, pushing his hand under his boxers to do so. This was horrible. I shouldn't be watching him when he thought he was alone. *Just a poor sap*, Felicity had said. But then I thought of the way he had been when he had found me in the park, trailing Jason and Poppy. *You don't like me*, he had said, and there had been something menacing about the way he looked at me then.

I had to move.

I took one step, then another. I knew that with the next step I would be fully visible to him, framed in the doorway and just a few feet away from him. I took the step and felt a nightmarish temptation to look up and reassure myself that he wasn't looking. But I just took one more step, then another. Now he was out of sight, just the sound of the TV.

I looked back up the stairs and Roxie was standing there, fur bristling. She gave a sharp bark.

But the front door was ahead of me. I was almost there. One step. Another step. Roxie barked again.

I was close enough to reach the handle of the front door. I twisted it as slowly as I could, stepped through the small gap and pulled it shut with both hands.

I eased one shoe back on and then the other. I couldn't believe it. I wanted to cry. I was out.

I walked down the path, stepped onto the pavement, turned to the left almost gagging with relief, and found myself in the way of two people. I apologized and then looked into the faces of Jason and Emily.

It was like the ground had fallen beneath my feet. I couldn't think of anything to say. Jason apparently felt the same. I thought he would be angry but now, at this moment, he just looked confused.

I desperately tried to think of an excuse and then thought I shouldn't seem guilty. I had a right to be there, didn't I? Or at least I should act as if I did. I greeted them in as casual a way as I could manage, as if I'd just bumped into them in the street.

"What are you doing here?" Jason asked.

An idea came into my head. I didn't have time to decide whether it was a good one.

"I just wanted to talk to you about the arrangements with Poppy. I was in the area, so I thought we could talk in person. If you were at home. Which you weren't."

"But you knew that, didn't you?" Jason said this with a smile that wasn't a smile, as if it were some kind of shared joke between us. It was difficult for him to get cross with me in front of Emily.

"I forgot. I've got so many arrangements in my head at the moment."

"We came back early. As you can see."

"Lucky for me."

"Not so lucky for us. Emily's got awful morning sickness."

"Oh, I'm sorry," I said. "That's terrible. I know what it's like. I had it really badly with Poppy."

"Emily's is much worse," said Jason.

"No, I bet it was just as bad for Tess."

I wasn't sure whether I was more irritated by Jason's opinion about my morning sickness or by Emily speaking up for me. I looked at her and saw that she was pale with an almost greenish tinge to her cheeks. Her lips were trembling.

"You need to get inside," I said. "I'll leave you."

"You came here to talk."

"I don't want to be any trouble."

"It's no trouble," said Jason briskly as he opened the front door from which I'd just emerged and stepped inside.

Emily ran past him and clattered up the stairs and into the bathroom. We could both hear the sound of vomiting. We looked at each other.

"You might want to go and help her," I said.

"I think she's managing on her own," said Jason.

"I meant comfort her."

"I think what she wants at a moment like this is privacy." He looked around. "Hey, Ben."

"What's up?" said Ben.

Jason explained why they were back.

"Why didn't you hear when Tess rang the bell?" he asked.

Ben looked at me with frown. "I didn't hear anyone ring."

"I just rapped at the door," I said. "It was probably drowned out by the TV."

"TV?" said Ben. "How do you know I was watching TV?"

"I didn't," I said, flushing up to my hairline. "I know now. Anyway, I was thinking about what to do and then you two arrived."

It was too much explanation. The less I said the better.

"Let's go through to the kitchen so we don't disturb Emily," Jason said.

There had been a tiny, knowing smile on his face, but once we were in the kitchen he turned to me with an entirely mirthless expression.

"All right," he said.

"All right, what?"

"You came all the way across London to talk to me," he said. "Oh no, sorry, I forgot. You were in the area. But anyway, what did you want to talk about?"

"The arrangements for tomorrow."

"Have they changed?"

"No."

"Then I know them. I'm collecting her and then she's spending the night here."

I thought of what I'd seen in the house, Ben sitting in his boxer shorts watching darts and scratching himself and belching, and I felt almost sick at the idea of my daughter being unprotected.

"I also wanted to say that Poppy is in a delicate state. She's not sleeping well."

"You've told me that before. Many times. Why do you think it is?" Jason spoke in a slow, even tone.

He didn't ask me to sit down. He didn't offer me a coffee. It's not that I wanted any of that, but I was aware of the two of us simply standing there, warily.

"I think that the breakup has been bad for her. I think she's picking up on the bad feelings and it's affecting her sleep and it's affecting her behavior and I want to do anything I possibly can to protect her from it."

Jason opened a cupboard, took a glass tumbler, filled it with water from the tap and drained it.

"Can I get you anything?" he asked.

"No, thank you," I said. "But maybe Emily would like a glass of water."

"You can leave that to me."

"I feel a bit awkward having this conversation here while your wife is upstairs feeling ill."

"I'll decide what's awkward in this house."

"I think I'd better go."

He held up his hand. "Wait. Just a moment."

"What for?"

"I thought you wanted to have a talk with me. So let's talk."

I swallowed and tried to calm myself. I didn't want to talk. I just wanted to leave.

"I've said what I wanted to say. I'm worried about Poppy. I want us both to pay attention to her."

Jason stepped forward and raised his hand. I moved away from him.

"What is it?" I said.

He shook his head. "Honestly, Tess, I don't understand why you're here. Is there something you're not telling me?"

"Like what?"

"I know it must be difficult for you, me being married to Emily, Emily expecting a child, us living in our old house. I appreciate that."

I had to stop myself from reacting. The thought of him thinking he knew things about me and telling me them made me want to howl with rage.

"I'm just thinking of Poppy," I said as calmly as I could manage.

"I understand," he said in a voice that sounded like he was calming an anxious child. "I know that we had a relationship that didn't work out and you blame me for that. I know that I may have strayed once or twice, but perhaps one day, when you can see things more rationally, you'll look at yourself and see why I behaved like I did."

I wanted to shout something back, I wanted to scratch his face, but I silently told myself: *It's all about Poppy. It's all about Poppy.*

He looked at me more closely. "I hoped you'd say something in reply."

"I don't want to have an argument."

"We're not having an argument. I'm trying to have a discussion. As I've said, we're separate now, but we're linked by our child. I thought we were handling it so well. But things have changed. Now you're interfering in things that haven't anything to do with you. If it were happening to someone who didn't still care for you the way I do, then that person might become angry. Very angry indeed."

He was still speaking in a calm tone that I found more menacing than if he had been obviously enraged. I couldn't help remembering the evidence that was sitting up in his computer. All he needed to do was check the "sent" mailbox. The thought of it made me want to throw up.

I felt a wave of relief when Emily came into the kitchen.

"Are you all right?" I asked.

"I still feel sick. Even though there's nothing more to come up."

She was speaking in a mumble as if even the effort of speaking clearly might make her feel nauseated.

"It'll go soon," I said. "You'll get through it."

Jason put his arm round his wife and kissed the top of her head. She flinched. Even that touch seemed to be toxic to her.

"Have you made tea?" she said. "I'd like something herbal. Ginger maybe."

"I'll do it now."

She looked at me. "Haven't you made Tess tea?"

"I would have, but she's about to go."

"Don't let me drive you away," Emily said.

"That's all right. You get better."

"Did you get everything sorted?"

"Everything was already sorted," said Jason. "There wasn't much to talk about."

I had the disconcerting feeling that he knew everything and that he was toying with me.

I waved a little goodbye to Emily. I didn't want to hug her and I was sure she didn't want to be hugged by me. As I walked toward the front door, Roxie emerged from the living room and barked at me just as she had done before.

"You know, don't you?" I said to her, but silently.

FORTY-TWO

Back at home with Poppy, I watched over her as if she were a glass ornament that might break even when gently touched. I had a painful impulse to close the door, keep her with me and protect her forever and ever. But then I remembered that the very next day Jason was going to fetch her and take her away, back to that house. What if I ran away with her, somewhere where nobody could find us?

This was a ridiculous idea. If I tried anything of the kind, Jason would set the law on me and he would have the law on his side. The result would be not to save Poppy but to lose her altogether. It was terrible. I would do anything to protect Poppy. For the moment, I felt that was the whole purpose of my existence. But I didn't know how to do it.

As I gave her a bath, I asked her about the party I'd just collected her from. I knew it had been the fourth birthday party of a girl in Poppy's class called Alicia. But when I asked Poppy about it she said firmly that it wasn't a birthday party and when I asked if they sang

286

"Happy Birthday" to Alicia, she said, no, they didn't. I asked if there had been lots of people and she'd said no. When I asked her how many then, she just held her arms out and said, "That many."

I asked her what games they had played and she said they had played the elephant game. I asked did that mean pin the tail on the elephant and she said no. I asked if it meant making an elephant out of balloons and she said no. I'd recently read her a storybook about an elephant that gets returned to the jungle and I wondered if she had got her memory of that confused with her memory of the party.

And this was the witness whose memories I'd been relying on, whose memories had turned my life upside down.

But there was Skye. I had to hold on to that. Skye had fallen from a tower. Skye had been murdered.

I put Poppy to bed and read her a story that wasn't about an elephant. Afterward, I lay beside her for a bit and then suddenly came to and realized we had both fallen asleep.

I had to look around to recognize where I was. I got up and made myself a coffee. I knew that I should eat something. I hadn't eaten all day. I wasn't hungry, but I needed to stay in some kind of functioning health. But food could wait. I switched my computer on and checked my emails. There were advertisements from clothes shops and spam about losing wrinkles and dating online and there were the three messages I had forwarded from Jason's computer: Lara Steed, Nicole and Inga. One from each.

So I had them. What was I going to do with them? I
quickly saw that there was only one thing to do. Lara
Steed was the most recent, so I clicked on her address
and selected "new message." I considered how to do
this: breezy, casual, as if it were no big deal. Above all,
nothing that would suggest any connection with Jason. I briefly considered disguising my name, but then
I'd have to set up a fake email account. That would be
like an admission of guilt if something went wrong.
My own name would be simplest. I wrote:

> Hi Lara,
> Sorry to contact you out of the blue, but someone
> told me you might know a friend of mine: Skye
> Nolan. I'm trying to find people who knew her. If
> the name rings a bell, could you reply to this?
> All best,
> Tess

I stared at the message for a full minute. What could
go wrong with this?

So much, in so many different ways.

I pressed send.

FORTY-THREE

Jason's message was curt: *Bring Poppy to café by London Bridge. 3:30pm.*

Poppy didn't want to leave—she wanted to play chase in the park, she wanted to finish making her cardboard house, she wanted another drink, she wanted to change into different clothes, she wanted her hair in plaits and then she didn't, she wanted to have another story, do another drawing, talk to Sunny, she wanted to play hide and seek and stood behind the curtains and was cross when I found her. So we were late to arrive. But when I pushed open the door to the café, Jason wasn't there. Emily was, sitting at a little table drinking herbal tea.

"Hello," she said timidly. "Jason was a bit held up, so he asked me to come."

So he didn't want to see me. That was fine, I didn't want to see him either—except of course, it wasn't fine, because we had a child together; we had Poppy. I thought back to that list of rules we had agreed on, which were based on the principles of collaboration and mutual trust. That felt long ago.

"No," said Poppy.

"It's OK, honeybunch. Daddy's waiting," said Emily. She looked tired, and she'd lost her peachy luster. Her skin was pale and dull, her hair was lanky.

"Do you feel rotten?" I asked.

"I'm sure it'll pass. That's what Jason says. He says I should just keep going and not give in to it."

"He's never been pregnant." I turned to Poppy. "I'll see you tomorrow."

"No," she said again, and she wrapped her arms round my legs.

I bent and undid her grasp, put her unwilling hand in Emily's outstretched one.

"You have a lovely time, darling."

"No," Poppy repeated. "No, no, no."

"We'll make a cake together," said Emily in a pleading voice. She sounded as if she was about to weep.

Poppy lifted her head and glared at her suspiciously.

"A chocolate cake?"

"All right."

"With chocolate buttons?"

"Buttons. Good idea!"

"And I did walk on Ben's feet. And feed Roxie. And no bath."

"Fine," said Emily helplessly.

"Right," I said. Then before I had decided to say it: "Do you know anyone called Inga?"

"Inga. I don't think so."

"Or Lara? Or Nicole?"

"Do you mean Nicole Drake?"

"I don't know."

"I know her a bit. Lara's my best friend. I've known her since we were Poppy's age pretty much." Emily gave a small, girlish laugh, as if remembering them when they were tiny, and then her face suddenly clouded. "Why?"

Suddenly I couldn't speak. I didn't know whether to cover up the secret or to warn her. But how could I, her husband's ex-partner, tell her? Would telling her, or not telling her, be selfish and wrong?

"No reason." My tone was breezy, unconvincing. Emily gazed at me with her blue, innocent, worried eyes. "Maybe Poppy said something."

"No," said Poppy crossly.

I watched them walk away, hand in hand, Poppy's little red backpack bobbing into the distance.

I made myself go to a friend's party that evening, but it was a mistake and I didn't stay long. I went home and opened my laptop to see if anyone had replied. Above me, Bernie and a woman were shouting in pleasure.

I don't know anyone called Skye Nolan, wrote Inga. *And btw, who are you? How did you get my email?*

I hesitated, then replied: *I used to live with Jason Hallam. Does that mean anything to you?*

This time there was no answer.

The following day was Poppy's last day of half-term holiday. I collected her from Brixton. Jason passed her over at the door, putting his hands on her shoulders and giving her a push over the threshold, like she was an object on wheels, and we went straight to London Fields for a picnic.

I'd arranged to meet Gina, Jake and maybe Nellie there, but Laurie turned up as well. I'd bought a collection of M&S food, miniature Scotch eggs and falafel and sticks of carrots, cans of lemonade and some strawberries, but Laurie was carrying a proper wicker hamper which he opened triumphantly to reveal Tupperware containers of homemade salads, chicken drumsticks that he'd obviously roasted himself, neat whole-wheat sandwiches with hummus, also homemade, and a bottle of elderflower cordial.

"Did you make this too?"

"The first of the season," he said, pouring it out into plastic glasses. "Cheers."

He'd bought a soft ball as well, and after we'd eaten, we ran around on the grass kicking it, while the sun poured down, thick and warm, and Poppy and Jake shrieked.

I watched him. The perfect stay-at-home dad, with his dimply chin and charming smile. Too good to be true? He put an arm round Gina's waist and she smiled at him, while Nellie, perched on his back in the child carrier, peered over his shoulder.

We lay on the grass. All around us there were people spread out, sunning themselves.

"I'm taking next week off," I said to Gina, quietly so no one else could hear.

"Are you? Good idea!"

"I've a doctor's note, actually."

"Are you ill?"

"Stress," I said.

She opened her eyes, turned her face toward me. "Are you OK?"

"Things to sort out," I said.

"I'm glad you're taking time for yourself," she said. "If you want to talk—"

"Yeah. Thanks. Anyway, we can keep to the arrangements with Poppy and Jake."

"Sure."

Walking back to the flat, we met Bernie walking in the opposite direction. He was with a woman I hadn't met before. Where did he find them all?

"Pops!" he called from a distance.

Poppy shrank back as he got closer. "Go way."

"One of those days, eh?" he said cheerfully.

He held up his hand that was missing two fingers and waggled it in her direction. Poppy stared at him in fascinated horror. Playfully, he bared his teeth. The woman beside him tugged on his arm.

"Don't scare her," she said.

"You're not scared, are you?"

Poppy contemplated him, her tongue on her upper lip as it was when she made drawings.

"Yes," she said.

FORTY-FOUR

I thought of what Peggy Nolan had said: there was a Hannah Flood, who used to be Skye's friend; a Hannah Flood, who had a shop off Marylebone High Street selling candles. I googled the name and found nothing, and nothing about candles and Marylebone either. But it was my only possible connection so the next morning, after dropping Poppy off at school, I went there by bus and underground.

I wandered aimlessly up and down the neighboring streets—past well-heeled houses, past shops that sold designer wear and simple, scarily expensive pottery, a place that mended and sold violins, past little cobbled courtyards and a florist with its cool green interior beckoning. No candle shops, until I went down a narrow street whose apartment buildings blocked out the sky. A newsagent. A shop selling electrical items. A shop called Rainbow that sold aromatic oils and candles.

I stepped inside. There were pillar candles and taper candles and tea lights and floating candles and scented ones and ones carved into the shape of a skull, an elephant, a pyramid and a water lily. There was an incense stick burning on the wooden table that served as the counter and behind it stood a tall, strong-boned young woman. She wore a dress that looked like a tent and her brown hair, centrally parted, reached almost to her waist. Her face was a smooth, surprised oval.

"Hannah?" I asked.

"Sorry, do I know you?"

"Peggy Nolan told me you were a friend of her daughter Skye."

Hannah Flood's face closed down on me, became a blank surface. She looked down at her hands, which were resting on the table, and blinked several times.

"Who are you?" She seemed suspicious. Rightly.

"My name's Tess. I knew Skye a little bit and since her death I've met her mother and Charlie."

"You know Charlie?"

"A bit."

"He's nice. She should have stayed with him. I always told her that." Hannah gave a sigh, and her shoulders slumped. "But then, when did Skye ever listen to anything anyone told her?"

"I'm trying to find out about her last few weeks and months," I said.

"Are you a journalist?" She was twisting a wooden bangle round and round on her wrist.

I told her my connection with Skye and she seemed convinced—or convinced enough.

"I didn't see her that much," she said wretchedly. "We'd drifted apart a bit. You'd think that would make it easier but it doesn't. I wasn't there when she needed me."

"Peggy said you knew her from when you were children?"

"I never knew why she chose me. She was quick and clever and one of the popular ones. I was slow and clumsy and hated the way I looked. I was like a giant beside her. They called us Little and Large. She was the naughty one. She used to get me into such trouble." Hannah managed a smile at the memory of this.

"And then?"

"She went off the rails, but you probably heard about that. I tried to help, but she was difficult. She'd turn on me. She could be really cruel.

"After she met Charlie, it got better for a bit. When I moved down to London, I saw her again. I'd see her from time to time. She was nicer to be around when she was with Charlie. She could be really generous. She'd see some madly expensive thing she thought I'd like and buy it without thinking about the price. She bought me a dressing gown once and a big book about trees. I love trees. I always did, even back when I was a kid."

"What went wrong?"

"I don't know. She got restless or bored. It's like that saying, you don't know what's enough until you know what's more than enough. For her it always had to be more than enough."

"Did you stay in touch?"

"Just about." Hannah gave another sad smile. "I think I was too boring for her and she was too scary for me but we always kept a connection."

"When did you last see her?"

She thought for a moment. "About ten days before she died, I guess."

"How was she?"

"She was fizzing and manic and it made me feel panicky just to be near her. If it sounds exciting, it wasn't, it was horrible. I just wanted to get away from her." She caught her lower lip between her teeth and screwed up her face, hearing her words. "Like it was catching or something."

"What did she talk about?"

"Dogs," said Hannah bitterly. "And how she wanted to be a foster parent, which was ridiculous. She couldn't even look after herself. And the old days a bit, when we were kids and she got me into scrapes. We always talked about that. And she told me about this man she'd met—that was another thing we always talked about."

I went still.

"Man?" I asked.

"Someone she'd met in a bar when she was out of it. Except being Skye, she didn't think he'd picked her up. She thought he'd rescued her. He took her back to her flat and she didn't really know what happened between them, but she said he was nice to her. I'll bet. And then he came back to see her. She told it like it was a big romantic story."

"Do you," I said in a voice I tried to keep neutral, "do you know his name?"

She wrinkled her brow. "I don't think so. It sounds like something I should remember, but she told me this kind of story pretty much every time we met—how she'd met a man and he wasn't like the others. He was different. This time it would work out."

I nodded. This was exactly what Charlie had said too.

"Was it a common name, or unusual?"

"Probably common, or I'd remember it, don't you think?"

"Jason?" I suggested.

"Hmmm. Maybe. I can't say yes and I can't say no.

"Or Ben?"

"Could be."

"Or Aidan? Or Bernie?"

"Honestly, I can't say. She probably didn't tell me his name."

"Or what he did for a living?"

Hannah shook her head apologetically. She spread her hand at the base of her throat and leaned toward me.

"Do you think he could have killed her?"

"I don't know. It happened in her flat so it might have been someone she knew."

"I thought it was a robbery."

"Yes, that's what the police think."

"Who were those men you mentioned?"

I didn't answer that, saying instead, "Is there anything else she said about the man? What he looked like? Anything about what he did, where he lived?"

"She just said he was nice."

"Nice."

"Yeah."

"And it was only a couple of times?"

"I think they met somewhere else as well. I don't know if it was more than one time. Also—" She stopped.

"Yes?"

"Well, I think she kind of followed him. She knew where he lived; she said it was a nice place. And she knew he was with another woman. Or maybe she said women, plural. That didn't put her off. She was sure they had something special and they'd be together in the end. I think he was angry with her, but she said she had to be patient." Hannah gave a laugh. "Though patience wasn't exactly Skye's strong suit."

"So basically she stalked him?"

"I wouldn't use that word; it makes it sound too creepy. But I guess so."

"Where did this man live?"

She made a helpless gesture. "I don't know. I don't think she said."

"A house, a flat?"

"She just said it was nice."

"This other woman, did she live with him?"

"I assumed that's what she meant, but I don't know. I just thought it was Skye, doing her thing again—taking a sleazy encounter and turning it into romantic destiny."

"Children?"

"I don't know," said Hannah slowly, frowning. "All I know is that I felt this man had a whole other complicated life and Skye was deluded enough to think he would leave it for her."

"She thought he'd come to her?"

"Skye always thought that. She never learned to protect herself. She was always bright and shiny with hope."

Without warning, Hannah's face crumpled. She leaned her body over the table and started to cry, her brown hair swinging and fat tears falling.

"I always thought I was the one to get let down by her," she gulped out between sobs. "Now look."

Cautiously, I put a hand on her shoulder and waited. Gradually the sobs halted and she straightened up, wiping the back of her hand across her smeary face.

"Sorry," she said. "Sorry."

"No. I'm sorry."

"Do you want to buy a candle? As you can see, I don't have many customers."

"I'd love to," I said.

I selected a bag of tea lights, four taper candles, six floating ones, and a candle in the shape of an elephant that I thought Poppy would like.

"If you think of something," I said, "this is my number."

I wrote it on a scrap of paper that she pushed at me and then keyed hers into my mobile.

"If you see Peggy," she said, "tell her I'm thinking of her and I'm going to write a proper letter. I should have written. I didn't know what to say. And tell her I'm sorry."

FORTY-FIVE

As if Hannah had conjured her, my mobile started to ring as soon as I left the shop and Peggy's name appeared on my screen.

"Tess? It's me, Peggy. Is this a bad time?"

"It's a good time."

"I tried calling Charlie, but he hasn't answered."

"Are you OK?"

"Yes. No. No, I'm not. I've just collected Skye's things."

"Her things? I thought you'd already done that?"

"No. The things she was wearing. When she fell."

"That must have been horrible."

"I can't bring myself to look at them."

"You don't need to do it at once. Give yourself time."

"Will you help me?"

"Me? Well, yes, I mean—what can I do?"

"I mean, will you look at them with me?"

"Of course. If you want me to. I can come to your house again, if that's good. I'm not working this week."

"No, I mean now."

"Now! Where are you?"

"I don't know. I'm just walking. I've been walking for ages. Wait a minute." There was a pause. I could hear traffic in the distance and the muffled sound of footfalls. "Farringdon Road," she said eventually. "The junction of Exmouth Market."

"Do you want me to come and find you?"

"Would you? Would you do that?"

"Stay there," I said. "I'll be with you as soon as I can."

Peggy was wearing a long dress and sandals and a scarf tied round her purple hair. She had a capacious embroidered bag hanging from one shoulder and was clutching another bag in her arms like a newborn baby. I called her name and she spun round toward me.

"Thank you," she said. "Thank you so much. I didn't know what to do."

I took her arm and steered her away from the busy road and soon we found ourselves in a small leafy churchyard. People were eating picnics on the grass and there was a man juggling three grapefruit.

We sat under a tree and I saw how her face was so thin that it looked like it was falling in on itself, her eyes deep in their sockets and red-rimmed.

"You really don't mind?" she asked.

"Of course I don't mind."

"It was different from what I expected. It felt all right going through her flat. Maybe I was still in shock so it didn't sink in what I was doing. But this . . ." She gestured at the bag she was still cradling. "I can't. These are what were on her poor little body when she died."

"You really want to do it now?"

"Yes. I have to."

Her fingers trembled as she opened the bag and pulled out a sealed package. She tore at it, splitting the plastic and laying the bundle onto the grass between us.

Skye Nolan had been wearing a long wrap-over dress in a paisley pattern, all oranges and browns. It had short sleeves knotted at the side. It seemed weirdly unblemished. Peggy laid it out in front of her and stroked it.

"She would have looked so pretty in this," she said. "What shall I do with it? What shall I do with all her things?"

I was thinking that Skye had dressed up that evening, like she was expecting a visitor.

She'd been wearing simple wedge sandals, lacy knickers, a flesh-colored bra size 32A. A watch with a large face and brown leather strap. A lucky charm bracelet, with tiny silver objects hanging off it—a bell, a horseshoe, a star, a cat, a top hat, a shell … Her mother touched each charm in turn with the tip of one forefinger.

"She had this when she was nine. I'd buy her a charm on each birthday. Then she stopped wearing it and I stopped buying charms. But some are new. This is." A hummingbird. "And this." A wishbone.

There was a heart-shaped silver locket.

"I don't recognize that," said Peggy. "She loved jewelry, though."

"Can I open it?"

She nodded and I pried open the heart with a fingernail. There was a miniature inscription on the inside: *Always.*

"I don't know how to do this," said Peggy. "I don't know."

I put a hand over hers. There was nothing I could say.

"I can imagine her getting into these clothes. Standing in front of the long mirror, turning this way and that, examining how she looked. Putting on the jewelry. Smiling at herself. That reminds me. I've got something for you."

"What do you mean?"

Peggy took something from her pocket, an object in tissue paper. She unwrapped it and held it out to me. It was a copper bracelet, decorated with light blue stones. I could imagine a teenage girl wearing it to a party.

"Was it Skye's?"

"It was. And now it's yours."

"I couldn't."

"You must," Peggy said. "Something to remember her by. And me. Skye took such pleasure in all of that. Whatever else happened, she was still a child really."

Her face was a sheet of tears.

"That's what Hannah said as well."

"You've talked to Hannah?"

"Yes."

"She's a good girl."

"She loved Skye."

"Shall we put these away?" Peggy carefully folded the dress, collected up the watch, the locket, the charm bracelet, then held them in the cup of her hands and stared down at them.

"Here."

I held out the bag and she poured them in.

"Do you need to go?" she asked.

"Not particularly."

"Do you want to see some photos of Skye? Charlie sent them to me. She looks really happy in them." Her voice snagged.

"I'd like that."

Peggy fumbled in the embroidered bag and brought out her phone. She swiped to the left a couple of times.

"Here," she said. "Here she is."

Peggy slid them past me. There were the photos that Charlie had already sent me, and then there was Skye on a bridge, gazing down at water; Skye in old jeans and a turtleneck sweater, looking like a young boy; Skye heavily made up, barely recognizable; Skye from a distance, a dog by her side; Skye in swimwear, in a Santa Claus hat, walking in a park, sticking her tongue out, waving, standing with Charlie, standing arm-in-arm with a group of young women. Skye in the dungarees she'd been wearing when I saw her that evening, and I remembered her smiling at me, pointing at me, doffing her cap. Skye in that same cap, the peak turned sideways.

That cap. Corduroy with a maroon brim.

"I think I'll print some of them out," Peggy was saying.

"That." I jabbed at the photo with a finger. "Where did she get it?"

"What?"

"The cap."

"I don't know." She looked bewildered. "Why?"

"I've got to go," I said. My voice was guttural. "Sorry."
I staggered to my feet.

"Now?"

"Sorry." I saw her stricken face. "I'll come and
see you tomorrow, if you want. We can go through
her things."

"Will you do that? Yes. Yes, please."

"I'll come late morning. I'll ring if something
changes." A thought occurred to me. "Can you forward
me that photo—the one of Skye in a cap?"

I ran to the bus stop where I waited, unable to keep
still, pacing the short length of it, until the bus appeared. I jumped on board and sat at the front, willing
it to go faster. My mobile pinged and there was the
photo of Skye, grinning in the cap.

I got out near Broadway Market and pelted along
London Fields and up the road to my flat, dropping my
keys, scrubbing for them, clumsy with terror.

"You look like you're in a hurry," said a voice.
Bernie.

"Later," I said.

Down the stairs, into the little kitchen. To the fridge
where drawings and photos were attached by magnets. The Polaroid. The Polaroid of Poppy that Lotty
had given me. Where was it? There was one of her on
the slide at school, mouth open in a shout of glee. But
where was the other? I'd put it up here; I was sure of
it. I pulled off the drawing of the sun and an over-

sized flower. I pulled off the postcard from my friend Magda. The shopping list. The list of tasks.

The picture of Poppy had gone: the one in which she was wearing, pulled down over her eyes, a corduroy cap with a maroon peak.

I crouched on the kitchen floor, put my hands over my eyes and forced myself to remember.

Last week, Poppy had come back from Jason's with a bag of dressing-up clothes that Emily had sorted. The cap had been in with those—or no, it had been in Poppy's backpack along with beads and bangles and scarves.

Poppy had tried it on in her room—I could see her now, laughing because it came down over her eyes— and I had put it in the bag with the other things she had selected and I'd handed it over to Lotty's assistant.

And then Lotty had given me a few photos of Poppy, including one of her wearing the cap. I'd put it on the fridge. I was certain I had.

Now I'd seen a photo of Skye wearing the identical cap. The one she'd worn that night we'd met.

But the photo of Poppy in the cap had gone.

I lay down on the floor and squinted under the fridge in case it had fallen. I sat up and gazed around helplessly.

If it was gone, it meant someone had taken it.

I went into the garden, paced up and down its small threadbare lawn. I thought back over the days since I had put the Polaroid on the fridge. That had been— when? My brain hurt with the effort of remembering.

Tuesday, yes. The day that Poppy had talked about going to the zoo and I had realized she often mixed her tenses; the day I had gone back to see Kelly Jordan with my revelation. That afternoon, Lotty had given me the handful of photos of Poppy, including the one of her in the cap. And that evening, the detective had returned and told me the name of the woman who had died and I'd seen her picture and remembered.

So, there were five days between that Tuesday and today. Who had been to the flat? I squinted up at the flat blue sky. What had happened on Wednesday?

Kelly Jordan had come round in the morning with the other police officer, Madeleine Finch, and they'd questioned Poppy.

And then—yes, then Aidan had come round with his colleague, bringing peonies. They'd come into the kitchen and conservatory. I could see it now—Poppy and Jake in the garden, and Aidan and his friend with me, drinking cordial in the warmth of the late afternoon.

And Bernie: he'd met us in the hall and come into the flat as well, making himself at home, stretching out his legs as he sat in the chair and grinned.

And then Jason had arrived. And Laurie, just in time to see Poppy pushing dirt into Jake's mouth.

Any of them could have seen the photo and removed it.

But the cap came from Jason's house.

FORTY-SIX

When I dropped Poppy off at school the next morning, I bent to hug her, but she pushed me away crossly and I watched her dart forward, away from me. Before leaving, I stepped into her classroom and looked around for Lotty.

"Can I help?"

It was the nursery assistant.

"Yes. I left a load of dressing-up things here before half-term and there was something I wanted back."

"Changed your mind?"

"Sort of."

She pointed to the dressing-up corner and I went and started pulling items of clothing out of the old trunk. Bright and silky cloth slid through my fingers, flouncy skirts, an old Spider-Man costume ... There it was. My hand closed on the cap.

I stood up with it. I clicked on the photo of Skye that her mother had sent me. There she was, grinning from under the maroon peak that was tilted sideways.

Behind that image was the image of Poppy, the cap pulled down over her eyes.

I put the cap in my bag and left.

On the train to Chelmsford, I considered my recent behavior. I had messed around with people's private lives, I had virtually broken into my ex-partner's house like a burglar and spied on his private email. I told myself that I hadn't exactly broken into the house. I'd had my own key. But I didn't even manage to convince myself. All right, so Jason was betraying Emily, the way he'd been betraying me; I was sure of that from those emails. I had it in my power to tell Emily the truth. Perhaps to protect her.

I'd done it all to protect Poppy, but perhaps I hadn't even managed that. I'd gone around creating trouble. It may be that I'd made life more dangerous for myself and Poppy, not less. Someone had killed Skye. Someone had broken into my house, searched through Poppy's room, I was certain of it. Could it be that I'd caused this by kicking up dust, lifting up stones? And for what? What had I actually found out? And now I was going to spend more time with a grieving mother, forcing myself into her life, into her grief.

I told myself that I would allow myself this one last chance. I would spend this time with Peggy, I would listen, I would be her friend, I would find out whatever I could and if I didn't find out anything, then that would be that. Even thinking it, it felt like I was an addict, lying to myself. Just one last time, one absolutely last time, I really mean it. I started to think that maybe the best way to protect Poppy was indeed to stop and give her a happy life and gradually her bad dreams and waking fears might cease. I would be kind to Peggy, but I would also keep my eyes open. If nothing came of it, then I would go back to work and put my arms around my daughter and try to keep us safe.

At a stall outside Chelmsford station, I bought a bunch of flowers and then took the taxi once more to Peggy Nolan's house. I pressed the front doorbell and rehearsed in my mind questions I needed to ask her without seeming too intrusive. I waited for the sound of footsteps but none came. I rang the bell again and heard the chime at back of the house. Could she have forgotten I was coming? Or was she asleep? Or had she gone to the shops? I called her number and it went straight to voicemail. I left a mumbled, incoherent message saying I was outside her house and wondering where she was and if she was all right.

I had a thought. She could be in the garden without her phone and maybe not hearing the doorbell. I stepped back and looked at the front of the house. The right side was detached and a passageway led through to the back. I looked around, almost guiltily. There was no fence or gate blocking it. It must be all right.

I walked along the passage and reached the garden. She wasn't there.

I felt a puzzlement that quickly became irritation. I'd come all this way. Would I really just have to call for a taxi and go straight back to London?

Possibly she had fallen asleep. She was on medication and it might have knocked her out. I looked at the door leading into the kitchen. If she had gone out, she would have locked it and that would be that.

I tried it and the handle turned. The door was unlocked and moved inward. I stepped inside and heard voices. It seemed that she had visitors and that was why she hadn't heard the front doorbell, but then I realized that the radio in the kitchen was on. I switched it off and expected to hear the sound of footsteps or anything, the little creaks that show someone is somewhere in a house.

"Hello?" I called out, my own voice sounding strange to me. "Peggy? Are you here? It's Tess."

Nothing.

My first impulse was to turn round and walk out the way I had come in and go back home. But I had the strange sensation that a thread was pulling me forward and into the house, into somewhere I didn't want to go, to see something I didn't want to see. And so, when I stepped out of the kitchen, took a couple of steps and walked into the living room, it was almost with a sense of inevitability that I saw the body of Peggy Nolan lying facedown on the rug, one arm under her, the other splayed out to one side.

My brain was working slowly, as if everything was in a thick fog, but I had the dimmest memories of a first-aid course I'd been on, years ago, of chest compressions and blowing into the mouth. I knelt down by the body and said Peggy's name and touched her neck, but she was so obviously cold and dead that there was no point in doing anything at all.

I wondered at first whether she could have died of

grief, of a broken heart, or perhaps just stumbled and cracked her head, but then I looked around and saw a bureau drawer that had been pulled out and tipped upside down, the contents scattered. Someone had been here and done this. Could they still be here? I listened, but could only hear my breathing and feel the beating of my heart.

I had to do something.

I took my phone out. What was the number? 999? Or had that changed? Did it depend on the kind of emergency? Then I thought: no. I looked through my saved numbers and made the call.

It took some time for Kelly Jordan to answer. She sounded immediately irritable.

"Yes?"

"You know Peggy Nolan? The mother of Skye Nolan?"

"What about her?"

"She's been murdered."

There was a pause.

"What do you mean? How do you know?"

"I'm standing next to her body. I'm looking down at it. It's cold."

Jordan began some kind of a question and then stopped.

"OK," she said, in a clipped, official tone. "Where are you?"

I had to think for a few seconds before I could remember the address and give it to her.

"Are you safe?" she said. "Is there anyone else at the property?"

"No, I mean, yes, I think I'm safe, I don't think anyone else is here."

"Fine. You stay there. Don't do anything. Above all don't touch anything. Have you got that? Nothing at all."

I murmured something in response and she broke off the call.

Don't do anything. Don't touch anything. What would I do or touch, anyway?

I looked around. I hadn't taken in at first the sheer extent of the mess. Books, magazines, documents, mugs, cutlery, random objects, were strewn across the floor. Then I saw the bag I had seen the previous day. The bag that had been filled with the clothes and objects that had been on Skye's body. We had looked at them one by one yesterday and then replaced them. I knelt beside the bag. Clearly it had been tipped upside down and emptied onto the floor. I noted the lovely dress, the bra, the sandals. I picked up the charm bracelet and as I looked at it the sound of Peggy's voice came back to me as vividly as if she were speaking to me. I put it back down. The locket, the knickers. They were all there.

And then dully, through that dark fog, something dim, a kind of a memory: not quite all. There was something missing. What was it?

There were flashes of light on the ceiling and I looked up and round. The lights were coming from outside, there were cars and the sound of running feet.

FORTY-SEVEN

I was in a room with no windows. Everything was of an indeterminate color. The lino on the floor was a sort of flecked gray. The walls were a kind of drab green. The molded plastic chairs were gray as well. The table was laminated wood. A young officer brought me a cup of tea and ginger biscuits wrapped in cellophane. I never bought biscuits and I hadn't eaten these ginger snaps since I was a child. But I felt like I needed something that would stop my feeling of trembling and faintness. I tore open the packet and dipped a biscuit into the tea and ate it and then did the same with the next.

I made a few feeble attempts to make sense of what had happened, but I kept being overwhelmed with the thought of Peggy Nolan and her grief for her daughter and that she had been alive yesterday and now she was as dead as Skye. Had she joined her daughter? Is that what she had wanted? Could I make myself believe that?

The door opened and what felt like a crowd of people came in. It took an effort for me to focus and see that one of them was a uniformed female officer and the other two were Ross Durrant and Kelly Jordan. Ross Durrant placed something on the table but I was looking at their faces. Kelly Jordan looked concerned; Durrant was frowning.

"Are you all right?" Kelly Jordan asked.

I nodded.

The two detectives sat down opposite me, the uniformed officer stood in a corner to one side. Durrant's eyes bored into me.

"Are these your clothes?"

I looked down at myself, as if I needed reminding.

"What? These? Yes."

"What the—" he began and looked round at the officer. "Why wasn't this done at the scene?" He turned back to me. "In a few minutes some officers are going to come here. They are going to take your clothes and give you others. They will take a DNA sample and they will also take some scrapings from under your nails. And so forth. Do you understand?"

"Yes."

"Do you agree to it? You have a right to refuse."

"No, it's fine."

He leaned forward and pressed a button and then stared down at it.

"Is it working? I can never tell if it's working."

The officer stepped forward. "The light should be flashing."

"I think it's flashing." He looked at his watch. "It's fourteen twenty-seven on the third of June. Present are

316

Inspectors Ross Durrant and Kelly Jordan. And Sergeant ..." He looked round.

"Woolley," said the officer. "Elinor Woolley."

"Elinor Woolley." He looked up at me. "Interviewing Tess Moreau. So, Ms. Moreau: what the hell were you doing there?"

"I met her at the inquest. We became friends."

He seemed to consider my answer for few seconds.

"Let me rephrase that: what the fuck were you doing in Peggy Nolan's house?"

"I've just explained. Had to be there. I'm as upset as anyone. I feel terrible about it all. Absolutely terrible."

"Is that all?"

"I felt sorry for her." I took a deep breath. "I also thought I might learn something about why Skye had been killed."

Ross Durrant looked round at Kelly Jordan and then back at me and nodded slowly.

"You became involved in the Skye Nolan murder, didn't you?"

"If you mean that the police assumed that it was a suicide until I got involved, then the answer is yes."

"That's not what I mean. Were you explicitly warned not to get involved in the investigation?"

"I *am* involved," I said desperately. "I only wish I wasn't."

"As you well know, Ms. Moreau, we have found no evidence connecting you to Skye Nolan."

"There are strange things happening," I said.

Durrant ignored me. "But we have found a connection between the two murders, a connection that seems worth pursuing."

"Good. What is it?"

He leaned forward. "You."

"What do you mean?"

"You involved yourself in the Skye Nolan case, against all advice. You've been persecuting my colleague and taking advantage of her *kindness*." He made kindness sound like a dirty word. I saw Kelly Jordan flush. "And now you were at the scene of Peggy Nolan's murder."

"That's ridiculous. I was the one who reported it."

"I'm simply making an observation."

"Why were you there today, Tess? I mean, apart from being her friend, if that's what you had become. For what specific reason?" It was Kelly Jordan this time, her voice level and dispassionate.

I turned gratefully toward her.

"We met yesterday. She had collected the things that Skye had been wearing when she was found. She wanted company to go through them. She thought it would help."

"I didn't ask about yesterday," said Kelly Jordan. "I asked about today."

I thought about this. It suddenly sounded rather lame.

"I was going to carry on helping her sort out Skye's things."

"But you said that's what you did yesterday."

"But that was just a little bag of the things Skye had been wearing when she died. There was everything else."

Now there was a long silence. The two detectives stared at me. I felt I could tell what they were doing. They were leaving a silence for me to fill, just out of a need to keep talking. Perhaps I would give something away.

Then, seemingly out of nothing, I remembered something.

"The watch," I said.

"What?" said Durrant.

"The bag with the things she had been wearing. Whoever did this tipped it out on the floor. When I went through it, I felt that something was missing, but I didn't know what. It was the watch. The watch isn't there."

"Went through it?" said Kelly Jordan. "Did you touch anything? Please tell me you didn't touch anything."

"I may have lifted some things," I said, haltingly. "Just to see if it was all there."

"I told you—specifically told you—not to touch anything."

"I needed to be sure."

"For fuck's sake," said Ross Durrant. "All right, that's enough for now. While this is being written up for you to sign, you need to be checked over before any other clues get accidentally lost."

"No," I said. "I have to go."

"You will go when we have finished with you."

"My daughter's at school," I said. "I need to collect her. What time is it? It must be nearly three o'clock. If I leave now, I can still get there on time."

"Absolutely not."

"You can't stop me."

"Really?"

"Tess," said Kelly Jordan. "Please try and be reasonable. You've found a body. A woman has been murdered and we need your help."

The words were friendly enough, but the tone in which she spoke was not. I could see that she was furious with me.

"I have to get Poppy."

"Isn't there anyone you can ask to look after her until you get there? Presumably you have arrangements for when you're working?" A crease appeared between her eyes. "Why weren't you working today, by the way?"

"I'm ill," I said. "I've got a doctor's note saying I'm suffering from stress." As soon as I'd said this, I regretted it. I knew it made me look even more irrational and unstable.

"So who normally collects Poppy?" asked Kelly Jordan.

"No!" I heard the wildness in my voice, and saw Durrant and Jordan glance at each other.

I didn't want Laurie anywhere near Poppy. Or Jason, or Emily or Ben for that matter. My mind scrabbled. My mother was too far away. Gina was at work. I couldn't ask Bernie. I couldn't ask Aidan.

"I can ask Lotty, her teacher, to wait with her," I said at last. "But it mustn't be for long."

Kelly Jordan nodded and I took my mobile out and found the number of the school and, after a few minutes, was talking to Lotty.

"Sorry," I said. "So sorry. There's been an emergency and I'm going to be a bit late. But I'll be there as soon as I can."

"Are you all right?"

Lotty's voice was concerned. I took a steadying breath and tried to speak calmly.

"I hate being late. Is she OK?"

"Poppy's fine. Hang on." There was a pause. I could hear muffled voices and then Lotty was back again. "Jake's father's here and he's offering to take her, like he often does, right?"

"No! No, please—I mean—"

My mind was clotted with thoughts. I desperately didn't want Poppy to be left with Laurie, but to refuse his offer would be to show him that, and then what? Which was worse—to let her go with him, or to not let her go with him? I couldn't decide and stood with the mobile pressed to my ear, frozen in indecision. In front of me, Ross Durrant drummed his fingers on the table in loud impatience.

"Tess?" I could imagine Lotty and Laurie standing together while she listened to my silence. "Shall I hand Poppy over to Laurie?"

"Yes," I blurted. "OK. Tell her to be good and tell her I won't be long."

"Sure."

I ended the call. Now Lotty would think I was crazy as well.

They took my clothes and gave me others, drab, the trousers slightly too short, the top smelling of floral fabric conditioner. They scraped beneath my nails. They took a swab from the inside of my mouth.

I didn't know how Peggy had died. There'd been no blood, no obvious weapon, her head hadn't been turned at an unnatural angle. She'd just been dead. So unmistakably dead, her poor slight body splayed out on the floor, her long skirt around her knees, her optimistic purple hair framing a face that was blank as stone.

I was taken back into the interview room where I signed my statement without reading it through. Ross Durrant reappeared, this time without Kelly Jordan. He put his hands on the table and leaned toward me, his expression grim.

"You may go and fetch your daughter now," he said. "But before you do so, you need to hear this. In my opinion, we have been far too accommodating of you and your whims and panics and deluded imaginings. You have taken up our time, you have interfered with our investigation, you have thrown sand in our eyes, you have tampered with evidence."

"That's not—"

He plowed over my feeble attempt to defend myself.

"All that ends here. You found the body of Peggy Nolan and you are now a witness in a murder inquiry. That is all you are. You are not a victim, you and your daughter are not at risk, you are not a detective, nor are you a fucking soothsayer. You do not have special insight. You are not permitted to go poking round, creating your own paranoid dramas, ringing DC Jordan up at all hours. And she's too soft-hearted to tell you to bugger off, making our job next to impossible."

Durrant leaned closer so his eyes were boring into mine. I could smell his meaty breath. "Do you hear?"

"I hear," I said. "But—"

His hand lifted and crashed down on the desk.

"No fucking buts. If you do anything else to impede our investigation, you will be charged. That is a promise. Now get out of here."

FORTY-EIGHT

Poppy was in bed and I had showered and changed into my own clothes and was in the garden in the soft dusk. I could smell next door's roses. The rind of a moon hung above the rooftops. I thought of pouring myself a drink, of getting a cigarette from my secret stash, but instead I just sat, limp and exhausted after the day. The rush of images had ceased and I felt empty, ransacked of emotions.

Dimly, I heard a sound and then realized it was the front doorbell, barely audible from the garden. It was late, I wasn't expecting anyone and I thought of ignoring it, but when it rang again, I heaved myself out of the low chair, went through the conservatory, up the stairs, and opened the door.

"Hello, Tess." Aidan spoke awkwardly. "If you tell me to go away, I will." I didn't reply at once. "Sorry. This was a mistake. Stupid. I just couldn't . . . I didn't . . . forgive me."

He turned.

"No," I said. "Don't go!"

He stopped, his back still turned to me. The sight of

324

him, with his defeated shoulders and his thinning hair, made me feel painfully tender.

"Come in. Just for a few minutes."

He faced me then, taking me in.

"You look awful."

"Well, thank you!"

"No, I mean—what's happened? Are you OK?"

"Come inside."

"If you're sure."

"Of course."

We went back into the garden together. I didn't offer him a drink. I didn't know why he was there or what he wanted. I didn't know anything.

"What happened?" he asked again.

"I'm not sure I'm ready to talk about it. Things have been rough, that's all. Today ..." I faltered to a halt.

"Today?"

I looked at him properly for the first time, letting our eyes meet. His face was thinner than I remembered.

"It was awful," I said. I didn't want to cry in front of him.

"You don't need to tell me. But is there anything I can do to help?"

I shook my head. We were both silent.

"I didn't mean to come," he said at last.

"I'm glad you did."

"Really?"

"Yes."

"I've missed you." His voice was low. "I've missed you so much."

"I've missed you too," I said.

"Does that mean ... ?"

"No," I said. "I need to sort things."

He nodded several times. "Do you think, in the future, when you're ready ... ?"

"Mummy!" Poppy's voice cut through the air. "Mummy Mummy Mummy."

I jumped to my feet.

"Sorry," I said. "Let yourself out."

"Of course."

I ran up the stairs and into Poppy's room. Leaning over her bed, pushing her damp hair off her forehead and murmuring to her, I heard the front door open and then I heard it close.

FORTY-NINE

The next morning, it rained heavily, water clattering
down on the leaves and running off cracked earth.
Poppy and I dashed to school under an umbrella but
still arrived soaked. When I got home, I changed into
running clothes and headed for London Fields, barely
able to see through the downpour, my feet splashing
through the rapidly forming puddles, houses and trees
damp smudges on the drenched horizon.

I ran for more than an hour, as fast as I could,
chasing along paths, blindly retracing my footsteps.
I wanted to wear myself out; I wanted my lungs to
hurt and my legs to ache. When I finally got back to
my street, I saw there were two figures standing at the
door of the flat, one of them holding an umbrella. I
slowed down and squinted through the driving rain. A
man and a woman.

I drew nearer then halted. The man was Jason—
here when he should be at school. I had never seen the
woman before.

"Jason?" I said, walking up to them. My sodden

top and shorts were plastered to my body, my hair was dripping.

They turned. The woman was wearing glasses that had misted over, so I couldn't see her eyes.

"I tried calling. I need to speak to you," Jason said.

"Is something wrong?"

"Can we come in?"

I put my hand up to retrieve the key that I hang round my neck when I go running.

"Shit."

"What?"

"I forgot my key. We're locked out."

The woman took off her glasses and blinked at me. She was older than me, severely thin and neat.

"So what do we do?" said Jason.

"I'll see if my neighbor's in."

I rang Bernie's bell and to my relief heard his unmistakable thumping down the stairs.

"Tess," he said. "You got caught in the rain."

"I know. I forgot my key."

He raised his eyebrows. "You're in a bit of a pickle then, aren't you?"

There was a horrible moment where I tried to remember whether I really had given him the spare key or whether I had borrowed it back from him and not returned it and wondered what on earth I was going to do. And then I looked at him and saw him smiling.

"It's OK," he said. "Of course I've got your key."

He ran back up the stairs.

"You know the song about good neighbors," he said cheerfully when he returned with the key. Nobody responded. "Becoming good friends. Anyway." He clapped Jason on the shoulder. "We met before. The other day. Poppy was rubbing mud into her little friend's face. I'm Bernie."

"Jason."

"I know. The ex." He looked at the woman. "Is this your new—?"

"I'm sorry," Jason said. "We're in a bit of rush."

I opened the door to my flat and we stepped in, shutting it on Bernie's grin.

"Is it all right if I change?" I asked when we were in the conservatory. "How much of a rush are you in?"

"It's fine," said the woman.

I was puzzled. She was speaking as if she were in charge.

"I'm sorry, who are you?"

"My name's Fenella Graham. I'm a friend of Jason's."

That didn't feel like a proper answer, but I was beginning to feel cold and clammy and also grimy and disheveled compared to them in their smart, dark clothes and me with wet bare limbs and goose bumps. I hastened into my bedroom, peeled off my clothes, toweled my hair and pulled on a tee-shirt dress.

Back in the room I offered them tea or coffee.

"We'll only be a minute," said Jason.

We sat at the kitchen table, me on one side, Fenella and Jason facing me. I laughed nervously.

"It feels like an interview," I said.

"I wanted to make this informal," Jason said. "Fenella is a friend and she's doing this as a favor. It's very generous of her. To you as well as to me."

"What do you mean?" I said. My mouth suddenly felt dry, but I didn't exactly know why except that I felt something bad was coming. Jason looked at Fenella and nodded and she nodded back and then looked at me.

"As I said, I'm a friend of Jason's."

I gave another scratchy laugh.

"I thought I knew most of Jason's friends." As I said the words, I remembered that there was a whole other category of Jason's friends that I hadn't known. Was Fenella another of them?

"I'm also a solicitor. But I'm not here officially." She lifted her eyebrows. "I don't normally make house calls."

"After your recent behavior," said Jason, "I thought I should get some legal advice."

"What do you mean?"

Jason held up one hand. He spoke calmly, drawing out his words, watching them land. I could imagine him talking like this at one of his meetings at school.

"I've tried to be patient," he said. "I know you're under stress. I know that my marriage to Emily has caused you jealousy and distress and the fact of her pregnancy has been very painful for you. And I accept that there have been faults on both sides."

"What is this actually about?"

Jason looked at the solicitor. She smiled at me, as if we were two new friends, sitting over coffee.

"You know, Tess," she said, "I work in family law and, as a lawyer, one of the main pieces of advice I would give a friend is, don't bring in lawyers. Once they get involved it quickly becomes very unpleasant and very expensive."

"You *are* a lawyer."

"As I said, I'm here as a favor. To you as well as to Jason."

"You're here as a favor to me?"

"Yes."

"I'm sorry," I said. "Could you explain that?"

Her smile faded; her face was stern again. "Jason has told me about the events of the last few weeks. He has told me about things you have said, about things you have done and accusations you have made. Jason is understandably upset by this. He feels threatened, he feels that his family is threatened, and he feels that his daughter is unsafe. Nevertheless, when we talked about this, he was sure that you could settle it like reasonable people."

I looked at the two of them, first one then the other. I felt I was under attack and I didn't know how to defend myself.

"What do you mean?"

"I think a useful first step would be if you agreed not to approach or go near Jason or his wife or her brother."

"This is ridiculous. We have a daughter together."

"Emily can collect her for the time being," said Jason. "Not tomorrow, as it happens. She's not well and I don't think it's a good idea for Poppy to come to our house. But she can collect her from school on Friday, and in the future, we can make arrangements for an efficient exchange."

"It's all about being sensible," Fenella Graham continued. "You need to stop making it difficult for Jason to see his daughter. And you mustn't make contact with his colleagues or acquaintances."

I shook my head.

"This is all rubbish," I said. "I'm not going to be told what I can and can't do."

She smiled again. I hated her more when she smiled and pretended to be friendly than when she was serious and businesslike.

"Look, Tess, I don't think you realize how tolerant Jason is being. Based on my understanding of what he has told me, he would have no trouble in obtaining a restraining order against you. If he wanted to pursue it, I'm confident he could successfully press charges against you. More than that, with his new marriage and family, his stable household, I believe a family court would be likely to award him sole custody of your daughter."

"You can't. No. You can't."

All of a sudden, my throat thickened and, for a moment, the two figures blurred. For I had remembered that I hadn't deleted those emails I had sent myself from Jason's computer. They were there in plain sight. If he happened to look through the sent items, he would see at once that I'd broken into his house and into his laptop. Nothing more simple, nothing more incriminating. I put a hand across my mouth to stop myself howling.

"Are you all right?" Jason asked.

"I just . . ." I couldn't continue.

"I'm simply describing the situation as I see it," said the solicitor.

I was filled with fear. I could taste it in my mouth and feel it rolling in my stomach. I had broken into Jason's house. I had hacked into his computer. I had sent emails that I found there to my own computer, private and intimate correspondence. If he found that out, and it would be so easy for him to find that out . . . I couldn't continue the thought. Jason turned to me. I could see the bones of his face, the curve of his jaw, the tiniest grimace, or perhaps it was a smile, tugging at his mouth.

"Keep away from me, Tess, from all of us. This is your final warning."

FIFTY

For the rest of the day I felt numb. I wrote the last of my reports, did some tasks around the flat and then in the afternoon I couldn't remember what they'd been. I collected Poppy from school and she ran out and gave me a picture she had painted. It was of a fish in the sea and I looked at it suspiciously to see if there was anything ominous about it, but the sea was bright blue and the sun in the sky was bright yellow and the fish had a big smile on its face that stretched beyond its body.

"It looks like a happy fish," I said to her. I wanted to pick her up and crush her to me and never let her go.

"Lily fell on her head," Poppy said.

I didn't answer at first because I was thinking of something else. I was always thinking of something else. Then I realized what Poppy had said.

"Really? Is she all right?"

"No," she said, not looking at me but straight upward at the sky. "She cried."

I looked around and saw Lily and her mother and walked across to them. Yes, it turned out, Lily really had fallen on her head. Rather proudly she pointed at the bit of her head that had a bump on it.

"They don't keep them safe enough," Lily's mother said to me in an undertone. "I'm going to complain."

"I think they're doing their best," I said feebly.

"It's not good enough. Anything could have happened. Lily could have hit her head on the corner of a table."

I didn't say anything more. I wasn't the person to lecture anyone about overreacting.

The rest of the evening, part of me was cooking and giving Poppy a bath and playing a game with her and reading her a story, but all the time I was thinking about what Jason and Fenella had said. Thinking about what it would be to lose Poppy. Thinking how I would go mad with grief. My whole body hurt at the idea of a life without her; my heart would break.

Poppy made the evening almost more painful for me by being happy and chatty and, apparently, untroubled. When she was in bed—she fell asleep almost immediately, with a smile on her face—I found a bottle of whisky and poured a glass and then stopped just as I was lifting it to my lips.

I could hear banging. I frowned. It sounded like someone was banging at the front door. Why would they do that, when there was a bell?

I waited, because whoever was out there was not someone I wanted to see. There was no one I wanted to see. I wanted to be alone in my flat with Poppy: just the two of us. I heard a voice and the banging stopped. My doorbell rang. I stayed where I was, the glass of whisky still in my hand. It rang again. I groaned and made my way upstairs, pulled open the front door and stepped into the hall.

Bernie was standing there and, beside him, a man I didn't at once recognize. I couldn't see his face because he had his forehead pressed against the door that led to Bernie's flat. As I looked at him, he drew his head back and then struck it twice against the wood.

"He said he's a friend," said Bernie. "If so, he's a friend who is not in a good way. Stop that, mate. You'll injure yourself. Do you know him or shall I tell him to get lost?"

I stepped forward and put a hand on the man's arm. He turned and looked at me wildly. I could smell alcohol and sweat and in the dim light of the hall I could see the whites of his eyes.

"Charlie," I said and then to Bernie: "Yes, I know him. It's OK."

"Sure?"

"Sure."

I led Charlie down the stairs and into the conservatory. I practically pushed him into a chair and poured him a glass of water.

"Drink," I said.

He obediently lifted the glass and drank it down in thirsty gulps. I could see his throat jerking. He was wearing a heavy jacket that was far too hot for the summer evening.

"Another?" I asked.

He shook his head from side to side. I saw that his cheeks were wet with tears. They were draining into his beard, which had been neatly trimmed last time I saw him but now was longer and a bit frizzy. He wasn't wearing his glasses and his eyes were red-rimmed.

"Coffee?"

"Maybe. Thanks. Sorry."

I could barely make out the words. I took the glass from his hand and went over to the sink, where I filled the kettle and turned it on. Behind me, I could hear him blowing his nose several times. I ground the coffee beans and shook them into the French press, poured in the water.

"Milk?"

"And one sugar," he said.

I put the mug in front of him, sat down myself, took a sip of my whiskey.

"Peggy," I said.

He nodded, gave a short sob.

"I can't seem to stop crying," he said. "I don't know why. I didn't cry like this over Skye. I never cry. Skye cried all the time. She cried when she was upset and she cried when she was happy, when she was angry, when she was tired."

Charlie was crying at he spoke, his face puckered up so that he looked like a little boy, his words coming out in bursts.

"It's just so sad," he said. "*I'm* so sad. I'm so fucking sad I don't know what to do with myself."

And then he put his face in both hands and let himself cry properly, his shoulders in the heavy jacket shaking, tears seeping through the cup of his hands.

I waited. I couldn't remember ever having seen a

man cry like this before and it felt oddly intimate, like he had undressed in front of me. I remembered him in the swimming pool, his strong legs and arms and his small pot belly.

"Sorry. So sorry," he managed at last, lifting his head and dragging the back of his hand across his smeary face. "Jesus. I don't know what's wrong with me."

"Grief," I said, and for a moment his face contorted once more. He made a visible effort to hold back more tears. He picked up the cooling mug of coffee and swallowed some.

"You found the body," he said.

"Yes."

"Was she—?" He stopped. "I don't know what I want to ask."

"She was just dead," I said, seeing again those open eyes.

"Why?"

"Why what?"

"Why would someone kill Skye and then Peggy?" He put the half-full cup down, pushed his fingers through his slightly greasy hair. His face was puffy from crying. "They were so ..." He searched for a word. "Nice," he said eventually, hopelessly. "They thought well of people. They trusted people. I used to tease them for being so unworldly. Even when Skye was taking drugs and doing whatever she did, she was like a little kid. I remember ..." He squinted at me, as if the light was hurting his eyes. "I remember when I was first together with Skye and she took me home to Peggy's, they would fuss over me and tease me and make me feel special and looked after. And if I did anything for them, they were so *grateful*. As if they weren't used to people putting themselves out for them. I remember thinking they would be in my life forever: Skye and Peggy. I was really happy then."

He stood up and stared around him. I saw him taking in the room—Poppy's drawings on the fridge, the sewing machine on the table, the whiskey bottle, the garden outside in the fading light.

"I let them down," he said. "I let them both down. I gave up on Skye and she died. Then I wasn't there for Peggy when she needed me the most and if I had been maybe she would be alive now. I've always thought of myself as a decent kind of guy—not particularly handsome or clever or successful or anything. Ordinary, but OK, you know. Someone who'd do the right thing when push came to shove. But I failed the test."

"What test?"

He shrugged. "I didn't save them. I didn't even try to save them. I'll feel guilty for the rest of my life."

"No," I said.

"No?"

"You will go mad if you think like that."

"How should I think?"

"Someone is out there who killed Skye and then killed her mother. That's how you should think."

"Who?"

"I don't know yet."

"Will you know?"

339

"Yes."

"Tell me what to do."

"How can I tell you that, Charlie? We hardly know each other."

"No, I mean: tell me what to do to help you find him."

"Ah."

"I'll do anything. Just say."

"OK. If there is anything, I will just say."

"You promise?"

"I promise."

He didn't look so out of it now, just tired and crumpled.

"It's time for you to go home."

We went up the stairs together. The door to Poppy's bedroom opened and there she was, in her cotton pajamas, eyes wide open, but not really awake. I took her hand and held it, but it was like a soft warm object that didn't belong to her. She gazed at us, through us, as if we were made of glass.

"Hello," said Charlie awkwardly. "Did I wake you? Sorry."

"What big ears, big teeth you've got! All the better." Charlie looked bewildered.

"Bye," I said.

He hesitated, then held out his hand. I hesitated, then took it.

"Remember," he said.

That night, Poppy sleepwalked, racing round the house, her bare feet thrumming on the wooden boards, her eyes staring fixedly ahead, seeing and not seeing.

I took her to her bed and pressed her back against the pillow. Her hair was sticking to her forehead. I sang her a song about the moon and she mumbled something, made a feeble attempt to join in, then her body softened and her bright eyes closed at last.

FIFTY-ONE

On the way to school the next morning, Poppy and I sang songs together and made up extra verses and silly rhymes and giggled madly. On the way back I thought about Charlie's visit, which now had the quality of a dream, and about Jason. With a cold clutch of fear, I thought about losing Poppy. That was impossible, it couldn't happen, it would be the end of me.

When I got home I felt a sudden sense of purpose. I made myself a pot of coffee and took a stack of paper from the tray of my printer and wrote notes of everything I could remember, underlining names. They filled several pages. I took a fresh sheet and started to construct a flow chart. I wrote "Poppy's drawing" then "Skye's flat" and drew an arrow from one to the other. I wrote "Peggy's house" and "watch" and drew an arrow from the watch to Peggy's house and another from Skye's flat to the watch. The watch. Had Jason been wearing a watch? I tried to remember, but it was impossible. My mind had been on other things. I put a question mark next to "watch." Then I wrote "home" and "cap" and drew an arrow between them. I wrote "Poppy's school" and drew an arrow from the school to the cap.

I stared at it. Skye's flat. My flat. Peggy's house. All the arrows between them just looked like a cartoon of confusion.

I pushed the paper aside and found a fresh one and wrote "Jason's house" on it and underlined it. What next? Under it I wrote Jason's name, then Emily's name, then Ben's name.

I wrote a timeline, starting from the Sunday that Poppy had returned from Jason's house with her drawing in thick black crayon. I looked at the calendar on my phone to work out the exact dates. It had been going on for three weeks and five days. It felt longer than that, a lifetime, or no time at all.

I cleared a space on the table and then spread out all the sheets I'd written on and looked at them. I moved the sheets around, rearranged them in different shapes. I'd hoped that by doing this a pattern would emerge, but it was just the same old mess, the same places and objects and fears. I'd taken them out of my brain and put them down on paper, but it hadn't made any difference. It wasn't like a jigsaw puzzle that didn't fit together. It was worse than that. I was starting to think that they were pieces that didn't fit together because they were from different puzzles.

I picked up my phone and looked at the time. It was twenty to three. I had missed lunch. I had been so lost in this that I had forgotten to be hungry. I checked for messages. My emails were the usual rubbish, about perfume and miracle cures and fake offers, but there was also one from a name I recognized: Inga Haydon. She was one of the women I'd found on Jason's computer. The one who had written to me saying she didn't know Skye Nolan and asking how I'd got her address. I'd assumed I'd never hear from her again. I clicked on the message. It was just a short question: *Can I come and see you?*

I stared at the sheets of paper on my table then back at my phone. It felt like something magical had happened. It also felt too good to be true. Could there be something wrong? I made myself think of the worst that it could be. Was it possible that it wasn't really from Inga at all? Jason had only just threatened me with interfering in his life. Could this be a trap? Could he be luring me into doing it again and that would give him the evidence he needed to take Poppy away from me? I looked at the message. The email address was in the name of Inga Haydon. I looked back at the previous message from her. It was the same address. Could that also have been from Jason?

I felt like I was driving myself insane. I considered it and made up my mind. I couldn't see Inga now. I was about to collect Poppy. But later? I typed a message: *What about this evening at 8 at my flat?* I wrote my address. There was nothing incriminating in itself about responding to a message like that. I took a deep breath and pressed send.

Barely a minute passed before I got a message back: *OK*.

FIFTY-TWO

Miraculously, Poppy was in bed and asleep when the front doorbell rang. I opened the door and found myself looking at someone different from what I'd expected. Inga was a woman of about my own age, in jeans with a brown suede jacket. Her hair was short with a parting on the right, neatly combed, almost boyish. She wore thin wire-rimmed spectacles and her face was smooth. Everything about her seemed clean and neat and organized.

As she stepped inside, she looked at me and then around at the flat with obvious curiosity.

"And you are?" she said.

"Tess Moreau."

"Yes, I know that. I mean who *are* you?"

"Can I get you a coffee? A glass of wine?"

She shook her head slowly. "I'm fine."

"A glass of water?"

"I just want to say something and then I'll go."

I gestured her toward the sofa and when she sat, she remained perched on the edge. She made no move to take her jacket off. It was like she wanted to make it clear to me that she could leave at any moment.

"Why did you get in touch with me?" she asked. "What do you want?"

As briefly as I could, I told her of my relationship with Jason, how it had broken up, how we had certain ongoing problems. I didn't specify them. I felt I needed to be careful, to take one thing at a time. As I talked, I saw her face change, a flicker of different emotions passing across it. She had probably heard all about me, but not my name: Jason's version of our breakup; the story he told to women he wanted to captivate.

"And you," I said, when I had finished. "You had an affair with him."

"How do you know that? I never told anyone. I thought nobody knew apart from the two of us."

I explained how I'd had a false view about my relationship with Jason and that I'd learned a lot about him in recent days. I didn't say I'd hacked into his computer.

"You didn't answer my question."

I thought for a moment of those words you hear in films: anything you say may be used against you. I needed to be careful what I admitted to. I didn't want to tell Inga Haydon anything more than I absolutely had to.

"I just know," I said. "Let's leave it at that. But I'm surprised you're here. I wrote to you asking if you knew anything about a woman called Skye Nolan. You said you didn't. So why are you here?"

Inga looked down at the floor and when she looked back up, I noticed that her cheeks were flushed.

"You know you have an idea of yourself and you do something and it's not who you are?"

"What do you mean?"

"I'm not someone, you know, who has . . ." She hesitated, like she was having difficulty actually saying the words. "Casual sex. I don't. I've never been comfortable with that. And I'm not someone who would have an affair with a married man. And I don't think you should get involved in that way with colleagues. I think it's just wrong."

I tried to make sense of what she was saying. "So you're a colleague of Jason's?"

"I'm a teacher at his school. I've only been there since September."

"And you had an affair with him."

She took several quick, deep breaths. She looked like she was suddenly feeling faint.

"Are you all right?" I asked.

"I was lied to," she said. "Humiliated."

"I thought you said nobody knew."

"You can feel humiliated by yourself." She looked at me more directly. "When I got your first email I felt like I was suddenly being punched on a bruise, over and over again."

"I'm sorry," I said. "I didn't mean it."

"You weren't to know."

I thought of myself entering Jason's house, breaking into his computer, reading his private email. I thought that maybe I was to know.

"At first, I wanted to have nothing to do with it. I wanted to pretend to myself. Then I decided I had to see you. I had two reasons. The first was that I wondered if you had been through what I had been through and, if you had, I wanted to sit opposite you and look at you."

I did indeed feel her looking at me and I didn't enjoy the experience. I had felt shamed by what I'd learned, but that didn't make me want to be part of some kind of sisterhood of shame.

"You said there were two reasons. What was the other one?"

"You know the expression to 'get someone into bed?' "

"Well, yes," I said, "I suppose so."

"Jason got me into bed. He made me feel things and believe things and then once he had got me into bed, he made it clear that it was nothing to him. Just a bit of excitement."

"I'm sorry," I said. "Was that the second thing?"

She shook her head. "I've got information about him."

"What kind of information?"

"Emails."

"To you?"

"To another colleague."

"What about?"

Now her voice sounded calmer, harder. "You know, sexual ones. Harassing ones."

I thought for a moment. "How did you get them?"

"Someone gave them to me."

"And you think if they were made public, they would be damaging to his career?"

"Oh yes," she said. "Very."

"Why don't you do something with them yourself?"

348

"I am. I'm offering them to you."

"I mean, do it yourself, make them public yourself."

"I don't think it would look good coming from me."

Before I could answer, she looked round sharply. I followed her gaze, and saw Poppy standing in the doorway. I expected her to say something about not sleeping or being thirsty or wanting a story but she was staring at Inga, her eyes wide, her mouth open, immobile.

"Poppy," I said and she ran across to me and almost jumped at me. I held her in my arms and she clung to me, her face buried in my sweater, her hands gripping me so tightly that they felt like claws and almost made me cry out. I murmured consoling words into the top of her head and carried her back to her bed.

As I laid her back down, she started to sob and then almost to howl like an animal that had been cornered. I tried to soothe her but she cried and wouldn't let me go. Finally I told her that I would just say goodbye to Inga and then I would come back and lie down with her and hold her and sing to her.

I returned to the living room and found Inga standing up, apparently ready to leave.

"I'm sorry," I said. "I don't know what's got into Poppy but I need to go back and comfort her. I'll get back in touch with you about all of this."

"We've met before," she said.

"What? When did we meet?"

"Not me and you. Me and your daughter. We didn't exactly meet."

"What do you mean?"

"I was once outside the house with Jason. Saying goodbye, kissing a bit. I looked up and she was in the window, looking down. She looked like a sort of ghost."

I stared at Inga and felt nauseated by the thought of it, of Poppy noticing everything, the three-year-old girl, trying to make sense of her world, taking everything in. Was this woman trying to help me or was she getting me to do her revenge for her so she could pretend to herself it wasn't her.

"I'm sorry," I said. "I'm going to have to see you out."

"Of course."

"One thing, though. The really important thing is Skye Nolan. We haven't talked about her, but really she's the reason I got in touch in the first place. Do you know anything about her? Anything, however trivial?"

Inga didn't hesitate.

"I told you in the email. I've never even heard the name before."

FIFTY-THREE

That night I lay stretched out, tense and aching and fearsomely awake, while the events of the day streamed through me, in my heart and in my brain and in my blood.

Jason's threats—he couldn't, he couldn't, he couldn't—and the lawyer's instructions, Inga's revelations, the emails of other women he had harassed that she offered to me as—what? Ammunition? Revenge? Something to bring him down?

Behind all of this, beneath it, overarching it all, like the air I was breathing, the fear I was living with, was the image of Poppy. Poppy standing at the window and staring out through the darkness at her father kissing a stranger, while her stepmother was in the house and her actual mother was far away. Poppy burrowing into me, gripping me with her hands like claws. Poppy bent over her drawings, giving me clues I couldn't properly read. Poppy shouting. Poppy stumbling around the house like a terrified ghost. Poppy asking me if I had died. Poppy calling my name, night after night,

Mummy Mummy Mummy. Asking for help, for rescue. Handing me a knife. Her ears like a hawk's, her eyes on stalks, taking in the world and all its messed-up, conflicting meanings.

What should I do? Should I play safe, do nothing, sit out this terror, and trust that it would gradually blow itself out until the horror was just a memory, a nasty stain across the past? But was doing nothing actually playing it safe, or was it a way of closing my eyes and putting my hands over my ears and pretending there wasn't a monster in the room, coming to get us?

I turned in the bed, rearranged the pillow, held my breath and listened for Poppy, but there was only thick silence.

I could instead continue my investigations, despite warnings from the police, from Jason, from Fenella. Investigations: what a grand word for my blundering attempts to find out what Poppy had seen, had heard, had foretold. I thought of the timelines and drawings and notes I had made earlier that day: anyone looking at them would say they were the indecipherable scrawls of a madwoman.

I am not mad, I am not mad, I am not mad.

I felt mad, infected with fears, prey to every ghastly image that blew through me.

At last, just before five, I got out of bed. I looked in on Poppy. She was deeply asleep, her breath slightly puffing at her lips, her lashes thick on her cheeks.

I went downstairs. It was already light and Sunny was lying curled up on himself in a rectangle of sun in the conservatory. I made myself a pot of tea and tidied things up. I picked up the thick bundle of papers on which I had written down everything the previous day and pushed it into a drawer. I chopped up strawberries for breakfast and put birdseed into the feeder. I walked into the garden, still damp from dew, the lawn mossy and the smell of honeysuckle carried by the warm breeze.

Today mustn't be like yesterday. I dressed with care: I wanted to look orderly, sane, in control of my life. I brushed my hair and tied it into a thick braid, put on a blue cotton dress and gold stud earrings, then looked at myself in the mirror. Would I pass? Tess Moreau, a mother, a teacher, a woman on the brink.

I woke Poppy and we ate breakfast in the garden, flaky croissants and strawberries, as if it were a Sunday or we were on holiday. She held up a forefinger and said, "I will be a bumble and stripe and sting."

Bernie looked out of his window above us and said, "Oh, a picnic. Can I join you?"

"No," said Poppy. "Go way."

He simply laughed; the laugh went on too long.

"I will be a worm," said Poppy.

We walked hand in hand to school. At the door to Poppy's class I bent down to kiss her. She put her face against mine and gripped the braid of my hair as if it were a rope and she could pull herself up on it. Rapunzel, I thought.

"Don't blink," she said.

We stared into each other's eyes and then she gave me a small push. I blinked.

"I did win," she said triumphantly and was gone without a backward glance.

"Tess!"

I turned to see Laurie, standing just a bit too close, Nellie staring beadily over his shoulder.

"I could have taken Poppy for you, no problem."

"Thanks. But I like to. I'll be back to normal on Monday."

"Sure. Are you feeling recovered?"

"Kind of."

Nellie reached out and clutched my hair with her plump, sticky fist.

"Hey there," said Laurie, laughing and prying her fingers loose. "Let's walk back together. It's such a beautiful day; we can go through the park."

I fell in beside him. He talked. I saw his mouth opening and closing, his mouth smiling. Every so often he reached out and touched me on the arm.

"You're very silent," he said. "What are you thinking?"

I've always hated that question. I was thinking that Emily was going to collect Poppy from school and take her to Jason's house. I was thinking of Jason kissing Inga while Poppy stared down at them; of Ben sitting in his boxers watching darts and scratching his belly and belching; of Emily smiling and pale and pleading. How could I let her go there? How could I prevent it?

"I wasn't really thinking of anything."

"Still waters run deep," he said. "Come and have coffee."

I went. It felt different when Gina wasn't there, or Jake and Poppy. Just Laurie and red-faced Nellie who, whatever she saw, could never tell. I put my bag down on the floor and remembered that the cap I'd collected the day before was still in there. I pushed the bag further under the table, out of sight.

"Do you like dogs?" I asked Laurie as he poured coffee beans into the grinder.

"Dogs? I guess so? Why?"

"You walk your mother's dog, don't you?"

He turned on the grinder. Nellie began to yell and without pausing he passed her half a banana to chew.

"Winston?" he said, when he'd finished grinding the coffee. "Sometimes."

"Do you meet other dog walkers?"

He shrugged. "Sure. One of the things anyone will tell you is that when you have a dog, people come up and talk to you."

"Yes, that's what I've heard."

"If I was lonely, I'd get a dog." He poured boiling water onto the grounds and stirred. "But I'm not lonely."

"No, I guess you're not."

"Gina said you'd broken up with Aidan."

I didn't say anything. He passed me a mug of coffee and I half-perched on a stool and took a mouthful.

"You'll meet someone else," he said.

I shrugged. My mind was full of thoughts that were broken and wouldn't fit together.

"I lied," he said.

"What do you mean?"

"This life. I love it, of course, don't get me wrong." He gestured around him, the tidy kitchen, the little girl he had lifted off his back, her face smeared with bananas. "But sometimes I do get a bit lonely. Don't you, Tess? Don't you sometimes get lonely too?"

I stared at him. *Don't blink.*

"No." I put the mug down and stood up to leave. "I do not."

I went home. From the garden I kept seeing Bernie in the windows above me, passing to and fro, and in the house I thought I could hear him, like hearing a mouse scrabbling and scratching. Did he have no work to do? Probably not.

I took the cap I'd collected from Poppy's school and gazed at it, as if it could give me an answer. My mobile rang and it was Charlie.

"I'll call you if there's anything," I said.

"The police have been round twice." He sounded rattled. "They keep asking me questions about my private life, my sex life, when I last saw Skye, if I slept with her. Do they suspect me?"

As if I was the one who would know.

"I'm sure it's just procedure," I said blandly, meaninglessly.

"Do you?"

"What?"

"Suspect me?"

"Why would I suspect you?"

"That's not an answer."

"I don't suspect you."

I took the cap out of the bag and looked down at it.

"That photo you sent Peggy, of Skye in a flat cap," I said.

"Did I?"

"Yes. Where did she get it from?"

"How would I know?"

"It didn't belong to you?"

"I don't wear things on my head. I don't even know what cap you're talking about."

"It's on your phone."

"Hang on."

There was a silence. I knew he was scrolling through his photos.

"It didn't belong to me," he said. He sounded suddenly somber, perhaps because he was looking at Skye's face laughing out at him.

I went into the garden, turning my back to the window so I couldn't see Bernie. I took out my mobile and found the number. My finger hovered above it.

Emily was young, younger than her years even, and she seemed guileless and nice. She was living with—was married to—a man who had been serially unfaithful when he was with me, and who was serially unfaithful now he was with her. He was having affairs and he was sexually harassing a member of his staff. She was pregnant and there he was, kissing one of his teachers while parked outside the house. Again, the image of Poppy standing pressed against the window, staring down, came to me and I felt that someone was clutching my throat. I thought of Emily's face, puffy from crying.

The right thing to do was to tell her what I knew. But at the same time, I thought that if I told her

357

and she told Jason, he would do what he had said he would do.

I put the mobile into my pocket, feeling boneless with dread and indecision. All that I had done was cause damage. I had found reasons to distrust every man I knew. Shouldn't I have found reasons to *trust* people? The very idea made my head spin, it was so novel and strange. How did you do that? I tried to remember the circumstances of Skye Nolan's death. I wanted to be sure but how could I be? Who had an alibi for the early hours of a Monday morning?

I took out my phone and looked at the calendar, scrolling back through the weeks until I got to the day of the murder and then, for the first time in what seemed forever, I smiled. I almost laughed.

But it wasn't enough. I rang Kelly Jordan. When I had finished, I rang another number.

"Aidan, it's me. Sorry, this is probably a bad time to ring. But I need to talk to someone. I don't know what to do."

"Of course," he said. "This evening."

"If you're busy—"

"I'm not."

I knew that even if he had plans, he would cancel them and I felt a small spasm of guilt.

"Shall I come to yours then?"

"Six-ish?"

"Good."

FIFTY-FOUR

I watched the clock. It ticked past the time that Poppy would be finishing at school, that Emily would collect her and lead her away, that she would be back in the house in Brixton. Ben would be there—he was probably always there, padding from room to room, staring at the TV, opening the fridge—and his dog, which I had last seen growling at me from the top of the stairs. Soon Jason would arrive home and Poppy would run to him and he would pick her up and lift her high.

I left the flat at half past five, even though it was only a fifteen-minute walk, and meandered along the road in the warmth of early evening. There were crowds of people clustered round pub doors and outside little restaurants.

I hadn't often been to Aidan's, he had almost always come to mine, even when Poppy wasn't there. His flat was on the first floor and small—one bedroom, one tiny bathroom, a galley kitchen tacked onto the living room—and he kept it very tidy. There was a calmness about the space, books in alphabetical order, work piled neatly on the end of the table, a fridge where nothing was past its sell-by date, a spice rack next to the block of knives.

When he let me in, he didn't try to hug me or anything, just led the way into the living room where there was a bottle of white wine, beads of moisture on its cool glass, and a bowl of olives.

"Or would you prefer tea?"

"No—"

"Or I have tomato juice, or cordial."

"A glass of wine would be lovely," I said.

I felt suddenly awkward and self-conscious; I was very aware of his eyes on me.

He poured us both a glass of wine and we sat on the sofa. He was wearing a gray soft-cotton shirt and jeans and his hair had been recently cut. I was seeing him double: as someone I knew intimately and as a stranger.

"Maybe this was a bad idea," I said.

He didn't answer, just raised his eyebrows slightly, waiting.

"The truth is, I'm scared and I don't know what to do. I needed to talk through it all and now I don't know what to say."

I picked up my glass, but my hand was trembling and wine slopped over the brim. Aidan leaned over, took it from my hands and put it back on the table.

"I know some of it already," he said. "But why don't you start from the beginning."

I nodded.

"When did it start?"

That was easy.

"It started with a drawing," I said. "Poppy's drawing in black crayon, of a figure falling."

I told it like a story, but it was a story with holes and gaps in it, one that didn't fit together, and all the time I looked down at my hands, as if I were in a therapy session and talking only to an audience of myself, and all the time I was aware of his eyes watching me.

I didn't leave anything out: I told him about Poppy's mangled swear words, her night terrors, her strange behavior; about going to see Alex at the Warehouse clinic, my trips to the police station, my investigations into Skye, meeting Charlie, meeting Peggy, seeking out dog walkers, trying to find connections. I told him about the cap, the photo of Poppy that had disappeared from the fridge. I told him about the watch.

And then, taking a deep breath and looking away so I wouldn't see his expression, I told him about breaking into the Brixton house, creeping around, hacking into Jason's computer, seeing Ben in his underwear. About the emails I'd read, the women Jason was having affairs with. About how I'd sent those emails to my own computer. And then Jason's visit with the lawyer and the threats he had made and how he didn't yet know about me breaking into the house but might so easily find out, and if he did, I was done for. At this point my voice became thick with tears. I told him about Inga coming to see me, with her tale of humiliation and her offer to pass on the emails of other women.

I told him about going to Peggy's house and finding her dead—my voice cracked at this point. I had to stop for a moment. Aidan still didn't say anything, just waited. I told him about realizing that the watch Skye had been wearing when she died had gone from Peggy's house.

I took a hefty mouthful of wine, then another. I cleared my throat and said that I had been suspicious of every man in Poppy's life—Jason, Ben, Laurie, Bernie, Charlie ... and Aidan himself. I didn't look up when I said this, but I paused and the silence was like a skin stretched between us.

When I finally came to a halt, he didn't speak immediately, just poured us both more wine.

"Well," he said at last. "You have been through the mill."

"You don't think I'm mad?"

"No, Tess, I don't think you're mad."

"So you believe me?"

"Wait a minute. Before I answer that, I want to ask you something?"

"Yes?"

"Do you still suspect me?"

This was the question I had been waiting for him to ask me. I knew the answer I was going to give but I still found it difficult to say out loud.

"What would you like me to say? Would you like me to say that I trust you because I love you?"

He seemed to find it difficult to answer this.

"Well, yes," he said. "That is what I'd like you to say."

"I felt I'd lost my trust in everyone. I was looking for some reason, any reason, not to distrust someone and then I remembered. I checked it in my calendar. On the day when Skye Nolan was murdered, we weren't together. I took Poppy to visit my mother. And you went to a conference out of London."

"And that's enough to trust me?"

"No," I said.

"No?" said Aidan, looking shocked. "What do you mean?"

"Anyone can *say* they're going to a conference. I rang the detective. I knew that after the Peggy Nolan murder, they'd checked people's alibis. I know that you really were there. You signed in at an event." Aidan half-turned away. "I'm sorry."

"I don't know what to say."

"It was the only way forward. I'd stripped my trust in everyone I know. I've almost driven myself mad. I wonder if I can now do the opposite. If I could show that people were innocent, one by one, then I'd be left with the one person I can't prove innocent and he would be the one."

There was a long silence. Aidan was looking dissatisfied.

"I don't know," he said. "It's difficult to prove people innocent." He looked at me more intently. "What if I hadn't been at that conference? What then? Would you be here?"

"I didn't mean to hurt you. I thought I should be honest."

"Is that what a relationship means to you? Assume the worst unless it's proved otherwise?"

"I'm sorry," I said. "I think I can learn to do better than that. But it will take time. All I can say is that when I was thinking about whether to call Emily, and awful thoughts and pictures were going round and round in my head, I desperately needed to talk to someone. I thought I would go mad if I didn't. And you were the person I wanted to talk to."

"Because I was at a conference when this woman died. I'm honored."

"That sounds sarcastic."

"Sorry, it *was* a little sarcastic."

"So now I've said I believe you. Do you believe me?"

There was a pause. He had a pleat between his brows. He took his glasses off, rubbed his eyes, put them back on again.

"I believe that Poppy witnessed something," he said slowly, carefully. "And that it was connected to Skye Nolan's death in some way. Yes."

"Is it Jason? Does it sound like it was Jason?"

"Honestly, Tess, how can I answer that? I don't know the man. I know he deceived you, but that doesn't mean he's a murderer."

"I guess not."

"I can say that you are well out of his life. And I'm sorry for all you've been through."

"Thank you." I stared down at my plaited hands. "This is not about us getting back together, you know." It came out more brusquely than I intended.

"I know that."

"I need to sort things out."

He nodded. "After everything you've just told me, of course I see that. I just—"

He stopped, passed a hand in front of his face.

"Me too," I said softly, because he looked so frail and because I shouldn't have come. "I just too."

I don't know who kissed who, who took the other by the hand and led them into Aidan's orderly bedroom, dove-gray duvet cover and white pillows, a black-and-white photo of a man skating in top hat and tails above the bed. I know that he undressed me as he had done so many times in the past, folding my clothes neatly, watching me with his serious eyes. And then he took off his own clothes and folded those too, taking off his glasses last and putting them on top of his shirt. We held each other, whispered the other's name; we said we were sorry, we said it was all right now. It didn't feel like desire, not exactly—more like a kind of rescue. But I don't know who was rescuing whom.

And after, tangled in each other's arms, Aidan lifted himself onto one elbow and looked down at me.

"Jesus, I've missed you."

"I've missed you too," I said.

It was still light outside. I thought of Poppy in Jason's house; I thought of her standing at the window staring out at the mysterious world.

"And I've missed Poppy," he added, as if he could read my thoughts. "How is she?"

"Maybe a bit better than she was."

"When's she back?"

"Tomorrow mid-morning. I'll meet Emily halfway."

"Shall we go on a picnic after that, the three of us? I can bring everything."

"That would be nice," I said, though I wasn't really

listening. Instead, I was hearing how he assumed it was just going to go back to the way it had been—we'd broken up and then we'd made up. I was hearing how happy he sounded.

"Are you hungry?"

"Maybe. I don't know. What time is it?"

He reached out for his phone and looked at it.

"Just gone nine thirty. There's some cheese and smoked salmon in the fridge—we could have that."

"OK," I said.

"Or we could go out and grab something."

"No. I'd like to stay here."

I watched him as he got out of bed, pulled on a dressing gown, put on his glasses; he smiled over his shoulder as he left the room. I lay under the duvet, listening to him in the kitchen, the chink of knives, of glasses. I felt neither glad nor sad, waiting to know what had just happened and what it meant.

FIFTY-FIVE

I went to sleep early, wiped out by emotions, and when I woke, soft gray light was showing through the thin curtains. For a moment, I wondered where I was and then I remembered. I turned over and saw Aidan, deeply asleep beside me. He looked young and peaceful. I reached across him for my phone, to look at the time. It was not yet half past five.

Aidan shifted, put a forearm across his eyes. He had thin wrists. A memory—or a memory's fragment—reached into my mind like a long finger. Something about telling the time, something that belonged to the past. A barbecue. Aidan in a denim shirt, the sleeves rolled up to the elbows, looking at his wrist and telling me when the food would be ready.

The way he always took his watch off before he got into bed, laying it on top of his folded clothes. Such a neat man. A man of habit.

I lay still. Very, very still, like an effigy. I didn't breathe. Hook in my throat. A jam of fear, and my heart stuttering and my skin crawling.

I told myself I was going mad, I had gone mad, would always be mad now.

It wasn't true. Of course it wasn't true. I feared it only because if it was true, then every last thing I trusted would be reduced to ash. I had turned myself into a creature of paranoia, an echo chamber of my own fantastic dark imaginings, and every dread was chaotic, free-floating, attaching itself to whatever object lay at hand.

Aidan had been at a conference when Skye had died. His missing watch was just a missing watch.

But I held the thought in my mind and around it, things gradually clicked into place. Skye had stalked the man she thought had rescued her, followed him, found out about the "complications" in his life. And Skye had come to the restaurant where we were having a meal, had stood in front of us, and what if all the time she hadn't been speaking to me but to him?

Skye had died after I had shown him the mutilated rag doll. I remembered his expression as he stared at it.

He had come to see me on the evening of the day that Peggy had been killed, because he knew, or thought he knew, that he was in the clear now.

He had stood by the fridge, pouring elderflower juice out for everyone that day, right next to the photo of Poppy in the cap.

And Poppy—my chest ached—Poppy didn't like him. I realized in a rush how every time he had come to our home, she had refused to be with him, had clung to me.

I looked again at Aidan. He was almost smiling, as if his dreams were pleasing ones. He shifted slightly and his breathing deepened.

Slowly, I slid from the bed. My mouth was open in a silent yell. My legs felt hollow, a string puppet's legs, disarticulated. I picked up the clothes and tiptoed from the room. If I turned round, he would be sitting up in bed and watching me creep away, as if I could ever escape from the horror that was growing inside me.

I had brought out Aidan's clothes, not mine. Edging into the bathroom, I took a large towel from the hook on the door and wrapped it round me. I sat on the edge of the bath and tried to take long deep breaths, but they hurt my throat and my lungs. I was having a panic attack, I told myself. That was all. It will pass. Breathe in and breathe out; only think about your breathing.

I screwed up my eyes and tried to picture the watch that had been among the things Skye had been wearing when she fell. Nothing was clear to me anymore; nothing made sense.

I stood up and stubbed my toe against the base of the sink, almost cried out, stuffed a hand to my mouth to stop sound escaping. The towel loosened and fell to the floor and I bent to pick it up. My breath was coming in little whooshes and I was aware of moving jerkily. The ends of my fingertips were tingling, as if I had pins and needles.

I went into the living room and stared around. I needed to find Aidan's watch, even while at the same time I knew there probably wasn't a watch to find and I was stumbling fraily around in the dim light like a fool.

His desk had lots of small drawers. I pulled one open. It was full of stationery: a stapler, paper clips, Post-it notes, highlighters, a bundle of thin-nibbed pens held together by a rubber band, a book of first class stamps.

I shut it, pulled open another. Receipts. Bank statements. Everything orderly, methodical.

Next drawer down. Passport. Paper driving license. Membership cards to various art galleries and theaters.

The bottom one. A few photos. I pulled them out. Stop now. I shuffled through them. One of me in a raincoat, smiling. What did I think I was doing?

I laid the photos on the little table and turned to the cupboard beside the television. A few DVDs, a coil of chargers and connectors, a pile of instruction manuals.

On the bookshelves just books. What did I expect? Technical ones about solar power and wind turbines; a few novels; some biographies; a couple of unexpected volumes of poetry. If Aidan hadn't killed Skye and Peggy, I'd never be able to prove it. I couldn't prove his innocence by not finding a clue to his guilt.

A sound and I froze, my hand against my bumping, jolting heart.

A car door banged shut.

It was getting lighter. I didn't know what time it was because my phone was still in the bedroom, on the table next to Aidan.

In the kitchen cupboard were just kitchen things: pots and pans, plates and bowls, a hand-held whisk, a colander. Higher up, a cupboard with glass doors: glasses, tumblers, a nice earthenware jug. Drawers of cutlery, of tin foil and plastic wrap and parchment paper. Shelves of flour and sugar and pasta and rice. Spices and herbs in alphabetical order. Honey, marmalade, jam. A bottle of whiskey and another of gin. A bread bin in which I found the remains of a whole-wheat loaf. I stared at the knives, gleaming sharp in the block.

The most likely place to hide a watch—if there was a watch to hide—was in the bedroom, among the shirts and jerseys, in the pocket of a jacket or at the back of the wardrobe, under the bed. I imagined slithering along the floor like a snake with arms outstretched, or ferreting about among his clothes, while he watched me through half-closed eyes.

I went into the little hall. It was nearly full light now. I tried to work out what time it was, but couldn't tell if minutes or hours had passed since I'd crept from the bedroom. I didn't even know if Aidan was a light or heavy sleeper: we'd barely spent a night together, because I had always insisted he leave. There were beads of sweat on my forehead as I put my hand on the doorknob.

Then I saw the coats and jackets hanging from the hooks by the front door to the flat. I put my hands in each pocket. On the last hook was a small, soft leather duffel bag. I reached in and touched something soft, like a cloth, and then something cold and smooth. I took it out.

A watch, with a worn strap, a large face and Roman numerals. Classy.

I stared at it as it lay in the palm of my hand and the minute hand quivered forward. Eighteen minutes past six.

Not a watch: the watch. The one I had last seen in the bag of Skye's possessions, and then not seen at Peggy's house, the day she had been killed.

Dead sightless eyes, brave purple hair.

The minute hand quivered forward again.

Clutching the watch in the same hand that held the towel, I opened the bedroom door and slid into the room. I needed to push it deep into my backpack, retrieve my clothes and phone, then get out. I tripped over shoes, gathered up my trousers, crawled on all fours toward my backpack, towel unraveling as I went.

"You're up early."

I stopped dead, feeling the watch press against my collarbone where I clutched the towel.

"Morning," I managed to say. I lifted my head: Aidan was half-sitting on the bed, regarding me with tender amusement.

"What time is it?"

"I'm not sure." The watch ticked against my skin.

"What are you doing down there? Have you lost something?"

"I was looking for my knickers. Ah, there they are."

I fumbled my clothes into a pile and pushed the watch inside it, held it against me like a baby.

"I'll just get dressed."

"Come back to bed. It's so early."

"I couldn't sleep. I need to get back. Turn myself around before I get Poppy."

He swung out of bed and crouched beside me, put his arms around me. I breathed in his particular smell—fennel, I thought, or aniseed. He kissed my neck, his lips cool.

"Coffee?"

He stroked my hair, still tangled up in its unraveling braid, and I crouched there like a sweaty animal with nowhere to hide.

"OK. I'll put my clothes on then have a quick cup."

Clutching backpack, shoes and clothes, with the towel still around me, I backed out of the room and into the bathroom. I locked the door, put the watch at the bottom of my backpack, hurriedly pulled my clothes on, then was hit by the sudden realization that I'd left the pile of photos on the living-room table.

I got there at the same time as he came into the room, knotting his toweling robe around him.

"I could make us breakfast," he said.

"I'm not hungry," I said and sat down on the table, feeling the slide of photos beneath me.

He ran his fingers down my cheek. I bared my teeth in what was meant to be a smile.

"Just coffee then," he said.

"You know me. It takes me time to get going in the morning."

I was trying to remember how a normal person behaves, but it felt sketchy and transparent. I swept the photos into my backpack when his back was turned. I wrapped my hands around the cup and heard Aidan talking about a friend of his who was a family lawyer: would I like him to ask his advice, in confidence of course, about Jason's threats?

"Maybe," I said. "But wait a bit first to see what happens."

I need to be careful, I said to him. One step at a time. The stakes are so high. Perhaps it will all just blow over.

He knows everything, I thought. I told him every last thing.

And then, finally, I was at his door. He held my face in both hands and stared into my eyes and I tried to gaze at him, not to look away, but I thought I wouldn't manage it. I wanted to scream and howl and strike out with all the strength in my body.

He kissed me again. I let him kiss me. I kissed him back. Bile rose up in me, a physical recoil that it took all my will not to give in to. When I got home, I would scrub my teeth until my gums bled and shower until my skin was raw.

I smiled at him and left.

And when I was out of sight of his windows, I ran and ran.

It had been in my house all the time. It had never been outside. It had been inside. It had been me: I had brought the danger home.

Poppy, I thought as I ran, my breath tearing like strips of adhesive tape being ripped from my lungs. Poppy Poppy Poppy.

FIFTY-SIX

I was in a police interview room. Another police interview room. An officer had asked me if I wanted to make a statement, but I said I needed to talk to the detective in charge of the inquiry. I told them that it was about the murders of Skye Nolan and Peggy Nolan. I knew who had committed the murders and it was urgent and I would only talk to the detective.

The young police sergeant looked confused and also irritated. He said that it was a Saturday, people were at home. I said it didn't matter what day it was. I could see him thinking hard. If this was all rubbish, he would get into trouble. But what if it wasn't?

"You'll need to wait a long while," he said. "I'll have to reach someone. And they'll have to come in."

I said that I could wait and so I found myself in another interview room where there was nothing to do and nothing to look at. I supposed that must be deliberate. Pictures on the wall would be a distraction. And there were nails and pieces of string that could be dangerous, maybe.

While I waited, I took the photos I'd filched out of my bag and leafed through them. At first I didn't see it, but then I did: a group photo of Aidan and his colleagues on some work outing, Aidan at the back. He was wearing the cap. I put the rest of the photos away and kept that one out on the table.

Finally the door opened. I'd hoped that it might be Kelly Jordan, but I wasn't sure if she was formally connected with the inquiry—only connected with me. It wasn't her. It was Ross Durrant. He was wearing trainers and blue trousers and a polo shirt with a blue and white wavy pattern. He looked like he might have come straight from the golf course. I expected him to be angry but he was entirely expressionless and simply sat down opposite me.

"Go," he said, in a quiet voice.

It didn't take very long to explain. I told him about the things that had been found on Skye Nolan's body that Peggy had shown me and how I'd seen them scattered on the floor when I'd found Peggy Nolan. He interrupted to say I had already told him that. How I'd known that something was missing and then I realized it was the watch. He said I'd told him that as well. I described my feeling when I'd remembered that Aidan used to wear a watch but now did not. And then how I'd discovered the watch hidden in his bag, a trophy perhaps, or why would he have had the nerve to keep it. It was entirely distinctive. It would have led back to him. So he must have gone to see Peggy Nolan and killed her and taken the watch.

While I was talking a uniformed officer came into

the room and handed a cardboard file to Ross Durrant. He laid the file on the table in front of him and nodded at the officer who sat down to one side.

When I had finished, there was a long silence.

"Aidan Otley," said the female officer. "That's your boyfriend."

"That's right," I said. "I trusted him."

I looked across at Durrant, but he seemed to be ignoring me. He had flicked open the slender file and was looking at the contents—apparently just a few sheets of paper. He tapped on them with a pen. He took out a piece of paper and looked at it with a frown and then turned to me once more.

"I make that ten interactions with the police force," he said. "Eleven, including this one."

"What about what I've just told you?"

He continued as if he hadn't heard me.

"You first made a report that involved no crime and no perpetrator, but there was a vague accusation made against your ex-partner. Secondly, you contacted Inspector Jordan about a crime that you said was the one you had reported on the previous occasion, even though it hadn't yet been committed."

"I've explained that."

"Thirdly, Inspector Jordan did you the courtesy of coming to your home to inform you about the inquiry."

"And I told her about the doll that had gone missing and reappeared."

"Yes, there's some mention of a doll," said Durrant in a steely tone. "Fourthly, your daughter was interviewed by a child protection officer. Fifthly ..." He paused and looked at the female officer. "Fifthly. Is that a word?" She shrugged in response. "I met you for the first time and we actually diverted officers to interview a number of men that you mentioned. Nothing productive emerged from this. Six: Inspector Jordan once more did you the courtesy of informing you about the progress of the inquiry."

"It wasn't just informing me of the progress of the inquiry," I said, feeling angry now. "You'd discovered it was murder, just as I said it was."

"She also told you that no connection with Skye Nolan had been found with any of the men we interviewed. Seven: you phoned Inspector Jordan about a supposed break-in. Nothing was stolen. It says here in Jordan's report: 'Ms. Moreau said: "I know that your heart must sink every time you hear my voice."' I'll leave that there. It doesn't require comment. Next, as an added bonus, you pitch up at the inquest and engage with the mother of the victim."

"What's the point of all this?"

"It's a useful exercise. It helps clarify the mind. Eight: you phoned Inspector Jordan once more after seeing Peggy Nolan. And then, nine: you phone Inspector Jordan from the scene of Peggy Nolan's murder. She tells you not to touch anything but, by your own admission, you interfere with the scene anyway. It also emerges that your child is at school and that you haven't arranged for anyone to collect her." He looked up from the file. "I assume that someone is looking after your child now. Or have you left her in front of the TV with a packet of crisps and a fizzy drink?"

"She's being looked after," I said. I had a feeling of dread. What if he found out about me breaking into Jason's computer? What if he found out about the legal threat?

"And ten, which is in some ways the most significant, you phone Inspector Jordan, who you seem to be practically stalking by now, and who has not done her career any good by the way she has gone along with your paranoia, to confirm that Aidan Otley has an alibi for the day of Skye Nolan's killing and she confirms that he does indeed have an alibi. He was at a conference in Birmingham. He checked in, he attended a seminar and he spent the night there."

He put the file down and closed it and looked across the table at me.

"That was what confused me," I said. "So before coming here, I phoned a colleague of his. A man called Frederick Gordon. He went to the conference with Aidan. He went to the seminar. But he can't remember seeing Aidan in the evening and he wasn't at breakfast the next morning. He remembers Aidan telling him that he'd overslept."

"He's still been proved to be at an event fifty miles away."

"He could have got back," I said. "Easily."

"So let me get this straight: you've accused your ex-partner, you've accused his housemate—"

"I never accused anybody. All I did was to try to do what was right. I reported a crime. I was asked who Poppy might have interacted with and I answered. I didn't want to cause trouble to people."

"You accused your ex-partner and now you're accusing your current partner. Is that something worth thinking about?"

"I don't know why you're saying all this," I said desperately. "Didn't you hear what I've been saying? I found the thing that you've been looking for all along: the connection between Aidan and Skye Nolan."

Durrant tapped the tabletop several times with the pen and then laid it down.

"All right," he said. "The watch."

"Yes, the watch."

He thought for a moment.

"Whose watch is it? I mean originally."

"I told you. Aidan's. That's the whole point."

"So we go to Aidan's house and find Aidan's watch in Aidan's drawer. What good does that do us?"

"You don't need to go there. I've got it. Look." I bent down and felt in my bag, feeling the slide of photos under my fingers, then finding the smooth round face of the watch. I pulled it out and held it toward him, expecting him to take it, but he drew back.

"You took it?"

"I thought you'd want to see it."

"You've committed an act of theft."

"But it's evidence."

He rested his eyes on me; there was an almost-smile on his lips.

"According to you."

"I told you. I saw it among the possessions that Skye had on her body. That was why he had to get it. That's why he killed Peggy."

"Do you have any record of it? A photograph?"

"Of course I don't. But I'm absolutely certain. I saw it. But what about you? Don't you have photographs of her body? Don't you take photographs of the crime scene?"

Now Ross Durrant looked slightly evasive.

"As you know, it wasn't considered a crime scene at first. It was treated for some days as a suicide. The possessions would have been collected at the hospital. There'll be an inventory of some kind, but it's just a list. There's no photograph."

"As far as you know."

"I do know. There's no photograph."

"But I saw what I saw. Don't you believe me?"

Durrant looked above my head as if he had seen something interesting behind me, but I knew that there was nothing interesting behind me. Only a blank wall.

"I've got this as well," I said and slid the photo of Aidan and his work colleagues across the table.

"I fail to see the relevance of this," he said, glancing at it.

"He's wearing the same cap that Skye Nolan is wearing in a photo her mother sent me. I can show you."

I started fumbling with my mobile, but he put up a hand.

"You know what I think?"

"No, what?"

"This is unproductive meeting number eleven. You know what the rulebook says? It says I should charge you with wasting police time. That can be punished by a fine or up to six months in prison. But some people looking at you carrying out your little battle with your boyfriend and your ex-boyfriend, and getting involved in an inquiry and talking to witnesses and interfering with a murder scene, might think it's not just wasting police time but perverting the course of justice, and then we're talking some serious consequences. You can get anything up to life in prison for that."

I looked at the two officers. I had thought it was going to be all over and I was just starting to realize I'd made a terrible mistake.

"Do you really think I made all of this up?"

Ross Durrant shook his head.

"You know, over the years I've gone into court with eyewitnesses, fingerprints, DNA, and I've still seen the cases fail. The eyewitness was too far away, the fingerprints were smeared, the DNA may have got contaminated in the lab. And what have we got in this case? A child's drawing and a watch that you say you saw in one place and then in another place and now you've stolen it."

"I'm not expecting you to immediately charge him with the two murders," I said, feeling defeated. "Although I'm absolutely certain that Aidan committed both of them. Are you just going to do nothing? Except maybe punish me for trying to be a good citizen."

Ross Durrant looked away from me, glancing at the female officer, and when he turned back to me, he spoke in a tone that didn't sound quite so much as if he hated me.

"Our investigation is continuing. We will investigate anything that seems productive. In the meantime,

Ms. Moreau, maybe you just need to sit back and look at your life. I'm not a psychiatrist, but if you think your ex-boyfriend is a murderer and then you think your current boyfriend is a murderer, then possibly it's not about the boyfriends. I suppose there are people you can talk to about that. And also you've got a little daughter to look after."

"Is that it?" I said. "Are you going back to the golf course?"

His expression darkened. "I was in the park playing football with my two little boys," he said. "But thanks for asking."

He closed the file.

"Aren't you going to take a note of what I said?" I said.

His expression turned sarcastic. "I'm glad that you're taking an interest in police procedure."

"It's not that," I said. "I want you to write down what I said here today." I looked at the female police officer. "In her presence. What's your name?"

"Steiner," she said. "Jan Steiner."

"I'm going to make a note of the meeting myself," I said. "Because in one week, or two weeks or a month, if I'm found dead with my daughter—" I had to stop and swallow because the picture of that suddenly became vivid in my mind. "Then, if that happens, I don't want you two to mysteriously forget that we sat here today and I told you what I've just told you."

Ross Durrant looked at me warily and inclined his head very slightly.

"A note will be made."

"I'll make a note too," I said. "Where people can

find it." I stood up. "And now I have to go back to my life and this man who has killed two women and I don't know who to turn to."

Ross Durrant stood up as well.

"You've worked yourself up," he said. "When you've calmed down a bit, then maybe you can start looking for some help."

"That's why I came here," I said.

FIFTY-SEVEN

Poppy had her hair in pigtails; one was higher than the other, which gave her a lopsided look. She had a thick scratch down one cheek. I knelt and gathered her into me. For a moment, I shut my eyes and felt her heart beating against mine, her breath hot on my neck. Then I held her back from me.

"What happened to your face?"

"Roxie did bit me." She put a finger against the livid line with a tragic air. "She did hurt me."

"Roxie?" I stood up, still holding on to her warm hand like it was the only thing that could keep me safe, and turned to Emily.

"She tried to ride on her back," said Emily. "I put antiseptic cream on it. Jason says it's fine."

Emily wasn't looking as fresh and healthy and pretty as she usually did. Her hair needed washing; there were bruised shadows under her eyes. She was wearing a man's shirt over cotton trousers, and looked more like a child than a pregnant woman.

"Are you OK?"

Her gaze shifted from me, rested on the window of the café where a fly ticked and buzzed uselessly.

"Jason said we shouldn't really talk." Her voice was low.

"And you always do what Jason says?" My voice came out harsher than I intended, almost a growl.

She turned her eyes back to me. "We're married."

I gave a small laugh. "Is that what marriage means?"

"I should go."

"Emily, don't you go to work anymore?"

"I'm taking a break from working," she said.

I wanted to shake her, tell her to open her eyes and see what was happening to her. Who was I to talk, to tell anyone what to do about anything? I looked down at Poppy's burnished head, then picked up her overnight bag.

"I'm sorry that I didn't have time to wash her clothes from yesterday."

"That's not a problem. We'll be off then," I said.

"Tess?"

"Yes?"

"Oh . . . it's nothing really. Bye."

"Take care," I said and saw tears spring into Emily's eyes.

"What shall we do today?" I asked Poppy as we walked hand in hand toward the bus stop.

I was so crowded out with fears, I could barely speak. Because what should *I* do today, any day? My breath was raw in my chest, my legs thin and shaky as reeds. My body—the body that a few hours ago had been in Aidan's arms, had been touched and entered by Aidan—now felt corrupted and broken.

"Grandmother's Footsteps?" she said hopefully. "Hide and Seek, and I'll hide and you will find me."

"OK," I said in a bright voice.

But maybe, I thought, we should go and stay with my mother, or Sylvie, who lived in Newcastle. I had a friend living in Hamburg, another who'd moved to New Zealand. Or I should go to Gina and tell her everything, or Nadine perhaps, who was always so calm and practical and laid a soothing hand on the most seething of troubles.

But would they believe me? Would anyone? I didn't know if I would believe me, if I were them.

We boarded the bus. Poppy sat close to me, swaying against me as the bus rounded corners. When we got off, I tried to hold her hand, but she pulled away and skipped in front of me, her small backpack bumping against her body, her pigtails bouncing.

"Tess!"

Bernie was coming toward us, striding rapidly.

I found myself almost glad to see him. He was irritating but just a normal kind of irritating—making too much of an effort and hitting the wrong note. OK, so he stood too close and wasn't good at respecting boundaries, but really he just wanted to be liked. He hadn't killed anyone.

"And how's Pops?" he asked, grinning at her, his teeth yellow.

Poppy stared at his left hand, raised in greeting, at the rounded nubs where his fingers used to be.

"Where are they now?" she asked, pointing.

"That's a good question."

"Did they die?"

"I suppose they did, in a way."

"Are they in the ground?"

"I don't think so."

"Do they hurt?"

"No, not anymore."

"Roxie did hurt me." Poppy put a finger on her cheek.

"A dog," I said.

"Going home?"

"Yes."

"See you later." Bernie gave his wheezing laugh at some private joke.

We turned into our road. There was a figure sitting on the doorstep and as we approached, the figure stood. Aidan.

I halted, took Poppy's hand and held it tight.

"Mummy? Mummy, you're hurting."

He was waving at us, his hand high above his head. Then he came loping toward us down the road. He took my face in his hands and kissed me full on the mouth, then bent toward Poppy and touched her gently on the shoulder. I remembered how I used to like the way he was respectful with her, a bit awkward.

"I've missed your mother, and I've missed you," he said. "But I'm back now. We're going on a picnic!"

Poppy stared up at him, her eyes round. She backed

against my knees. Why had I never sensed that she was scared of him? I had searched desperately for signs and clues, and not seen what was in front of my eyes.

"I'm not sure—" I began.

"I've probably brought way too much," he said. "But whatever we don't eat now, we can save for later. I thought we could go to Epping Forest. Do you like climbing trees, Poppy?"

"No."

"I've looked at the buses. They go every ten minutes."

"I'm quite tired," I said.

Aidan took my hand and kissed the knuckles.

"So am I," he said softly. "We didn't get much sleep, did we?"

"I think I may be coming down with something."

"It's all been too much for you," he said.

"Coming down from where?" Poppy tugged at my hand. "Where are you up?"

Perhaps I actually was ill—the ground didn't feel steady under my feet and when I tilted my head to the blue sky and small clouds, the trees seemed to tip toward me. I wanted to fold up on myself—fold up over Poppy and close her into my embrace.

How could Aidan not see? How did he not know? He was smiling, saying things about how he'd spent the morning thinking of me. I thought of running past him with Poppy, getting into the house and slamming the door shut.

But in the reeling nausea of my thoughts, I understood—and it was the only thing I understood—he must not know that I knew. Our safety lay in Aidan thinking he had got away with it.

"Let me drop off Poppy's stuff and get a picnic blanket," I said.

Aidan pulled out his mobile and looked at the time.

"Sure. There's a bus in a minute and then another in twelve minutes—we can get that one. We're not in any hurry." Again, that tender, knowing smile.

I rummaged in my bag for the door keys and felt the photos, the watch, under my fingers. I let us into the hall, then into the flat. Poppy picked up Sunny and held him so he dangled from her.

"You won't hurt me. You're my friend."

She put a fat kiss on his shabby orange head and I saw his tail twitch ominously.

"Let's go then," said Aidan.

"I don't want to," said Poppy.

"It's OK, darling. We can play Grandmother's Footsteps."

"I want Sunny."

"Sunny will be here waiting for you."

"I want Milly. I want chocolate. I want a banana. I want my crayons. I want ice cream."

"I'll buy you an ice cream," said Aidan good-naturedly. "There's a little café near where we get off the bus."

"I want a paddling pool."

"We'll swing you," said Aidan. "Swing you high all the way to the bus. Won't we, Tess?"

I nodded. Part of me was thinking this wasn't real, part was thinking I had to run away with Poppy right now, run and run and never come back. I imagined us tearing down the road together; I imagined him calmly walking after us, reaching us. Then what?

Aidan took Poppy's hand. I looked down, seeing the way his larger hand curled around her small one. She was so little.

FIFTY-EIGHT

We swung Poppy to the bus stop. We swung her as
we walked into the forest. We looked like the perfect
little family. I had a blanket and Aidan had the picnic
in his backpack. He was wearing a green tee shirt and
gray cotton trousers and he looked relaxed and happy.
He identified trees, gestured to a buzzard wheeling
above us, pointed out the elderflower growing thickly
along the path.

"We should make elderflower juice," he said. "Would
you like that, Poppy?"

"No."

He grinned as though her answer pleased him.

When we spread out the picnic, he had brought a
bottle of champagne and two glasses wrapped in newspaper to keep them safe. He had fizzy drink in a can
for Poppy and lots of miniature foods—tiny falafels
and sausages and salmon rolled up with cream cheese.
There were cherries as well and strawberries. Chocolate biscuits, which were sticky in the heat.

He poured out champagne and we clinked glasses

and he said, "Here's to us," and tapped his glass against Poppy's drink as well.

She edged toward me. I took a sip of the champagne, and when he wasn't looking tipped the rest onto the dry mossy ground. He reached up and delicately removed a twig from my hair. I couldn't do this. If he touched me again, I would lash out. If he touched Poppy, I would claw at his face.

He put his hand over mine and I let him. I turned my head and I smiled at him and felt disgust in my throat like thick silt. How could he not tell?

On the way home, Poppy went to sleep curled up against me and I carried her from the bus stop, refusing Aidan's offers to take her from me. He followed me into the flat and waited while I laid Poppy on her bed.

"How asleep is she?"

I knew what he meant and pretended not to.

"She'll wake in a few minutes. She doesn't usually nap in the day."

"I understand, of course, but she doesn't seem that happy I'm back in her life."

"She's tired."

"She wants to have you to herself. I get it." He smiled at me—that small half-smile I used to find so sympathetic. "I'm sure she'll get used to me in time."

I couldn't do this. I felt physically incapable of meeting his eye, of returning his smile, of letting him lay his hands on me, of kissing him back. I turned toward him.

"Aidan. It was lovely, but you know that nothing's really changed, don't you?"

"Everything's changed."

"No. I mean, the reason that I ended things—it was because I wasn't in a good state. I needed to sort things out and I still do."

"I know. And I know what you're going through and I can help, I can be there for you. I can be your rock, the person you can always turn to."

"I think," I said as firmly and kindly as I could, "that we should put things on hold. Just till I'm ready."

Never never never never.

"No," Aidan said. "I think in the past I sometimes felt a bit raw because you always put Poppy before me, but one of the reasons I fell in love with you in the first place was that you are such a fabulous mother. Of course you have to put her first. I understand that now in a way that I didn't before."

"But I have no room in my life for a relationship."

"I don't think that's true. Think of last night. To me it felt like coming home. And I believe it was like that for you as well."

Then he put a hand on my naked arm. I looked down at his four fingers, slightly apart, pressing into my skin.

"You trusted me," he said, speaking slowly, each word distinct. "You trusted me with *everything*, Tess, everything you've been thinking and feeling. Everything you've done. Things that you can't tell anyone else, mustn't tell anyone else. I will always remember that."

What was he saying? I blinked; my eyes felt scratchy and sore.

"I would never tell a soul," he continued. "I know what you stand to lose if, for instance, Jason and his lawyer found out about you breaking into his house, hacking into his computer, sending yourself those emails, seeing Inga after they'd given you that final warning. I know how completely terrifying that must feel."

He meant Poppy: that's what I stood to lose. I stared at him, unable to turn away.

"You're in a horrible position." His voice was mild and tender; his eyes were on me. "People haven't believed you: Jason, the police. They think you are hysterical, mad, dangerous. I don't think that. I know you. I know what a fierce, loyal and wonderful woman you are. You'd do anything to protect Poppy. I know that. You're on a knife edge."

I tried to speak, but my voice faltered.

"I'm here for you," he said. "Come what may. So don't say we should end things or put them on hold. Don't say that, my lovely Tess, because what would I do if you said that?"

I understood and I saw him seeing I understood. His gaze never wavered and his warm hand remained on my arm, his fingers pushing into my flesh. Slender fingers, like a pianist's.

"Mummy! Mummy Mummy Mummy."

"Coming now," I called. I pulled back from Aidan, tried to give him a smile that wouldn't look like a snarl of fear and disgust. "Sorry," I said. "You need to go."

"No worries," he said. "I'll call you later. We'll make plans."

Poppy and I played Grandmother's Footsteps in the little garden that I could cover in five strides. Poppy stood with her back to me, her body tense with the effort of not turning.

I took a small step.

Aidan had killed two women because of me. He killed Skye because she must have threatened to tell me about their fling, if *fling* was the right word for a man "rescuing" a woman when drunk, taking her back to her flat and having sex with her. I remembered Aidan and me at the party after I discovered Jason's infidelities, me wrapping my arms around his neck. I heard my words: *If you ever cheat on me, we're over. No second chances.*

Another step. Poppy was practically vibrating with her desire to look round.

I saw Skye in the restaurant, pointing a finger at me, smiling and smiling, and opposite me sat Aidan.

My small world had been bristling with acts of domestic surveillance: everyone had been watching everyone else, tracking everyone else, keeping their own secrets and prying into other people's.

I thought about the cap that Skye had held in her hands that evening, Aidan's cap, and Aidan, sitting beside me with his unwavering expression, had seen it. She must have slipped it into Poppy's little backpack that day in the park with Jason: the cap he was wearing in the photo I had, the cap Skye had worn in that photo on my phone, the cap I had upstairs. The whole thing had been a show she had put on for him.

Another small step. Poppy turned and I froze and she grinned and turned back again.

Skye must have followed Aidan to my house after

the second time he'd gone to hers. She had watched us and tracked us. She had retrieved the mutilated Milly from my trash and she had sewn it back into a mockery of a beloved rag doll and returned it to me via Poppy. I had shown the doll to Aidan, and Aidan had gone the following night when he was supposed to be at the conference and killed her, pushing her from her balcony as if she were a rag doll herself.

Aidan had also spied on us, kept track of me when I thought I was free, and I in my turn had spied on Jason, trailing him, breaking into his house and his computer.

My daughter had been a spy in her own life as well, though she hadn't been able to decode the things that she had heard and witnessed. Poppy had watched her father kissing a strange woman. Poppy had watched Aidan with Skye, maybe from her open window or maybe from the top of the stairs while I slept. I would never know how much she had seen and heard and taken into her crowded imagination.

I will kill you, you fucking cunt. I will push you from your balcony and no one will know. Except my daughter had known, with her eyes like saucers and her ears taking in everything.

Again. I could almost reach out and touch Poppy now.

Skye and then, when he realized that he wasn't quite safe, Peggy. Coming to see me after he'd done it, looking tired and peaceful. He had thought it was all over and now we could be together again.

I stood quite still in the little garden, the sun beating down and the birds singing, thinking, tiptoeing forward. Aidan wanted me. He wanted us. He thought in some horrible way that we belonged to him, and now he believed he had us: *You're on a knife edge*, I heard him say.

Poppy had watched and Poppy had listened and Poppy had tried to tell me with her drawing, her obscenities, her night terrors, the way that she clutched at me with pincer fingers, her high-wire anxiety and need. I'd seen all the signs and misread them all.

Now she whirled round, her hair flying and her mouth agape in a shout of laughter.

"I do see you move!" she shouted in triumph. "I do see."

FIFTY-NINE

Later Poppy was so fiercely tired that she couldn't go to sleep. I read her a story and switched off the light and lay beside her on the bed, stroking her hair, but I could feel her tense, springy little body. The doorbell rang. I went to the door and Aidan was standing there smiling, holding up a bottle of wine.

"I ordered a takeaway," he said. "I thought you wouldn't feel like cooking after a day like today."

It felt like a test. I'd sent him away. I'd said I would call him and now here he was. It was a demonstration of my powerlessness. I stepped aside and he walked through.

"I'm trying to get Poppy to sleep," I said weakly.

"Don't mind me," he said. He took a wine glass from the cabinet and twisted the cap off the bottle and poured himself a drink. "Can I get you one?"

"Not just now," I said.

He sat down on the sofa and picked up a magazine, a free one that was pushed through my letterbox once a month and that I normally put straight in the trash.

"This will probably take some time," I said.

He smiled and raised the glass. "No hurry."

I went back into Poppy's room. I felt unsteady. I sat down on Poppy's bed.

"Don't you want to cuddle up and go to sleep?"

Poppy loudly insisted that she wasn't tired and wanted to play with me and she wanted me to stay with her forever and ever. I noted that she didn't want to sleep and she wanted to play, but she wanted to play in her room and she only wanted to play with me.

"I want to be with you."

"You are with me, honey?"

"Only you."

"We need to be nice to Aidan as well," I said.

"Only you," she said firmly. "For ever and happy after."

I leaned over and told her to hush and kissed her on her forehead. I tried to tell her a story from memory and she told me I was getting it wrong, so I had to admit defeat and turn the light back on. I read a book and then another book and tried to make my voice gradually quieter and more soothing until finally I looked up and Poppy's eyes were closed. I turned the light off and went into the living room, which didn't feel mine anymore. Aidan looked up and smiled.

"I poured you a glass," he said. "I thought we'd both earned it."

"Thank you," I said.

"I opened a bag of crisps as well. I hope that's all right."

"That's fine." I felt like an actor in the play of my

own life and I had to perform the part perfectly. I took a sip of wine and it felt corrosive. I ate a crisp to disguise the taste and the crisp felt like cardboard and my mouth became so dry I couldn't swallow, so I needed to take another sip of the foul wine. "I think she's finally asleep."

"She was overexcited," said Aidan. "Don't you remember that from when you were a child? You become so tired that you can't sleep."

"Yes, I do. It's—" I stopped. My mind was a blank. I had forgotten my lines. I literally couldn't think of a single thing to say.

He leaned forward with an expression of concern and touched my cheek.

"Are you all right?"

"I'm tired as well." I laughed. It sounded convincing. "Just like Poppy." I took another sip of wine while I thought of something to say. "You should have phoned to let me know you were coming." I said this in the lightest tone I could manage. "I might have had people here?"

"You didn't mention it," he said. "Anyway, what would it matter? You know, like in those films where the hero surprises the heroine in a restaurant and sings to her in front of all the customers and everyone applauds at the end."

I thought of how I'd always hated scenes like that, even in films I liked. I could never push away the idea of how embarrassing it would be in real life, however much you loved the person who was doing it. I made myself smile.

"Please don't ever do anything like that to me. I've got a very low embarrassment threshold."

Aidan laughed. "I can't guarantee it." He picked up the magazine. "I was just looking at the property ads in here. There are a couple of lovely places on the market."

I didn't answer.

"What we need to talk about is what's best. I'd been thinking that the question was whether you two should move in with me or I should move in with you. Probably I should move in with you because my flat is tiny and has no garden. But maybe we should both sell our flats and buy somewhere bigger together, make a new start."

"I couldn't," I said immediately, unable to stop myself. "I just couldn't."

"Why?"

"There are lots of reasons. I found moving here unbelievably stressful."

"But you were doing it on your own."

"I couldn't do it to Poppy. She's in such an unsettled state. She just needs stability."

He smiled again. "Don't you see, Tess, that's all the more reason we should do this? It would make her part of a proper family. It would give her a feeling of safety and security." I started to make a stammering attempt at answering this, but he carried on speaking. "Don't you understand? I didn't just fall in love with you. I fell in love with you and Poppy together. I want to protect you both. I won't let anything happen to you. I won't let anything come between us."

I was saved from having to say anything at all by the doorbell and the delivery of the food. I took the bulging plastic bag from the young woman in the motorcycle helmet.

"You don't need to tip her," Aidan said from behind me. "I added a tip online."

I started to distribute the containers of food on the table. I fetched plates and glasses and cutlery from the kitchen. When I opened the cutlery drawer, I saw the bread knife and—with a sudden vividness that horrified me—I imagined picking it up and walking toward Aidan, holding the knife behind me, and then plunging it into his chest. I was sure I could do it. I wanted to do it. But other images followed this in my mind: Poppy just a few feet away; years in prison or a mental institution for me; Poppy with her father, lost to me forever.

Aidan had ordered Thai food, which was normally a favorite of mine: the lime and the chili and the garlic and the lemongrass. But either there was something wrong with the food or there was something wrong with me because there was a sour under taste to everything and it felt both too salty and too sweet. I drank tumbler after tumbler of water from the tap.

"I think we should go away together," Aidan said.

"You mean, just us two?"

"No, the three of us. That's what I mean by 'we.'"

"It's term time."

"We could go on a weekend. I'll find a cottage. Somewhere remote, maybe by the sea, where we can go for walks and build sandcastles with Poppy. I think it would be good to spend some intense, quality time together."

Now I did look Aidan full in the face. I knew what he had done, but I still didn't feel I understood this man opposite me. I imagined a stranger eavesdropping on this conversation. Would they think they were witnessing a touching love scene? Perhaps for him it really was a touching love scene. But what kind of love was it? How was it going to be expressed when Poppy and I were with him in some remote place, out of sight, out of earshot?

When he'd finished eating, he started to pile up the plates and the food containers.

"I'll do it," I said, but he shook his head.

"I insist. You just sit there."

I did just sit there. I didn't look at my phone or pick up a book. I listened to the sound of cleaning in the kitchen, the kettle, the coffee grinder, until Aidan came back with the French press and two mugs and some chocolate biscuits arranged on a small plate.

I was grateful for the coffee in the way I might have been grateful for a sudden cold shower. As I drank it, no milk and very hot, I felt I was jolting myself back to life. He chatted while we drank and I nodded at the things he said. Then he got up and walked behind me and took the cup from my hand and put it on the table. I felt his lips on the nape of my neck and his hand moved down the front of my shirt and inside my bra and I said to myself: am I really going to go through with this? Can I? I thought of the old cliché: not tonight, I've got a headache. Tonight I really did have a headache that was located just behind my forehead and was radiating waves of nausea down through my jaw and into my neck.

I was an object, a thing. It was not me; I was not here. I let myself be led through to the bedroom and undressed and pushed back on the bed and kissed and pawed and licked and my limbs pushed apart and the weight of him on top of me. I held him tight so that he couldn't see my face and I could look past him up at the ceiling.

Afterward he lay back and I turned the light off and felt sleepless like my daughter, except that I thought I would never be able to sleep again for the rest of my life. Aidan murmured a few things, but I tried to breathe in a rhythmical way that mimicked sleep and after a few minutes I could feel the slow coming and going of his breathing next to me in the darkness.

Wasn't he going to leave?

I got out of bed and went to the bathroom and peed and then got into the shower and washed my hair and all over my body, scrubbing and scrubbing. I dried myself and got back into bed, as close to the edge on my side as I could manage. I turned on my side with my back to him and stared into the darkness.

This man lying peacefully beside me had killed two women and was threatening to tell Jason and his lawyer about behavior that would cause me to lose Poppy unless I stayed with him, in a monstrous charade of a relationship.

I was in no doubt that he would do that. He would destroy me rather than lose me: that was his version of love. That was the man whose chest rose and fell in easy sleep.

Who could I turn to? Who would believe me now? I was like the girl who had cried wolf too many times. The police didn't believe me; to them I was bitter and paranoid and a nuisance. Jason thought I was jealous, vengeful and unhinged. My friends, sympathetic and supportive, saw me as a woman under stress, who wasn't really coping with the life of a single mother. My GP had told me I needed to meditate and see a therapist, because the horror was in my imagination, running amok.

It was real. This was my life. There was nobody who could rescue me.

I thought of telling my mother. Then I thought of what had happened to Peggy, Skye's mother.

I knew that I had only one task: to protect Poppy. Nothing else mattered, including myself. So how could I do that? Could I lie, night after night, year after year, next to the man who had strangled Skye Nolan and then strangled her mother? I would do anything for Poppy. But that?

I imagined again running away with Poppy, leaving the country and never coming back. It took only a few seconds of thought to see that as a hopeless fantasy. Where would I go? What would I do? In this world of computers and credit cards and passports and CCTV cameras, someone like me couldn't possibly escape.

But what if Aidan simply got tired of living with Poppy and me? Could I just wear him down, making him sick of me the way so many husbands get sick of their wives and wives get sick of their husbands? But I felt sure that nothing I could do would make him bored with us. He would remain fixed in his unyielding sense of ownership. He would never tire of having a woman and a little girl in a cage, to do what he wanted with.

I turned in the bed and looked at his dim outline in the darkness. I could hear him, I could smell him. At this moment, he was entirely in my power. If it were just me, would I be able to do something to him? To make myself safe from him forever? The knife lay in the kitchen drawer. But I wasn't alone. What would it be like for Poppy to be the child of a murderer?

I felt like I was staring into a deep mist, that there was an answer somewhere in that mist, if only I could find it. As I lay there, all through that terrible night, I felt I was getting nearer to it, that it was gradually hardening and taking shape as I got closer and closer and then I fell asleep.

SIXTY

Aidan was up early. I lay in bed and listened to him in the shower, singing to himself. Through half-closed lids, I watched him pulling on his clothes. He sat on the bed beside me; I could feel him watching me and I wanted to scream, kick out, drag my nails over his face, obliterate him. I pretended to be asleep and at last he stood up again.

He went to the shops and came back with a disproportionate number of croissants and pastries that he warmed in the oven. He put a cloth over the little table in the garden and laid it with plates and a jam jar of yellow roses that were bending over our fence from next door. He put strawberries in a bowl. There was a French press of coffee for the two of us, with a jug of heated milk on the side, and a mug of foaming hot chocolate for Poppy.

"And guess what?" Triumphantly, he produced a packet of marshmallows, ripped it open and dropped two pink and two white ones into her steaming mug. "How's that for a Sunday breakfast, Poppy?"

Poppy looked at her drink, looked at Aidan, looked at me. Her face was blotchy; her mouth was a thin, straight line.

"No."

Aidan laughed. I put a pastry on her plate and she pushed it away. I could feel the fury building inside her. Inside me.

"What are the plans for today?" Aidan asked.

"We will play a game," said Poppy imperiously. She pointed a finger at me. "You have to be the mummy. I'm the baby."

"So what am I in this game?"

Poppy flicked an angry glance at Aidan. "You aren't in the game."

"Oh dear," he said mildly.

Poppy slid off her chair, breakfast untouched, and stomped to the end of the garden, where she squatted to look for worms, jabbing her fingers into the soft earth.

"I'm sorry about that. But she'll come round to you," I said.

"I hope so. What am I doing wrong?"

"You're doing nothing wrong." I took his hand under the table. "You're doing everything right."

He leaned toward me slightly. "God, you are beautiful," he said in a low voice.

I lifted his hand and kissed the knuckles. I saw us from the outside: a man and a woman sitting close together in the fresh summer morning, intimate, murmuring softly to each other, while a little girl played a few feet away. I just had to act that woman, smile when she would smile, reach up and touch the man's face when she would. My role was a woman in love, while my skin crawled.

"Come back tonight," I said softly, as ugly thoughts crammed in my throat. "I'll ask Gina to have Poppy for a sleepover and she can take her to school tomorrow morning."

"Really?"

"It's not good for us to always have Poppy around. We need some time when it's just you and me."

I felt his hand on my thigh.

Smile, I told myself. I smiled. Kiss him, I directed myself, and I put my lips on his lips and felt his mouth curve beneath mine.

"Now go," I said. "I'll give Poppy my undivided attention and tonight I'm all yours."

He went and I could breathe again.

Sixty-one

I looked at the dinner table and took a deep breath. Everything had been done. All the arrangements had been made. As for the dinner itself, I had never done anything like this in my life before. I'd placed knives and forks and spoons precisely around the plates and folded patterned paper napkins on both plates. I had two different wine glasses and a tumbler for the water all placed just so, like in the sort of restaurant that had always made me feel ill at ease. I struck a match and lit the single orange candle in the middle of the table. I wondered if it was all a bit too much.

The front doorbell rang. I looked at my watch. I had told Aidan to come at about 7:30 and the time was now 7:27. I took a deep breath and opened the door.

"You look fantastic," he said and leaned forward and kissed me on the lips. He held up two wine bottles. "I wasn't sure what we were eating."

As he stepped inside, he took a bunch of keys from his pocket and smiled again as he shook it.

"Time I got my own key," he said.

"I'll get one cut for you."

Though I knew he already had one. He'd let himself in to search through Poppy's room; he'd probably come at other times as well.

I opened one of his bottles and poured wine for us both. We clinked glasses. He smiled at me and I smiled back at him. I could do this. I felt icy with hatred and rage.

"We've got so much to talk about," he said.

I sat down next to him on the sofa and offered him a dish of almonds, which I'd roasted and sprinkled with salt.

"These are great," he said.

"You're right," I said. "I mean, not that the nuts are great, but that we've got a lot to talk about. But can I make a suggestion?"

"Of course."

"Can we not talk about anything big this evening? I think we've earned ourselves an evening where we just eat and drink and don't talk about anything important. I mean, we've got time, haven't we?"

We finished our first glass of wine and then we sat down at the table. I had made salmon blinis for a starter and for the main course I had fried two duck breasts and accompanied them with just a green salad, from a bag, tipped into a bowl and sprinkled with salad dressing from a bottle. I had gone to the supermarket and looked for what was as simple as possible while seeming like plausible dinner party food.

As we ate we made conversation. I asked him about

where he had been on holiday in recent years and where he would go on holiday now, if he could go anywhere.

"Are you planning a surprise?" he said.

"I'm just curious. We still have so much to learn about each other."

I felt myself forgetting what he said almost as he was telling it to me. I think he wanted to go somewhere in South Africa where you could walk and swim in the sea. Or was it Australia?

I found it possible to smile and nod and ask questions and move the conversation on, but I found it completely impossible to eat anything at all. I knew that I couldn't swallow any food and if I tried I would instantly gag and vomit. Instead I made a show of cutting up the food and shifting it around on my plate and then, once or twice, stabbing a piece of duck breast with my fork and raising it toward my mouth and then seeming to think of something to say and putting my fork down again.

I took one or two very small sips of wine. I could drink, but I had to keep my head clear. Mainly I drank water, glass after glass of it. Afterward, I cut up some strawberries and mango on to a plate and I was able, just about, to eat a couple of pieces, even though they felt toxic in my mouth, stinging and sickly sweet.

I made the coffee and we sat on the sofa together. I managed to drink some coffee. I liked that it was too hot. I liked the way it scalded my tongue. It was like deliberately giving myself electric shocks or cutting myself.

And then I led him to the bedroom.

I had given into sex before with boyfriends, with Jason: easier to let it happen than say no. This was different. Now it was like being a prostitute, without any sense of shame, without pleasure but without pain as well. I had dressed for it. I had worn a red dress that I had bought years earlier and didn't much care for because it was bright and sexy and drew attention to me, but it was the sort of thing that Aidan might appreciate. I wore lacy black underwear that just about matched if you didn't look too closely. I would rather have turned the light off, but I left it on. Seeing everything that was happening made it worse for me, much worse. But I decided it might make it more exciting for him.

The sex wasn't exactly an out-of-body experience. As I did things to him and let him do things to me, I experienced a certain level of disgust but it was controllable. It was like when you leave some fish remains in the kitchen trash for a day too long and you have to deal with them. The smell is awful but manageable as you pull the trash bag out of the trash and tie it up and carry it to the trash can outside. I still managed to smile and groan and gasp and cry out at the appropriate moments.

When it was over, I was able to lie on the wet patch and not be overwhelmed by repulsion.

"That was wonderful," he murmured, stroking me.

I murmured something in reply and then got out of bed. As I left the bedroom, I didn't put my dressing gown on. Why would I put a dressing gown on in my own flat, just to go to the bathroom? Casually I pushed the bedroom door shut behind me. As I took a couple of strides across the living room, I felt his sperm trickling down the inside of my thigh.

His jacket was still over the back of the chair where he had hung it when he arrived. I put my hand into one pocket and then the other. Good.

I crept into the little hall and eased the front door open to put the envelope half under the pot but visible. I was still naked. I didn't have time to put anything on, but I crouched down so that nobody could see me. Then I closed the front door, very, very gently, and went to the bathroom and peed and washed as much of him out of me as I could and then went back to bed.

Aidan was already asleep, almost with a smile on his face, one arm flung back.

I got back into the bed with him. I had to. If he woke up in the night, I had to be there beside him. Before turning off the light, I looked at him and I was struck by a strange idea: he looked truly contented. This awful rubbishy, sleazy charade that I had performed, so crude and overdone, was exactly what he wanted from me.

I set the alarm on my phone and made sure it was plugged in and charging, and then I rechecked that the alarm was set to the right time and switched on, and that the phone really was connected and wouldn't run out of battery.

Of course there was no chance of me sleeping. I

was sure of that. How could I possibly sleep? But I switched the light off, lay back and immediately fell asleep and had a night not of turbulent nightmares but of calmness, of floating in a warm sea, safe and warm and looking up at the stars.

SIXTY-TWO

The alarm woke me with a start and that strange feeling of a day that isn't like a normal day, a day when you have an exam or the beginning of a holiday, a wedding or a funeral. As I sat up, Aidan stirred and murmured. He opened his eyes and smiled at me.

"Hi, honey," he said.

I got out of bed. I wanted to get into the shower, but I couldn't. He might have joined me and that would be disastrous. I went into the bathroom and quickly washed my face and under my arms. That would have to do. I returned to the bedroom and pulled on knickers and jeans and a tee shirt.

"I'll make coffee while you're in the shower," I said as casually as I could manage.

"Sounds good."

I went into the kitchen and put the kettle on. When I heard the shower, I ran to the front door. The envelope was there. I felt a tremor of alarm, but it was in a slightly different position. I closed the door once again as quietly as I could. After some desperate fiddling and rearranging Aidan's jacket, I looked around. There was nothing else, was there?

Just one thing.

I picked up my mobile and dialed 999.

"Which service?"

"Police," I said. There was a pause. Please hurry, please hurry, I silently prayed. I heard a voice. I gave my name and my address.

"I'm in terrible danger. My partner has said he's going to kill me. I'm going to be killed."

"Is your partner in the room?"

"He's in another room. He'll come in any second."

"A car's on its way. It'll be there in a few minutes. Can you leave the premises?"

"No, I can't. It's not safe."

I repeated my address to make sure they'd got it right.

"Another thing: you need to contact Inspector Kelly Jordan and Inspector Ross Durrant. Kelly Jordan and Ross Durrant, in charge of the investigation of Skye Nolan. They must come as well. It's really important. Have you got that?"

"Why?"

"Just give them the message. Say I'm in danger. Matter of life and death. I've got to stop, I think he's coming."

I put my phone down on the table. I could hear Aidan, up in the bedroom. He was dressing and while he was dressing, he was humming something. The kettle had boiled, but I ignored that. I opened one of the drawers and took out a pair of kitchen scissors. I pulled the collar of my tee shirt away from my neck and cut through the seam. I put the scissors back in the drawer. I grabbed the cut pieces of the shirt with both hands and tore the material, just an inch or so. It wasn't really necessary, but it might help in the first couple of minutes.

Aidan came into the room, all fresh and scrubbed from the shower. He looked like he was glowing. He moved into the space like he owned it.

"Is the coffee ready?" he said.

"Sorry," I said. "I was in another world." I wasn't going to make any coffee. "What time do you need to be at work? I can make you breakfast. Would you like some toast or I could fry some eggs and bacon. I think I might have some pastries in the freezer." I had no bacon, I had no pastries. I could have said anything: kippers, eggs benedict, kedgeree, deviled kidneys. We weren't going to have any kind of breakfast.

He looked puzzled. "What happened to your shirt?"

I looked down at it as if I had only just noticed it. "It got torn."

"I can see that. But you only just put it on. What happened?"

"It got caught on something."

He continued to look puzzled, but also the first stirrings of suspicion showed on his face. "Is something up?"

For a moment, I was at a loss. Why weren't they here yet? Hadn't they heard my message properly? Could they have taken it down wrong? I'd said it twice. Was this all about to go in utterly the wrong direction?

"No, everything's fine," I said. "So what do you want for breakfast?"

"I don't know. Just a piece of toast. And coffee."

"Yes, of course. I'll make them."

I wondered whether I was going to have to go through the performance of finding bread and grinding coffee when I heard a car outside and heard voices and footsteps and then a ring on the door.

"What's going on?" Aidan asked.

I didn't answer. I opened the flat door and then the front door to two uniformed police officers. I stepped aside and gestured them inside. They were tall men and they bowed their heads as they entered, as if the ceiling was too low for them. In fact, the two of them in their visibility vests with all the straps and buckles and paraphernalia did make the room look small. They stared around quizzically. Aidan stared at them, his face almost comical with surprise.

"There was a call," one of them said.

"It was from me," I said. "My name is Tess Moreau." I gestured at Aidan. "This is Aidan Otley. He said he was going to kill me. He said he was going to kill me, the way he killed Skye Nolan and Peggy Nolan."

Aidan gave an uneasy laugh.

"Is this a joke? A crazy sick joke?"

"No," I said. I felt tall and strong.

Aidan's eyes flickered between me and the policemen; his mouth was pulled into a kind of quivering smirk.

"This is ridiculous," he said. "Ridiculous and insane. She's insane. I didn't say anything like that. I haven't killed anyone. This is all rubbish ..." He pointed at me. "That shirt. She did that to herself."

The two officers looked at me.

"What's all this about?" said one of them.

"Two detectives are on their way," I said. "They should be here soon."

"What do you mean? Why are they on their way?"

"Just wait."

The two officers didn't seem happy about the idea of just waiting. They started to ask Aidan some questions, but he was dismissive:

"This is all rubbish," he said. "I don't know why you're even here. I'm going to be late for work."

"Apparently this young woman reported an emergency."

"When?"

"About ten minutes ago."

Aidan opened his mouth and closed it. He looked behind him toward the bedroom and the shower and then back at me. He stared at me directly and gave a very slight shake of the head. Even with the two police officers there it made me shiver.

"What have you done, Tess?" His voice was gentle.

I didn't reply. I didn't even look at him.

It was a few minutes before I heard a car pull up outside. I hoped it would be Kelly Jordan or at least the two detectives together, but it was Ross Durrant on his own and he didn't look at all happy to be here. He had a murmured conversation with the officers during which he occasionally looked over at Aidan or at me. When he was finished he walked across to me, leaned in close and spoke in a whisper:

"I swear that if you are playing games with us—again—I will arrest you and charge you with perverting the course of justice. Do you understand?"

"Is Kelly Jordan on her way?"

"I don't know anything about that."

"When she gets here, I'll explain everything."

This seemed to make Durrant even angrier. He asked Aidan to take a seat, but Aidan said he was happy to stand.

"Why are you here?" Durrant asked him.

"I spent the night."

"Were you and Ms. Moreau intimate."

"Oh yes." And Aidan turned his head and smiled at me.

"Was the encounter consensual?"

"It was."

Ross Durrant looked round at me.

"None of that matters," I said.

"Is he lying?"

"Wait until Kelly Jordan gets here. Then I'll explain everything."

His face had gone red with anger.

"Five minutes," he said. "Five bloody minutes. Then we'll talk, whoever's here."

Kelly Jordan arrived in three minutes. She didn't look much more pleased than her colleagues to be here. She made no attempt at a greeting and she didn't smile.

"What's this about?" she said.

This was it. This was the moment I had been waiting for. Now that it had come, I felt tranquil, even though everything depended on what I was about to say.

"Aidan Otley threatened to kill me," I said. "He said he'd kill me just as he'd killed Skye Nolan and Peggy Nolan."

"This is all rubbish," Aidan said in an almost amiable tone. "I never knew these women. I'd never even heard of them."

"Aidan said that he had trophies. He had a trophy from Skye Nolan's flat and he had a trophy from Peggy Nolan's house and he had kept them in his flat and he would show them to me as a sign of what he would do to me."

There was a silence. Aidan looked at me in shock and then his expression changed to a smile. He actually laughed.

"OK," he said. "I get it. Two objects?"

"That's right."

"One belonging to Skye Nolan and one belonging to Peggy Nolan?"

"Yes."

He looked at the two detectives. "She thinks she's framed me. She's put two objects in my flat and then she's phoned the police with this completely made-up accusation."

"What do you mean framed?" I said. "When would I have done that?"

"You've been there. Or you could have got in when I wasn't there."

"I don't have a key to your flat. I've never had a key to your flat."

"You could have managed it somehow."

He looked back at the two detectives.

"Do you want me to tell you about those two trophies?" Aidan closed his eyes, clearly trying to remember. Then he opened them. "Yes, that's it. The mother gave Tess two presents and she showed them to me. One was a bracelet that had belonged to her daughter. It was copper with swirly engraving on and some kind of light blue stones in them. The other was a square little clay thing, enameled on top, yellow and green. It's the sort of thing you'd put a hot drink on, what's it called?"

"A coaster," I said, in a low voice.

"That's right, a coaster. It had the daughter's initials carved into the clay at the back. Tess kept them here, but somehow I don't think they're here anymore. I think they're probably in a shoebox under my bed or in a shelf in my cupboard, somewhere a bit hidden but easy to find. Do you want the police to have a quick search or is it a waste of time?"

I started to speak, but Aidan interrupted me.

"I'll save you the trouble. She keeps them in her knicker drawer."

I looked at him sharply. "Have you been going through my things?"

He only shrugged. "I needed to check on you," he said. "And it's lucky I did. And when you don't find them, we can go and retrieve them from the place in my flat where Tess put them."

"Any objection?" Ross Durrant said. "Not that it matters what you think."

"If it doesn't matter," I said, "you'd better go ahead."

One of the officers—the red-haired, fresh-faced one—left the room and Aidan looked at me.

424

"When this is over," he said, "it feels like we've got a thing or two to talk about."

Ross Durrant looked at me coldly.

"Anything you'd like to correct?" he said.

"Do you mean these, sir?" said a voice behind me.

I turned. The young officer was standing with outstretched hands. In one was the bangle with lapis lazuli and in the other was the coaster. Aidan looked like he had been punched in the stomach.

"You bitch," he said. I waited for the words Poppy must have heard him say to Skye, and sure enough, he said them. "You fucking cunt."

SIXTY-THREE

They left me with the red-haired officer. As Aidan passed me, he leaned toward me.

"You'll never get rid of me," he said in a whisper.

I asked the officer what his name was.

Thorpe, he told me. Ronnie Thorpe.

"OK, Ronnie, would you like some coffee?"

His eyes darted around as if he was expecting Durrant to emerge from a cupboard.

"If you're making some." He couldn't meet my eye.

"I am."

I made us both strong coffee, taking my time over it. Then Ronnie sat stiff-backed and perspiring at the table, while I rang my school to say I wouldn't be in until the following morning. I'd been a victim of a crime, I said, and heard the intake of breath at the other end.

I fed Sunny. I washed up the dishes from last night, sluicing the congealing duck fat off the plates, sloshing the glasses under hot water for ages and then rinsing them several times. I scrubbed at the kitchen surfaces. Every trace of him. Anywhere he might have touched.

"How long will this take?" I asked Ronnie.

Ronnie didn't know. He only knew I was to stay in the house; his job was to keep an eye on me.

I went and had a shower. The water was tepid, but I stood under it until it turned cold, washing every inch of my body, scrubbing at it, and even that wasn't enough. I cleaned my teeth, gargled with mouthwash. I pushed the torn tee shirt and the knickers I'd been wearing into the wastepaper basket. I did the same with the red dress and the lacy underwear from last night. I put on drawstring linen trousers and a crisp white cotton shirt, soft on my skin. I stripped the sheet off the bed, pulled the duvet cover off, the pillowcases, and threw them onto the landing, to take to the trash outside later. I had a sudden impulse to cut off all my hair, but thought that Poppy might be alarmed to see me shorn so I just coiled it into a tight knot at the back of my neck.

I went downstairs again and Ronnie was still sitting hot and stiff on the chair, nursing his coffee and gazing steadfastly in front of him.

I went into the garden, which I had neglected recently. I put birdseed in the feeder and crouched down with a trowel and dug out the ground elder, a stubborn weed with thin deep roots. I deadheaded the roses, then sprayed the buds with soapy water to keep the bugs away. I tipped out the rainwater that had gathered in the little paddling pool, rinsed it out with a couple of buckets of water. I got rid of the ash in the barbecue.

I understood that I was thinking nothing, feeling

nothing. I was waiting. Behind me in the conservatory, Ronnie waited too.

Just before midday, I saw him get to his feet and move heavily toward the stairs, so I rinsed my hands from the outdoor tap and went back inside, just as he came back down again, with a figure behind him.

It was Ross Durrant. He strode into the conservatory as if he were on his way somewhere else, then came to an abrupt halt just in front of me. I could see a small tic in his temple and realized that he was angry.

"Well?" I asked.

He rested his eyes on me. I felt he was looking at me the way I looked at a snarl in the thread when I was sewing.

"I am here to take you to the police station," he said and I felt a trickle of dread run through me. Had something gone wrong?

"Why?"

"To make a statement."

"What's happening?" I asked. "Did you find the things I told you you'd find?"

"We did." His mouth snapped shut.

"What were they?"

"There's a car outside for you."

"I was right, wasn't I?"

"All right," he said, unsmiling, "you can have your moment of triumph."

"I don't feel any triumph."

"I'm not going to apologize, if that's what you want."

"What I want is for Aidan to be put away where he can't harm me or my daughter."

"It looks like you'll get your wish."

I picked up my denim jacket and bag, took my keys from the table.

"A small silver goblet with Skye's name engraved on it." His back was to me; I couldn't see the expression on his face but his shoulders were square and unyielding. "A christening or a naming mug, I imagine. And an old copy of a poetry book that Peggy was awarded as a school prize for best improvement or something in 1986. It has a bookplate inside its front cover with her name on it and she's scribbled in the margins."

"Is it enough?"

"We're about to turn his life upside down. There's nothing we won't know about Aidan Otley by the time we're done. But it doesn't really matter. We've already got enough to charge him with double murder. Which we will be doing imminently."

"Good." My hands were trembling; my stomach felt hollow. I felt as if I was very hungry or about to throw up. "That's good."

Ross Durrant looked at me with a more humane expression.

"And all because your little girl saw something or heard something and put it in a picture."

"That's right. Poor little thing."

"Any idea where it happened?"

"I've gone over and over it. She barely spent any time alone with him. It might have been in the park or Skye may have come to the flat one day when I was out at the shops, or maybe at night after I was asleep. Looking back, I can see that Poppy didn't want to be alone with him after that. I think in her way she was trying to protect me."

"Can't you just ask her?"

I shook my head.

"She's been asked about it so much, there's nothing real left. That picture—that was her memory: a girl falling from a tower."

SIXTY-FOUR

Poppy marched up to me like a soldier going into battle. She looked cross and hot and full of the importance of what she had to say.

"I did cry at Jake's," she said.

I squatted down. "Why did you cry, my darling?"

"I wanted Teddy."

"You had Teddy. I put him in your bag."

"I wanted my special mug. I wanted Sunny. I wanted my unicorn tee shirt. Gina brushed my hair."

I took her hand. "Let's go."

"Just me and you."

"Just me and you."

"We can dig for worms," said Poppy with satisfaction.

"OK."

She looked at me suspiciously. "No bath," she said.

"We'll think about that."

"And it can thunder and lightning and I will see a fox and Sunny will sleep with me."

"I can't promise the weather."

I bought us each an ice cream on the way back and we sat on a bench to eat them, the sun on our backs. Then we went back to the flat, hand in hand, and Poppy played in the paddling pool, dug for worms with intense and scowling concentration, told Sunny a story about a girl called Poppy who could fly, and I watched her. I watched her and marveled.

Soon enough, the news about Aidan would be public. It would be in papers, on news channels, online. More to the point, everyone in my life would know, would look at me differently, look at me hungrily, would talk to each other about it in appalled and reveling tones. *Did you hear? Did you know? Isn't it awful?* Not yet, though, not this evening, which was so warm and luminous and peaceful. Not while Poppy splashed in the paddling pool, throwing handfuls of water into the air, and ran in her knickers round the garden, muddy and enthralled, and the birds came to the feeder and the light fell through the leaves and left rippling shadows on the ground.

I didn't know what to tell her and what to leave alone. Should I simply let time wash away her memories and her bad dreams, or should I say to her: you witnessed horrible things, but they are over now? You were confused and scared, but now you don't need to be. I let a bad man into our home, but he will never come again. Your world is safe once more.

But the world is never safe, not for a little girl who is unfiltered and wide open, who sees everything, hears everything, lets everything move through her; is like a wind chime that the lightest breeze will set chinking.

"Bedtime," I said.

"Stories," she replied. "Till I say stop. Owl babies and the tiger at tea, and little bear and the moon and the cow jumped over it and this little pig. All the way home."

SIXTY-FIVE

The next day, Jason was waiting outside school when I emerged with Poppy.

"When were you going to tell me?" he asked.

"How did you hear?"

"The police called me. They assumed I already knew."

I was about to reply that he had forbidden me from contacting him, but I felt Poppy's warm hand in mine and I stopped myself. I didn't want to be that woman anymore. He was Poppy's father; I had let danger into his daughter's life.

"I am really sorry you had to find out like that," I said. "You're absolutely right. I should have told you at once. It was just that everything was—" I stopped. My eyes were hot with tears and I didn't want to cry in front of Poppy. I didn't want to cry in front of Jason either. I wanted to lie in a dark room and let tears course down my cheeks and into my pillow, weep with anguish and guilt and relief.

"Where do I be now?" asked Poppy, looking up at both of us.

"With me tonight," I said. "You're with Daddy tomorrow. Today is Tuesday and tomorrow is Wednesday."

"I can do it, I know it: Monday Tuesday Wednesday Thursday Friday Saturday Sunday," she yelled in a frantic singsong voice.

"Brilliant," I said. Then to Jason, "Can we have a little walk, the three of us?"

He nodded and took Poppy's other hand. I couldn't read his mood. He was a handsome stranger.

"Swing me," commanded Poppy as she always did, sinking down so her bottom was almost on the pavement. "Swing me high."

So off we went, Mummy and Daddy and our little red-haired daughter swooping up between us.

"Aren't you going to apologize?" asked Jason.

"Yes, I am."

"You pretty much accused me of murdering a woman. You set the police on me. And then it turned out to be your boyfriend all along. It was all happening under your own roof."

"Again! Again!"

"One, two, three, up! For the rest of my life I will have to live with that. I was wrong. I was looking in the wrong direction. I didn't see what was right there—in my own home, as you say."

And in my bed, I thought, and that familiar nausea rose in me.

"So from the bottom of my heart, I apologize. I'm

sorry I suspected you of being connected with Skye's death. I'm sorry that I trusted someone who turned out to be a murderer. I'm sorry that all the time I thought I was protecting Poppy, I was in fact putting her in danger."

I put my hand against my throat. My whole body felt raw and sore; my eyes stung. I waited.

"I could ask for custody, you know," he said.

Here it was, what I had feared.

"Again!" cried Poppy imperiously.

Up she flew, our red-headed daughter.

"I'd fight you every inch of the way," I said. "Why not run to the corner, Poppy?"

We waited while she raced away from us.

"I was wrong about you and Skye, but I wasn't wrong about you."

"What the fuck is that supposed to mean?"

"It's true you didn't kill anyone," I said in a low voice. I turned to face him. "But you bullied me, you cheated on me, you lied to me and when we split up you made me think it was something we were doing together in a civilized way. And now you're doing it to Emily and to other women as well, even people who work for you." I saw his startled look. "Yes, I know things about you that you really don't want anyone to find out. It wouldn't look great in court, would it? And you've let Poppy witness your treachery. You're not a murderer, I was wrong about that, but I wasn't wrong about you. And I think any judge, given the evidence, would see that I was foolish, but I acted in good faith, whereas you—you were faithless."

"So that's how it is."

"Jason, I want us to behave in a civilized way together, for Poppy's sake. I don't want us to be enemies for the rest of our lives. But I swear I won't be civilized if you try and take Poppy away from me."

He stared at me. I could see tiny red veins in the whites of his eyes and a faint speck of spittle at the corner of his mouth. Then something shifted in his expression.

"We used to be good together," he said. "What's happened to us?"

"We were never good together. I was young and foolish. But we can try to be good parents."

We caught up with Poppy, and I took her hand.

"Home," I said.

SIXTY-SIX

Months later, it was a cold February day and I was on my own, walking through Covent Garden and I saw him, walking in front of me. I could recognize him even though I could only see him from behind, just as I'd seen him from behind that first time, sitting next to Peggy Nolan at the inquest. I sped up my pace, caught up with him and tapped him on the shoulder.

Charlie stopped and looked at me with surprise and then with obvious dismay.

"It's been a long time," I said.

He only mumbled something in response.

"You don't have time for a coffee?"

"I don't think that would be a good idea." He looked around. "What are you doing here? I didn't think we'd ever meet again."

"It's all right," I said, trying to sound soothing. "I'm sorry if I gave you a shock. I wasn't following you."

He looked suspicious. "Has something happened? Did someone tell you where I was?"

I held up my hands in protest. "Honestly. I'm meeting a friend."

We looked at each other for a moment.

"I was surprised you weren't at the trial. When I was giving evidence, I looked for you in the public gallery."

"I couldn't face it. Obviously."

"And then afterward. I tried to get in touch. I thought you might want to talk. Maybe you didn't get my emails."

He leaned forward and spoke in a hoarse whisper so that I could barely hear him against the traffic.

"I got them," he said. "And I pretended I hadn't seen them. What would I want to talk about? About breaking into your boyfriend's flat and hiding the mug and the book that Peggy gave me? Is that something we're meant to have a chat about?"

"You didn't break in. I gave you the key."

"It's still a crime. You know, I've never even taken a pen home from my office if it didn't belong to me and now I've helped frame a man for two murders."

It was my turn to look around and see if any passerby might have heard what Charlie was saying.

"Do we have to have this conversation in the street?"

"I don't want to have it at all. I just know that I committed a crime."

I put out a hand to him and he seemed to flinch from it.

"Charlie, the reason I wanted to contact you is that I wanted to thank you. Aidan killed the woman you loved and he killed the mother of the woman you loved. You know it wasn't the mug and book that got him convicted, it was a wealth of evidence. They found his prints at Skye's flat; there were several people who had seen him with her in that bar. We just made the police look in the right place, which is what they should have done anyway. If you hadn't done what you did, then not only would he have got away with killing Peggy and Skye, but at some time he would have killed me and he would have killed my little girl. I'll owe you that forever."

"It was you," said Charlie. "I just collected the key and ..." He hesitated. "Well, all the rest."

"Yes, all the rest. And I owe you my life for it."

"Yes, all of that is right. But will God forgive me for it?" said Charlie. "For the lying, for the law-breaking."

I was stunned by the question. For a moment I couldn't think of anything to say.

"I don't know," I said. "I don't know much about God's forgiveness. I don't know much about God. But I know that I was in a dark place and everybody I turned to had let me down. Except you." I thought for a moment. What could I say that would comfort this man? "Maybe that's what makes it good. It would be too easy if you were just doing what you were meant to do. To help me, you had to go against what you believe and you had to break the law. To do right you had to do wrong. That was a real favor because it was so difficult. I'm sure God will see that."

Charlie gave a slow smile. "You think that's what God will think?"

I managed a smile as well. "I don't know. I'm just trying to make you feel better."

His smile faded. "You know he'll get out one day. What then?"

"He made it pretty clear what then, that day in court. But the judge said he should serve a minimum of thirty years. He killed two women and both murders were premeditated. By that time, it'll be Poppy's turn to look after *me*."

He nodded, shifted from foot to foot. "Well, it's over at least."

"I suppose we won't meet again."

"I suppose not," said Charlie. "Unless you're wearing a wire."

I smiled. "I'm not wearing a wire. And you should be proud of what you did for Skye and Peggy."

"Maybe," he said, but I wasn't sure he was convinced.

SIXTY-SEVEN

On a cool and blustery Sunday in May, I took Poppy to Alicia's fifth birthday party. I looked back to Alicia's fourth birthday party. I remembered how Poppy had worn the tulle skirt I had run up on the sewing machine, and the golden witch's cloak I'd made, which now lay abandoned and shabby with overuse at the back of a drawer. I couldn't bring myself to throw it away.

Today she wore faded jeans, desert boots and a bomber jacket Jake had grown out of. Jake had shot up in the last six months, all gangly limbs and clumsiness; Poppy was still little, one of the smallest in her Reception class. Her red hair seemed even redder; her pale skin more freckled. Her eyes gleamed; she crackled with energy.

"If we were driving in your car—" she said.

"I don't have a car."

"Yes, but if we were in it, and I shouted and jumped out of the window and did a somersault over the pavement and then ran to the seaside, what would you do?"

"I suppose I'd have to stop the car and follow you."

"All the way to the seaside?"

"Of course, if you got that far before I reached you."

"But what if I can fly and you can't fly?"

"That doesn't seem fair. If you can fly, why can't I?"

"Grown-ups can't fly. Only children."

We reached Alicia's house and I handed the birthday present we'd brought to Poppy and rang the doorbell. Alicia's mother opened it; she already looked exhausted. Behind her, I glimpsed a jumble of excited children.

"Have a lovely time," I said to Poppy, but she didn't move. Her hand gripped mine tightly and she stared up at me.

"I'll be back soon," I reassured her.

"Promise till your crossed to die heart?"

I resisted the urge to pick her up and hold her tight against me.

"Yes. I cross my heart."

She let go of my hand and stepped over the threshold.

"Good luck," I said to Alicia's mother.

"I got crayons for you!" Poppy was yelling as she charged into the little crowd. "Open it. All colors of crayon."

It wasn't really worth going back home and so I walked through London Fields and into Broadway Market. I wandered round the stalls and thought about buying a lovely bronze pendant for myself, but knew I wouldn't. I went into a café and ordered a flat white and an almond croissant, damp and warm, and sat at a small table near the window.

My mobile was turned off. No one knew I was here and it felt like an illicit pleasure. I took my time, sipping at the coffee, dabbing up the last flakes of croissant with my forefinger. That was something I was gradually learning to do: take time, give myself time, let the world settle around me and feel myself, if only for brief moments, at the center of my own life.

It had been a year, and there were hours and even days when I let myself forget what had happened to us last summer, what Poppy and I had been through and what we had escaped. But there were things I must never forget. I had met Jason shortly after my previous boyfriend had left me for my friend. I had met Aidan shortly after Jason had left me. Both men had sensed my vulnerability and been like burglars coming across a window open, a door unlocked, a house wide open for violation.

When I'd said this to Gina, she had looked alarmed. "You don't want to become all defended," she said.

But I didn't want ever to be so defenseless again, either.

I thought about how I'd let Aidan into my home, into my bed, into my heart. And into Poppy's life. Her safe place had been made into a place of danger and fear.

Poppy still had bad dreams; quite often she would pad into my room in the night and curl up beside me, pressing her hot body against mine. She was still clingy and didn't want to let me out of her sight. But very slowly, the fear was leaving her, as mist dissolves, leaving only floating shreds behind. She had a little brother now, called Arlo. She had a bicycle I'd given her at Christmas and which she rode to school every morning, with me running beside her, ready to catch her if she fell or stop her if she careered out of control. She had a small group of friends that she bossed around, dragged into her complicated imaginary games and showered with affection. She had learned to read. Often at night, after our story time, I would leave her bent over a book, her tongue on her upper lip, her mouth moving to the words. She wrote stories as well, her wonky script spilling down the page, but I could decipher it: stories about adventures, about dragons and unicorns and mysterious caves, mountains and green seas, and about a little girl called Poppy. She drew pictures in bold bright colors to go with her stories: houses, flowers, rainbows, suns, cats, and elephants—which she called by their proper name now.

Gradually, day by day and week by week, I was ceasing to be continually anxious about her, or be gripped by dread in the small hours when something woke me and I would lie in the darkness, hearing the house creak or the wind sigh outside, or Sunny at the end of my bed whimper in his sleep, dreaming of whatever old cats dream about.

And sometimes what we had lived through barely felt real, like a tale that a child tells, or a picture they draw: a picture in thick black crayon, and they can't tell you what it means, only that it's scary, only that they are scared, and you need to listen. Because a child sees and a child hears, and all the great and menacing world pours into them unmediated.

*

I walked back to the party and got there a bit early, but other parents were beginning to gather. Alicia's mother took me into the living room, which was a scene of chaos: crisps and biscuits and chocolates trampled into the carpet, and sticky children squirming on the sofa or throwing cushions at each other, while out in the garden, other children were trampling the flower bed, high on sugar and excitement. Poppy was there; I could see her bright hair and hear her voice, which was louder and more carrying than anyone else's.

"It got a bit out of hand," Alicia's mother said grimly. "I'd planned all these games, but the children got through them in no time and then—well. Mayhem. I need a drink."

"We can help you clear some of the mess at least," said the man beside me as a child hurtled by, knocking into him and then spinning off again like a rogue satellite.

I recognized the man. He was the father of a boy newly arrived in Poppy's class. He'd become quite friendly with Laurie, and Gina had told me that his partner had died of a rare cancer when their son was only two.

"I don't think we've properly met," he said. "I'm Baxter, Leo's dad."

"Tess," I said, and he smiled and said he knew that. Then, to hide his self-consciousness, he bent to pick up paper plates covered in the sludgy remains of cake and cracked plastic cups.

"Why did I think buying meringues was a good idea?" said Alicia's mother. "Look!"

She left the room. Baxter and I looked at each other, suddenly awkward.

"Leo says that Poppy's wicked. In a good way, that is."

"Sometimes she's wicked not in a good way," I said. "Is Leo settling in OK?"

"Yeah. It's been hard for him, but it's getting better." He seemed about to say something, then changed his mind.

"Good. That's good."

"Maybe you and Poppy would like to come over after school one day," he said. "To play with Leo."

"I'm sure Poppy would love that."

He coughed, rubbed his cheek.

"I'm not very good at this. That is, I'm out of practice. But what I'm really trying to say is maybe you'd like to come over. Or meet up. With me, I mean."

I looked at him. He was a bit taller than me, with hazel eyes, and he had a kind face. His partner had died; he was a single father of an anxious boy with jug ears; he cleared up mess in other people's houses. He was my kind of man. Something stirred inside me.

What should I say? I'd spent a lifetime feeling apologetic, sparing people, putting myself in other people's shoes, considering their feelings, letting them down gently or not letting them down at all. How should I put this?

"No," I said, shaking my head. "No."

About the Author

NICCI FRENCH is the pseudonym of English wife-and-husband team Nicci Gerrard and Sean French. Their acclaimed novels of psychological suspense, including the internationally bestselling Frieda Klein series, have sold more than eight million copies around the world.

MORE FROM NICCI FRENCH

HOUSE OF CORRECTION
In this heart-pounding stand-alone, a woman accused of murder attempts to solve her own case from the confines of prison—but as she unravels the truth, everything is called into question, including her own certainty that she is innocent.

THE LYING ROOM
In this thrilling stand-alone, a married woman's affair with her boss spirals into a dangerous game of chess with the police when she discovers him murdered and wipes the crime scene.

DAY OF THE DEAD
The final novel in the internationally bestselling series featuring London psychologist Frieda Klein—a gripping cat-and-mouse thriller that pits one of the most fascinating characters in contemporary fiction against an enemy like none other.

SUNDAY SILENCE
In this thrilling novel from the master of psychological suspense, Frieda Klein becomes a person of interest in a horrifying murder case, trapping her in a fatal tug-of-war between two killers: one who won't let her go, and another who can't let her live.

DARK SATURDAY
Enter the world of Nicci French with this electrifying, sophisticated psychological thriller about past crimes and present dangers, featuring an unforgettable protagonist.

WHAT TO DO WHEN SOMEONE DIES
In this ingenious stand-alone thriller from the internationally bestselling author and "razor sharp" master of suspense (*People*), a grieving wife is forced to ask: Which is worse—infidelity or murder?

THE OTHER SIDE OF THE DOOR
Everyone tells lies. But is anyone prepared to tell the truth to uncover a murderer? A sexy, intricate thriller about the temptation of secrets, the weight of lies, and the price of betrayal and suspicion.

UNTIL IT'S OVER
In this steamy and suspenseful stand-alone thriller a group of housemates must determine who in their midst is a killer when a series of murders occur.

LOSING YOU
From the bestselling author of the Frieda Klein series, a suspenseful stand-alone novel in which a woman's frantic search for her missing daughter unveils a nefarious web of secrets and lies.

DISCOVER GREAT AUTHORS, EXCLUSIVE OFFERS, AND MORE AT HC.COM